For Mary, Emma and Robin

Foreword

Every family has stories about its more colourful members, both living and dead, and mine is certainly no exception. But I had always assumed that the family legend that my many-times-great grandfather was a member of the original Robin Hood's 12th-century gang of outlaws – that he was, in fact, the renowned medieval trouvère and swordsman, Sir Alan Dale – was no more than a charming fairytale passed down by successive generations of the Westbury family with their tongues firmly in their cheeks.

However, after the death of my father Professor Roderick Westbury-Browne last year, and the discovery of a mass of papers in a dusty school trunk in his neglected attic in Albert Street, Nottingham, I have changed my view. The papers, which are typed out on faded yellow A4 paper, purport to be a collection of ancient manuscripts transcribed to a modern format from the original decaying vellum by my father in his spare hours, when he was not engaged in teaching Medieval History at the University of Nottingham. Of the original vellum, no trace now remains, but the type-written pages appear to be nothing less than a series of fresh stories composed in the early 13th century by Sir Alan Dale in his later years at his manor of Westbury.

I had long known that my father was an old friend of Angus Donald, the popular historical novelist, and I vividly recall the two of them sitting up late into the night over a bottle of whisky discussing matters of mutual interest. However, perhaps rather stupidly, I had not connected Mr Donald's splendid series of eight novels about Robin Hood and Alan Dale – collectively known as The Outlaw Chronicles – with my father's own stories about my family and their antecedents in Nottinghamshire as well as his own long-term interest in the many legends surrounding the Holy Grail.

Sadly, it is too late now to ask my father about the truth or otherwise of his claim to kinship with Alan Dale, the Knight of Westbury, and Mr Donald has been unable to tell me anything more than that my father was convinced the connection was genuine. Mr Donald did, however, admit that the origin of his Outlaw Chronicles was indeed the extraordinary set of thrilling stories that he and my father discussed at length some decades ago.

    It seemed fitting, therefore, to hand over my late father's typed-up manuscripts to Mr Donald for editing and publication. And the fruit of this, the first instalment of a new collection of adventures of a long-dead hero, is contained within the following pages. I trust that all these newly discovered tales will one day be published, and the travails of a man who may well be my ancestor may prove both edifying and entertaining to the general reader.

Michael Westbury-Browne
The Old Grange, Lichfield, Staffordshire
June 20, 2019

PART 1

October, Year of Our Lord 1191

Chapter One

The storm came out of Africa, a ravening beast of wind and water and fury. It drove up from the south in a black wall and smashed into the side of the ship; one gigantic wave lifting and canting our vessel – the Tarrada – far over on the starboard beam.

The rain lashed the ship in freezing torrents, hard as hail, filling the air so completely with moisture that it became almost impossible to breathe. I seized hold of a backstay with both hands as the deck beneath my feet surged upwards. And choking, spluttering in the suddenly blinding wet, I struggled to keep my feet on the slippery, heaving planks beneath me.

The kindly sunlight of a Mediterranean afternoon was immediately extinguished as the ship was thrust into this roaring waterfall. The wind howled about me, the ship plunged and slewed a quarter turn, hurling my body in a short arc to crash into the ship's rail. Had I not been gripping on to the rope, I'd have been swept away to my doom.

One poor fellow, our company's only priest, who had been standing unwarily by the starboard rail, was indeed snatched up and hurled overboard, immediately lost to the ocean. I caught one glimpse of Father Simon's white terrified face, and wide, silently screaming mouth, before he disappeared for ever, and my first thought was: *This is Robin's fault! He is entirely to blame.*

After that I had no time for musing, nor for more than a passing sorrow at the priest's fate. I was clinging for my life to the taut backstay as the ship danced beneath me, soaring as a wave bore it upwards, dropping like a stone as the seas hollowed out a space below its timbers, and smashing into the water. A green wave crashed across the deck, slapping the breath from my lungs, wrenching the rigging from my grip. I dropped and slid, panicking like a child, bashing once more into the rail but, by God's grace and my own desperate lunge, finding a hold, hugging the hard wood into my armpit.

Another wave smashed into me and its horrible power sucked at my body, but I gripped harder, squashing my body into the corner between deck and rail, until the wave's grip slackened, released me and the ship righted herself.

When able to look up again, I saw a dozen men on deck in similar poses to mine: huddled, soaked, clinging on for dear life. But surely there had been at least twice that number on the deck when the storm had struck. *How many were lost?* I thought, and then again: *This is all Robin's fault.*

A spike of white lightning split the black sky, and vast groan of thunder followed immediately like the grinding of two mountains. The iron cascade of freezing rain battered my head without mercy. I lifted my eyes to the aftcastle, the raised platform at the rear of the *Tarrada*, which housed the massively thick steering oar, and saw Robin Odo, Earl of Locksley, lord of this company, owner of the vessel – and the man responsible for this torment. He and the ship's captain were wrapped like drenched monkeys around the steering oar, or the tiller, as I had also heard it called, struggling to keep their course as the ship was madly buffeted about by the storm.

Yet I could also see that, despite the bellowing of the tempest and the desperate prancing of the ship, Robin and the captain, a stocky piratical type called Aziz, were arguing furiously about something. I could see mouths opening and closing, exaggerated facial expressions of mutual disagreement.

Captain Aziz was occasionally gesturing quickly with one hand towards the north, when he could afford to release the long wooden tiller for an instant. It was quite obvious that Robin did not at all agree with him. But after a few moments of screaming back and forth – the meaning of their words stripped away by the wind before they reached me – I could see that Aziz had won the dispute. Robin nodded reluctantly and I saw them lunge together, their weights combined, and heave the tiller over to the right.

There was a squealing of whistles, just audible over the howl of wind, and a stamping of bare feet on the rain-slick deck as the crew ran to their stations. I watched with awe as the nimble sailors scrambled up the various rope spider-works that held the three masts and their yards in place, quite contemptuous of the whip and fury of the weather. They loosed this sail and tightened another, hauled tight on that rope or line – despite many years of maritime travelling, my understanding of the intricacies of seamanship is still lamentably poor – and the ship came around, the canvas of the sails snapping angrily in the tumult; more ropes were pulled in, tied off, and we began to run north more calmly with the wind and the storm behind us.

The noise dropped immediately, our passage became smoother and, although we were still regularly battered with rain bursts and the ship buffeted with great swells, my deep terror that the *Tarrada* was about to be plunged to the bottom of the ocean slowly began to subside. We were still travelling at a vast lick, being thrust remorselessly, so it seemed, by the very sea itself in this new direction of travel. I was drenched, dripping and chattering with cold, but when I finally released my death grip on the rail, got unsteadily to my feet and wiped the running water from my eyes, I found that Robin himself was standing beside me.

"Aziz says we must make for dry land. He says we must find shelter."

"Where?" I shouted over the still-considerable din of the elements.

"He thinks the island of Crete is only a dozen miles to the north. We can ride out the storm there. I think we should battle on but Aziz knows these waters. He says we'll be ripped in two if we do not make landfall."

"It's the storm season," I bellowed. "It's mid-October, too bloody late in the year to start a long voyage. We should all have stayed safe and dry in Jaffa. But you insisted, *you* said we must sail now, or we'd never get..."

"Don't start with me, Alan," my master yelled back. "This isn't the time. Go below and check on the horses, will you. They'll be in a rare state."

That stopped me. My own beloved mount, a fine grey gelding called Ghost, was stabled below. I took a hard breath and, as usual, meekly obeyed my lord's command. Robin turned away and walked forward beside the rail, balanced like an acrobat and riding the wild heaves of the ship with irritating ease. I started to work my way aft through the splash and spray, clinging to the ship's rigging whenever I could, stumbling, slipping, creeping slowly towards the hatch that led down to the hold. The deck bucked beneath my feet with every cautious, landlubberly step. God knew what our beasts must make of this mad agitation of their cramped quarters below. Horses cannot vomit, of course, but in their distress the other end of the animal can certainly make up for this natural deficit. Above me lightning cracked, the thunder roared out its terrible pain; rain hammered the deck without mercy.

We very nearly made it safely to land. The coast of Crete was a brown looming shape on the horizon, visible through the veils of rain, rushing towards us with alarming speed. The sailors had taken down most of the sails by now and we were scudding along under a single foresail, pulled down to half its normal height, a bed-sheet sized scrap of canvas, no more. This reckless speed, driven by the rolling waves, was still too great for my comfort yet, as we entered the mouth of a narrow bay, with a grey beach in its back teeth, I began to feel that we might possibly live to see the dawn.

I was plastered with sprayed horseshit and hay, only half washed clean by the ceaseless rain, but feeling easier in my own mind. Below-deck had been a hellish shambles: one huge destrier, with a white-flecked mouth and creamy withers, had been bucking, kicking and biting everything and everyone within reach. It had been driven completely insane by the storm, kicking out the wooden panels of its stall, ripping the skin and flesh of its legs badly in the process. It had to be dispatched; and I sliced through its neck with one clean blow of my sword. The poor animal's death seemed to calm the rest of the herd substantially. Ghost was still trembling, skittering and rolling his eyes in his stall, but I soon managed to soothe him. Softly murmuring in his wild, twitching ears, gently stroking his sweaty satin neck.

Back on deck I watched the rocky coastline approaching, measuring with my eye the distance at which I believed I could swim to safety, if absolutely necessary. Once that point was passed, I felt my own body relax, just a fraction. We were inside the bay, only a stone's throw from the semi-circle of the beach, swooping in and I was turning to say something to the man standing next to me, when there was a tremendous screeching noise and the whole ship jumped and shuddered, coming to an abrupt, awful stop.

We were all thrown forward, the man beside me a short, heavy fellow called Edwin landing with his knee in my back, pinning me to the deck. We disentangled ourselves and stood. Aziz was screaming at his crew in a fury, and suddenly a dozen Arabs were crowded along the larboard rail and peering over the side at the churning ocean. The beach was only thirty yards away but the rolling waves were still pounding at us, each wave that smashed into us causing a scream of wood. We'd hit something, apparently, some outcropping of rock; a little submerged island in the centre of the bay.

"Get all the hatches open, Alan," Robin was yelling at me from the aftcastle. "Get the horses swimming; and save as much of their gear as you can." Then he was calling to Little John and others. I grabbed Edwin and we began fighting our way through the panicking crowds of men – ours and the Arab crew, some of whom were already throwing themselves off the stricken ship into the churning sea and paddling the short distance to land.

We hauled back the hold hatches, all of them, throwing them wide and got the ridged loading boards in place, the rain still hammering down, and with the help of a dozen of Robin's men we started leading the terrified horses out of the dark hold. Some men, following Robin's directions, were seizing sacks and boxes, and barrels of goods, and hurling them over the sides; many of them sank immediately, others bobbed sluggishly in the waves and swimming men guided the containers that floated to the beach.

The lower decks of the vessel were awash and, at the front on the larboard side, I could see by dim light a jet of sea spurting like a severed artery, pumping saltwater deep inside the shattered body of the round ship.

I swung on to Ghost's bare back, got him clattering up the loading ramp on to the deck and urged him with my heels to jump into the white-whipped sea. He balked only once, then as a massive bolt of lightning bleached the sky; he gathered all his courage and made a truly heroic leap and splashed down heavily into the cold roiling water. A dozen heartbeats later we were shaking seawater from ourselves on firm sand.

Behind me, I could hear the grinding of the *Tarrada*'s torn-open planks against the submerged rock over the dreadful noise of the storm. But we were, all praise to Almighty God, now on land, if not particularly dry land, and I took a moment to say a grateful prayer and thank my personal patron Saint Michael, the great warrior archangel, for my safe deliverance.

We worked until nightfall to get all the men and horses and as much of the goods, food and war gear as possible off the stricken ship. Then we anchored the *Tarrada* with three lines attached to trees and rocks on the small beach.

We piled the pitifully few barrels and boxes that had survived on the beach under a lashed-down tarpaulin and led the sick and trembling horses to the shelter of a thick wood on the northern side of the bay. We tethered the exhausted creatures under the trees, a strange type of local pine with thick gnarled trunks, long drooping limbs and delicate, almost feathery green leaves that turned white-brown at the tips. I thought we ought to camp beneath them; if we wove the branches overhead together, I reckoned, we could make a nearly waterproof ceiling for our camp. However, Hanno, an iron-tough, shaven-headed Bavarian man-at-arms, loudly disagreed with me.

"I know a better sleep-place," he said, in his unique kind of English. Hanno had joined our company of English and Welsh men-at-arms in the Holy Land, after being abandoned by his own lord, Duke Leopold of Austria, and he had not only become my friend and comrade but had also appointed himself my mentor in all of the dark and varied arts of warfare.

Hanno had scouted the bay while we were busy unloading the ship and had discovered, apart from a few ramshackle fishermen's shacks, apparently abandoned by their owners for the winter months, an extensive series of dry, spacious caves burrowed into the sandstone of the bay's northern headland.

By midnight, all of the ship's surviving men were ensconced in dry warm caverns under a sandstone roof, with fires already lit and the soup simmering, the salvaged goods and gear piled around us, steaming gently, and our exhausted men preparing to spend the night in relative comfort. I stood at the mouth of the cave, sipping a welcome mug of barley broth, with a cheery blaze crackling behind me, and looked out through the drifting curtains of rain at the *Tarrada* stuck in the middle of the bay like a beached whale on its invisible perch. The fury of the storm seemed to have slackened somewhat but I wondered how we were going to get the ship off its rock and fix it up well enough to continue our journey. It seemed an impossible task.

"God's great bulging balls," said a rumbling voice. "I don't know if I've ever been more grateful to have hard ground under my boots. I near shat my braies when we came barrelling in and ripped out our arse on that reef."

I turned to look at a huge looming shape, a man nearly seven feet in height, standing behind me. A flash of lightning lit up his vast, cherry-red face, framed by two fat, plaited ropes of sea-bedraggled blond hair. I very much doubted he had truly been close to soiling himself in fear: for my friend John Nailor, also known as Little John, was Robin's trusted lieutenant and right-hand man and one of the most courageous warriors I'd ever met.

"Get comfortable, John," I said. "We're likely to be here for a long time. Heaven knows how we're going to fix that great big hole in the hull."

"Aziz will know how," said Robin appearing out of the gloom of the cave to stand beside Little John and stare out into the lashing rain. "He has some fine carpenters among his crew. He'll know just how to patch her up. But first thing in the morning, when this blow has passed, we need to get the remaining stores out of her, salvage as much as we can. Might even be worth diving for the sunken flour sacks. This little lot . . ." he waved at a pile of still-dripping barrels and boxes stacked at the rear of the caves " . . . won't feed us for more than three days. By the end of the week, we'll be hungry."

A little later, I wrapped myself up snugly in my large forest-green cloak, which was still damp from the sea but also warm from the fire, and curled in a dark sandy corner of the cave. I was tired, all muscles aching, and very dispirited, too. I thought then about our poor priest, Father Simon, who was snatched from the deck by the storm. *Had God deserted us? Was He punishing us? Why would He take up to Heaven His servant and not another man?* As I prepared myself for sleep, I listened to the rattle and crash of the wind in the trees of the dense wood below us and the hiss of rain on the rocks outside the cave, and thought longingly of the warm, sun-lit land we'd sailed from a week before, the land where Jesus Christ himself had walked.

The *Tarrada* was a dismal sight, even from a distance. She was tied up at the end of long, rickety wooden jetty that speared out into the Mediterranean Sea from the harbour of the port of Jaffa. She was the kind of vessel usually known as a round ship, or a cog, a type of craft used for transporting large numbers of men or large quantities of goods by sea over great distances.

She was big and slow, round as her name suggested, rather than fast and sleek, and she projected an incongruously sad, despondent demeanour in the bright sunshine of the Holy Land. Like a large, plain girl at a country wedding who cannot find a young man to dance with her. She was dirty too. Her sides were streaked with filth where her sailors had carelessly relieved themselves, year after year, into the big ocean. The paintwork on her two square fighting castles, one each at bow and stern, had once been glorious gold and imposing black but was now a faded yellow-orange and a sludgy brown. All her visible ironwork – cleats, bolts, chains, nails – was rusty.

In short, she looked neglected – and mainly because she had been.

"Yet he does swear in the Name of Allah that all her timbers are sound?" said Robin to Aziz, who passed on his enquiry to a skinny, elderly Arab man, who was acting for the ship's owner. This owner was rich a Jaffa merchant who, for a variety of good reasons, had not wanted to be seen to trade directly with the infidels of the Great Pilgrimage – the Christian knights who had arrived in the Holy Land in their thousands over the past year and who, under the command of lion-hearted King Richard of England, had trounced the great Muslim warlord Saladin at the bloody Battle of Arsuf only a few weeks before. I listened to Aziz's question and its answer, having picked up a decent knowledge of the language from an Arab girl whom I'd loved and very painfully lost – a skill that neither Aziz nor the seller's agent knew I possessed. Robin glanced over at me, and I gave him the merest suggestion of a confirmatory nod, which meant: "He is speaking the truth".

Robin did not entirely trust Aziz – he was not an original member of our company but a local seafaring man with wide connections whom Robin had had several murky dealings with in the past. There were ugly rumours about his true allegiances and I'd been brought to this meeting at the harbour to use my language skills to make a discreet test of the captain's good faith

"He swears they are all sound," said Aziz. "I've looked below decks myself – there is some rot and a little sea-worm damage but I believe the ship will carry us to Messina and then on to Marseilles. However, I consider his price too high. I shall offer him only half the sum he has demanded..."

I left Robin and Aziz to their haggling with the Arab, listening with only half an ear, and wandered away along the jetty towards the *Tarrada* to get a better look at her. She was about two hundred feet in length, the size of a moderate hall in England, and it seemed to me that she was too small, old and tired, to carry a hundred Welsh and English men-at-arms and archers and all their gear, as well as a handful of our women folk, three children, twelve horses, a few goats and pigs, a cock and five chickens all the way across the Mediterranean. Then there was the dry stores, too, sacks of flour, salted meat and pickled vegetables in barrels, fodder for the horses, water, ale and pipes of wine, and all of Robin's possessions too...

On top of that there would be Aziz's crew of sailors – how many would they be? A dozen? A score? That would make a total of a hundred and forty souls, more or less. I could not imagine that great mass of living, sweating human flesh fitting into the space enclosed by this little round ship – enough people to make a village, indeed more than the number of folk who lived in my own manor of Westbury, just outside the town of Nottingham, in England, which had been given to me by my lord for loyal service to him. All these travellers, human and animal, would be crammed on this leaky casket for weeks, the time it would take us to travel from the Holy Land to Marseilles, in the distant County of Provence. And if there was a storm...

This was another point of great concern for me – one that I had raised several times with Robin. The sailing season in the eastern Mediterranean ran from early March to the end of September. But we were already in the first week of October. For centuries, the local peoples had recognised that it was unwise to entrust your life to the treacherous waves during this stormy period of the year. Yet that was exactly what my lord intended to do.

Robin had dismissed my concerns. "I know you hate sea travel, Alan, but there is a risk attached to everything we do in this life. We might both catch an ague right here in Jaffa and die of it tomorrow..."

"I do know a certain amount about risking my life, lord," I said, through clenched teeth. I had fought for Robin many times, and by his side too, and I did not like the implication I was merely terrified of putting to sea.

"Look, Alan," he said, "we need to go home. The men are exhausted; some are wounded. I have completed the task I set myself in this land – and Richard has asked me personally to hurry back to England and act as his eyes and ears in the matter of his treacherous brother Prince John. You know what *he* is like. The King has *requested* that I do this. And a royal request is, in fact, an order. Do you want me to ignore the King's wishes? And look at the sky, Alan – look! We'll be fine, we'll be absolutely fine, I promise you!"

The sky was an irreproachable blue. The glorious sun blazed down upon us. And, while Robin had not mentioned it, I knew that he himself was very tired and had also been wounded in the thigh at Arsuf. I gave up trying to persuade him. For I also knew that if we did not leave now, we would not be able to sail before spring. He was right, I told myself; I'm behaving like a silly old woman who is frightened of dipping a toe in the sea.

I slept badly on the hard sand in that damp, chilly cave on the south coast of Crete. At some point in the night I sensed that the storm had increased in its power and malignancy, the noise of the wind was louder and higher in pitch, the crashing of the waves on the rocks below a constant music, and it occurred to me that I should rise and see that all was well with Ghost, who was tied up with the other horses in the wood below the caves. But I was thoroughly worn out by the voyage and the rigours of the storm and for once I indulged my natural laziness, rolled over and sank back into a deep sleep.

In the morning – the quiet, bright morning – I stumbled to my feet and joined a handful of men at the mouth of the cave looking out at a perfectly beautiful sunny day. The sand had dried to a pale yellowish-brown, the sky and sea, a pure and innocent azure. There was no sign at all of the *Tarrada*.

On the strand below us, I could see Aziz, standing alone, forlornly at the edge of the water, waves lapping his boots, as he looked out at the empty bay. There were a few pieces of torn wood floating on the dark blue rippled water – but nothing more. All that had remained of the round ship was gone.

Chapter Two

The dazzling Cretan knight on the fine white destrier was accompanied by six men-at-arms on foot. The small procession of warriors came plodding up the rough cart track that ran alongside the storm-swollen river between the two spurs of mountain towards our beach. On the northern side of the river was the dense wood of twisted Cretan pines and brushwood undergrowth, that side quite impenetrable to man or horse, unless a squad of axe men were prepared to cut a virgin path through the thick vegetation. Between the river and the sheer cliffs of the southern mountainside there was a space no more than fifty yards wide that allowed for a passage, and the marching men, led by the shining mounted knight, came straight down this avenue towards us.

Since the morning when we had lost the round ship – two blazingly hot summer-like days – we'd built a chest-high barricade of brushwood cut from the pine forest, more of a big fence really, and set it across the track between the river and the southern cliffs. That was the extent of our defences.

I was standing guard at the rough gate in the brushwood that served as the entrance to our camp, with two spear-carrying English men-at-arms in sea-swollen leather cuirasses and three of our Sherwood archers – who had only a handful of shafts between them in their arrow bags.

The disappearance of the *Tarrada* in the storm had meant we were left with little food or drink and few serviceable weapons – a shortage of arrows, being the most urgent problem, since more than half of our men were archers. Robin had ordered me to make a collection of all our serviceable arrows, and share them out equally; then he put us all on half-rations.

In contrast, the approaching Cretan knight and his men were beautifully equipped. The mounted man was clad in a shining coat of tiny steel plates, each plate shield-shaped, thumb-nail sized and sewn on to a leather garment that fell almost to his ankles. The effect was to make him look as if he was covered in glittering scales, like a fish. His right hand held a long lance with a large shining leaf-shaped blade; a long, jewel-hilted sword hung from his belt, and a mace, a great spiked iron club, hung from his ornate saddlebow. He had a shield shaped like a huge teardrop and painted a brilliant white, with a golden device that resembled a bull. His horse, a mighty charger, was draped in a pure white trapper, and the bull device was echoed on its chest and flanks. In the bright Cretan light, he dazzled us like a second sun, and his men were only slightly less splendid – each soldier in iron mail coat and white surcoat with the bull-device on his chest and shield, and equipped with an ash-shaft spear, a round shield, a dagger and long, straight arming sword.

I hungered for those fine arms – a part of me wished to take them forcibly from the Cretans. For, despite their glittering splendour, I did not feel that the approaching strangers posed much of a threat to us: I believed myself the match in battle of any knight, no matter how dazzlingly clad. And my archers – even with only a handful of arrows – could take out at least four of the men-at-arms before they got within fifty yards, if I gave the order. Moreover, there were more than a hundred Locksley fighting men within earshot and, poorly armed or not, I was confident we could dispatch this small band of intruders in the time it takes to scoff down a mutton pie.

I was fortunate, in that I had a good iron mail coat, just a little rust-stained from the sea air, and a well-worn old arming sword buckled around my hips – pure luck, really. I had been wearing both items when the storm had struck the *Tarrada*, having just completed a vigorous combat-training session with Hanno, who was also similarly accoutred. It had been our daily habit on the long, dull voyage from the Holy Land to practice our swordplay on the forecastle for an hour or two in the afternoons. I also had a back-up weapon stuck in my left boot, a long, thin dagger known as a misericorde, from the Latin for "act of mercy" because it was used to give a quick death to mortally wounded knights. Hanno had been giving me lessons in how to best use that murderous tool: how to end a man silently from behind, exactly where to strike to disable him at a blow and leave him at *my* mercy. I had thought I was a fairly competent warrior. Hanno regularly showed me how much I still had to learn.

The Cretan knight stopped his horse at the barrier, a dozen yards from me, and holding up his hand, he halted the six accompanying footmen too.

He said something in a loud voice: a proclamation of some kind, of which I did not understand a word, though I recognised the language as Greek – the language spoken by some of the inhabitants on Sicily we had encountered on the outward journey to the Holy Land. We had called them Griffons and held them in contempt for their greed and cowardliness. I was prepared to feel the same way about this shining horseman. Then he repeated his message in excellent French: "Who are you, stranger, who presumes to enter my lord's land uninvited with men garbed for war? Name yourselves!"

I straightened my spine, looked directly into the slit in his helmet visor and said: "I am Alan Dale, of Westbury in the county of Nottinghamshire, liegeman of the Earl of Locksley.

My lord serves King Richard of England."

"You are truly servants of the King of England?" The knight had a note of incredulity in his voice, perhaps even respect – but what was even more surprising was that he spoke in English. "The noble Lionheart who made the long pilgrimage all the way from his northern realm to save the Holy Land?"

I wished then I wasn't wearing a dirty, salt-stained tunic under my rusty mail; that I'd bothered to comb my cropped blond hair before going on duty.

I said: "We are holy pilgrims and protected by order of Pope Celestine in Rome. All who call themselves true Christians are bound to aid us, if they can, and to respect our right of passage if they cannot. We were thrown upon this desolate shore, unwillingly, not two days hence. Our ship was caught in the recent terrible storm and has sunk. We have lost most of our goods and possessions. Who are you to question us, knight – and whom do *you* serve?"

"We are indeed true Christians – yet we do not recognise the authority of your Latin Church. We honour, instead, the high and holy Patriarch of Constantinople and all his bishops. Nevertheless, in the Name of Christ, I swear that you will not be harmed or molested while you abide lawfully in our land. I am Kavallarious Nikos Phokas and I am here to invite your captains to come to the House of the Archon, half a day's ride from here. You are summoned to the presence the ruler of this province, Lord Phokas."

I knew, of course, that the island of Crete was part of the sprawling Greek empire ruled from Constantinople – the great ancient city on the Bosphorus known since antiquity as Byzantium. But I was unsure of exactly how things stood between these so-called Orthodox Christians and our own true Christian forces of the Great Pilgrimage. In May, King Richard had captured Cyprus, which under a rebel scion of the Imperial noble family had declared itself free of the Byzantine Empire but, instead of returning the island to the rule of Constantinople, after capturing it Richard had sold it to the Knights of the Order of the Temple so that they might use it as a base for future operations in the Holy Land. And the Byzantine lords had sent no armies to assist us in the fight against the Saracen chief Saladin, who was our common enemy. This seemed to indicate ambivalence, at least, if not hostility, to our holy cause. Yet this dazzling, English-speaking knight, this Kavallarious, as he called himself, seemed perfectly civil, even friendly.

I bade him wait outside the brushwood barrier, watched closely by my archers and men-at-arms, and went to consult with Robin.

"We'd better do as he asks," my lord said. "This is their land, after all, and we could not resist them if they came at us with their full strength. We need help, Alan. Perhaps this great Lord Phokas can provide us with a ship."

So, less than an hour later, Robin and myself, suitably armed and dressed for travel, with half a dozen men-at-arms, came out to join the waiting Kavallarios and his men. We left Little John in charge of our beach encampment – which the Cretan knight told me was known as Matala by the locals – and formed up beside the strangers, holding ourselves as proudly as we could in our bedraggled state. To be honest, it felt good to be on Ghost's back once again – and the grey gelding now seemed fully recovered from his watery ordeal and the wild and stormy night in the wood.

The sun was high as we rode off along the dusty track between the arms of the mountains, leaving the beach and our friends behind us as we climbed steadily, heading generally northeast, I reckoned by the passage of the sun. It was a hot day, hot as an English summer noon, but a cool breeze off the mountains made the air comfortable and the journey rather pleasant.

I had no sense of danger from our Cretan escort who trudged along ahead of us in their brilliant white surcoats. Robin was walking his mount beside our six men-at-arms at the rear of the column, discussing something with Gareth, one of the senior members of our company. All was peaceful.

The landscape we rode through was of golden-brown

slopes, some covered with scorched strands of long yellowish grasses but there were also plenty of gnarled, tough-looking silvery-green olive trees dotted here and there to give shade, as well as more of the twisted local Cretan pines.

The steady buzz of insects that filled the air was strangely soothing. I scanned the ridges and skylines of the little round-topped hills we passed, purely out of habit, looking for danger of any kind, but I could feel my senses being caressed and lulled by the warm sunshine and, in truth, I saw nothing on that two-hour ride more threatening than a few capering goats.

"You have not seen this island before?" asked the Kavallarious, who had manoeuvred his horse to walk it next to mine. His English was excellent with only the very slightest Greek accent. I saw that he had removed his pointed helmet in the heat and slung it from his pommel by the leather strap. He was a handsome young man, perhaps sixteen or seventeen years of age, with a long thin straight nose and curly jet-black hair, now glistening with oil or sweat. I was bareheaded myself, but with a steel helm and mail coif in my twin saddlebags, which were slung over Ghost's haunches.

"I've seen Crete before but only from the deck of a ship," I said. "We made a rendezvous on the north coast off Chandax during the voyage to the Holy Land. But we stayed only one night before continuing our journey."

He nodded. "It is a very beautiful island," he said. "But quite often overlooked – travellers such as yourself often pass us by without remaining very long. They see Crete as a . . . a backwater, is that the correct word?"

He sounded rather wistful, even a little ashamed of his homeland.

"How is it that you speak such good English?" I said. It was a question I had been longing to ask.

"I had excellent tutors," he said. Then stopped.

"But why English?" I persisted. "What need of it is there in Crete?"

"I learnt French, too, and a little German. But I wished to

speak all the different tongues of the fighting men of the Great Pilgrimage so that I... well... I wished to join the holy cause, to fight at the side of the knights of Christendom; to recapture the city of Jerusalem for the sake of Our Saviour."

"Why did you not do so?" I said. "I'm sure King Richard and his nobles could have found a use for another brave knight such as you."

He smiled at me shyly. "You are kind, sir," he said. "I wished to join the pilgrimage but my father forbade me. He said I was too young. It was too dangerous... So I stayed in my schoolroom studying obscure languages, and mathematics, and rhetoric. While other, better men battled the heathen."

We rode on in silence for a while. I had never really thought of English as an obscure language. But then we were very far from home. I decided not to take any offence at his words. Indeed, I was warming to the lad. He was clearly intelligent and seemed eager to please. I found that I rather liked him.

Then he said: "I heard there was a glorious battle about a month ago in the Holy Land, a great fight, at a place on the coast called Arsuf. And there the forces of Christ triumphed over the wicked Saracens, is this correct, sir?"

I told him it was, and with no small measure of pride I recounted my own part in it – and brave actions of Robin's men, too; and the activities of the other contingents of the Christian army, as well. Indeed, as we rode along, I found myself giving him a full description of that bloody day of slaughter – and when I had finished his eyes were shining with excitement.

"So victory was the result of the Hospitallers' impetuousness," he said. "That is strange: I have always admired them for their iron discipline. Indeed, I once considered defying my father and applying to join their ranks. But you say they charged the Saracens without King Richard's permission? And he was forced to support their attack and commit to a full assault?"

"That is one way of looking at things. Richard had planned to wait until Saladin attacked him, but... well, the King always says that in war no plan ever survives the first contact with the enemy. The point is, we triumphed."

"You know the Lionheart personally? Are you then a great nobleman?"

"Not I. Merely a captain of men in the Earl of Locksley's service, and the holder of one small manor in England. But the King has been most kind and generous to me, and we have made music together – which I believe creates something of a bond between men, even of vastly different rank."

He frowned at that and said: "That would not be the case in Crete – my father would not dine, or make music, or spend his leisure time with a man who is not of noble blood. He would be dishonoured by that close contact."

I decided not to take offence once again. "The King did offer to knight me himself," I said, "if I joined his retinue. I would have been given honours too. But I chose, instead, to continue to serve my lord, the Earl of Locksley."

He seemed perplexed by my claim to have refused a knighthood and lands but still impressed, nonetheless, with my royal connection, which was not an unpleasant sensation for me. Then he began to tell me about his own wealthy family, and his illustrious lineage, although I confess I did not pay close attention. He spoke at length about his honour and how he cherished it, and how he desired glory above all else in this life, and I was left with the impression of a boy who desperately wished to distinguish himself in battle.

Even at my tender age – and I had seen roughly the same number of years as him – I could have told him that there was little glory in bloodshed. But I was content to listen to him babbling about honour and sacrifice, and a Christian knight's duty, nodding politely, as we rode along through parched landscape. He seemed a pleasant, eager, enthusiastic fellow. And he clearly meant well in his charmingly parochial Cretan way. As I say, I liked him.

At last, we began to climb a very steep slope up a part of the road that doubled back on itself as it rose in a series of tight zigzags. At the very summit of the hill, I could see what looked like a collection of tumbled ancient ruins, shattered columns and huge blocks of tumbled stone, and off to the side one large square newly built house, covered in shining white marble and topped with a red tiled roof. There were several outbuildings and many shady cypress trees and the whole establishment was surrounded by a man-high white stone wall, topped with a row of spearheads set in mortar.

"This is the House of the Archon," said Nikos, "palace of my father Lord Ioannis Phokas, Governor of Phaestos, Mires and the Messara Plain."

I had gathered from Nikos's ramblings on the journey that, since Crete had been liberated from cruel Saracen rule two hundred-odd years ago, it had been governed by twelve aristocratic Greek families, sent down from Byzantium by the Emperor himself – each family controlling a particular region of the island. Lord Ioannis Phokas, Nikos's father, was the head of one of these twelve noble families and the Governor – or the Archon, as it was called in their tongue – of this richest southern province of Crete.

As we approached the gate in the white marble wall, I was struck by two things – first the astonishing view over the Messara Plain stretched out below us to the north of the House of the Archon: a lush bowl of a valley filled with small fields and neat orchards, of olives and barley, of oranges and lemons and figs, the land as green as a jungle in places, and well watered by a long brown river that snaked through the middle. The sight of the valley from this vantage point was breath-taking: I felt as if I were suspended cloud-like over this bountiful landscape with its ripe fields of plenty, which was quite clearly the source of the local Archon's wealth.

The second thing I noticed was that some of the spear points set on the top of the wall around the House of the Archon were adorned with the severed heads of men, of varying disgusting degrees of corruption. There were some fresher polls, lifelike and recognisable, perhaps, by their friends and families, but there were others that were just black, shapeless masses, with shifting crowds of flies swarming eagerly over them. Still others had lost all their flesh and were no more than yellowish, toothy skulls lolling emptily on the spikes, retaining only a few dried scraps of gristle and hair.

It was a revolting sight, at odds with our pleasant sunny ride through the golden hills, the magnificent view and my amiable, rambling chat with young Nikos. It struck a horrible, jarring note; a note of pain and horror in a near-idyllic landscape. But it was not as shocking, nor as deeply disgusting, to me at least, as what I saw on the final part of the road leading up to the Archon's gate. As we turned a corner, I saw that on the far side of the road, the southern side, three huge wooden crosses had been set up.

And they were occupied.

The forms of three naked wretches were nailed up there in a row in gross imitation of Our Lord's Passion at Golgotha. And at least one of the poor victims, the fellow in the centre with blood-crusted iron nails pinioning both wrists and feet, was still alive. I saw him flex his knees and shove his emaciated body up the wooden plank at his bare back, extending his crossed, pierced feet, pushing painfully upwards against the iron nail to take a great tearing breath into half-collapsed lungs, before slumping again. I was almost as shocked at the blasphemous nature of the punishment, as by its cruelty.

"Who are these men?" I asked Nikos.

"What? Oh, them," he said, nonchalantly, as though he had barely even noticed this seeping obscenity right on his doorstep. "They're criminals."

"What sort of criminals?" I asked. I had thought the laws of England were harsh. I had once been threatened with losing my hand by the sheriff just because I had stolen a pie in a market. This seemed even more extreme.

"They are pirates. Just some Saracen pirates. The waters around Crete are infested with them. My father is a scholar – he is fond of reading the classics, the works of Julius Caesar, you know. Caesar famously ended the scourge of piracy across the

Mediterranean by hunting down and crucifying all the pirates he could find. The Archon seeks to emulate the great Caesar."

Chapter Three

Our horses were led away by grooms to be brushed, fed and watered, and the six Locksley men-at-arms were ushered into a low building on the far side of a large courtyard, where they were told they would be given refreshment.

When Robin and I had washed the dust from our hands and faces in a splendid golden bowl filled with rose-perfumed water, and had been given watered wine to irrigate our throats, Nikos asked us if we wished to bathe or change our clothes. I looked at Robin: we had brought with us no clothes but the dusty, salt-stained ones we stood in. When we politely refused, Nikos told us to wait until we were called into the Archon's audience room.

After about half an hour, sitting in silence in a long hallway filled with fine works of art – vases, statues, silk-woven tapestries – we heard the clattering tramp of nailed boots on the stone floor and a squad of spearmen came through the door. The soldier's faces were grim as iron, and not one of them spoke. Robin and I immediately rose to our feet, and still without a word, the six spearmen formed around us in a tight circle, and we were marched through a set of doors into the presence of Lord Ioannis Phokas.

I was astonished to see that the Archon was lying down, perfectly relaxed as if it were his bedtime. Neither did he rise to greet us. He was in the centre of a large airy, richly appointed room, dressed in a long, loose white robe with a purple stripe, reclining on a padded bench, his upper body propped up with several large brightly coloured cushions. A wreath of green leaves adorned his sparse white hair like a crown. It was obvious that he had just eaten a substantial meal in this extraordinary prone position, for there was a large round table in front of the bench, which bore the stripped carcass of a game bird, several dishes containing sauces of some kind, the bones of a fish, the gnawed crusts from various pies, a few heels of bread, bowls of nuts and olives and one of peeled boiled eggs, and half-eaten citrus fruit.

The honour guard of spearmen retreated to the walls of the chamber and, joining a dozen of their fellows, they took up positions all around us. Robin and I stood straight-backed in the centre of the room and observed the Archon of Phaestos, Mires and the Messara Plain as he lounged before us.

I wondered, since he seemed unable to rise, if the Archon was suffering from some terrible illness. I could think of no other reason why he would choose to greet his guests from the confines of his day-couch. He was a huge man of later years, billowing with fat, his saggy face sweat-slimed and an unhealthy beetroot colour. He did, in fact, look seriously unwell, rather than merely glutton-ish. It also occurred to me that he also might be a deaf-mute. He stared at us for a good long while in total silence, after we had entered the room and made our most elegant bows and then, after a painful silence, he clapped his pudgy hands together and a servant appeared from nowhere with a jug and refilled a vast jewelled goblet on the table in front of him.

The Archon offered us nothing to eat or drink. He just stared at us over the rim of his jewelled cup, sipping his wine noisily. I suddenly had an unpleasant thought: that we were on trial; that this grossly fat, sickly old man, lounging on his bed was a judge, about to pronounce sentence on us.

"You claim to be pilgrims," the Archon said at last, and in French. He spoke in a high, sweet, fluting voice; a beautiful voice in fact, and his accent was impeccable. "My son tells me you are warriors of great renown. And that you came here from the Holy Land, shipwrecked by storm, and claim my protection under the general edict of the Pope in Rome. Is this the case?"

"My lord," said Robin in the same language, stepping forward, and making another elegant bow. "That is indeed the truth. We are noble English men of the sword who, having fought bravely and at great personal cost for Christendom in the Holy Land, are attempting to return to our homeland."

"I do not acknowledge that upstart priest in Rome," said the fat man, giving a dismissive little sniff. "The true Roman Empire, the true Church of our Lord and Saviour Jesus Christ lies here in the East. And you don't look much like noble warriors to me, either. You look like vagabonds; you look like the usual type of penniless flotsam that is washed up on my shores."

Robin stiffened at this insult but said nothing. I glanced around the room. There were more than twenty spearmen lining the walls now, surrounding us, and, while we still had our swords, I knew we would not stand a chance of fighting our way out. I looked at Robin and saw he was smiling. A brittle grimace: "Your Excellency is pleased to jest," he said.

The Archon said nothing. He took another great slurp of his wine.

"Our ship was destroyed by the great storm two days ago, along with almost all our possessions," Robin continued. "We were indeed washed up on your most hospitable shores, this is quite true, and it is also true that we no longer possess the clothes and jewels worthy of our rank. It was all lost."

Robin paused. The Archon remained scornfully silent.

"Yet we are indeed who we say we are: I am the Earl of Locksley, a companion of the King of England, His Highness Richard the Lionheart. I am not without wealth and status in my own lands. My friend here, Alan of Westbury, is a famous swordsman, who makes music with the King, and is a great favourite at his court. We're willing to prove our prowess, if required."

I felt that Robin was over-egging this more than a little – he was, in fact, very short of coin, having spent vast sums to take his armed company of former outlaws to the Holy Land. My swordsmanship left a lot to be desired and I was far from being a "great favourite" in Richard's crowded court. For all I knew, the

King might have completely forgotten me by now.

"Never heard of either of you," said the Archon, and sipped again wetly from his huge cup. "And I may require you to demonstrate your prowess in due course. You have no actual proof, I assume . . . " Here the Archon's French took on a thoroughly unpleasant, sneering tone . . . "of your true name and rank. No? You could, for all I know, be a gang of Godless pirates, masquerading as pilgrims: prowling these waters like the wolves, preying on honest Christian shipping. We know how to deal with pirates in Crete. And just because you have been shipwrecked on my shore does not mean you are entirely guiltless. Who knows what crimes you have committed in the past?"

I felt a chill at these words. And thought of the three men nailed to the crosses outside this blubbery oaf's gates. I flexed my sword hand discreetly.

"You may not have heard of us," said Robin, still grinning away like a village simpleton, "but we have heard of *you* – Lord Ioannis Phokas, the Cretan Caesar, Lawgiver of Messara, Scourge of all sea-borne Saracens."

The Archon half-smiled. Robin's sweet words were hitting the mark.

"Your bold actions against the heathens in Crete, lord, are spoken about with deep respect, even awe, in the Holy Land. Not two weeks ago, the Lionheart himself spoke of your methods with approval. 'He nails them all up, Locksley,' the King said to me, 'we should honour Lord Phokas's example; do the same with Saladin's men when we capture them.'"

Phokas half-sat-up. "Truly? King Richard said that?"

"I would not lie to you, my lord," lied Robin. "And while it is most unfortunate that we cannot prove our identity with our possessions," he continued smoothly, "we did manage to salvage a few of our most precious items. And I am pleased to be able to bring you a gift today of great value – a relic from the Holy Land, one sanctified by the holy blood of Our Saviour – should you graciously choose to accept it, O great Caesar of Crete."

I could see that we had the Archon's full attention now.

"It is a mark of our great esteem for you and your illustrious House," said Robin. He reached into the purse at his belt and pulled out a small box of walnut wood, with polished silver at the corners and studded with a pearl on the top. It looked like a container for some of the paints and powders that a lady of fashion might use to beautify her face, indeed my former lover, a stunningly lovely young Arab girl, had possessed a similar-looking object.

Robin opened the box and inside I could see, resting on a thick pad of sheep's wool, a long, square-cut, rusty carpenter's nail.

"This," said Robin, "is one of the nails that penetrated the blessed feet of Our Lord Jesus Christ himself on the hill of Golgotha. I acquired it from a Greek hermit near the city of Acre, a very holy man named Peter of Galilee, or sometimes Petros Stylites, a living saint who once remained atop a pillar for seven years, and who assured me that he had been told of its provenance in a holy visitation from Mary, the Mother of God. He has performed many miracles after praying on this relic. He is a wonderworker of some renown."

The Archon sat up completely now. He seemed suddenly to come alive. He stared at the little box in Robin's palm, with an expression almost of hunger, or perhaps lust. He opened his mouth and licked his fat red lips.

"Would you condescend to accept this trifle, Excellency?" said Robin. "Hmm, perhaps not. Perhaps it is beneath your noble dignity. I see that I have made a gross error. Accept my humblest apologies." My lord snapped the wooden box shut and began to tuck it away back into his belt pouch.

The Archon swung his massive feet off the bed, twisting his gross swollen body around on the cushions. For a moment I thought he would attempt to rise fully upright, but instead he clapped his fat hands. When a servant poked his head around a curtain, Phokas began screaming at him.

"Bring wine and food for our esteemed guests, imbecile;

bring them immediately. Why have you so disgracefully neglected our visitors? You bring dishonour upon my House. Why have these fine English lords been forced to stand here like grubby peasants? Bring couches. Bring wine. I shall have you flogged bloody for your discourtesy..." and so on in this vein.

A pair of couches appeared; we sat on them – I decided that I was not about to lie down flat in front of this preposterous man – cool white grapes and sweet red wine were brought, figs and oranges, bread and meat grilled on skewers, a procession of servants came back and forth, and while Robin and I picked at the food, I could not help but think that the nail he had just shown the Archon looked remarkably similar to one of the rusty fixtures from the timbers of the *Tarrada*. I said nothing, of course; I ate some grapes and listened while Robin and the Archon struck up a congenial conversation.

I do not remember exactly the ebb and flow of the discussion between my master and Lord Phokas, the cut and thrust of the bargaining; the terse haggling, in truth. There were offers made and counter offers. I ate the food – which was perfectly delicious after two days of the watery soup of half-rations – and drank the excellent wine. But the gist of the negotiation was this: Robin wanted a ship and sufficient food stores, and fresh water, barrels of ale, wine and so on, and preferably some arms to replace the ones that had been lost. The Archon, quite obviously desired the "holy relic" in the walnut box – but it seemed he also wanted something else from us. A service.

There was a troublesome nest of evil Saracen pirates, Phokas said, less than ten miles northwards up the coast from where the *Tarrada* had struck.

"They are a bold, murderous crew, wolves of the sea, the foulest kind of sea-borne scum," the Archon explained in his strange fluting voice, "and they swarm in these parts like fleas on a dog. There are perhaps a hundred and fifty of these heathens there, maybe more, well armed, with many boats and small ships kept in a little natural harbour. They're protected by a fortress – the Red Fort, is its name – and when my knights draw near to them they either flee into the vastness of the sea, or retreat inside the fort and slam its gates in my face. I long to bring these evil Saracens to justice but..."

I thought of the crucified men on the road outside the House of the Archon. I knew that if I were a pirate, I'd stick very close to the safety of my stronghold, too, when the Archon's shiny knights came galloping into view.

Robin insisted that his men were exhausted, and that their fighting days were over. They had spent all their strength in the Holy Land, he claimed.

Next, Lord Phokas tried to appeal to Robin's sense of Christian duty: "You came on the Great Pilgrimage to kill the Saracens. I applaud your endeavour and here are some more of their ilk for you to exterminate..."

I wondered what the Archon would say if he knew that Robin had been forced to come on the Great Pilgrimage against his will and that, in truth, once in the Holy Land, his objective had been to take control of the lucrative market in frankincense; moreover, that he was just as happy to deal with Saracens, men like Captain Aziz, as he was to deal with Jews, like his friend Reuben, or indeed with Christians. It made absolutely no difference to him. Furthermore, he was not a Christian in any true sense and, despite dabbling in some pagan rituals in Sherwood, he had no religious convictions at all.

But Lord Phokas did not know this. What he also did not know, but which was plain to me, was that Robin would almost certainly accept his offer, once he had wrung all he could out of the fat man in terms of stores, food, drink and a good weatherly ship to complete our journey home.

"We should need to be properly equipped with new arms and armour, of course," my lord said musingly, as if this had only just occurred to him, "and we must be compensated appropriately as well – with a generous extra payment for the families of any unfortunate man who falls in battle..."

I took some more wine and ate a little more of the food. The immediate danger seemed to have passed and I sank into a reverie, losing myself in my own dark thoughts as I waited for the two men to come to an arrangement.

Ever since we had departed from the Holy Land, there were two terrible crimes, insults to all common decency and humanity, which had regularly poisoned my daily happiness, and upon which I was inclined to brood.

The first crime had been committed by my lord – in the Holy Land, in pursuit of the riches of the frankincense trade, Robin had callously murdered a good friend of mine, a brave and true Templar knight called Sir Richard at Lea. He had ordered Little John to slit his throat – and the big man had done so without a moment's hesitation. Sir Richard at Lea had not transgressed in any way against Robin, nor against any of us. In Robin's own vile, exculpatory words, the Templar had simply stood in his path; he had been an obstruction, no more, and so my lord and master had casually destroyed him.

I had not exactly forgiven Robin for this appalling crime but I had, in a small way, made a kind of peace with his actions. I reminded myself that I had sworn an oath to Robin to be loyal until death, and that this oath was binding and sacred, and it overrode any duty I might have had to seek justice for my poor dead friend. However, it was not a comfortable accommodation I made with my conscience. I took the trouble to remind myself, from time to time, what I knew to be true: that the Earl of Locksley was capable of monstrous cruelty, of murder and worse, whenever it served his interests.

The second crime on which I regularly brooded had been committed by me. My Arab lover, a girl named Nur, had been captured by an enemy of mine and appallingly mutilated – her ears, lips and nose had all been sliced off rendering her once-perfect face perfectly hideous, in fact, quite terrifying to behold. I had sought bloody justice for *this* affront, and had killed the man who did this, a creature called Malbête, but the crime was mine because it was on *my* account that she had been so horribly mutilated: Malbête had been seeking to punish and humiliate me by striking at her. And I had failed to protect her. Worst of all, when she had presented her ruined face to me, I had screamed in terror and rejected her. An instinctive reaction, yes, but I knew in my heart I could not truly love someone with the face of a monster.

That was my crime. And, in a way, by recognising my own failings, my own selfish shallowness, I gradually came to accept and understand Robin's.

As we rode back to Matala in the late afternoon, I asked Robin how he had known that the Archon would be so interested in his "holy relic".

"Believe it or not, Alan, there really was an old Greek hermit in Galilee called Peter who lived on top of a pillar for seven years."

"Truly?" I said. "For seven years? How did he . . ."

"He had a bucket. His acolytes emptied it when they brought up food."

"Oh, I see, and why did he stay up there so long?"

"Who can fathom the mind of religious folk? I imagine he thought the height brought him closer to God. The ninny. But the point is, there is such a man and he has a certain amount of fame among members of the Orthodox Church. Never met the fool myself but I took a chance that the Archon had heard of him. If you are going to sell a man a lie, Alan, it's always best to mix in as much truth with it as possible. I also knew we would have to give that fat bumpkin a gift of some kind, and I had nothing, so when I saw that rusty old nail sticking out of a plank on the beach, it seemed perfect . . ."

"Will he find out the nail is a fake, do you think?"

"Maybe. But he wants to believe it is a true relic. He is, after all, paying a hefty price for it." Robin then explained to me the finer points of his deal.

"He has provided silver, of course, but says he doesn't have a ship he can spare at this time. However, the lardy oaf says he knows a sea captain now refitting up in Chandax whom he can persuade – by which I assume he means bully or bribe – to take us on to Messina in a week or two. We'll have to make our own way on from there. But I've contacts in Sicily, through the frankincense trade, friends of Reuben, so I can get credit there quite easily."

"What about arms for the men?" I said. "We have almost no arrows left – just six bundles, I think, about two shafts for each archer. If we're going to fight a hundred and fifty Saracen pirates, we'll need a deal more than that."

"The Archon has no arrows at all," said Robin flatly. "Why would he have? The Byzantines don't use the war bow. But he's lending us six of his Cretan knights. And he has promised me swords and mail and shields and other sundry equipment. They'll be delivered to us tomorrow and then..."

"Then we go to war," I said.

"There is one more thing. And you won't like it, Alan. But I don't want you to make a silly fuss about this. Promise you won't go soft on me, yes?"

I frowned. "What is it?"

"He wants us to take prisoners, as many we can manage, and hand them over to him for summary punishment. For what he calls Caesar's justice."

I stared at Robin, horrified. An image of the man nailed to the cross, outside the Archon's house, struggling to take a breath, swept into my mind.

Chapter Four

There were three of them, sitting on upturned barrels beside a small crackling campfire, drinking wine and laughing. I did not know if they were actually sentries, for they paid no attention whatsoever to the surrounding night. Perhaps they had just decided to take their little party a little distance from the main gate of their enclosure. I could not tell. If they were supposed to be on guard, they were making the worst job of it that I had ever seen. By staring into the fire they destroyed any hope they might have of seeing beyond their circle of light. Yet, whatever they were, criminally incompetent sentries or just carefree partygoers, they were all already doomed to die.

I was lying with my shoulder pressed against Hanno's, in a patch of long dry grass, a dozen paces from the three men and their jolly gathering. It had taken us a full two hours to approach the spot in which we now lay, crawling painfully on elbows and knees through the night over hard, rocky ground. A yard behind my boots lay the huge form of Little John, still as death; behind him – fifty yards back – was Robin and the rest of our force.

When we had set off that morning from Matala, we mustered sixteen well-mounted, well-armoured men-at-arms, six of them scale-clad dazzling Cretan knights, including my new friend Kavallarious Nikos Phokas. Our ten Sherwood riders had all been provided with swords and shields, and even twelve-foot, ash-shafted, needle-tipped lances – the Archon had proved to be as good as his word in this respect, at least. We also had thirty handsomely equipped Locksley men-at-arms on foot and a company of twenty archers – each with a long bow and each *now* with six or seven good straight arrows.

When the meagre supply of shafts had initially been shared out between the sixty-odd bowmen who had survived the wreck of the *Tarrada*, the archers had begun to grumble and moan about going into battle with so few missiles, only one or two shafts per man. Robin had gathered them together and told them bluntly that there was nothing to be done about the situation.

Owain, who was the long-time captain of the Sherwood men, a mature and sensible Welshman of middle years, had then come up with a solution. The sixty bowmen were divided into three equal-sized groups, according to their skills. All the serviceable shafts we had – one hundred and thirty-five arrows, if I recall correctly – were collected up and given to the twenty best shots in the company, men Owain had picked out personally. Another score of archers, the least skilled and least intelligent men, were told to put away their bows for now and were given arming swords and shields, daggers and spears and were designated – with a few accompanying good-natured jeers – as temporary men-at-arms. These men were ordered to remain in at Matala beach with Aziz and his handful of Arab sailors to safeguard the camp, the women and children, our remaining food stores and our few possessions.

The last group of twenty bowmen – those who were the tallest and strongest in body, and perhaps the toughest minded – were issued with stout clubs hewed from pinewood and bundles of rope cut into one-yard lengths.

Their task was to take the prisoners.

This squad of twenty were to come in behind the main assault. They were ordered not to attempt to take part in the fighting but, instead, to knock down and subdue the wounded enemy with their heavy clubs, being careful not to slay them or smash their skulls, and to bind the prisoners, so they could be subsequently delivered up to the Archon for his "Caesar's justice".

I wanted nothing to do with this club squad, which was commanded by the vintenar Gareth. I had not made a "silly fuss" – as Robin had so unfairly described it. I didn't go "soft" on him at all. I just kept my mouth firmly shut while the anger boiled in my belly. I resented the cold-bloodedness of our plan to pick out enemies, fellow warriors, albeit of a different faith, club them, capture them and turn them over to a tyrant for unspeakable torture and a slow death. If we had not been desperate to get the Archon's help in finding a ship, I believe I'd have refused my lord, and stayed away from this dirty, dishonourable fight. But, to my shame, I did not. I struggled into my rusty hauberk that morning, slung sword and shield, slid the misericorde into my boot, saddled up Ghost and joined my comrades mustering on the beach.

Robin gave us a brief address: "We have an unpleasant task at hand, gentlemen; dangerous, too, but necessary to get us off this island. So may we all do it with brave and willing hearts. Now, men of Locksley, let us march."

And we were off, heading north towards the Red Fort – and battle.

The three sentries, or whatever they were, were still sitting around their cosy fire about thirty paces west from the main gate in the high pinewood fence that surrounded the castle courtyard to the north of the Red Fort. The gate to the courtyard, astonishingly, was propped wide open and earlier that evening, in the last blaze of the setting sun, Hanno and I had observed the casual comings and goings of the bedraggled men who held the Red Fort.

They were mariners, for sure, identified as such by their comic rolling seaman's gait, and well armed with scimitars and knives, a few with short-hafted axes. These dangerous "wolves of the sea" were also mostly dirty, bearded, slovenly, and many of them were apparently extremely drunk.

The whole settlement had the appearance of a sleepy sun-drenched market in the Holy Land. As true night fell, and the moon began to rise, stalls were set up both inside and outside the courtyard fence offering fruit and grilled meats and fish, griddled flatbreads, and drinks of different kinds, and scores of men – there were no women that we could see – wandered between the stalls, chatting, gossiping and sampling the various wares.

The Red Fort itself – a square, two-storey tower constructed of blocks of a blood-coloured stone thinly veined with white – was situated at the base of a short rocky peninsula, only a hundred paces long, that jutted out south into the dark Mediterranean, and curled round a little to the east to make a natural harbour. In the shelter of this shallow bay, anchored fore and aft, was large round-bellied trading cog, not too dissimilar to the *Tarrada*, although a little smaller and leaner, which looked as if it might well have been captured from Christian merchants. There was also a medium-sized Arab ship, of the type known as a dhow, moored beside the cog, and several smaller craft. Beyond the little harbour, to the right of the Red Fort and some miles out to sea, I could just make out in the moonlight, the grey shape of an island, which resembled a giant beast with a long snout slumbering in the water.

The fort had crenulations on the flat roof, which also supported a sentry – at least it had had one by day – a sleepy fellow in a dirty white robe and straw sunhat leaning on his spear and drinking from a large yellow gourd. The sentry disappeared with the sun – and he had not been replaced. Another indication that discipline in this shambolic lair was disgracefully lax.

To cap it all, the double door to the Red Fort itself was also left wide open; probably, we surmised, to allow a cool breeze into the dark interior.

As far as we knew, the enemy had no inkling of our presence, which I was glad of because our plan rested dangerously on the element of surprise.

Hanno whispered, "Go!" in my ear and I jumped to my feet and began to sprint towards the open gate. I pelted straight past the three sentries at their cheery fire, running like a hare despite the weight of my weapons and mail, and was peripherally aware of them all leaping up with wild cries of alarm.

I could hear Hanno pounding along behind me, and further behind him, John keening softly as he thundered on like a charging bear in our dust.

Now, behind me, arrows were flying out of the darkness, pfft, pfft, pfft, and could easily imagine the trio of sentries skewered, writhing on the sand.

We ran straight through the courtyard gate. A tall, oily fellow, bare-chested with baggy silk trews, shouted something and put out both his hands as if to try and restrain me. I hit him with my left shoulder, low and hard, thumping him in the upper belly, knocking him down in a tangle of limbs.

I didn't even break my stride. I was halfway across the courtyard already – I was very swift on my young legs in those far off days – market stalls and boozy browsers all around me, Arab men, frozen, mouths open in the act of eating, or surprise, or just pouring out a jug of cool drink.

There ahead of me was the big, iron-bound double door of the Red Fort. Still open. There was a pair of large, semi-alert guards, mailed and armed with fat, wickedly curved swords; they instantly saw me and Hanno and John, charging straight at them. And did exactly the right thing.

They began to haul at the doors of the fortress; pushing them closed.

But their slovenliness was again their undoing. The heavy double doors were not well oiled, hardly cared for at all for some months, perhaps even for years; the big slabs of wood screeched and stuck, and despite the yelled oaths and straining muscles of the two strong door-keepers, by the time I was within striking distance, they were still a quarter-way open. I yanked my slim misericorde from my left boot top, mid-stride, and leapt on the left-hand man. We both went tumbling to the ground, his curved sword flying, and me ending up crouched on top of him, snarling like a leopard. He was terrified, screaming for help, batting at me with his bare hands; I was struggling to get the point of my blade under his chin. I pinned his shield to his chest with my left knee, swiped aside a flailing fist and shoved the sharp point once, hard up under his jaw-line, punching through the bottom of the tongue, up higher and feeling it crunching through the palate and lower skull and right up into his brain. He went suddenly limp. I breathed out a lungful.

Hanno was savaging the other door guard with a pair of hand-hatchets, cutting him apart like a butcher at a carcass, and Little John had burst past us, roaring, and was dealing with two men-at-arms inside the Red Fort itself.

I wrenched my misericorde free of the dead man's lolling head, wiped it clean on his long grey robe and returned it to my boot-sheath. I took off the fellow's shield, slipped my left arm through the loops, stood up and drew my arming sword. Hanno tucked away one of his pair of blood-smeared hatchets, and drew his own long blade. John was growling and panting over the two bodies inside the fort and we prepared to defend its part-open portal.

The first element of our task was done. We had taken the doorway to the Red Fort. All we had to do now was hold it till Robin could come up.

They came at us then, their slack ways and drunken casualness all gone; blasted away by the brutal shock of our intrusion. They took a moment or two to organise themselves, and then a pack of them – maybe half a dozen men, although it was impossible to count, charged yelling towards us.

Behind me I could hear the clang of steel on steel, and the occasional scream, as Little John protected our backs against a slew of pirates who had come clattering down the stairs inside the fort. I heard John say clearly in plain English, "Come on, then, you arse-munchers! Come on, I haven't got all night. One at a time, or come all at once: I care not! Let's get this done!"

I was too busy to turn and watch. A scimitar lashed down from out of nowhere towards my head, and almost simultaneously another dark-faced man lunged from below with a three-pronged spear. I got the shield up to take the sword blow, just in time, and ducked in the same movement and felt one of the spear tines screech over the steel dome of my helmet. An inch lower and it would have punched a hole through the centre of my forehead.

My own sword licked out an instant later in response and I felt the long blade sink into his unarmoured belly, and a jolt as the steel tip hit his spine.

The man was screaming then, anger and pain, right into my face, his big red mouth wide; his breath reeked of greasy meat with too much garlic.

I shoved him away, and he staggered and fell to his knees. Another man in a snowy white turban tried to grapple me, pecking at my mailed chest with a long dagger; I fended him off with my shield, but too weakly, and he came bouncing back, slicing at the mail on my shoulder. I smashed my forehead out, the steel helmet cracking into the bridge of his nose like a hammer, and he stepped back dazed, on jelly legs. I whipped my sword across and slashed half-through his dirty neck.

Out of the corner of my eye, I saw Hanno split the skull of a balding fellow and an instant later lop the forearm clean off a semi-naked pirate who was lunging at him with a long jewel-encrusted dagger.

Behind me Little John was roaring like a madman; I felt his broad back knock lightly into mine. I stood panting: the crush had gone; there were still three or four men now squared up to us, but they had seen the carnage we could inflict and flinched from our long, wet blades.

I looked over their heads and saw, with vast joy and relief, that the courtyard gate was still wide open, four of our Sherwood men guarding it with shield and spear. Somewhere a brass trumpet was sounding, and then sounding again; sharp calls, brash as morning sunlight, out in the inky night.

Then they arrived, at the gallop: sixteen men on huge horses, two by two, lances high, the front ranks in dazzling scale armour, dyed yellow and red by the flickering torchlight in the courtyard. Kavallarious Nikos Phokas was in the vanguard – at least I assumed it was him from his golden bull insignia, I could not see his face with his visor down – and he and another knight burst straight through the open gate in the fence, followed by four other Cretan knights, then a raggedy pack of green-cloaked Locksley horsemen. The cavalry exploded into the courtyard, splitting up into shards of dazzling steel and flapping green as each rider sought and found a target.

Nikos – the bull knight – slammed his lance deep into the back of a running man in a long violet robe. I saw the bloody point burst out of the front of his chest like a red flower. The other Byzantine knights were doing equal damage, skewering the foe, puncturing frail bodies, blades licking out again and again until lances jammed in ribs, spines or sucking flesh. Then the horsemen drew swords, found new targets and the butchery continued.

There had been perhaps forty or fifty men in the courtyard when I ran through it with Hanno and Little John, but when the cavalry column erupted among the crowd they were like a sack full of rats released to the terriers in the pit. They ran everywhere, scattering in all directions, the cleverer ones running for the harbour or the little grey rocky beach on the western side of the little peninsula, splashing into the dark sea and swimming for safety.

The dull ones who remained too long in the courtyard were doomed. The horsemen were in and among them now, ranging all over the space, slashing and skewering, cutting up and charging down the frail bodies of the men on foot; killing joyously, shouting with zeal, hunting them like vermin.

But the battle was not all one way: I saw a Byzantine knight dragged from his horse by five enraged pirates, and their curved blades rose and fell and came back up again bloody to the hilts. Another scale-clad knight was shot in the belly with a crossbow at very close range, close enough that the black quarrel penetrated his shiny armour. The knight tumbled right over the back of his saddle, and lay stunned in his spreading blood on the torn earth.

Now there was a mass of pirates mobbing the entrance to the Red Fort too, seeking its safety. I was stabbing, shoving and cursing the impossible crush of men around me, hacking about wildly with my red-dripping sword; Hanno beside me slicing and slaying like a fiend from Hell. Little John – seemingly having vanquished all his foes inside the fort – turned about and joined us with a wild excited yell, his huge double-headed axe arcing over the top of our helmets to sink deep into the crowd of snarling, scar-faced, blood-splashed pirates, again and again, his broad steel falling on them, his blade splitting skulls, slicing flesh and severing heads from grimy necks.

I was sprayed with hot gore time and again. My arms were leaden now, I could barely lift the sword, my strokes were slower, clumsier, poorly aimed, my eyes blinded by other men's spit, blood and brains. I cursed and cuffed at my sticky face with my hard mailed sleeve, and just blocked a blow with my shield, as a mace crashed down. I smashed my cross-guard into a man's face; and took a crunching blow to my ribs. I was lifted off my feet by the press of men. Something bashed into my helm from the side, the world tilted and swam. I could feel all the strength draining from my legs...

Then Robin of Locksley himself and a squad of dozen howling foot men crashed into the back of the heaving scrum around the door of the Red Fort, cutting unwary men down from behind, crunching them with swung steel, hauling our enemies bodily away from the portal. I saw my lord cut down a huge red-faced pirate with one elegant flick of his shining sword; stab another man straight through the eye-socket immediately afterwards.

The archers had come in to the courtyard now, too, and their arrows were making their weird hissing music... and then it was done. The last of the unmarked foes fled into the darkness; melting away like frost in the sun.

I could see the bow-less archers, too, Gareth's grim squad, clubbing the wounded pirates to the earth, knocking them senseless, bending down to lash their limp arms together. Collecting the dread harvest for "Caesar's justice".

I was done in. I sat on the ground with my bloody sword across my knees, my poor aching back against the blood-splashed stone wall of the Red Fort and watched the squad of clubmen at their terrible work.

Robin had led a party of ten fresh Locksley men-at-arms into the Red Fort, for there were still half a dozen or so Saracens hiding upstairs in the darkness, hoping to escape our notice and somehow creep away. I could hear the occasional horrible scream and clash of steel emanating from inside the walls behind me. But in essence the battle was now over. Hanno came to sit beside me. He had found a large full skin of wine somewhere and having sucked down several huge draughts, he passed it over to me. It was good. Very good. I found my mouth was horribly parched from the exertions of the battle. I gave silent thanks to God and Saint Michael for my survival. It had been touch and go: if Robin and his men had not attacked the crush round the door, Hanno and I, probably Little John too, would have been corpses.

"Perfect," said Hanno, belching long and soft, and reaching over to take the wine skin from my hand.

"What do you mean, perfect?" I said crossly. "Look at the carnage out there," I said indicating the scores of bodies, wounded and dead, lying in their blood and filth on the courtyard floor – some of them our people. As usual after battle, I felt a crushing black weight of sadness on my shoulders.

"We make a plan. We execute the plan. It is successful." He took another long greedy swallow of drink. "Now we have wine. It is perfect."

A little time passed and we sat there in companionable silence, Hanno and I, too tired to talk; we cleaned our weapons, then rested, sipping our wine, eating grilled meat on flatbreads scavenged from an overturned market stall and watching the courtyard, and our men dealing with their wounded comrades. Robin emerged from the Red Fort with John and a few men-at-arms. Their blades were sticky with blood and they brought out no prisoners.

Was that better? I wondered. *What would I prefer?* To be killed in battle, even hunted down inside a fort from which I could not escape; surely that was preferable to the slow, painful death by crucifixion that awaited the poor Saracens who had already been captured. It was better. It was infinitely preferable to crucifixion. Yes. But it still did not feel right to me.

The prisoners from the courtyard, about twenty men, had been gathered together by the side of the fence. They were sitting on the ground, most of them battered and still bleeding, some still unconscious. On the far side of the courtyard, the three surviving Cretan knights – my friend Nikos among them – were praying over the bodies of two of their fallen comrades.

The sixth knight was badly wounded, lying propped up against the sagging fence, his surcoat drenched with blood, his pain-filled eyes were wide open.

I saw Nikos kneel beside him and give him a drink from a cup.

I looked round at Hanno, who had fallen asleep, his head tilted back against the wall of the fort. He was snoring gently. I got slowly, very stiffly to my feet, and plucked up the half-empty wine skin from his loose hands.

I picked my way through the dead and wounded, stopping from time to time when I saw a stricken Sherwood friend, and giving him a good draught from the skin; our casualties had been light, thank merciful God, only half a dozen dead and a dozen wounded in varying degrees of severity.

Unwounded men naturally gathered round their wounded friends, making them as comfortable as they could in their pain; praising their acts of valour. A few of the worst injured, those with untreatable belly wounds, for example, would be given the option of the knife; a swift end, if they chose it.

"Hey, Blondie, give us a drink," said a harsh, scratchy voice. "For the love of all that is holy, give me a little sip or two from your wine skin."

I looked quickly all around me but the nearest Sherwood man was twenty paces away. "Here, mate," said the voice, "sling us over the skin; don't be a tight bastard. I'm about as dry as a Mother Superior's privates."

I looked at the speaker. He was gathered with the rest of the prisoners against the courtyard fence. His dirty hands were tightly bound. Large round eyes glittered in a hairy monkey-like face, which was burnt the colour of old oak by the Mediterranean sun; his head was wrapped, Arab-style, in a grubby turban, and he wore a long robe that covered his small, skinny body to his ankles. But the words coming from his mouth were English; and in the unmistakable tones of a man born on the banks of the Thames.

Chapter Five

I gave him the wine skin and he drank a good pint without pausing. Raising it in his bound hands and pouring the liquid in a red stream into his open mouth. The vintenar Gareth, who was in command of the squad of clubmen, came over to me, and stood beside me, slapping the head of his bludgeon into his open palm, and staring at the little man drinking from my wine skin.

"Is this one giving you any cheek, Alan?" he asked. "Want me to teach him some better manners?"

"No. Tell me, Gareth, any of these men been given meat and drink?"

"Meat and drink – a-ha-ah-aha . . ." Gareth convulsed with laughter. I stared at him. "Meat and drink – for heathen prisoners – and maybe some soft cushions to sit on, oh, ha-ha-ha . . ."

I began to find him more than a little irritating.

"I'm not joking, Gareth," I said, putting a hand on his shoulder. "Go on now, and organise some water and food, if we have it, for all these prisoners. We don't want them expiring of thirst during night. The Earl would not be pleased. Neither would the Archon. Go on, bread, water, whatever you find."

A confused Gareth nodded obediently at me, his mouth drooping, then he stumbled away to dig up some suitable sustenance. I went over to the man clutching my wine skin, and took it back from him. It was sucked quite dry.

"Thank you . . . sir," he said. " 'Twas good of you. Nice vintage, too."

"Who are you?" I said sitting down next to him.

"I'm generally called Rashid al-Bahar in these parts."

"And in other parts?"

"Well, I used to go by the moniker Richard Seaman, or plain Ricky."

"You're English? How did you find yourself among these

rascals."

"Luck," he said, and grinned at me. "All of it bad."

Then the little Englishman started slowly, a little reluctantly, to tell me his story. He had been born in the parish of Dowgate, in the City of London. He had grown up, in his own words, a "filthy wharf rat", and he had run away from his dirt-poor, drunken whore of a mother and gone to sea about a dozen years ago. He had started on the trading ships, bringing great tuns of wine from Aquitaine to London, but restlessly moving from ship to ship, employed as a cook's assistant here, and then as a deck hand there, then as a helmsman and navigator. However, on one voyage on the *Mary Magdalene*, a fat, slow Norman cog out of Rouen, his ship had been attacked in the Bay of Biscay – attacked by swift-sailing Moorish pirates up from Salé on the African coast, rapacious and cruel men but very fine seamen indeed, he said.

The ship had put up a fight but had been easily taken – the cog had only a handful of men-at-arms on board – and all the crew who survived the short bloody sea-battle were enslaved. They were taken in chains to Spain and, after a long brutal land journey, to the country of Al-Andalus in the south of that sunny peninsula. They were treated very badly, Ricky said, because they were both Christians and slaves: branded, abused, whipped and beaten...

I held up a hand to stop Ricky's painful flow of words, for I saw my lord coming towards me. It was very late now; the night was almost done and dawn could not be very far off.

"I see you can speak pretty well with these Saracen prisoners, Alan," said Robin, stifling a yawn. "I'm for my bed soon but, before I go, please ask this evil-looking bantam why the two larger ships in the harbour are fully loaded with stores and provisions, even with barrels of fresh water. I've been looking inside all the vessels in the bay and it seems they were about to set off on a long voyage. I'd like to know where they were planning to go – and why. Can you ask this little fellow that?"

I turned to Ricky, and said loudly in plain English: "You

were about to set off on a journey, is that not so? What was your intended destination?"

"Alan?" said Robin. "What . . ."

"We had a right juicy target in mind, sir," said Ricky. "Good plan, too."

Robin stared at the man, digesting this. But he said nothing.

"What sort of target?" I said.

"Just told you: juicy."

I frowned at him, and he sighed: "It was to be a rich target, sir, very rich indeed; I'm talking about wealth beyond the dreams of money-lenders."

"Very well, man, you have my full attention," said Robin. He sat down cross-legged on the ground beside Ricky and me.

"Tell me more about this juicy target."

Ricky shook his head. "I'll willingly tell you all I know, my lord, but only in exchange for my life and freedom – and a drop more of that wine."

Robin laughed: "I don't think so. Maybe I'll just put you to the question now with fire and the knives. You would talk to me soon enough, I warrant."

I snapped my head round and glared at Robin.

"You could certainly try that, yes," said Ricky, nodding seriously as if he was mulling over a knotty problem with an old friend. He showed no fear at Robin's threat of torture at all. "It might even work but, you know, my lord, torture is very tricky. People will tell you whatever you want to hear, when they're in bad pain – regardless of whether it's the truth or not. Your best bet, I'd say – and this is just my humble opinion, like – is to promise me my freedom and hear what I have to say. If you don't like it, well, then you can always break your sacred word, besmirch your honour, and have me executed on the spot. But you *will* like it, sir. I know you will appreciate it."

Robin laughed again, a kinder sound – the sound of genuine pleasure.

"I like this fellow, Alan. Let's hear what he has to say."

"No," I said. "No. Absolutely not. I will not allow this – I will oppose you, my lord, with all my strength and will!"

Robin and I and Little John were sitting at a candle-lit wooden table inside the Red Fort. We had wine and bread and salty white cheese before us but nobody was breaking their fast; nobody was eating a crumb. In a corner of the small room, slumped on a bench was Hanno, snoring again. Upstairs the three Cretan knights had commandeered a room of their own, and were snug abed. Their badly wounded comrade had died about an hour before. At dawn, in an hour or so, we were due to set off for the House of the Archon to deliver the wretched prisoners to Lord Phokas and claim our reward.

"It's the logical thing to do, Alan, if we are actually going to follow this new course," said Robin. "It is the only correct choice."

"No," I said again, banging my fist on the table. "I will not stand for it."

"I'll do the actual killing, if you are going to be a girl about this," said Little John. His big red face was frowning at me in perplexity from the other side of the small table. "It would be the work of a mere moment, nothing more. Hanno would lend me a hand, if necessary. What is your problem?"

"My *problem* is that is would be the cold-blooded murder of our friends and allies, three innocent Cretan knights, who have done us no harm at all – indeed, who have fought with us, who have aided us and promised us further aid. It is evil, immoral. It is just plain wrong. I will not allow you to do it."

I was feeling desperate. I truly did not want to go against my lord and Little John. Quite apart from the danger – I knew they would kill me if it became necessary – we had a bond between us I could not bear to sunder. I was thinking of Sir Richard at Lea and his casual murder at Robin's hands.

"Alan, just listen to me," said Robin, he fixed me with his extraordinary silver-grey eyes, and said: "If we adopt this plan of action, your new friend Ricky's plan, that is, to take the . . .

well, let's just call it the Target, for now, the less we mention our objective the better . . . then we'll be breaking the contract agreed between me and the Archon, the dread power in this little part of Crete. Personally, I think we *should* go for the Target. No question. Little John agrees. The Archon's promise of finding us a ship was vague at best. And we have two ships, right here, right now, loaded with stores and fresh water, ready to go on a voyage. A bird in the hand . . . you agree?"

I nodded. I couldn't deny his argument.

"When the Archon finds out we have accepted his silver and his fine weapons and armour, accepted his hospitality – and then broken our solemn word and cheated him of his prisoners, he will be angry. Yes? He will seek to punish us; he will wish to nail *us* up on those monstrous crosses outside his big vulgar palace. But, with luck, we can be far away by then; we can thumb our noses at the fat slug and his warped notions of justice. In order to escape, though, and get far enough away, we have to delay the news getting to him that we have, uh, changed our minds. Yes? Do you agree with me?"

I could not fault his logic.

"So *if* we are going to do this – *if* we are going to make this choice – we must kill the three Cretans to give us sufficient time to escape. Yes?"

I looked into Robin's long, drawn but still handsome face; and Little John's big red shiny moon. I thought about what the slyly grinning prisoner Ricky had told us about "wealth beyond the dreams of money-lenders".

"I have an idea," I said.

We crept up the stairs, wincing with every creak of the wood, Hanno, Little John and me, and behind us came three of the clubmen. In an instant, I was beside the cot that held Kavallarious Nikos Phokas. I slapped a hard hand over his mouth and put the point of my misericorde under his jaw. His eyes snapped open, and he made to rise. I shoved the point in a little further, breaking the skin and he ceased his struggling. He glared at me, his black Cretan eyes filled with fear and hatred. I moved my hand from his mouth to his shoulder, allowing him to breathe.

"Believe me, friend Nikos," I said, "I do not do this lightly. But it is a far, far better thing to do than the alternative, trust me."

"Take your filthy hands off me, Englishman," he hissed.

I shook my head, and let him feel a little more of the sharp point. Behind me, Hanno and John were busy subduing the other knights. I jerked my head to summon Will, the nearest clubman with his lengths of rope.

In a few moments, all three Cretans were tightly trussed.

"My father will crucify you for this, Alan of Westbury," said Nikos. "And I will stand at the foot of your cross and jeer you into Hell. I swear it."

"I am truly sorry – but we have no other choice," I said. And meant it.

Hanno came over to my shoulder, he looked down at the Greek lying in the bed with his hands and feet bound, and idly scratched his shaven head.

"I give you two advices, knight-ling. Don't make threats when helpless. And never threaten my friend, Alan. You'll get yourself killed you do that."

We left the knights there, in the upper storey of the Red Fort, in their sweat-stained nightshirts, lashed to their beds. And later, much later, I wondered if that dire humiliation had been wise. At the time, I was busy congratulating myself on having preserved the lives of Nikos and his knightly comrades.

Robin made the captured Saracen pirates, eighteen of them who survived until the pink-grey dawn, swear an oath that, if we freed them, they would not attempt to harm us, and that they would obey Robin's commands.

Ricky – or Rashid al-Bahar as they called him – arranged this ceremony and translated my lord's stern words about their terrible punishment if they dared to cross him into the Arabic dialect they all used among themselves.

The former English wharf rat addressed his words mainly to a portly, middle-aged cove with a thin, curved nose like a falcon's beak and great bushy beard dyed orange-red beneath it, who was their captain, a fellow named Iqbal. As far as I could tell with my imperfect grasp of their tongue, Ricky spoke true and did not attempt to play us false – but I was also very careful not to display my knowledge. Plump red-bearded Iqbal nodded along, seeming to agree wholeheartedly with the scheme Ricky proposed

As Ricky made his pitch to Iqbal and the rest of the captured Saracens, I thought about his extraordinary life story, which he had completed for me in the first streaks of the new day, when I had brought him another skin of wine – his reward for revealing to Robin all that he knew about the Target.

As a Christian slave in Al-Andalus, Ricky had been sentenced to the galleys – a fearsome fate, almost a death sentence, in truth. He had been chained in a flat-bottomed craft with a hundred other wretches, fettered to their oars, and there he had laboured for *two years*, exposed to the elements day and night, barely fed, slops from a bucket, often whipped, and labouring all day at the oar, sitting in his own and his fellow slaves' filth, which was washed away only when it rained. I could imagine the horrors he'd endured.

The galley was owned by a man named Khalil, a wealthy prince of the sprawling Almohad dynasty, the emir or lord of the Moorish province of Valencia on the eastern coast of the Iberian Peninsula. Even uttering the name of the galley owner, this Prince Khalil, seemed to strike terror into the little wharf rat's heart. And Ricky was no coward – he had not turned a hair when Robin had threatened him with fire and knives. But whenever Khalil's name was mentioned, he stammered and seemed to grow pale under his tan.

The Almohads were a powerful, warlike Moroccan clan from the Atlas Mountains, fanatical followers of their Prophet, Ricky said. The Almohads had risen in a single generation from obscurity to ruling an empire that stretched from the sands of the Sahara desert to the plains of central Spain; from the Atlantic coast of Iberia to the borders of the ancient land of Egypt.

When Ricky told me about the Almohads, and their supreme leader, the Caliph Abu Yusuf Yakub, and the vast reach of their mighty armies, I was astonished. Indeed, I was inclined to disbelieve him. I had heard rumours of this African empire, whose rulers were the sworn enemies of Christendom, and close allies of our enemy Saladin, and yet confronted by an Englishman who had seen it at first hand, I was assailed by doubts. Could this monstrous, sprawling heathen powerhouse really exist? Why did God allow it to exist?

Prince Khalil – and once again Ricky's voice shook with fear as he mentioned the name – travelled the Mediterranean coastlines ceaselessly on behalf of his cousin the Caliph. His slaves rowed his personal galley from Valencia to Tangiers, from Algiers to Tripoli – places of which I had only vaguely heard. The swift black galley stayed close to the land, if possible, stopping each night at a suitable beach so the prince could sleep on dry land.

But the Almohads' grip on the waters of the western Mediterranean was not absolute. A powerful Sicilian pirate ship surprised Ricky's black galley in the waters off the little town of Bougie; and the Almohad prince's vessel was boarded and taken, after a short sea chase. The crew of Valencian sailors and slave-masters was slain outright or thrown overboard to drown. Yet Prince Khalil was treated with great respect – his name was well known, as was his connection to the mighty Caliph – and he was held and ransomed back unharmed to his family for a fortune. The way Ricky told it, it was the wise thing to do: the Sicilian pirates would certainly have been hunted down without mercy if they had murdered the Caliph's beloved cousin.

So the pirates treated Khalil with the utmost respect – and made a vast pile of silver from the Almohads. And when the deal was completed, the Sicilians – most of them Arabs but with a sprinkling of a few Greeks and Italians – offered the hundred or so galley slaves a simple choice: they could be set ashore at the next port, or they could sign up as members of the crew.

That had been seven years ago.

I felt a deep sense of satisfaction when I saw Gareth and his clubmen cutting the bonds of the eighteen surviving Saracens, and watched them rubbing their wrists and standing up in the slanting golden sunlight of early morning.

Robin had decided that we would take the two largest ships – which were both fortuitously already prepared for their own mission to attack the Target – and that we would depart as soon as we could. I understood why – the sooner we could get to Matala and pick up the rest of our people the better. The angry knights were still tied up like hogs in the Red Fort but they would get loose sooner or later, and then the hours were counting down till word reached the House of the Archon of our unexpected change of heart.

I knew from a long, pleasant conversation with Nikos the day before on the way to the Red Fort from Matala, that Lord Phokas had at least a forty knights under his command, as well as several hundred well-trained men-at-arms, and a company of javelin men and slingers – and even more Cretan troops available from his fellow archons in the neighbouring districts, should he choose to call upon them. The Archon could crush us like a frog under a stone, if word of our betrayal reached him before we were safely at sea.

I had assumed in my sea-ignorance that we would then simply jump into the ships, haul on a few ropes, drop the sails, lift the anchors and be gone. But the process was far more complicated than that. Our own Arab sailors, under Captain Aziz, were still in Matala and Robin judged it too time consuming to fetch them to the Red Fort. Matala was ten miles away by sea – surely with our combined skills, we could shepherd the two ships that far.

However, it meant we were totally dependent on little Ricky and the surviving Saracens – all men we had been trying to kill a few hours before – and on their captain Iqbal, to unmoor the two ships and get them under way.

Although they had eagerly agreed to the new plan – it was that or crucifixion – they did not love us. Iqbal said he wished to speak to Robin.

There were courtesies to be observed. Robin and Iqbal, attended by Ricky and me, sat at the table in the dark, stuffy room on the ground floor of the Red Fort, and an infusion of mint, honey and boiling water was served out by one of the Saracens, a skinny, silent boy of about twelve years of age in a grubby blue robe and turban, who it seemed was Iqbal's personal slave.

We sipped our hot, sweet mint infusion, and Iqbal, speaking through Ricky, praised Robin for his efficiency in capturing the Red Fort so swiftly. He must be much blessed by Allah to have been so successful in the battle.

Robin asked him what he wanted.

Iqbal then spoke of the glories of the Mediterranean Sea, her beauty, her moods, her occasional treachery, the difficulty of navigating across her. He commiserated with Robin for the loss of his ship *Tarrada*, and said that he understood what a blow to our fortunes, and our joy, that must have been.

Robin thanked Iqbal, and told him that time was pressing, then politely suggested that perhaps they might continue this interesting discussion at sea.

The Saracen then spoke at great length of the blessing of children – he apparently had a great many scattered all along the sea lanes – and enquired about Robin's own family. He had taken a wife, yes? Ah, but only the one?

Robin stood up from the table. "Tell your friend," he said, looking at Ricky, "that if he does not tell me what he wishes to discuss, I shall have him bound, gagged and thrown in the bilges of the dhow, and we will work out ourselves how to sail the ships to Matala. I cannot waste any more time."

Iqbal, apparently, wished to discuss the division of the spoils from the successful attack on the Target. He suggested that since Robin had no precise knowledge where the Target was to be found – only Iqbal possessed that information – that

Robin should receive only one eighth of the booty; the other seven parts to go to Iqbal, to be divided among his remaining men.

I was impressed with this red-bearded chieftain's coolness: he clearly understood that we were in a tearing hurry; he also knew that his men were needed to sail the ships; and only he knew exactly where the Target was. I half expected Robin to explode with rage: this fellow was pushing him hard.

Yet my lord did not. Instead, he whistled; a couple of short notes. And Little John, Hanno and a couple of burly archers came bursting into the low room. Suddenly, the space seemed very hot and crowded. John, particularly, seemed to loom like a fairytale ogre over every man in that small room

Robin said: "Get a good firm grip on him, John. And place his right hand on the table. Alan, you keep your little Dowgate friend out of this."

There was a flurry of movement. Hanno clamped Iqbal to his seat. Little John pinned the chieftain's hand to the table and brandished his axe, the double-blade held menacingly only a foot above the pirate's right wrist.

I had my sword out in a flash and the point an inch from Ricky's Adam's apple. The wharf rat did not move, he just looked calmly up the length of my steel blade and smiled, his dark eyes twinkling merrily at me. The boy servant cowered in the corner, his hands pressed over his mouth.

Robin said: "I hope you will forgive this crude approach but I have no time to dispute with you." Iqbal showed no fear or surprise. He glanced down once at his hairy wrist under John's blade, looked at Robin and smiled.

"I am going to make you a fair offer," said my lord. "It is the best offer I'm prepared to make – you must appreciate this. I know that things are done differently in your lands. But I mean this most sincerely. There is no trick, no subterfuge. This is the offer. The only offer. Do you understand me?"

Ricky made the translation and Iqbal nodded, still smiling calmly.

"I will give you half of the spoils from our mission – only half – if the Target is a rich as your man here says, there should be plenty for all of us. You will immediately, right now, without delay, help me get the two ships to Matala to pick up my friends. Then you and your man Rashid here will accompany me to the Target and aid me, freely and fully, to accomplish this task. You will not betray me. You will not hinder me. Nor will you quibble at all about the division of the loot. You get half, that is all – understand?"

Robin paused to let Ricky translate. Iqbal was still as cool as snow. "Furthermore, you will instruct your sailors – under my captain Aziz – to safely transport the women and children, the horses, my goods and a portion of my men to Marseilles in the cog, while we head for the Target in the other ship, the Arab dhow. When my people have been delivered to Marseilles, and safely landed there, your men may keep the second ship – the cog. They may return it to you, or do what they please with it. This is the only deal."

Robin let this sink in. "You must agree to all of this now, at this very instant, without any attempts to bargain or change the terms, or . . . I will cut off your hand, right now, right here. And I will deliver you and all your men to the Archon for his punishment. And I will forget any notions of taking the Target, and make my own way to Marseilles and home with my people with Lord Phokas' most generous aid. Now, answer me, sir. Do you agree?"

Ricky conversed for a while with the red-bearded captain and then gave his reply: "Iqbal says, if you will keep faith with him, he will keep faith with you. He is an honourable man, he says, and fully agrees to your proposal."

Chapter Six

It took no more than three hours to reach Matala and by the early afternoon the cog and the dhow were both beached and anchored to stout trees between the two headlands. However, despite the speediness of our departure from the Red Fort – Iqbal had been most active in encouraging his men to rouse themselves and get the two ships under way – two things worried me deeply.

Firstly, the weather had grown wilder on the ten-mile journey from the fort to Matala, the sea swell rough and choppy; even in the big cog I was travelling in – with Ricky and half a dozen of the Saracen pirates tending the rudder, ropes and sails – had been alarmingly buffeted and knocked about. Once again, in the south, somewhere towards the African coast, there was a band of purple, brown and black, like a vast bruise. It was advancing on us.

The second troubling thing was that during the short voyage, I had spotted a score of horsemen in dazzling white and silver trotting along the road by the coast, heading towards the Red Fort. Part of me was glad that Nikos would soon be released from his bonds; part of me was apprehensive that his cruel father would too quickly discover our perfidy.

There was a small chance that Lord Phokas would do nothing. After all, the nest of Saracen pirates in the Red Fort he had complained about to Robin had been extirpated. We had completed that part of our bargain. On the other hand, he had paid us, given us stores and arms, yet been deprived of the victims he demanded; he would have no bodies to nail up outside his house.

It depended on what sort of man Lord Phokas was – would he seek to strike at us for denying him his pleasures? Would he risk attacking us, with the inevitable casualties among his knights that would ensue, purely out of a petulant desire to punish us? I had a horrible feeling that I knew the answer.

Moreover, how long would it take the Cretan knights to discover what had happened at the Red Fort, to report back to the House of the Archon, and for Lord Phokas to raise a force to come against us. By my calculation, if the Archon moved briskly, he could have troops here very soon, any time now.

I went to Robin with my problem, and it seemed that he had been thinking along the same lines. I found him in one of the caves with Elise, a strange Norman woman, tall and young-ish but with a great fluffy mane of grey-white hair. She was the unofficial leader of the half dozen women in our company. She had been briefly married to a young friend of mine called Will Scarlett, an outlaw who had been killed in the great battle at Arsuf.

She was crouching over a very large dead seagull, which had been split open from beak to fundament. And Elise was rooting around with bloody fingers inside the corpse of the bird. I frowned at Robin – was he indulging in his foul pagan practises once again? He saw my look and held up a hand to stop my questions, reinforcing it with a single long finger held to his lips.

I watched in silence as Elise tugged out a bloody scrap of purplish meat from the bird's interior, and examined it closely.

"Hmmm," she said, cocking her head on one side. Then, to my disgust, she palpitated the morsel, sniffed it and took a tiny bite of the meat.

She spat the gobbet out on to the sand of the cave floor.

"And?" said Robin.

Elise looked up at him. "The liver is bitter as wormwood," she said. "But it is small and perfectly well formed, and not yet entirely putrid."

"What does *that* mean?" I said, fascinated despite myself. Elise had a reputation for possessing second sight, and for dabbling in other less savoury magical practices. The word "witch" was bandied about when people spoke of her. But it was never spoken to her face. She called herself a wise-woman.

Elise ignored me. She spoke only to Robin: "The storm is coming and it will be powerful. The bitterness tells me that. It will strike tonight. But the tempest will not rage long. By dawn the skies will clear, the sea will calm."

Robin thanked her and, putting an arm around my shoulder,

he led me away from the weird widow hunched over her dead seabird. We stopped at the mouth of the cave and looked out on a busy beach scene: the men were loading our possessions into the two ships, with Owain and Little John supervising the labour. I could even see some of the Saracens pitching in to help. Iqbal was standing facing Aziz on the deck of the dhow, discussing something with much waving of hands. I could not tell if they were arguing. The boy servant in the blue turban sat on a coil of ropes, listening intently.

"Do you truly believe in all that divining nonsense, my lord?" I asked.

"Which nonsense would you have me believe in?" he snapped back.

I said nothing. Religion had long been a bone of contention between us. And the exertions of the fight at the Red Fort had reopened the half-healed wound in his thigh that he'd taken at Arsuf. I knew he was in constant pain.

"My apologies, Alan," he said at last. "Do I believe in her divinations? Well, her predictions are correct, more often than not." He paused again. "I do not know if she is merely a good judge of the weather or, at other times, an uncanny judge of people and complex situations, but I do trust her. And, whatever her strange methods, her advice is almost always very useful."

"You saw the Cretan knights on the coast road to the Red Fort?" I said.

"Yes, they will be coming here soon, and in considerable numbers."

I remained silent. I felt strangely reassured that Robin and I were of the same mind about the Archon and the possibility of an imminent attack.

"I want you to take command of the outer defences, Alan. Your task is to protect us here while we prepare the ships for sailing. A storm is coming; a bad one, and we must ride it out on land. The moment it is passed, I want us ready to go. Do you think you can protect us till the storm moves away?"

If my lord had one quality over and above the rest, it was that he made men want to please him. When he gave you a task, no matter how difficult – and the task he had just given me was nigh-on impossible – you wanted to do it so well that he would praise you for accomplishing it. It is a kind of magic, I suppose; real magic, not the superstitious hocus-pocus that Elise indulged in.

Robin gave me a dozen archers, those who still had shafts for their bows, and thirty Locksley men-at-arms – and Hanno. He also promised that Little John and the rest of the arrowless archers and men-at-arms would swiftly come running to my aid when I requested it. But not until then. He needed as many strong arms as possible to complete the loading of the two ships, and particularly to get our beasts on board; and then to make sure the vessels were absolutely secure during the violence of the oncoming blow.

"I can't afford to lose any more ships," he said, with a wry smile.

The first thing I did was to post a reliable man-at-arms on top of the headland to the north, directly above the caves we had slept in, and one on the mountain to the south, to keep watch for the arrival of the Archon's men.

Then I set the rest of the men to digging.

We worked hard all that long, hot afternoon. I reinforced the skimpy brushwood fence that we had built on our arrival, which soon stretched north to south for fifty paces, chest high, across the donkey track beside the river, which was the only path by which a force of men could approach the beach.

Beyond the river, to the north, was the dense wood of Cretan pines and I felt able to leave that unguarded since it would take hours of noisy axe-work to cut a suitable path through the undergrowth. The pinewood forest spread halfway up the lower sandstone slopes of the steep headland, which contained the dozens of large caves we had sheltered in on our first night. On the southern side of the valley, to the right of the track, the mountain descended in a sheer cliff face. There was no way round the reinforced brushwood fence to the south without scaling that steep, bare mountainside.

By the time the sun was sinking, I had a reasonably secure defensive position, I believed, the thick barrier across the track should stop a charging horse, or make it pause anyway, and the brushwood would force a footman to take a little time to break through its spines and get to our defending men on the other side. The river, the wood and the headland protected my northern flank; the mountain with its sheer sides warded my southern flank.

I was wiping the sweat and dust from my brow, and glancing nervously to the south-west at the looming dark bar of the storm now only a few miles away, when I heard a shout from the northern headland. The man up there, a veteran archer called Gryff ap Bryn, bellowed down that a single knight was advancing up the track towards us.

"Only one man?" I queried.

It was indeed one man – it was, in fact, Kavallarious Nikos Phokas.

He walked his horse slowly up the centre of the track towards the brushwood barrier, much as he had done the first time we met – was that only two days ago? It seemed as if it had happened in a different age.

He was helmetless, and his long, black hair was streaming behind him in the brisk onshore breeze. I could even see the bloody mark under his chin where my misericorde had pricked him. He wore a look of white-hot fury.

"I am very glad to see you freed of your bonds, Nikos, my friend," I said from behind the barrier of the brushwood fence. "What news?"

"I have been sent as an envoy, a messenger, against my protests," said the Cretan. "I have a communication to deliver to you all from my father."

"I would first like to apologise, sir, once again," I said, smiling up at him with embarrassment, "for the way that we used you at the Red Fort. It was unkind, yes, and perhaps, even cruel.

But, believe me, Nikos, there were those among us who wished to do worse than bind you to your soft beds."

"If you are trying to prevent your approaching doom, Englishman, you can save your lying breath. Justice is coming for you. Here, this very night."

I stopped smiling and put my hand on my sword hilt.

"What do you wish to say, then, Griffon?" I had, at least, tried to mend things between us. But there was clearly no drop of forgiveness in his heart.

He didn't answer immediately. Then he said: "I used to respect you, Alan of Westbury, and your lord as well. I thought you were decent men who, like me, sought only honour and glory, men who fought bravely in the holy name of Our Saviour Jesus Christ for all that was right and good..."

He swallowed hard. "I even... I even admired you for your experience of the world, for your devout service in the Holy Land, fighting the infidel. And now... now I see I was a blind fool. You have made common cause with the Saracen – the enemies of our blood. You have sided with the Devil, against Christian knights. You are a traitor, sir. You have no honour. None."

I couldn't keep his gaze. I admit I dropped my eyes in shame. Had I been serving Robin so long that I had completely lost my own sense of right and wrong? Maybe. I could feel Hanno at my right shoulder, staring up at the knight in angelic shining white on the other side of the barrier. The wind had risen high; I could feel the breath of the storm on the back of my neck.

I looked up at him again. "You think yourself decent? You serve a man who would *crucify* his enemies and call it justice, who makes a mockery of Christ's Passion. I serve Lord Locksley, and only him. That is my honour."

"I am not here to bandy words, Englishman. Your lord is foresworn – an oath-breaker, and a liar, too. He broke the solemn undertaking he made with the Archon. And I have this message to relate to you from my father: Surrender to his justice, all of you, and he will be merciful. Lay down your arms and surrender now or, I swear it, you will all die very slowly in the most exquisite agony – your men-at-arms, your women, even your children."

"I've seen your lord's mercy. We defy you, sir. Do your worst."

"Then there is nothing more to be said." Nikos began to turn his horse.

"I say something," said Hanno. "You make many threats, little knight-ling. One day they come back and bite another hole in your arse. I swear it!"

They returned some hours later, when the full moon had risen high above the northern headland. I had hoped that they would attack us head-on with their knights, charging straight up the track into the jaws of our strong brushwood defences. But, as King Richard had told me, even the most brilliant of battle plans never survives the first crash of actual combat.

They sent javelin men and slingers, instead, to attack our right flank.

The first I knew of it was a loud cry of agony as I was bending down and checking the bedding in the earth of one of the new sharpened stakes that held the brushwood wall below the sheer cliff of the southern mountain.

I whirled and saw a man-at-arms called Joseph behind me with a five-foot javelin sticking from the hollow between his shoulder and his neck. The blood was spurting thick and black and he was coughing and trembling with the shock.

"Shields," I bellowed, "shields up now." And scrambled to get my own off its leather sling around my back and up over my head. The javelins were whistling down and fist-sized stones, too, from the slingers, a hail-storm of smooth round rocks that cracked against shields, thudded into unarmoured flesh and bounced up from the rocky ground.

An archer went down, struck on the back of the head by a slung missile, I heard the snap of bone breaking an a man-at-arms screamed ten yards way, and another fell to his knees, crying out in pain, a javelin wobbling from the muscles of his upper thigh.

We were being slaughtered. I peeked up from under the rim of my big shield and saw that a score of men were on the mountainside fifty feet above us – lightly armoured men in simple linen shifts slinging stones at us from leather straps like David against Goliath; or hurling down their javelins like thunderbolts. We had no cover but our shields and instinctively we huddled in a mass, a score of men, with more joining every moment, our shields held up over our heads, jammed together to form a carapace on which the hurled stones bounced and cracked and the spears clattered.

There was nothing we could do but huddle and endure, and every few moments another man at the edge of the mass of forty or so Locksley men would cry out and stagger away, stricken by a missile from above – no, not nothing, I knew we would have to try to get up the sheer mountainside and attack them. But how? We had no ladders and we could not fly!

Then something very heavy indeed thumped to my shield. It was a man, someone I had never seen before. Dark hair, dark skin, dark open eyes; dead as one of the smooth round stones in the leather pouch around his waist. And sticking from his chest, transfixing his heart, was a yard of ash. An arrow.

The rain of stones seemed to be slackening. I peeked out from under the shield-roof and saw, to my great relief, on the other side of the valley, and a little to the north, a group of half a dozen men standing outside the largest of our caves, lit by the glow of cooking fires behind them. And Robin himself was there, standing among them. Archers. The bowmen of Sherwood.

My lord had retained six of his finest shots for just such an emergency as this, and I saw them all in turn nock, draw and loose in the old familiar way and hammer the enemy on the opposite side of the valley. Robin also drew and loosed, and I jerked my head round and saw his shaft slice into the belly of a Cretan in the act of throwing his spear down on us. The javelin man dropped his spear and folded around his arrow wound, slipping, sliding uncontrollably down the mountainside and screaming like a soul in Hell.

The barrage raining down on us was slackening, and in a few dozen heartbeats it ceased entirely. The remaining Cretan troops on the mountain above were pulling back, retreating up the slope towards the summit, the lethal arrows hissing among them. I wondered briefly what had happened to the lookout man I had posted up there – and knew he must surely be dead.

A last stone clattered on my shield and they were gone.

I could see eight or nine dead and wounded lying up there. One man calling out for help; several others moaning and trying bravely to crawl up the slope to safety – all with shafts through their limbs or their torsos. But Robin's men outside the caves had ended their onslaught, were even now unstringing their bows. They knew better than any of us they must conserve their precious arrows. Robin's shadow, lined by firelight, lifted a long right arm to me and gave a cheery wave. And that was when the storm struck us.

There was a tremendous crack, like the breaking of a tree and a flash of blinding white. The rain immediately began to lash down, pelting, pounding, numbing in its sheer force, almost as thick and heavy as the sudden shower of javelins it had replaced – though thank God not nearly as deadly.

I had lost six men to the light infantry up on the mountainside, two of those dead. And I cursed my own stupidity. Why had I only sent one man as a lookout on to the top of the mountain, where he could be stalked by a local man who knew the land like the back of his hand, and swiftly silenced?

Two or three would have been much better: they could have watched each other as well as the road. I had been a fool and his death was solely my responsibility. No time, though, for recriminations. There was the sound of trumpets, and a pounding in the earth, a thunder even louder than the storm.

The Cretan cavalry was charging down the track towards us, suddenly there, a hundred and fifty paces away, like a white wave driving forward between the mountain and the river, charging spread out through the grey curtains of falling rain. A flash of lightning revealed five and twenty knights, more, perhaps even thirty, at the full gallop, coming straight down the valley between the mountains and towards the thin fence of cut sticks and fronds.

"Stand to," I was shouting madly. "Everyone! Man the ramparts!"

I stood with my men, shield up, a spear gripped in my fist, waiting behind the brushwood for the impact. Our barrier now seemed hopelessly feeble. The cavalry was seventy yards from us now, and with every beat of my heart they seemed to leap closer. I could see their lances coming down, all together in a ripple of steel – fine work, a demonstration of their skill. To do that at the full gallop was a feat indeed. These men had trained hard for many years. They were true knights, as honed as any I'd encountered.

"Archers, loose," I shouted and my handful of bowmen, their cords already soaked, made saggy by the rain, nocked and loosed and sent a frail dozen shafts against the wall of charging horsemen. I saw one knight yanked from his saddle but no others. They were almost upon us. Death was in our midst. "Loose again, for God sake," I yelled. "Loose, men, if you still can."

The leading horseman, a tall fellow on the left made unrecognisable by the lowered steel visor on his shining steel helmet, had a long red pennant flying from his lance, which even the black driving rain had not yet subdued.

His warhorse put a forefoot into one of the holes I had asked my men to dig that afternoon. Just a simple round hole, a foot in diameter, a foot deep, and covered with a few dry twigs and leaves to disguise it, but it was perfectly lethal to a charging warhorse. The animals' hoof plunged deep into the round hole; the momentum of the horse carried it forward and neatly snapped the animal's bone at the fetlock. The charger tumbled heavily to the earth, hurling its rider, over its neck to land with a sickening thump on the rocky ground forty yards from the barricade.

A second horse did exactly the same and a third ... I had dug more than eighty horse-trap holes on either side of the donkey track, leaving only a narrow path in the centre that was safe to traverse, and suddenly there were horses and men stumbling everywhere, tripping, flying and crashing to the earth. All across their line of attack, except in the very centre, there were horses breaking their legs, and riders flying, and other cursing riders and mounts becoming tangled in the carnage of the men and horses in front of them. The pure white wave of attacking Cretan knights had hit an unseen reef and had now broken and smashed itself into unrecognisable ruin.

We poured our remaining arrows into them, into the struggling mass of knights and their terrified, kicking, biting, eye-rolling mounts. The riders at the rear of the attacking formation, realising what was happening, began to try to halt their momentum, hauling back on their reins, the horses prancing and rearing high in surprise and fear, spraying water from their air-paddling hooves. But only a mere handful managed to avoid the tumbling carnage.

Two knights on the very centre of the track – the un-dug part that Nikos had rode in safely on – these two were still charging forward together at a gallop. Although they were now turning their helmeted heads, this way and that, bewildered, trying to see with the limited view through their visors what had happened to the now-absent comrades once galloping at their side.

Our final few arrows, loosed in tight volleys and concentrated only on these last two charging knights, stopped them dead, skewering man and beast, until they too staggered to a standstill, bristling shafts like a pair of hedge-pigs, slowing, faltering, flopping to earth, yards from the barricade.

I called out, "Now's the time, boys, now! No ransoms, no prisoners!" and a picked dozen of us slipped through the small hinged part of the barricade, our gate, if you like, and rushed eagerly forward, weapons raised.

We came running out from behind our defences to slay the

surviving fallen knights; to murder them, in truth. It was battle at its most foul, most ignoble – in ordinary circumstances a knight would be seized upon, captured and imprisoned until a ransom could be arranged. But *we* could not afford to hold any knight we captured – who would guard him while we fought the others? Would we have to take him with us on the ships? – yet we could not afford to allow him to limp away, perhaps to be remounted and rearmed and then attack us once more.

So we slaughtered all the Cretan knights we could get our hands on that night, as the rains came down on us like a hundred icy waterfalls; and it was nothing less than a muddy, bloody massacre. May God have mercy on us.

I kept my sword sheathed, at first, and mainly used the misericorde. The first knight I came to was on his back, half-stunned from the fall, still struggling to breathe. I pinned him to the earth with a knee on his soaking wet chest, seized his right arm, lifted it and jammed the misericorde into his torso though a hole in his shiny fish-scale armour under his armpit. The dazed man barely resisted me, and once I had stabbed him three or four times, he relaxed and was still, rain now puddling in his dark, open eyes.

I heaved myself off the corpse and, half-scrambling, I launched myself at a second knight, a few yards away, who was trying clumsily to get to his feet. I seized the man, who had lost his helmet, by the throat with my left hand. He tried to wrench my hand free but instead received the punch of my misericorde though his cheekbone, just below his left eye. He jerked once and fell back into the mud an instant later. Only then did I release his throat.

Another knight had actually made it, shaking like an old man, to his feet and was trying to hobble away down the track towards his departing comrades. I drew my sword, ran a few steps and swung low – cutting away his right foot. He screamed and splashed to the ground, and I stepped in and dispatched him with a lunge of my sword up and under his bearded chin.

I looked about me, then, and saw that the grim task was almost done.

Hanno and the other ten men, clothes plastered wet, their blades gleaming with bloody droplets, were dispatching the last of the knights, gleefully cutting throats and cracking skulls. In a few moments, it was all over. A handful of Cretans had managed to run back to safety – but most of the knights who fell prey to the hole-traps had by now been slaughtered. My men had killed the wounded horses, too, as an act of mercy, and by the time we hurried back behind the safety of the barricade, we left sixteen dead Griffon knights lying scattered across the track between rushing, rain-swollen river on the left of our line and the sheer mountainside on the right.

None of the dead men, I was glad to learn from Hanno, was Nikos.

While we had been dispatching the wounded knights, the remaining men behind the barricades, aided by some of Robin's reserves, had been busy building a storm shelter of sorts. It was little more than several large pieces of canvas stretched over a few long ropes, anchored with spears at either end, but it did get us out of the rain. Thank God – I was chilled to the bone.

I ordered hot soup to be served out in the makeshift tent and some bread and a few blocks of local sheep's cheese in barrels of brine, which had been kindly provided by our enemy. I ordered a small cask of the local resinous wine to be opened too. I dispatched a trio of good men up on to the mountainside, and kept a good watch on the track leading out of the valley. And for more than an hour nothing stirred. The enemy had pulled back out of sight – in the dark of night that meant only a few hundred paces. Still, we saw no sign of them. Not a single man. I guessed it was then about midnight.

I spoke to Edwin, the vintenar of my contingent of archers, and learnt with dismay, but no great surprise, that we had just three arrows left.

I hoped that Robin still possessed a few shafts but would not have been surprised if his cupboard were bare too.

"How soon 'fore we can fuck off from here?" asked Edwin, playing with one of the last arrows, spinning it between his thick, powerful fingers.

I looked up at the dripping inside of the canvas roof, tossing, snapping and billowing in the strong wind coming off the sea. The rain was scything down out of the wild night, drumming on the canvas as hard as ever.

"Dawn," I said. "Maybe. I don't know. When the storm has passed. The Earl will decide. Go out with three good men and see if you can salvage any serviceable shafts from the corpses of the Griffon knights or their horses."

"Done it already; we had a rummage while we was cutting throats..."

"Do it again, we need every single one. And keep your wits about you."

Edwin shrugged and went off out into the storm.

I stole a cup of wine out of Hanno's hand. Took a sip. It had been warmed and sweetened with honey. He snatched it back and drained it.

"What will happen now?" I said, reaching for a piece of bread.

"They wait a little, grow their balls; come again. On foot, this time."

"Maybe they've had enough?"

The rugged little Bavarian man-at-arms didn't bother to reply.

"How many you think they will throw at us this time?"

Hanno shrugged. "Hundreds. Many times what we have."

I looked out into the black, rain-lashed space across the brushwood barrier. I could just make out Edwin and two others stooping and tugging at arrows lodged in dead flesh; then angrily tossing the broken ones away. We might redeem two or three shafts from the dead knights, no more than that. The arrows tended to shatter against the Cretan's excellent scale armour, and against the big bones inside the human or horse's body. Rain also made the goose feather flights bedraggled and useless. Thunder snarled. A gigantic flash lit up the whole sky, making the valley bright as day for a split instant.

"We try a little trick, yes? I teach you something useful," said Hanno, unexpectedly. He reached out grabbed a passing archer by the shoulder; he pulled the man roughly towards him. "Gather me Big John here," he said.

The archer looked at him in confusion. "He means Little John," I said, "John Nailor, up in the caves. Hanno wants you to bring him here. Go on."

Hanno told me what he wanted to do, how he planned to stop the next Cretan attack. Once I understood what was in his mind, I shuddered – then reluctantly agreed. Unpleasant as it was, it was a decent ruse, a good plan.

Chapter Seven

The rain clattered down on my steel visor. My whole body was soaked to the bone and I was freezing. My feet felt like lumps of ice. I was having great difficulty in controlling my shivering. I had been lying here beside the dead Cretan horse for more than an hour now, dressed in a Griffon's helmet and garbed in his fine coat of scale mail, the horse's blood smeared all over my body but with my own weapons loosely clenched in my hands. It must have been long past midnight by then, perhaps only an hour or two before dawn.

Away to my left, Little John was also lying in the driving rain, his body curled up to disguise his height, a Cretan helmet over his distinctive blond plaits, a big Cretan shield marked with a snarling boar in gold over his tucked up body. We could find no scale armour to fit him but we also knew that, when they finally attacked, if the enemy chose to look closely at the dead bodies of their comrades lying before the barricade, we were doomed.

Beyond Little John, somewhere towards the steep slope of the southern mountainside, Hanno in his own looted scale-armour suit was lying next to his own dead Cretan horse. We were about fifty paces from the barricade, near the front of the swathe of enemy bodies felled by the hoof-holes. I could see through the slit in the visor, the warm, cheery candlelight inside the canvas structure on the far side of the barricade, and the shape of men drinking soup and eating bread and cheese, and wondered for perhaps the tenth time in the past hour, why I had agreed to the icy torture of Hanno's unusual plan. Could three men-at-arms really make a difference against hundreds? Now, shivering, wet and hungry, it seemed a ridiculous notion. I remembered a maxim of Hanno's that he repeated during our more gruelling sessions: "The more suffering *before* a battle, means less to suffer *during* it."

He meant that if you trained hard, the fighting was much easier. At least I think that is what he meant. Either way, I was certainly suffering now.

The Bavarian had insisted that we removed three corpses, roughly the corresponding sizes of the three of us, and we dragged them behind the barricade and stripped them of their arms and armour. He also said that we could substitute no more than three corpses in this fiendish *ruse de guerre*.

"If too many living men are pretending to be dead," he said, "the hazard is bigger they will smell us out. Three is enough to do this task."

I gripped my sword hilt tightly, trying to control my shaking limbs – corpses don't shiver – and wished the enemy would get out of their warm blankets, or wherever they were, and hurry up and attack us, if that's what they had in mind. Anything was better than this waiting. I strained my ears – all I could hear was the rumble of my own folk's talk behind the barricade.

Owain was behind there now, and perhaps Robin, too: for the loading of the ships was almost complete. Little John had told us that the women and children were already on board the cog, as well as the horses, and our stores; the sailors were making the last preparations on both vessels for a speedy departure.

All we had to do was wait till the storm passed and we could go.

All we had to do was hold off hundreds of angry Cretan warriors who knew this rocky terrain far better than us, whose noble comrades we had just wantonly murdered; all we had to do was hold them off until this raging October storm abated, hold them off till we could disengage from the bloody combat and get all our people safely into the beached ships, then launch those ships, and *then* we could all merrily sail away, live happily ever after.

Perhaps they weren't coming. Perhaps they'd seen their knights cruelly slain by our unfair tricks and our massed arrows and decided to wait out the weather in comfort under canvas. Perhaps they'd all gone home, just decided to cut their losses, and head for their own warm hearths.

My body erupted in a spasm of shivering. I clamped my teeth hard to ride out the bout of violent trembling. I knew that they had not gone home to their beds; they had lost sixteen high-born knights and a handful of slingers and javelin men so far, but they still had the vast bulk of their strength – and they would surely be looking for revenge. The Archon would be hoping for more hapless victims to adorn his crosses.

The spasm passed. For a moment my body was calm and still. And in that moment I noticed two things. First, the rain falling on my visor seemed to be slackening a little. I took four long, deep breaths, filled with hope – yes, the rain was definitely slowing. And now, it had stopped, only drop or two tapping on the metal over my face.

And the second thing: in the silence, I could make out, quite clearly, the throb of big drums coming from somewhere out in the darkness behind me.

They were coming for their revenge – at last.

I could clearly hear the tramp of many feet but dared not turn over and look. I lay as still as I could and listened hard. The deep bass drums were beating the pace, one-two, one-two, slow and steady, and now and then I heard a trumpet sound a stirring ripple of notes. The advance of the Cretans – for it could be nothing else – had not gone unnoticed by my comrades on the barricades. The line there was thickening; I suspected that Robin had drafted in all his men to try to hold our feeble brushwood defence. Sherwood men were mustering from wherever they had been sheltering from the rain or snatching a few hours' sleep. It occurred to me that I had not slept more than an hour or two for two days, yet I did not feel tired. I was very young, then, not yet seventeen years of age, although I'd seen my fair share of blood and suffering: I'd been fighting men, from the Humber to the Holy Land, since the first downy hairs sprouted on my parts. More than that, the approach of battle, at the beat of the drum, my young blood stirred, just as it always did.

I felt a little warmer, too, now that the rain had ceased.

I was ready.

The first Cretan stepped right over my prone body; a short fellow in a leather cuirass and a kilt of leather strips reinforced with beads of iron; he carried a spear, a round shield, and had a short sword at his side. He was shod with sandals and his skinny shins were protected with leather greaves.

Not a wealthy man, I thought, as I examined him through the slit in my visor, hardly daring to breathe, not a noble knight – a common foot soldier.

His comrades were all around me now, dozens, scores of them – maybe a hundred or more. They tramped all around, approaching the barricade in an unhurried regular march. There were dismounted knights among them, I could tell, the hems of their shiny scale coats occasionally swishing past my helmeted face. One knightly fellow, with a square-topped helm and a shield with a red sun-burst, paused, standing directly over me. I thought for a wild instant that he must know I was an imposter and tensed myself to spring to my feet. But he merely mumbled a loud prayer in Greek, made the holy sign of the cross over my prone, shamming body, and marched onward.

But the knights were few and far between: perhaps three passed over me in sixty heartbeats. For the most part, my head was surrounded by a forest of moving bare brown legs and my great fear was that a Cretan would step on me and I would cry out or move – and so be detected. But I need not have feared – who will willingly step on a corpse? And not a man did so.

The enemy passed quickly around and over me, driven forward by the pulse of the drums. Then a trumpet sounded and a great roar went up and the enemy began to charge at the barricade. I thought I could hear Robin's clear voice over and above the bellow of the enemy officers, and the pfft-pfft-pfft of arrows. A moment later a goose-feather shaft slammed into the ground beside my face – at least my lord still had a few shafts left, I thought.

The legs around my face had gone now, and I told myself I would count to a hundred and then rise and do my duty.

I could hear the fury of the battle at the barricade, the clang and clash of steel on steel, the shrieks and grunts of men striving for mastery; the animal howling of the wilder souls, the pitiful screaming of the wounded; a Cretan officer roaring incomprehensible commands in Greek. I could even hear my lord shouting at the barricade: "Hold fast, lads, we *must* hold them here ..."

Then, much nearer, another familiar voice, deep and jovial: "Up you get Alan, this is no time for a nap. The younger generation, eh, Hanno, what can you do with them? Lazy as hogs in a wallow, slug-a-beds every one ..."

I sat up, lifted my visor and looked up at Little John, seemingly bigger than ever, a double-bladed axe over one shoulder, a wide grin on his huge muddy face, Hanno by his side, grim in the darkness, sword and axe in hand.

"Shall we?" said John.

We charged together, the three of us, barrelling straight into the rear of the mass of struggling Cretans who were assaulting the brushwood barricade.

The first the enemy knew of our presence was Little John hacking the head off a man who was loitering at the rear of the scrum, a coward who did not choose to push forward into the press of his comrades and the bloody mash of battle. We sliced into them, the three of us, burrowing deep and deadly into their rear ranks, killing men whose backs were turned towards us – no fairness, no honour to this breathless fight. I stabbed a fellow in the back of his thigh, and chopped into his neck with my shield as he fell back.

Beside me, Hanno was killing with a controlled icy fury; dealing out death with both hands, axe and sword, swinging, stabbing, chopping. Little John seemed to be carving himself a kind of tunnel of blood through the enemy ranks, which were still three or four men deep against the brushwood.

I could see Robin and two score of our men-at-arms battling over the barrier, ducking the spear points thrust at them, delivering sword blows overhand, to batter at their enemies' helmeted heads. No man had broken through yet. And there were still a few archers loosing shafts; Owain, I could see, the master bowman, standing back from the fray, and with a man beside him calling out targets. Other Sherwood folk were thrusting blades, swords and spears through the woven brushwood, skewering men on the other side.

Hanno, John and I were still taking down unsuspecting rear-rank men, chopping into slow-witted fellows with their backs to us; but it could not last much longer. Even now many Cretans were becoming aware of us – scores of them turning, shouting, men whipping round to face us, dozens surging forward; in an instant we three former "corpses" were fighting for our lives.

A Cretan came for me, jabbing with his spear, short controlled lunges, forcing me to block with my shield; at the same time another man hacked at my head from the right. I got my sword up just in time, blocking his blow, and Hanno, two yards away on that side, reached out casually and sunk his axe into the back of the man's fat neck. I ducked another swinging sword then came swarming in myself, attacking furiously. I batted an importunate spear thrust aside and lunged with my sword, the blade sinking deep into the spearman's groin, under the lower rim of his swinging leather cuirass.

A Cretan knight engaged me, sword to sword, and the sparks flew as we chopped at each other and clanged our blades like blacksmiths. I ducked under one of his wilder slashes, half severed his left knee and he went tumbling down, yelling out in shock. The enemy were all shouting their darkest fears now. Not many could see clearly who it was who was attacking them in the darkness, but they knew they were being assaulted from behind.

This was Hanno's *ruse*, his trick of war. No man likes to think that he may be stabbed in the back while he is bravely fighting the foes to his front. Even a hundred brave men may feel the fear when attacked by only three. The press slackened a little at the barricade, the scrum became looser, men who had once been packed three deep against the brushwood were melting away in front of me, moving to the side, or even running backwards.

Little John was still laying about himself like a whirlwind, his axe a lethal red blur, and no man could approach him and live. A little bald man popped up in front of me and I blocked his swung mace with my shield; he disappeared just as suddenly; and I stabbed another man in the cheek, ripping open his face. Then I was at the barricade, brushwood at the height of my chest; the gore-spattered face of Robin not two foot from my own.

He appeared to be swinging his sword against me, and – utterly astonished – I was just raising my shield purely out of instinct when he shouted, "Down, Alan!" and I ducked, and his blade whistled over my head and chunked into the skull of a Griffon just to my right wielding a dagger.

I heard a roar from behind me and whirled and struck out with my own blade, hacking into the waist of a snarling officer with a pole-axe who was in the very act of slamming it down on my head. He fell away, and I noticed that there was now space on my side of the barricade where there had once been only a packed mass of shoving, jostling men. I turned and put my back against the prickly brushwood, lifted my eyes and saw that they were running, all of them, the Cretan infantry were splashing back across the muddy, blood-puddled, corpse-strewn, ground; streaming away, fleeing...

I lowered my gore-dipped sword, breathing hard like an old broken-down carthorse, and saw also that the air was lighter over the hills to the east; a paler grey after the black of night, a harbinger of blessed dawn. There was cheering right behind me on the beach-side of the barricade, and Robin was slapping my shoulder and saying, "Beautifully done, Alan, that was exquisitely timed – and executed. I could hardly have done better myself."

I watched the last of the Cretans trotting away in the distance – still many scores of them, still perhaps half their original numbers or more – retreating back to their camp, and I thought: *We did it. We actually did it.*

But there was no time for glorious reflection, no time for soaring joy and mutual congratulation. Robin said, "To the ships, everyone; right now!"

And we ran.

PART 2

Chapter Eight

We got off the beach with no more loss of life, mainly because Hanno had one more trick up his sleeve. He took a barrel of olive oil, kindly provided for our nourishment by the Archon before he became aware of Robin's perfidy, and chopping a hole in the top he poured it all along the brushwood fence, covering the rain-wet barrier in the light greenish flammable liquid.

We were almost all aboard the ships when the Cretans returned – once again on foot but cautiously now, feeling their way forward in groups of a dozen men, led by a dismounted knight. They examined every corpse of man or horse and, once determining that they were truly dead, hauled them away before advancing timidly under the cover of their shields, fearful of arrows.

They had no need to be so wary, since we were at last completely without useable shafts, but it slowed their advance on the barricade – for which I was profoundly grateful. When a force of them, maybe eighty or ninety men strong, was within twenty yards of the fence, Hanno fired the olive oil, and a line of flame danced along the top of the rampart, and the brushwood soon became a crackling barrier of fire across the bloody track.

It gave us just enough time to loose the anchor ropes holding the two ships, get the last men over the side and, as the sun came up over the gold-brown hills, we were gliding out of the bay, cheering ourselves hoarse. As I gazed back at the land from the rail of the cog's aftcastle, I thought I could make out the helmet-less figure of Kavellarious Nikos Phokas, standing on the beach, staring after us. *Farewell,* I thought, *I shall not see you again.*

We did not go far. We went north in our ships and dropped anchor in a rocky bay perhaps fifteen miles up the coast from Matala, near two small barren islands only a few miles away from the Red Fort. As we passed it, I was sickened to see that, in the courtyard in front of the tower, where we had battled some of the men now standing around us, four fresh crosses had been erected, and filled – the Archon's men had clearly captured some of the Saracens who had fled our attack. But there was no sign of his dazzling knights, nor his men-at-arms. But for the crosses, the place seemed deserted.

I was glad then we had broken faith with that monster. Good riddance to the Archon, his angry, glory-hunting son, and the whole filthy island.

A little before noon, Robin gathered his captains in the big main cabin beneath the aftcastle of the cog. The ship, incongruously for a Saracen pirate vessel, was called the *Santiago*, so named by its previous owners who were rich Christian merchants from the northern Spanish Kingdom of Aragon.

"Some of you know what we are doing, some of you don't – yet," Robin began. "So I shall tell you, all of you here, now, what we aim to do."

There were a dozen people crowded in the low, sun-filled cabin, which stretched right across the width of the cog: Robin, Little John, my lord's second-in-command, Owain the master bowman, Hanno, Gareth the archer vintenar, Stephen, the senior man-at-arms, and Aziz, our sea captain. The Red Fort crew were represented by russet-bearded Iqbal; his boy servant; a tall, lithe fellow of thirty or so years called Tariq, who I hadn't seen before but who was, apparently, his bodyguard, and Ricky, the former wharf rat.

They all fell silent when Robin began to speak.

"We are going to divide our company," he said. "Most of our number will be travelling in this good ship from here to Messina, where they will rest a few days before making the second leg of the journey to Marseilles."

I could hear Ricky giving a whispered and, in so far as I could tell, accurate translation to his plump master Iqbal and the tall bodyguard Tariq.

"The folk voyaging in the *Santiago* should reach Messina in a week or less, and be in sight of the coast of Provence a week or so after that; the beginning of November, about All Souls' Day. Once they reach Marseilles, they should disembark, find lodgings and wait for the rest of us in the port."

Owain put up his hand and said: "But, my lord, where will you be?"

"I'm about to tell you. But, just to finish this issue, I should inform you that you, Owain, and you Captain Aziz, with the help of some of our new friend Captain Iqbal's fine men, are to be given the task of sailing this good ship, the *Santiago*, to Marseilles. You are to be my representative, Owain, and will command all my people on the voyage, the men, women, children, horses and beasts are all in your charge, as well as my private goods – you are to keep them safe on the way there and during the wait in Marseilles.

"Aziz and his crew, and some of Iqbal's folk, will have charge of the actual sailing of the ship. You, Owain, will look after the rest. I will provide you with a little silver but, if you have difficulties, you may go to the Jews and borrow small sums in my name and, in that of my partner, Reuben. I'll give you a formal letter of credit to show to the Marseilles moneylenders."

Owain nodded but he didn't look very happy. Aziz clapped him on the back. "Worry not, my friend," he said, "we shall have a delightful voyage. Short. Calm. Little chance of a storm, after these last two big blows. In no time, we'll be sipping good Provençal wine by the harbour, watching the youngest, prettiest whores in the Mediterranean parading for our pleasure!"

"You do that, Owain," said Robin, "while the rest of us do a quick bit of work that will make us all wealthy beyond the dreams of moneylenders."

Everyone perked up at that remark, and I could see dark-tanned Ricky smiling to hear his own words repeated back to him by the Earl of Locksley.

"Thirty of our number are not going directly to Messina and Marseilles in the *Santiago*," Robin said, and the chattering room became quiet again.

"Twenty-five of my men-at-arms, picked by John and myself, and five or six experienced sailors of Iqbal's crew – will take the Arab dhow to the city of Tunis on the North African coast. We will wait a few days in the old city, then depart and will lie in wait and intercept a camel train a few miles outside the walls as it comes up out of the deep southern desert on its final approach to the city. Once we've relieved the camel train of its burdensome cargo, we shall speed back to the dhow and sail north for Marseilles."

"Tell them what is carried by the camel train," said Little John.

"I think they can guess," said my lord.

"Gold," said Ricky suddenly and little too loudly. "Five thousand ingots of the purest African gold."

The sudden quiet in the cabin was deeply reverential. It was as if a spell had been cast over the whole gathering. Robin's odd silvery eyes were gleaming. Little John was beaming like a drunkard with his very own barrel of wine. Naked greed shone from every man's face in that dim cabin. Except mine. I was utterly worn out – I had not slept for two days and I had fought several hard and bloody encounters during those hours. I was still wearing the scale mail I had appropriated from the corpse of a Cretan knight. My whole body ached; my head was numb and dull and seemed to be packed with wool. Yet the coals of my temper were stirred in to sparking, spitting flames by the shameless avarice on display before my tired and aching eyes.

"Would it not be a great deal simpler and easier," I said crossly, "and a far less likely to get us all pointlessly slaughtered, if we were merely to sail to Marseilles together, then . . . well, then just travel back home to England."

Hanno stared at me as if I were mad; Little John began to chuckle, then he laughed; then he guffawed until the tears were running down his cheeks.

"Oh, that's good, Alan," he said, between gasps of mirth. "Go home, forget about a pile of gold that's ours for the taking, oh, very good indeed!"

"I can see you're tired, Alan," said Robin, "and, if you wish it, I will not ask you to accompany me to Tunis. But think hard before you give me your answer. Every man with me will receive a triple share of the gold."

"I don't care about the money, I just wish . . ." I tailed off, my anger falling off me like a damp cloak. I truly wished only to sleep for about a week but, for some reason, I did not care to admit weakness to my comrades.

"Consider this, Alan," said Robin, "the gold shipment, which we plan to intercept, is heading east. It is supposed one of many payments made by the Almohad Caliph to his ally in the east, the Sultan of Egypt and ruler of other territories, father of the Ayyubid Dynasty. Do you know who I mean?"

I shrugged, as if to imply that I didn't care two pins about the multitude of grand Saracen potentates in this most complicated part of the world.

"We more often call the Sultan of Egypt by another name – we usually call him Saladin. He is the greatest enemy that our own King Richard has ever faced. It is Saladin's gold that we intend to steal. He receives it from the Almohad Caliph in exchange for shipments of wheat from the Nile valley."

I shrugged again. I believe I may even have ostentatiously yawned.

"You can confirm this, Captain Iqbal, can you not?" said

Robin, and after a brief flurry of Arabic words, Ricky said, "It is Salah ad-Din's gold – for now. But very soon it will be ours." And the cabin exploded into cheers.

Robin raised his hand for silence. "Well, then, Alan," said my lord, "if the idea of aiding our noble sovereign does not move you at all – for if we deprive Saladin of his treasure he may not be able to sustain the armies that stand against us in the Holy Land – then consider this: the share of the gold that will be yours, in just a few short weeks' time, would be enough for you – Alan Dale, once a penniless cut-purse of the Nottingham stews – to build a fine stone castle of your own at Westbury, and to extend your lands far and wide, to live the leisured life of a noble baron, if you so chose, doing nothing but hunting and feasting for the rest of your long and, I trust, happy life."

I had to admit that did not sound too horrible.

"But what happens, Robin," I whined, "if something goes wrong..."

"The raid will be quick and neat, a clean precise job, in and out, I am assured of this, then we'll be safely in Marseilles and heading for home; two, three weeks at most. We'll be home by Christmas, and rich, so *very* rich..."

"If you don't want to come, don't come," said Little John. "I'll not allow any man to say you failed your friends; no-one will call you coward."

Despite the kindly meaning of John's speech, I did not enjoy his use of the word "coward". But, in the end, it was Hanno who truly persuaded me.

"You cry like a baby sheep," he snapped. "Men fight for gold, yes, and for glory, yes, and for their comrades, also. You don't like it? You better run home and find a plough to follow. You say you want be a man-at-arms, heh? You choose the warrior's path? Then stop your bleating and come with us."

The sun was high, the sky a perfect blue – more like a fine, hot, summer's day, than the beginning of the autumn storm season – and the *Santiago* was hull down on the western horizon, bearing most of our archers, who were now, of course, largely ineffective due to a lack of shafts, the archers' and men-at-arms' women and children, who had accumulated over the past eighteen months in Robin's company like flowing weed on a ship's belly, as well as our horses – including Ghost – and Robin's possessions and goods.

Although both ships were aiming to travel almost due east from Crete, we had decided to split up and, at first, I thought this a very strange decision – would we not be much safer if both ships travelled in company?

Robin explained it to me. "If we meet any other ships on this voyage, they'll take one look at this dhow, and think: 'Big, fast, Arab-rigged craft, and crammed with armed men – must be a pirate!' What happens then?"

"We fight?" I could barely think straight for exhaustion.

"No, if they're small, they run like Hell from us; if they are larger and more powerful, we run from them. And Iqbal assures me this is one of the fastest vessels in the Mediterranean. In contrast, the *Santiago* is a very slow ship; it is a transport cog, its task to carry large quantities of goods safely and surely to its destination. If we had to run from our enemies, we would be forced to leave the *Santiago* at the mercy of whoever was chasing us. But the *Santiago* doesn't look like a pirate vessel – it looks exactly like what it is: a good, honest Christian trading vessel; furthermore, it will fly the flag of the Griffons and that will give her protection, since these waters are controlled by the Byzantines. Do you understand now why we must part company?"

"Where will they go?"

"The *Santiago* will sail up to the edge of the Peloponnese, then make her way across the Ionian Sea to the Italian shore, then down the coast to Messina in Sicily. She should be fairly safe on that route – Owain knows what to say, if stopped; they will say they're Christian soldiers returning from the Great Pilgrimage, which also has the advantage of being true."

"And us?"

"We're going to hop along the African coast until we reach

Tunis. Iqbal says he knows those waters as well as his own beard in the mirror: the small islands and the hidden sandbanks; the safe ports and the towns to steer clear of – he says we should be able to avoid other craft, if we keep a look out."

I was yawning by now in my lord's face – the height of rudeness.

"Go below and get some sleep, Alan. You look like a corpse. Between our folk and Iqbal's, we have plenty of eyes to keep watch. Go on, now, go."

The good weather held and, when I awoke after sleeping the whole of that warm day away in a stuffy corner of the hold, I went back up on deck to behold a magnificent sunset: the sun a golden ball floating on a red sea-lake far in the west, turning slowly to white as it dipped below the horizon and dyeing the streaks of fleecy cloud red and yellow and sullen blue-black. Somewhere out there, towards that gently sinking orb, was the *Santiago*, and with it all our friends and comrades, and I silently wished them Godspeed.

The long sleep had done me a power of good, for although I was still deep-in-the-bone fatigued – fighting is like nothing else for utterly depleting a man's strength – I was no longer the surly, whining, sheep-bleating youth of the morning. I was also extremely hungry and I was very glad to catch on the salty breeze the smell of some kind of rich meaty stew wafting up from the galley below along with the bellowed words: "Not enough peppercorns. And, Jesus, put a cup or two of wine in it, will you! God's bony bunions, this slop is as weak as kitten piss. No, not onions, you daft old witch! I said bunions – oh, never mind. More wine, come on, don't be mean, woman – this isn't one of your foul magic potions, put a good splash of red in there."

When it came to food, and indeed to many other things, Little John's tastes were uncomplicated: he liked strong flavours, plenty of meat, masses of rich gravy. I felt slightly sorry for the poor cook who had to put up with his so-called "help" in preparing the evening meal in the tiny galley.

The cook, the only woman to have come with us in the dhow, was Elise, the wise-woman who claimed to be able to tell the weather from the livers of dead seabirds. She had asked to come along with Robin, saying that she could be useful in countering any bad luck we had in the capture of the gold – she had foreseen, she claimed, some complications in the robbery.

Robin had frowned at her, with one leg over the side of the *Santiago*, the last man to board the smaller vessel. He saw some of the men-at-arms, those who heard her words, crossing themselves, and was about to say no, when she offered to cook for the company and tend to any wounded. So Robin had changed his mind and reluctantly agreed and handed her down into the dhow. Little John had offered to look after her if it came to battle, and he evidently felt that his offer included aiding her in preparing the stew.

I took up a comfortable position on a coil of rope in the waist, at the dhow's starboard rail, just below the elevated aftcastle, and watched the business of the ship's company, my empty stomach rumbling like thunder.

The dhow had an Arabic name that roughly translated as the *Royal Falcon*. She was about sixty-foot long, far smaller than the *Tarrada*, but more elegant, with a curved swooping shape, narrow of beam, with a square aftcastle supporting a long tiller bar under a canvas sun-awning, and coming to a sharp beak-like point at the front. I could well believe Iqbal's claim that the *Falcon* was fast, she had the lines for it, and the two big triangular sails, were taut and filled by the stiff breeze coming from over my right shoulder.

We were scudding along at a fair rate, faster than we had ever travelled in the *Tarrada*, with the deck canted over at a slight angle, the rigging twanging tight and throwing a fine white bow wave out before us. There was a delightful sense of exhilaration at this pace, a sense of driving energy under your body, like riding a galloping horse but much more comfortable.

The Arab pirates who sailed the *Royal Falcon* were a colourful gang of easily grinning rascals, leaning at their leisure on the ship's sides, when unemployed, and enjoying the speed of the dhow as much as me. Some of our men-at-arms were gathered there too: drinking wine; watching the sea.

We were heading southeast, with the wind coming up from the south, the actual direction we wished to travel in, and I dimly grasped that we would make a series of zigzags, heading southeast then turning southwest in several long stages, until we reached the African coast around midnight.

Iqbal was sitting on a pile of colourful cushions stacked against the main mast about fifteen feet away from me. He was being served a small cup of what I assumed was his honeyed mint tea by his body-servant in the blue turban. The boy was a delicate little thing, clear-eyed and smooth cheeked, with a slightly girlish kind of beauty and, as I watched them, I saw the pirate chieftain reach up and lightly stroke the side of the boy's face as he poured out the sweet tea. I was shocked, to be honest. I knew about these foul practises, of course; they had often been the source of many filthy jests among the outlaws of Sherwood. But I had never actually met a man who practiced the art of boy-love before, with the object of his sinful adoration.

The boy jerked away at the pirate's caress, spilling a few drops of the brew on the silk cushions – evidently the affection was not equally shared – and I heard Captain Iqbal gently scolding the pretty-boy for his clumsiness.

I stared at them – disgusted but also oddly fascinated, both emotions in equal measure. I wondered if I should do something about this, perhaps confront Iqbal, forbid him ever to touch the boy again, and decided against. It seemed a bad idea to pick a fight with our new ally, whatever revolting habits he indulged himself in. It was, I told myself sternly, absolutely none of my business what they did. I'd merely mention it in passing to Robin.

A dark shape loomed between me and the pair by the mast. I looked up and saw that it was little Ricky, smiling in a friendly way at me. He crouched down to my level and said, very quietly, "Word to the wise, mate."

"Yes?" I said. "What is it?"

"Don't be ogling, the captain's boy, like. Just a bit of advice. He's a lovely piece, no doubt. But old Iqbal gets jealous, murderously jealous."

"I'm not . . . ugh . . . no, you don't understand. I would never..."

"I'm just saying, mate, don't eye-fuck the captain's catamite. Last man who lusted after Abdul ended up with his throat sliced in the dark o' night."

Before I could protest, there was a huge shout from the aftcastle. A ship had been sighted, very low in the water, about a mile away to the north.

The placid, easy-sailing dhow was transformed. Robin appeared from below and bounded up on to the aftcastle. The Arab sailors lined the leeward side of the deck, shading their hands to try to make out the identity of the vessel. I climbed up to the aftcastle and stood under the awning beside my lord, who was gazing north at a black object just visible in the dying light.

It was a galley, a large sail-less vessel powered by oars. It was coming straight into the wind, heading due south, on a path to intercept us on this sailing leg, coming on at a terrific speed. I found Ricky was now beside me.

He said: "It's a war galley – a three-decker. Griffon ship, for sure. Crew and slaves, eighty men; and probably a hundred marines on board, too."

The galley was approaching fast. A shout from the lookout atop the mast confirmed it was a Byzantine vessel. I could now see a young man, dark haired, standing in the prow, he was clad in a dazzling suit of armour that flashed in the light of the setting sun. I knew immediately who it was.

It was Kavallarious Nikos Phokas. And he was coming for his revenge.

Chapter Nine

I assumed we would have to fight Nikos and his hundred Byzantine marines. But, due to my ignorance of sea-warfare, I couldn't have been more wrong.

We ran.

Whistles blew; the crew began running across the deck, leaping up the mast. The tiller was put across and the dhow swung around so that the wind was coming in from the other side of the deck, the larboard side, and we began sailing southwest on the opposite tack. The Griffon galley – which was by now merely a hundred yards away – changed its course to follow ours. But almost immediately began falling behind. They could row directly into the wind, which meant that they could travel in a straight line between two points, whereas the dhow had to work around the wind.

But we were faster.

We began to draw away from the Byzantine galley, only slowly at first, but with gathering speed. I could see Nikos turning to his captain and urging the man to lash more effort from the poor slaves. But Iqbal had not lied – the *Royal Falcon* was fast in the right wind and we sped away on the new tack, the stretch of blue sea between us grew larger with every beat of my heart.

It was nearly full dark and the Cretan galley was now invisible when Robin gave the order for all lights to be extinguished on the dhow. Captain Iqbal mustered his crew shortly after this and once again we changed our direction of sail – this time heading northwest, with the wind on our hindquarter.

"The Griffon doesn't know where we're going," Ricky told me. "He can't know. So he has to guess in which direction we might go in the dark. In all these thousands of miles of sea, there's no chance he'll find us again."

"How did he get here so fast?" I asked.

"I'd say that's one of the big Imperial galleys stationed at Ierapetra, fifty miles east of Phaestos. The Archon's son must have galloped like the wind this morning to get there from the beach at Matala by, say, noon today. But I guess he could have done it, with a change of horses. He would have had to immediately commandeer one of the galleys and her crew on the authority of the Archon – he probably greased a palm or two – and set off at full speed after us. He can't have wasted a moment. Our destination must have been obvious to him: due south to Africa. But don't fret too much, youngster, we've lost him now. He won't find us again, I guarantee it."

I was not so sure. Nikos seemed to be driven by a powerful, almost insane urge to punish us. But there was nothing to be done. I ate Little John's goat stew – which was delicious – drank some wine with it, then I curled up in my green cloak below decks again, and slept like a dead man.

I woke twice in the night – once to answer a call of nature, and once roused by the noise of running bare feet only dimly to recognising that the ship was changing course once more. But I was far too tired to work out in which direction we were now travelling. In the morning, a bright, brilliant but slightly colder day, there was no sign at all of the Cretan galley; there was, however, a low dark smudge on the southern horizon, several miles away, that Hanno told me with satisfaction was the continent of Africa.

By mid-morning we were nosing into a tiny bay, a fly-blown, dusty dimple in the rocky coastline, with high cliffs on three sides and a narrow entrance. It resembled a fishing port, with a scatter of buildings and a long wooden jetty. But it seemed a secret sort of place, enclosed and private. There were half a dozen ships and boats moored at the jetty, none of them bigger than the *Royal Falcon*, and all equally as rakish and disreputable-looking. The smell of rotting fish, oil and years of decay filled the salty air.

As we made fast the ropes, I looked out at the small waterfront. There was a warehouse with the door open and inside I could see untidy coils of rope, a jumble of ironwork, anchors and so on, a crate of oranges, a massive stone jar of olives or dates, and bales of canvas and other assorted goods. It functioned as some sort of shop, I assumed, as well as a place of storage.

Beside the warehouse was a tavern. Outside it, at a long wooden table in the brisk morning sunshine, there were half a dozen men – no women – a scarred, ill-kempt little group, some with eyes or limbs missing, most of them lacking some or all of their teeth. All of them armed, with swords and daggers, and the occasional spear and pole-arm leaning against the tavern wall. They greeted us casually in Arabic as we disembarked from the dhow, one man wishing that peace be upon us in a voice thickly slurred by strong drink. Our Saracen sailors replied to him politely in kind.

The seated men watched the dhow intently from twenty yards away, noting the efficiency with which we moored her, eyeing our weapons and armour. One man I saw nudged his neighbour and flicked a finger discreetly at Abdul the servant-boy, no doubt muttering some lascivious comment to his mate, but, by and large, they treated us with a non-committal respect.

Behind the tavern, I could see a dusty road that wound up the hillside, and which petered out into a goat-path as the hillside became the face of proper limestone cliffs. There was a noisy commotion behind the building and a very fat man in a long stained robe appeared, with a beggar-skinny fellow beside him in a raggedy loincloth and one eye as pure white as milk.

The fat man came puffing up to the side of the dhow, with the skinny fellow at his shoulder, and said in good Arabic, "Peace be upon you, my lords. Welcome to the beautiful and capacious port of Qatran, a garden of delights. May your time here be filled with the greatest happiness and joy!"

Iqbal popped his head up from below the rail, where he'd been coiling a rope and said: "Nasir, you old goat-fucker – upon you be peace, too."

The fat man stared at Iqbal. His smile died on his lips. His sallow face turned as pale as his servant's bad eye.

"You're alive!" he said. It seemed to be part statement, part question. The Arab dialect they used was reasonably easy to understand, and although I found myself baffled one or two new words, I could follow it well enough.

"Alive and well and equipped with a new ship and powerful new friends – as you can see, my old and trusted comrade. And I came here, with a lively anticipation of seeing your face again, Nasir bin Said al-Musrati."

"I meant to send you the money straight away, Iqbal," said Nasir tripping over his own words. "I swear by the Prophet, peace be upon him. But I found myself suddenly short of silver, there were some unexpected expenses, great losses, and... then I heard you'd been killed, ah, tragically murdered, in a great sea-battle..."

"Never mind that now. We can talk about all that at the feast," said Iqbal, his jutting red beard twitching as if he were laughing behind it.

"Feast? What feast?" said Nasir. He seemed to be trembling with fear.

"The feast you will honour me with today to celebrate my arrival."

"Oh," said the fat man, quite deflated. "That feast, yes, of course."

We had a drink of wine in the tavern while Nasir bustled away to prepare a suitable celebration for Iqbal's arrival. I was concerned that Nikos and his galley full of marines might make an appearance at any moment and said as much to Ricky, who was sitting on the bench beside me, already working on his second jug of the local vinegary red.

"Oh, they won't come into Qatran," he said casually. "They'd never come out alive – a Byzantine knight and his men? In here, in daylight?"

He pointed up at the skyline to the west, where I could see the outline of some timber constructions on the cliff top, beams arranged in a rough pyramid shape with long arms sticking out the side, and a solid block in the middle. The stark shapes seemed vaguely familiar.

"Nasir always has a crew up there – and sober lookouts – we are safe. Unless, of course, Nasir himself finds the balls to murder us in our sleep."

"Trebuchet?" I said.

"God bless you," he said and giggled into his cup of wine. Then, "Is that what you rightly call those ship-smashing machines? Don't know the name in English – we didn't see too many of 'em in Dowgate. Nasir has a pair of bloody great catapults that chuck down boulders the size of my head, accurate, too. They can put a big fucking hole in the bottom of a dhow. And any man who goes into the water wearing heavy mail – pff! – he's gone."

"What are we doing here, Ricky?" I asked. "No one tells me anything."

"Apart from enjoying a little rest and a drop of this nice, spicy red?"

"Should we not be making for Tunis with all possible speed?"

"Iqbal says he has some business here. We'll be on our way shortly. There is no hurry with regard to the camel train, so Iqbal says. We have a few days in hand. And your man Master Hood has agreed to this way-stop."

"He's Earl of Locksley," I said, "not 'my man Master Hood', he's a nobleman of high rank and renown. A famous hero in his homeland."

"Is he now? I heard he was just a murderous thief and deer poacher from the King's big old forest north o' Nottingham."

I put my hand on my sword. "You will not speak again of my lord with disrespect, Ricky, or you and I will have a very serious falling out."

"All right, youngster, calm down. I'll call 'im High Grand Duke of Nottingham or whatever you want. I'll tug my forelock like a good 'un."

"The. Earl. Of. Locksley. That is his correct title." I was close to fury.

"Thing is, Alan, in these parts we don't put all that much

stock in titles and old lineages and fancy coats of arms, an' other lordly bollocks. We're free and easy here – the brotherhood of the sea. All men are more or less equal in our ships, saving the captain and his quartermaster. If a man has a little power, well, you show him respect according to the muscle he has. Your man... Beg pardon, the Earl of Locksley, has twenty-five armed men at his beck and call, and a good, fast ship. He'll get enough respect for that."

I said nothing. Took a sip of the sour wine. In fact, although I would never allow Robin to be belittled in my hearing, there was not much of a
hierarchy among the Sherwood men, many of whom were former outlaws.

The rascally occupants of the sun-lit table outside the tavern had disappeared, perhaps called away by their master Nasir to help with the feast, and their places had been filled by our men. I saw Hanno and the tall warrior Tariq, their heads bent together over something. I knew that Hanno had picked up a few words of Arabic in his time in the Holy Land – though he was not as fluent as I – and the pair seemed to be able to communicate with reasonable success. I saw that Tariq was showing Hanno a long narrow dagger or slim short sword with a gold-chased black handle and they seemed to be thoroughly engrossed discussing its merits as a fighting tool.

Robin appeared beside me: "Come and see what I've found, Alan," he said. He seemed strangely excited. I nodded amiably at Ricky and got up, and my lord led me a dozen yards away to the door of the big warehouse.

"In here."

Once my eyes had grown used to the gloom, I saw the space filled with boxes and barrels of varying shapes and sizes, piles of equipment and stores.

"Apparently, the Emir of Qatran, as that fat cowardly fellow Nasir is pleased to call himself, owes our Captain Iqbal a monstrous debt in silver, which he cannot pay. So he says our ship's company may have a free run of the warehouse and pick out any items that we might take a fancy to. And I've already found a crate of a dozen poor-quality Genoese crossbows, and one of quarrels to match. There is nothing else of much value here, a few bits of rusty armour, and old sword or two, but I did find these..."

He pointed to what looked like a dirty cobwebbed tangle of sticks and poles and straps, but as I looked a little closer I saw that it was in fact three long bows – not good English yew but the lighter less powerful ash wood, and three dirty linen bags – which were all filled with dusty feathered shafts.

"Booty, I would guess, from some English archers who were taken captive by these pirates. God knows when, or from what ship. They must be more than a year old but some of those old shafts might still be serviceable."

I picked through the pile, selected one of the grubby arrows and held it up to the light looking along its length. It was warped into a distinct curve.

"If you wanted to shoot round a corner, I suppose..."

"I'm going to sort through this mess anyway. I'll warrant I can find a handful that I can use. And there is plenty of stuff that might be useful. Here, Alan, I found this and thought you might like it." He handed over a dagger with an ivory handle in an ornate leather sheath in a curious curled J shape.

I pulled the shining blade from the sheath and examined it with interest. I had seen these weapons before – and at very close range. Just days ago one of Iqbal's men – now our trusted companions, of course – had been trying his best to disembowel me with one. It was a thick weapon, as wide as my hand, with a pronounced steel ridge running down the centre of the viciously curved blade. It was also as sharp as a barber's newstropped razor – even after the many months it had been lying here neglected in the warehouse.

"Damascus steel," said Robin. "Much better than anything we make at home. Arab gentlemen like to wear them. Do you think you can use it?"

I nodded. It was a heavy, brutal weapon. And the wounds

it inflicted would be massive and deadly. I found it oddly beautiful – even without the extravagantly curled black leather sheath, which was inlaid with a pattern of tiny pearls. The ivory handle felt warm and comfortable in my hand – at home. It was beautifully balanced despite its heft. In fact, it felt wonderful.

"I can use it," I said, sheathing it and tucking the weapon into my belt.

The feast began in the middle of the afternoon. Although we were all invited to partake, I noticed that not everyone in our mixed company attended.

A large awning had been set up on a flattish piece of land behind the warehouse and several vast, thick, brightly coloured carpets had been laid on the sandy ground. Iqbal was seated, cross-legged, in the place of honour on a large pile of silk cushions, with Tariq on one side of him and Ricky on the other – the rest of his crew, including, I noticed, the boy Abdul – remained on the dhow, with Elise and half a dozen of Robin's men, guarding the ship.

It seemed that Iqbal did not trust his host entirely.

Nasir and a dozen of his followers sat on the left side of the carpets, and Robin, with myself, Little John, Hanno, Gareth, Stephen and two dozen other Sherwood men, sitting on the right hand side.

The feast began when two servants, with some ceremony and the ringing of little bells, brought in a vast tray containing a whole cooked sheep, brown, crisp and glistening with fat. The interior of the sheep had been filled with some kind of grain, millet, I believe, dyed yellow with saffron and lightly spiced. There were baskets of bread and fruit, soft curd-like cheese, and onions in vinegar, and little bowls of sauces, some fiery, some sweet or salty, and after a moment's awkward hesitation, in which at Iqbal's iron insistence, Nasir himself tasted the roast mutton and its filling and a selection of sauces, the whole gathering fell to eating with a will.

We filled our platters with the succulent meat and sauced

it as we chose and the plentiful food, while unusual for my tastes, with many strong smoky flavours, was good. Soon we had stripped the carcass down to the rib bones.

It felt very unusual to be eating sitting cross-legged on a thick carpet, with the black woollen tent keeping the hot sun off my back – but it was comfortable. I had left my sword in the dhow: one cannot sit cross-legged in any comfort with a yard of steel encumbering your legs. But I had retained my boot-sheathed misericorde and the beautiful new Arab dagger in my belt. I settled myself more comfortably on the silky carpet and for a moment I recalled the Archon and his odd habit of dining while lying on a bed. This was much better, if one could not have a stool and table of good English oak.

I leaned forward and helped myself to a piece of fruit, an orange, which I peeled with my fingers and slowly chewed, savouring its cool, sweet juiciness. When I had finished, a servant brought me a bowl of hot water and a cloth and I cleaned and dried my hands, trying to follow the intermittent conversation, slow and very formal, that took place between Nasir and Iqbal.

It was apparent from the start that Nasir was frightened of Iqbal – which I found interesting, for the captain seemed to me to be such a jolly and harmless fellow. However, I knew, of course, that he was a pirate and a captain of a gang of rogues, so he could not be entirely soft. Yet when Iqbal was not paying extravagant, flowery compliments to his host, and asking about his wives, his children, his business – the port of Qatran evidently served as Nasir's lair, from which he and his craft sallied out and ambushed passing shipping – he seemed entirely innocuous, as mild as a spring lamb.

There was, however, one moment when Iqbal showed a glint of his inner steel. The subject of the large debt of silver that Nasir owed Iqbal came up, when the servants were bringing round tiny cups of sweet mint and honey infusion, one for every man there. Iqbal listened to Nasir solemnly promise that the money would be available for his guest by the rising of the new moon, at the latest, three weeks away. And what, said Iqbal, if the new moon should duly come and Nasir still did not have the money?

"What would I do to you if that unfortunate situation came to pass?"

Nasir waved away his concerns. "I know of at least three ships – rich infidel merchant cogs, with supplies for the knights of the Holy Land – that are due to pass by Qatran in that time," he said. "I intend to capture them all, appropriate their cargo and sell the crew as slaves. Even one of these vessels would provide me with ample funds to make good on our arrangement."

Iqbal appeared to accept his reassurances; the conversation moved on.

I sat back and sipped my sweet, scalding brew. Most of the men had finished eating and occasionally one of two of them would rise and make excuses, or slip away to answer a call of nature. I was feeling delightfully sleepy, and wondered where we were to lay our tired heads that evening.

I noticed Tariq murmuring a few apologetic words, and rising to his feet. Keeping a low, humble posture, the tall man began to move to the side of the tent, to the bright evening sunshine outside. Full and comfortable, even drowsy, I could scarcely even comprehend what happened next.

Just as he passed behind the seated Emir of Qatran, Tariq whipped the long gold-and-black dagger from a sheath hidden beneath his robe, and in one smooth instant he plunged it vertically into the hollow between Nasir's neck and collar bones, sinking the blade a foot deep into his host's chest.

Nasir died instantly. The blade must have pierced his heart – indeed, it might well have severed the organ in two. And there was hardly any blood, even when Tariq ripped the red, glistening blade free of his limp body.

The whole tent erupted into noise and movement, with every man present immediately scrambling to his feet and reaching for a weapon.

Chapter Ten

I was on my feet a moment later. I saw one of Nasir's men throw himself at Tariq, who buried the long dagger he had so recently removed from the pirate chieftain into the attacker's belly, and ripped it wide, gutting the man.

Almost every pirate in that tent was shouting, brandishing a blade of some kind, looking madly about for the next threat. Tariq had closed up with Iqbal, who magically had a drawn scimitar in his hand by now – God knows where it had come from, I assume he must have planted it somewhere in the tent before the feast began. Little Ricky was beside his master with two small but vicious looking steel knives in his fists. We Sherwood men were all crowded around Robin, who had his short eating knife in his right hand.

I had my wide-bladed, curved Arab blade out of its sheath, and the misericorde in my left hand. Hanno had one of his small hatchets out, Little John just stood there like an ancient oak tree, his massive fists clenched.

One voice was bellowing louder than all the others – in Arabic. And I saw that it was Iqbal himself. It took me a moment to understand what he was saying, but he was actually yelling for calm.

"Peace, men of Qatran, peace. Peace. We mean none you any harm!" The twenty or so followers of Nasir glared at him, mouths open in shock.

"No need for more bloodshed," roared Iqbal, shaking his scimitar. "Your lord is dead. Do you love him so much you seek to join him?"

Astoundingly, it worked. A pause. An unexpected hush fell inside the tent. Iqbal spoke confidently and more quietly into the terrible silence.

"Your emir, Nasir bin Said al-Musrati, breathes no more. You owe him no further loyalty, O men of Qatran. I slew him for his gross..." and then a word I did not understand. "I was justified in seeking his death. He took my money and never returned it – nor did he ever intend to. He stole from me. Now he has paid that debt in full with his miserable life. But the rest of you have nothing to fear. Lay down your weapons; let us talk together of peace."

The men of the pirate port were looking wildly between Iqbal and Robin – the two sides were roughly equal in numbers, about a score in each camp. I took a deep breath. Any moment they would launch themselves at us. I could feel my heart battering against my ribs. Any moment now...

And nothing happened.

A big, bald pirate, a black man of Africa, took a step forward. He had been sitting at Nasir's right hand, obviously a lieutenant and trusted man.

"We will not lay down our blades, Iqbal bin Yusuf," he said, in a low, angry voice, "but we will hear what you have to say. Speak now, murderer."

Iqbal repeated what he had said about the chieftain's unpaid debt to him. "The killing today was a private matter between Nasir and myself; a matter of personal honour. Now it is settled. I have no quarrel with any of you. Let us not make war when there is no need. Have we not enough enemies – the Byzantine Emperor's men, the Christian knights, the legions of the Almohad tyrant? We are brothers of the sea – let us act like brothers."

"You murder your brothers in cold blood?" said the black man.

"As a matter of fact, Hamo, I *was* obliged to strangle my younger brother. He was a treacherous little worm. And my overbearing older brother Khalil, well, there are times when I would quite cheerfully slit *his* throat..."

There were a few chuckles. I could feel the tension seeping out of the stuffy tent. I lowered my Arab dagger, and slid the misericorde back into its boot sheath. I looked over at Robin's face and his expression was one I knew well: ice-cold fury; his mouth a thin grim line.

The black man, Hamo, was shaking his head in disbelief. But the risk of imminent battle had clearly passed.

"We will be leaving tomorrow morning," Iqbal said, his voice once more soft and amiable, "leaving you all in peace. And if you do not molest us tonight, there need be no more unpleasantness, no more bloodshed. Choose another emir – pick any man you wish with my blessing – continue your business as if this never happened, and let us part tomorrow as friends."

"Don't need your fucking blessing," muttered Hamo. But, apart from that, the matter seemed to be closed. A pair of burly servants came in and dragged the bodies away in a trail of blood. The carpet was a spongy ruin.

We all slept on the dhow that night, with alert sentries posted fore and aft. But the men of Qatran made no move to try to avenge their murdered emir. There was no battle, save one of words, and that between Robin and Iqbal, on the aftcastle, after night had fallen and most of our men were wrapped in their green cloaks, seeking sleep. I missed the beginning of the conversation, but took a few steps nearer when I heard the angry voices.

" . . . did it never occur to him that a number of my men could have been killed or badly wounded by his actions?" said Robin. "Ask him where our mission would be, if half our men had been injured in a pointless brawl."

Ricky, standing beside his captain, translated his words in to Arabic.

I drew a little closer, leaning on the ship's rail, a yard or two from Robin in case he should need me. I could see the tall shape of Tariq lounging by the tiller bar in the near darkness. The wind was blowing dry and warm, making the lanterns swing, and as the light washed back and forth across the deck, I saw that he was toying with his long dagger, now cleaned of its filth.

"And were any harmed? No. Not even one. I was always in control."

"If even one of them had been slain because of your treacherous desire for revenge," said Robin, icily, "you too would now be lying in your grave."

"Yet none were killed." Ricky relayed Iqbal's calm words to my lord.

"This recklessness must not occur again. I cannot allow it. If something like this ever happens again, I shall take my own action. Am I clear?"

"The affair is over. My captain apologises if you were alarmed," said Ricky. "But he also says this: our bargain over the gold stands. If you keep faith with him, he will keep faith with you. And his word is his honour."

Robin stared at the two men for a long moment. The lantern light swept across his face and I saw that his eyes were the colour of cold iron.

"That is all I will say for now," Robin said, and he walked away.

The next day in the mid morning, we sailed serenely out of Qatran, observed silently by a handful of the piratical inhabitants on the jetty. No goodbyes were said. No one waved. Yet we had been unmolested during the night. I kept an eye up on the cliffs to the west, as we traversed the harbour, in case any of Nasir's grieving followers should contemplate dropping a trebuchet stone on us as a parting gift, but there was no movement at all up there.

Once we were again on the open sea, and heading northwest, Robin called me to him at the prow of the boat. My lord was standing at the peak of the ship with his cloak blowing sideways in the wind. It was another beautiful day with no more than a line of fleecy clouds in the north and the blue Mediterranean adorned with row upon row of whitecaps. There were no vessels in sight, save a few fishing boats to the west close in to the land.

"Tell me, Alan, does your friend Ricky – or anyone else aboard – know that you can understand Arabic?" he said.

I thought for a moment. "I do not believe so."

"Good, then I want you to stay close to Iqbal, and to Ricky for that matter, and keep an eye on them for me. Listen to what they say in private."

"You don't trust Iqbal? He gave you his word…"

"The word of a pirate?" he said. "I believe he will keep his bargain with us. But I was taken by surprise by his murder of Nasir at the feast, and I don't wish to be surprised again. But I can't just toss him overboard. We need him, for the camel train, for the gold, and to sail this damned ship. I find myself in an uncomfortable situation. So, watch him for me, Alan, will you? And don't let them know you can understand their speech."

I said I would. Then, a little hesitantly, I said, "Iqbal is the lover of the young boy Abdul, I think. At least it looks that way."

"Is he? Eugh. Are you sure? Well, it's not unheard of. Christians – even some of our own churchmen – indulge in these habits, too – or so I am told."

His voice had a strange tone. He would not quite look me in the eye.

"Should I tell Iqbal to leave the boy alone?" I said. "We could have Little John give him a warning, maybe a bit of a scare. Make him desist."

Robin did not say anything for a long time. I could sense that he wanted to say yes. In the end he just sighed. "It is not our business – the boy is none of our concern. He is not one of us. And we would make an enemy of Iqbal."

He sighed again. Then looked directly at me. "Keep an eye on the boy, too, discreetly. And if… if you think he's being hurt, or ill-used, tell me."

When the midday meal, fresh bread and cheese, which Little John had acquired somehow in Qatran, was served, I went to sit beside Ricky beneath the starboard rail. I planned to discover if he knew I could understand Arabic. A first step to getting closer to Iqbal and, as Robin put it, keeping an eye on him. So I asked him to tell me about his years as a slave on the galley owned by the Almohad Prince Khalil.

"I don't rightly like to talk about it, shipmate," said Ricky and he gave a little shiver. "And trust me, you never want to discover what it is like. It is Hell – the cruellest Damnation – there is no other way to describe it. I would rather die – on my honour, I'd rather cut me own throat, rather than suffer that again. When I am done with this life, if Shaitan drags me down into the Pit for my sins, there is nothing he could do that would be worse than that."

"Is that where you learnt to speak Arabic?" I asked.

He laughed harshly. "Among other things. Want me to teach you, lad?"

I laughed too. "I don't think I could ever get my tongue around it."

"You might surprise yourself – the young learn easy. I could give you a few words to practice on, if you like."

"No, no thank you. I'll stick with plain English."

I felt a little bad about refusing his kind offer. But I did not want to risk revealing my secret. I changed the subject.

"What will you do when we have the gold? Your triple share will be a considerable fortune, will it not?"

After a pause, Ricky said, "I did think of buying my own ship, and getting a good, hard crew and setting up on my own as a rover. But speaking to you, to my own kind, in my own language – it's made me think again."

"Yes?"

"I have a powerful hankering for home just now, you see, Alan. And I thought, well, I thought maybe..."

"You want to go back to England?"

"Would you, would you do me a little favour, shipmate? Would you have a word with your captain – I mean with the Earl of Locksley – and ask him if, well, if I couldn't come along with you? Once we've the gold, I'd like to go north with your crew, go home to London. Maybe set up a tavern beside the Bridge, serve good English ale, meet a nice plump wench with great big... yes, I'd like to get myself home, if I can manage it."

"I'll ask Robin for you. I'm sure he'd gladly take you along.

But what would Iqbal say. Would he feel you were betraying him by leaving with us?"

"Once we have the gold, it will be every man for himself. Iqbal is looking to retire, anyway. This job was always going to be his last one."

We slept that night on an uninhabited stretch of rocky coast, with a small grove of palm trees and a stream that provided sweet, cool drinking water.

It had been a dull, sedentary day, and I had not managed to get any closer to Iqbal, who had slept through the afternoon in a folded blanket under the awning on the aftcastle. The boy Abdul was somewhere below decks. I had no duties, except for keeping watch for a two-hour stretch in the prow – during which time I saw nothing but a school of thirty dolphins who followed the dhow, leaping and sporting in the dark blue waves a stone's throw off out larboard bow. So when we dropped anchor by the shore, I stripped to my braies and took a cooling swim in the warm, shallow water. And drying myself on my chemise, I went to seek out Hanno. I felt it was high time we resumed our usual training.

I found him crouched down under a palm tree, shaded from the early evening sun, talking with Tariq – communicating after a fashion, at least. There was a good deal of antic play, grimaces and hand gestures, and a few simple words in Arabic, which I made sure not to be seen to comprehend.

I had not paid much attention to Tariq so far. My impression of him had been merely that he was a tall man. He was certainly that but now stripped to the waist, as he was, I saw he was very lean, finely muscled and with the solid air of a hard, competent man of action – not unlike Hanno, in fact.

His hair, I noticed, was a light brown colour, not tar black like most of the other members of Iqbal's crew, and his hairless skin was lightly sun-tanned. Indeed, in the right clothes, had I not known otherwise, he could have passed as a Griffon, or even an Italian. He regarded me calmly with his tawny eyes, and Hanno introduced me after a fashion, tapping my chest hard with a blunt forefinger and saying, "Alan. This is Alan Dale. My friend."

I had a notion of trying out the Arab dagger, and when I showed them the thick curved blade, Tariq's eyes sparkled with interest.

"*Janbiya*," he said, gently touching the weapon. Then he said in Arabic: "This is an honourable weapon, very old, even ancient. An emir's blade."

I tried not to show that I understood him. But I was secretly pleased that I possessed such a valuable object.

I asked Hanno if he was willing to mock-fight with me, he wielding an ordinary knife and I the *janbiya*. And while the Bavarian seemed happy to try a bout, Tariq was appalled.

"This is not a child's toy, to be played with," he said. "But I will show you its proper use, if you will allow it, young warrior."

He took the Arab blade from my hands, reverentially, and stood up.

Hanno and I sat in the shade, while Tariq stood perfectly balanced on the balls of his feet. He began to make a series of flowing cuts and jabs in air, at first very slowly then gradually faster and faster. After a little while he almost appeared to be dancing, the blade sliced through the warm evening, jabbing here and there, and sliding away, as if he were fighting an invisible and very skilled opponent. The steel caught the ruddy glow of the dying sun as it arced through the air and seemed to shine blood red, as Tariq stepped and stabbed and carved elegant shapes at a dizzying speed almost too fast to see. He was a master, clearly. And this was a fearsome weapon, I recognised that immediately, capable of ripping the guts from an enemy with a single movement, the curved tip acting like a hook to pull out the enemy's innards. To be honest, despite being confident in my skills, the thought of facing a man like Tariq with a *janbiya* in his hand sent a chill down my spine.

When he had finished, Tariq urged me to try to copy his

moves. I made a poor show of it. He exhorted me in Arabic, and I was forced to pretend that I did not understand his basic instructions. The movements with this heavy dagger were different, too, and being used to chopping with a long sword and stabbing with my slender misericorde, it took me a while to understand the sinuous flowing technique, cutting and wounding the enemy, then pulling back, making the opponent bleed and bleed to slow him down.

Hanno, who appeared to be enjoying the show, called out, "Imagine you fight a real warrior. Cut him, Alan, and move away. Cut and move."

By the time the sun had fully set, I had worked up a considerable sweat, and had a reasonable grasp of the basic *janbiya* technique. But I knew I would be no match for a man trained from birth in this Arab style of combat.

Tariq eventually bid us good night and wandered away towards the campfire fire and the cauldron of fishy-smelling soup that Little John and Elise were bickering over by the stream, and the scatter of makeshift tents.

"Not bad, Alan," said Hanno slapping my sweat-slicked back as we made to move back towards our comrades. "But not perfect."

A few paces later he said: "He is Hashashim, you know that?"

"What?"

"Tariq. He is one of this Order. Some call them Assassins."

"They're real? I thought that was just a tale to frighten children."

I had heard of the Assassins, of course; what fighting man in the Holy Land had not? There were many stories about them: superb Saracen warriors who used stealth and guile to track and murder their victims – sultans, emirs, even Christian lords. Some said they could fly, and turn themselves invisible and move like ghosts; others said they were made crazy by drugs that drove them into a killing frenzy. All agreed that they were superb, silent killers. Unstoppable. I had assumed that the tales were fanciful nonsense. But I was fascinated to learn that they were in fact real, flesh-and-blood men – and that our shipmate Tariq had once been numbered among their ranks.

"How do you know this? Surely he did not just admit it to you?"

"He has small tattoo. I see before. I ask him and he say yes: Assassin."

"I thought they lived in rare luxury in the high mountains of Syria," I said. "What is he doing with this crew of low-down and dirty pirates?"

"He tell me why, but I do not understand. He say he sent to kill an emir, an enemy of his lord, and he accomplish this death. But there was a woman who saw him make his kill, with a baby in her arms. And he say he could not silence them." Hanno shrugged at this incomprehensible act of mercy. "His lord would surely kill him for this failure, so he left the order. Joined Iqbal."

As I ate my fish soup by the campfire that night, I thought about Tariq and this revelation about his lethal past. And a truly horrible thought occurred to me. If Iqbal were to give the order, I had no doubt that Tariq would murder Robin as coldly and efficiently as he had dispatched Nasir.

And, if it came to that, I doubted my own ability to stop him.

Chapter Eleven

We sailed swiftly for three days: good, blustery weather, though growing a little colder; heading west along the coast of Africa, weaving in and out of the little islands and sand banks. We saw a big, slow trading vessel once on the horizon, heading northeast, and many small fishing boats, a few miles out from the towns and villages along the shore, and we made good time.

I learnt little during these days about Iqbal and his secret mind – and formed no opinion at all about his trustworthiness or otherwise. I spent as much time as I could within earshot of the pirate chief, hanging around doing small tasks beside his quarters – a small space below decks, directly beneath the aftcastle, walled with canvas for his privacy, which he shared with Abdul. Iqbal did not seem to be indulging in any carnal relations with the boy, at least he never did so when I was within earshot. Neither did he do any harm to Abdul, or punish him in the usual way, so far as I could tell.

He gave straightforward orders to his men, usually concerning the efficient sailing of the ship, and occasionally complained about the quality of the food, which he claimed was dull slop with too little zest or spice. He also made several unkind remarks to Ricky about the ugliness of Elise and her lack of appeal as a bed-mate. They joked that she must be barren. The young crone, they called her behind her back. None of this seemed serious enough to report to Robin, though I'd warned him about Tariq and his past.

Yet if I learnt nothing interesting about Captain Iqbal himself, I did discover something startling about his young servant boy Abdul.

On the fourth day of sailing from Qatran – when we were perhaps only a day's journey away from Tunis, by Ricky's reckoning, and in plenty of time to meet the camel train and achieve our objective – the wind, which had blown steadily from the southwest for days, faltered and then died. We were behind a long, narrow, ridge-backed island, covered in greenery, and it seemed to me that perhaps this landmass was blocking the slight breeze.

Iqbal seemed to think so too. In the sudden calm, with the two sails hanging slack as a pair of witch's dugs, he set about ordering his crew to set up the sweeps. There were four very long oars – twenty feet in length – used in an emergency to manoeuvre the dhow when there was no wind.

He asked Robin for some of his strong men-at-arms to help with the rowing, and my lord detailed off eight idle former outlaws to heave on the ungainly oars under the pirate chief's instructions. The dhow began to move again, painfully slowly, at a fraction of the exhilarating speed we had enjoyed in the days before, more like the pace of an elderly walking man.

"We should catch the wind again, *inshallah*, if we can only get our nose past Crocodile Island," I heard Iqbal tell one of his crew, who was sweating at one of the long larboard oars with Gareth and another Sherwood man. "I'm going to take a nap – but wake me if there is any change."

He went below.

I moved along to the prow, clambering out on to the bowsprit, a long pole that poked out from the end of the ship, to get a better look at the island. The sun was beating down and I suddenly felt very hot in my woollen hose and tunic without the cooling sea breeze. But it was a good spot, one that I had occupied before, away from the crowded deck and the incessant chatter of my comrades. I looked at the long island ahead, with its spine of dark green hills – it did indeed resemble a huge half-submerged crocodile – and after a moment or two, I saw movement on the sand-fringed northern flank of the long low landmass, a vessel coming round into sight from the west.

It was a big craft, sail-less, with dozens of pairs of oars on each side. From a pole set up on the aftcastle, a white flag was fluttering sluggishly.

Good, I thought, *there is some wind on the other side of the island.*

I looked again and as a strong gust extended the pennant to its full length, I made out the device imprinted on the flag. It was a huge golden bull on a white background. And my belly was suddenly filled with icy liquid.

It was Kavellarious Nikos Phokas.

I scrambled back from the bowsprit and sped back to the aftcastle to report to Robin. But my lord had already noticed the vessel and its device.

"Go and fetch Iqbal, Alan; hurry now. Tell him the galley is back."

I raced down below, jumping down the short set of stairs in

the waist of the ship, and sprinting to Iqbal's quarters. Not waiting to knock, I snatched back the canvas drape that served as a flimsy portal and stepped inside.

I was greeted by a scream and a vision that drove all other thoughts from my head. Abdul, naked but for a linen towel around his shoulders, was crouched over a large bowl of water, washing his body with a sponge.

Her body.

I found I was staring at a naked girl, a beautiful naked girl, at her toilet. Her hair, released from the turban she habitually wore, was as black as a bolt of silky midnight, and spilled down in a thick shiny plait over her milky shoulders and chest. Her bare breasts were small and pointed, easy to bind up and disguise, I realised. Her girlish beauty, most unsettling in a boy, now made a perfect kind of sense; like a missing piece fitting snugly into a child's puzzle. She screamed again, snatching the small towel and trying to cover her body and I realised I had been staring at her: grossly intrusive, unforgivably rude. I stepped back and aside, quickly, allowing the canvas flap to drop – and this small act of courtesy almost certainly saved my life.

I felt a presence behind me and something whizzed past my shoulder, slicing a long gash in the hanging canvas flap.

I was moving without thought by now. My misericorde was out of its boot sheath and in my left hand before I realised that it was Iqbal, with a long shining scimitar, who had so nearly opened my back to the spine.

He slashed at me again with the wide, curved sword, shouting, "Filthy beast! Predator!" I jumped back to avoid him spilling my guts on the deck.

He stepped in and chopped at my neck then, a hard downward slice, but I had the black, toughened steel misericorde up in time and blocked his blow solidly. Purely from habit, my right fist shot out, just as he was coming forward with the momentum of his strike and my knuckles connected hard with the point of his bearded jaw. He flew up and back and landed on his rump on the wooden deck. The scimitar leapt from his grasp, skittering along the deck towards me. I put my foot on the blade. Most of the wind was knocked out of Iqbal but he managed to whisper: "You shall not have her!"

My mind was spinning like a windmill in a winter gale. Then I grasped it all in an instant. His attack had been an attempt to protect the girl – Abdul, though that could not be her true name – from me. He saw me as a ravisher. I opened my mouth to deny it, to tell him in Arabic I had no such intention.

Just in time, good sense returned. I said, in slow, loud English, "My lord wishes you to know the Griffon galley has returned. The Archon's son has caught up with us again. Come on deck, up, up!" I pointed at the ceiling.

Then I turned and walked away.

The Cretan galley recognised its quarry immediately and changed course to come directly towards us. Meanwhile, we were as good as nailed to our position by the lack of wind. The men at the sweeps were ordered to re-double their efforts, more Sherwood folk joined them but there was only room for four at each oar. They hauled like heroes but Nikos and his galley, and his hundred elite marines, came steadily closer and closer.

We were edging due north now, striving to get beyond the blocking bulk of the island; Nikos and his slave-rowed galley was driving almost due east, straight to us, throwing a great creamy bow wave in her eagerness.

It was a horrible, helpless feeling, as with almost every ten heartbeats, the galley seemed to leap a hundred yards or more closer.

By the time I had hauled on my Griffon scale mail – it was lighter, and easier to pull on than the stiff iron links of my rusty Christian armour – girded myself with a sword, and slapped on a plain steel cap as a lighter helmet, and a shield, the galley was no more than a quarter of a mile away.

Robin ordered the men on the sweeps to be switched so that fresher arms could pull the long oars with greater strength;

Iqbal set about launching the dhow's small tender over the side – a small rowing boat that was used to ferry men from the dhow to shore, when the bigger ship could not come all the way in. At first I suspected that he was planning to make a run for it, flee from the oncoming galley – though that did not make any sense. The galley was moving at a greater velocity than a little four-man skiff could manage. But Iqbal did not climb down into the tender. Four men – three Sherwood and one from his crew – got into it, carrying a long heavy rope and I saw that they meant to tow the far bigger dhow with just the main strength of their arms. That surely must be a policy of desperation, I thought.

I readied myself to fight. I prayed, I tightened my shield and belt straps, loosened my blades in their sheathes. Filled my lungs with cold sea air.

Hanno had donned a hauberk, and picked up a crossbow and a handful of bolts. He came and stood beside me; and Little John too, was sitting calmly on a wooden crate a few feet away from me carefully sharpening his huge double-headed axe with long, slow strokes of a whetstone.

"They'll try to board us," John said, glancing up at me. "That means they will line up their men on the side, ready to leap across to our deck."

He made a few more scrapes on his already wicked edge. "But if we board them – just a few of us – we can maybe give them a bit of a shock."

"We jump on their boat," said Hanno, nodding. "Kill them all."

I admired his battle confidence but could not share it. Robin, who was standing above us at the edge of the aftcastle, said, "It's only a question of putting down Phokas. He is the money; he is the will that drives them."

As he spoke, my lord was sorting through a quiver of arrows that he had salvaged from the warehouse in Qatran, picking out shafts and looking along their lengths, putting them back. None of them seemed to please him.

"With their captain dead, they will fall away," Robin said,

holding a final shaft up to the sky. "Whatever rewards he promised will die with him."

That arrow seemed to be the best of a bad lot, for he nocked it to his bow, grimacing slightly, although he did not draw back the cord.

The galley was no more than a hundred and fifty yards away. I looked at our sails, which were just limp rags, empty sacks dangling from the masts.

The little tender was now at the full extent of the rope, pathetically attempting to pull us northwards. The four men on each of the four sweeps were straining mightily and yet the dhow seemed not to be moving at all. Every one of Robin's men who was not labouring on the long oars was readying himself for battle. Some had full hauberks, some leather cuirasses reinforced with strips of iron, some just padded wool and linen gambesons, but all had good swords and daggers, and most had shields and helms.

The galley was a hundred yards away now.

"This Griffon popinjay seeks to challenge us once more," said Robin, in his bronze battle voice. Every man on the deck turned his head to hear his words. "We handled him far too gently on the beach at Matala. So this time we'll give him more than a tickling. This time, we will show him how Locksley men fight. This time, we will not be gentle. This time, he will die!"

There was an answering roar from the dozen or so men on the deck. They shook their unsheathed weapons in the air and cheered like madmen.

I could see Nikos clearly standing bareheaded in the prow of his galley – now only fifty yards from us – a long drawn sword shining in his right hand, a shield in his left, the white-painted wood emblazoned with the golden bull of his House. Behind him were a thick mass of marines, dozens of knights in dazzling scale mail, with full-visored plumed helmets, spear-points gleaming. I heard the creak of Robin's bow behind me, and the hiss as he loosed his one good shaft. It flew, up, up and it smacked into the top right corner of Nikos's shield, knocking the Cretan back a step, and he was immediately swallowed by the mass of his own men – far more than the number who faced them on our own deck. It was a creditable shot, but it achieved nothing. Nevertheless, our lads gave a cheer at Robin's strike.

The galley was a mere thirty yards away now. I could plainly see the square individual breathing holes punched into the knights' steel visors.

"Get ready, lads," bellowed Little John.

I gripped my sword hilt, my palm already greasy. A trickle of sweat was running down the furrow of my spine. I longed to scratch my lower back but for some odd reason I could not move at all. There was a creaking sound from behind me. Wood and ropes under strain. I tensed myself, waiting for the crash of our two converging vessels, when I would leap on to the alien deck and begin to battle for my life and the life of my friends.

But the Cretan galley seemed to be no closer. Indeed, it seemed to be, if anything, a little further away. I could hear the crack of the slave-masters whips, their angry shouts for more speed, and the splash of hundreds of oars, churning the blue sea white. But – yes – I was sure now. We were moving away from the galley, slowly, surely, the distance between us was growing.

There was no sign of Nikos now.

I looked at the sails and saw that they were filling, swelling in the breeze now coming strongly from the southwest. The dhow was indeed moving. We had cleared the edge of Crocodile Island, and now, praise God, the sails were already drum-taut, drawing us away from the flailing galley. We overtook the little tender, willing hands hauling the rowing boat in and up the side of the dhow. We were running free, the full strength of the wind in our sails, the water hissing merrily along the side; the breeze on the left side of my face, wonderfully cool, and the galley floundering in our wake.

Four of us sat at a table set up on the aftcastle: Robin and I; Iqbal and Ricky. All the other crew members and Sherwood men were banished from the area, except Little John who lounged on the stern rail, looking at the sky. Iqbal and Robin sat opposite each other, each staring steadily into the other's eyes. I looked at Ricky across from me. He gave me a little smile and shrugged, as if to say: "What nonsense is this now, me old shipmate?"

"Who is she?" said Robin at last. "Why is she on this ship?"

Ricky translated.

"The captain says it is none of your concern. And you must leave her in peace. She will make no trouble and she is under his personal protection."

"Tell him, Ricky, that everything on this vessel is my concern. I do not know her. I must know this or I shall consider her – and him – as a threat."

"She is no threat. I guarantee it. I will care for her; she will remain in my quarters until we reach Tunis. She will be no trouble at all."

"This is your last chance to tell me . . ." I could see Robin was serious.

"This does not affect our arrangement," Ricky translated Iqbal's words as if they were his own, "It has nothing to do with the gold. On my honour. Our deal stands. We can all proceed as we intended and become rich . . ."

Robin turned to Little John. "Throw him in the sea," he said quietly

John sprang forward. He seized Iqbal by neck and belt and lifted him up, hauled him over to the rail. Tariq had suddenly appeared on the aftcastle, God knows where he had come from, his long gold-handled dagger in one hand and he was swiftly moving in on Little John, now encumbered by a madly struggling Iqbal. Hanno vaulted up on the deck, holding up a warning hand, and a short axe; he interposed himself between Tariq and Little John, who had the captain balanced on the rail. I'd only half-risen from my stool.

"Wait! Stop this!" Ricky too jumped to his feet and was shouting. "Be calm, everyone!" Robin had not moved. Ricky repeated his words in Arabic.

Then he said: "Her name is Tanisha. She is Captain Iqbal's

niece."

Everyone froze.

"The captain is trying to protect his kin – that is all," Ricky said in English, "be reasonable, my lord!" Then in Arabic: "The infidels will not harm Tanisha – trust them, Captain. Cease this stupidity, in God's name."

Robin nodded at Little John who allowed Iqbal to scramble back on to the safety of the deck. Hanno and Tariq faced each other for a few moments: both men crouching, coiled and absolutely still. Then Tariq straightened and went over to the rail, where he took up casual a position watching the table.

Robin rose from his stool. "Sit down, Captain Iqbal," he said calmly.
"Let us try this one more time. Who is the girl and why is she on this ship?"

Chapter Twelve

She is, as my wise friend Rashid al-Basan has already informed you, my brother's daughter," Captain Iqbal began.

The story, as told by Iqbal in Arabic and translated by Ricky, was as such: the girl was called Tanisha and she was the only daughter of Iqbal's older brother Khalil, who was high in favour at the Almohad court and was, in fact, the Emir of Valencia, a large region of the eastern Iberian Peninsula.

I looked at Ricky as he said this. *Was this the same terrifying prince who had imprisoned him in his galley for two hellish years?* Apparently so.

Tanisha's father had arranged for her to be married to a rich Moroccan lord, another distant Almohad cousin, an old man who lived at the base of the Atlas Mountains, but Tanisha – who had spent all her short life in Spain, did not wish to go to a strange country to marry a dotard the same age as her father. One who possessed three wives already, all past childbearing age.

"Wait," said Robin, holding up a hand. "Bring the girl herself up here so that she can tell her own story to me."

"It would not be seemly," said Ricky sombrely on behalf of Captain Iqbal, "to expose her to the gaze of so many lustful young men."

"Not a man will touch her – you have my word on that," said Robin. "But I would speak to her myself and hear her tale from her own lips."

"Lord, it would not be appropriate..." Ricky began.

"My patience with your master has worn thin. If he does not wish to enjoy an invigorating dip in the ocean, he should summon the girl – now."

Tariq was dispatched to fetch her and when she arrived, with a large piece of black cloth modestly covering her head, it was clear that she had been expecting a summons. I could see that she had lightly applied kohl around her dark eyes and perhaps a touch of something red to her full lips.

She reminded me, achingly, of my own lover Nur, before she had been mutilated. I told myself, however, that this night-eyed, ebony-haired Tanisha was not half as comely as the girl I had loved. The line of her jaw was not so fine; her skin more pale and ghostly than Nur's, her eyes far too large. Nevertheless, Tanisha made an impression on the men there, all except Little John, who seemed indifferent to her looks, and watched the blue sea instead.

Robin kicked me off my stool, I mean that literally – he put a boot on my hip and shoved me off – and told Tanisha to sit in my place. He spoke kindly to her, confirming the elements of the story, through Ricky, that Iqbal had told him. I watched the pirate captain during this exchange and, though he seemed a little tense, he did not seek to direct what she told Robin, even when she was scathing about her betrothed, a "drooling old baboon from the back of beyond", as she called him. It occurred to me that they could have agreed the story beforehand. But when – immediately after I discovered their secret? No. In the moments before Iqbal came on deck? Not possible.

"You did not wish to marry this man?" said Robin.

"I would rather lie down with a pig," said Tanisha, unexpectedly in good clear French. "I would be less defiled."

Robin seemed taken aback by her forthright attitude and her knowledge of the Frankish tongue. In fact, he seemed rather taken by her all together.

"You speak French?" he said, a rather obvious question, since she had already used that language to answer him.

"My mother was a noblewoman of Burgundy. She died two years ago,"

"She married a Moor?" said Robin. He almost blurted it out. He seemed ruffled by this beautiful young woman; far from his cool, controlled self.

"It was... political. Or so she often told me. The women in my family must marry where their fathers choose. Is it not the same in your lands?"

It was, at least for well-born ladies.

"And yet *you* refused. Did you tell your father," asked Robin gently, "that you would not be wed to this older Moroccan gentleman?"

"Told him? I told him a hundred times. He beat me and ordered me to obey. So I ran from Valencia. I left the Russafa Palace, my childhood home, I gathered my jewels and my clothes and fled the women's quarters. There was a captain of a dhow, a little vessel like this one, and I bought a passage to Egypt on his ship with a ruby. It came into my foolish head at that time to make a journey to the *Kaaba* – an *umrah*."

"What is that?" asked Robin

Tanisha evidently did not know the French word. Ricky exchanged a few sentences with her in Arabic and then he said.

"It is a journey to the city of Mecca. You've heard of the Hajj, lord?" Robin nodded – although I had no idea what Ricky was talking about.

"It is like that but less sacred and can be undertaken at any time of the year. I think just plain 'pilgrimage' is the best word for it, sir. To Mecca, to the Holy City. That's where she wanted to go and pray for God's guidance."

"And what happened?"

"The dhow captain tried to rape her and planned to sell her as sla..."

"Let Tanisha tell it," interrupted Robin.

"He was an animal," she said bluntly. "I pretended to consent and when he was lulled I stabbed him with his own dagger. In the eye. He soon died."

I could see that Robin was deeply impressed with Tanisha. She seemed so frail and modest, a true Arab maiden; indeed, she was only about my age. But the words she spoke painted a picture of a woman of courage and spirit.

"When Iqbal and the rest of us caught up with that dhow," said Ricky, speaking for himself this time, "Tanisha had barricaded herself in the captain's cabin, with the dead body, and a crossbow, and the dhow's crew were hammering at the door and trying to smoke her out with burning tar."

"You will be quite safe on *this* ship," said Robin gently. "I swear it."

Tanisha favoured him with a lovely smile.

"You plan to return her to her father?" said Robin to Iqbal.

"When we have the gold," the pirate replied, through Ricky.

"And do you consent to this?" Robin asked Tanisha.

The girl shrugged. "What choice do I have? I love my father dearly – and I know he loves me. He will not send me to that old goat. Not now."

Robin gathered the crew and showed Tanisha to them. He placed her in the charge of Elise, the "young crone" as Iqbal called her, and the pirate chieftain seemed to be content with that. Robin also made dire threats to any man who should disrespect her while she was with the company.

"You will treat her as if she were my sister," he told them. "I'll treat any man who fails to respect her as if he harmed a member of my family."

The next morning, when the rising sun had burnt off the

thick morning mist, we tacked past two small islands just beyond an enormous sandy headland, and now turning the dhow southwest, with a light breeze on our starboard beam, we came slanting down into the wide gulf of Tunis.

The ancient city appeared as a smear of red and white and brown on the right-hand side of a deep placid bay some ten miles across. But, as we came closer, I could make out the individual buildings, shops, low warehouses and dwellings, and a needle-slim minaret here and there, and some very grand houses with high walls, almost like fortresses, but inside the town itself.

We tacked again close to the bottom of the bay, near cultivated fields of bright shimmering emerald and lush darker groves of oranges and lemons, and were now heading northwest. Ricky at the tiller guided the dhow into one of the smaller of Tunis's several harbours, not much more than a fishing port, in fact, a suburb of this settlement, at the mouth of a slow green river.

The bulk of the city was now directly to the north and west of us, with two huge inland lakes, crammed with shipping and just visible from the aftcastle. These lake-harbours – or lagoons, I suppose – contained a forest of bare masts, some girded with rigging, and they held perhaps upwards of a thousand ships of varying sizes. And surrounding the nearest lake were the mud-brown walls of compounds connected by narrow winding streets, dark and warren-like, and some larger stone buildings, the red tiled roofs of villas and the many tall, slim glittering spindles of the Moorish houses of prayer.

We berthed at a broad stone quay in our cosy little enclave on the fringes of this great Arab city, and having secured the dhow, fore and aft, to a pair of massive stone bollards, and having collected our gear, we set off up a stony road, which wound uphill past the harbour master's grand house.

Iqbal led the way, with Ricky and Tariq at his side. The other two Arab crewmembers, along with two reliable Sherwood men, were ordered to remain with the dhow, to keep it safe and secure from any passing thieves.

I was intrigued to see that Robin walked alongside Tanisha and Elise as they climbed the hill, both ladies swathed in black from head to toe, as was the modest custom of the region for women in public. Yet all three of them seemed to be enjoying a lively conversation together, with much laughter.

I saw Iqbal turn and stare back at Robin and the two women from time to time, with a troubled expression on his face, but he said nothing and, after a short while, we came to the top of the bluff where there was a large house with high forbidding mud walls and a large wooden double-gated entrance, twice the height of a man. The dark brown double doors, oak or some other local hardwood, were the only entrance that I could see to this fortress – for that is what it truly was. There were no windows at all, not even a few arrow slits of the kind that you might find in a good Christian castle. There were crenulated towers on the corners of the building, square constructions and I could see men in black with spears or javelins posted up there, watching us.

They must have passed the word of our arrival for when we came to within forty paces of the double doors, they swung open, towards the inside, to reveal a broad, square, sandy courtyard, perhaps thirty paces on each side and stabling for at least forty horses over on the left against the outside wall.

A small, fat man greeted us, a fellow as bald as an egg, who was obviously well known to Iqbal. His clothes were fashioned from rich silks, brightly coloured, with small jewels sewn into them and intricate patterns of gold thread woven through the material. I should have taken him for a lord of men, a refined nobleman, but for the deference with which he treated the salt-stained Captain Iqbal, and his grovelling manner when he saw Tanisha.

"O lady," he said, bowing until he was almost bent double. "What a vast honour that you should grace our humble house with your presence."

Then the gates were closed behind us with an echoing thud

and, startled by the sound, I jumped a little and looked around the bare courtyard with its high walls on either side properly for the first time. The first thing that struck me, seeing black-garbed armed men on the walls on every side of the square, was that this courtyard was a quite obviously killing zone. A dozen archers – or good crossbowmen, or even slingers or javelin men – on the walkways above would be able to slaughter any men on the ground in here. There were no stairs, nor ladders that I could see. If those guards up there chose to rain down swift death, there would be nothing any men in the courtyard could do.

But the black guards on the walls did not attack us. Instead, the little egg-headed steward ushered us towards a smooth baked-mud wall at the back of the courtyard and a little arched door set into it. He opened it with a large key and we filed in, all twenty-seven of us, one by one. I was one of the last to enter, and when I did my breath was entirely stolen from my body.

In contrast to the austere mud walls and bare sandy courtyard, the grim guards on the walls, the mighty hardwood double doors, the interior of this Arab fortress, this humble home, was like a glimpse of an earthly paradise.

It was huge, far larger than the interior space I'd been expecting, and so light and cool and airy, it took a moment to remember that we were inside high walls at all. A large rectangular pool, tiled in shimmering turquoise and gold, occupied the centre of the large space, while a fountain splashed and tinkled pleasantly from a great bowl in the middle. There were well-trimmed trees, oranges and lemons, planted around the edges of the pool at regular distances apart, their scent perfuming the air, and couches set between them, enough room for a dozen men to lie by the cool waters and rest their bones.

There were servants in plain white robes waiting for us with large ewers of warm water, faintly smelling of roses, which they poured out into deep bowls for us to wash out hands and faces, and soft thick towels to dry ourselves on afterwards. One man held a tray of delicate glass beakers filled with the juice of various citrus fruits mixed with a dash of cold spring water.

Another man held a tray of small pastries containing delicately spiced meat.

I began to seriously doubt the evidence of my senses. Surely this must be what Heaven itself is like, I thought, as I washed the crusted salt from my sun-burned face, neck and hands and downed a cool draft of orange water.

The Sherwood men were all in a similar condition, staring about themselves, lost in wonder at this dream-like place. As well they might. Around the central pool and the white couches shaded by the orange trees, on all four side were arched colonnades, decorated with elegant Arabic script in gold and silver, the woodwork carved in intricate swirling patterns and repeating designs, more cunning and accomplished than any I had seen before. Beyond the shady colonnades, I could see into cool dark rooms, some set with tables and benches as if for a feast, and others filled with more soft beds and hammocks, little couches and piled of cushions. I saw doors that opened to other smaller courtyards, more tinkling fountains, more well-tended trees and flowerbeds. It reminded me of a high mountain monastery in its dedication to simplicity and quiet. I was suddenly struck by the urgent desire to remain in this calm, cool and beautiful palace for a long, long time – and perhaps never leave it until my dying day. It was, indeed, a paradise.

"What is this place?" I asked Ricky, who was sitting on a silk couch with his bare feet in the pool and munching a pastry. "Whose house is it?"

"They call it the Riad al-Mansur, which means the Pleasure Garden of the Conquerer – and it all belongs to . . ." he swallowed painfully, "to her daddy," nodding at Tanisha, who was in deep conversation with the steward.

We washed and changed our clothes and rested and some of the men slept. In a small courtyard off the main one, Hanno and I engaged in a little light sword practice, but neither of us was much in the mood for violent activity.

After half an hour, we stopped and sat and cleaned, sharpened and oiled our weapons. Hanno said, "You remember the monk's hospital in Acre?"

I nodded. It was in the quarter owned by the Order of the Knights of Hospital of Saint John, a calm, cool place of skilled and holy healers. It was where I had met Hanno, when both of us had been seriously wounded.

"This place is like that," he said. "But without the nights of pain."

"Do you like it here?"

Hanno waggled his scarred right hand, as if to say maybe, maybe not. "It is place out of time. It feel like there are no seasons. No past. No future. Rest of world is not real in here. There is no other world at all when you inside here . . ." He stopped.

I knew what he meant. The Riad was weirdly otherworldly, to be sure.

"That is dangerous. I feel sleepy here, and slow. There is danger here, and death, yet I do not care. Death seem like a very little thing in this place."

In the late afternoon, Tanisha, now our hostess, gave us a great feast. At a long, broad table in one of the rooms off the central garden, a lavish banquet was set out for us to enjoy: a spiced lamb stew with apricots, flat breads and pickled garlic, grilled vegetables, fruit, cheeses . . . We ate our fill, and I noticed that the Sherwood men seemed to be relaxed and rested even though they had been here less than a day. There was no wine or beer served with the meal, only water and the cool juice of fruits – apparently Tanisha did not approve of strong drink, and while Hanno grumbled, the rest were uncomplaining.

The white-clad servants served the familiar sweet mint infusion when the meal drew to a close, and Robin rose to address the whole company.

"We shall rest here for two days," he said. "We will take turns guarding the dhow down in the harbour, two men on a four-hour watch but, apart from that, you will have no duties – the time is your own. Eat, sleep and rest as much as you can – you will need your full strength in the days to come."

"Tell us about the gold," yelled out Gareth, from the benches, and his Sherwood neighbours on either side gave a joyful, but rather sleepy cheer.

Robin smiled. Night had fallen by now and many candles had been lit in the white-painted room, and his eyes gleamed like silver in the shadows cast across his long, lean face. "The gold... Yes, I think it time to tell you why we are here and how we shall proceed. Ricky, my friend, would you be so good as to translate for your steemed master, as he tells us of all the trials and challenges that lie ahead. Captain Iqbal, if you would be so kind..."

Iqbal was, in fact, still eating, but he gamely got to his feet, chewing furiously, and having wiped his red beard on a napkin that Ricky discreetly handed him, and swallowing down a glass of the mint brew in one gulp.

He began: "My Christian friends, my comrades, my brothers..."

He then told us how we were going to deprive the Caliph of his hoard of gold. It was neither Christian, nor friendly, and when I'd digested the enormity of his murderous plan, my belly felt as sour and sore as if I'd swallowed a whole bucket of boiling vinegar.

Chapter Thirteen

I have, in my long life, killed many men – and, to my great shame, a few women and even children, too, have fallen under my sword over the years; although I never took joy or satisfaction in their killing. Even then, as a tender youth, I had already removed many souls from the Earth. But all my victims had been killed in battle, or were folk who posed a threat to me, or my loved ones or my master. I believed I could face God on Judgment Day and answer for those deaths with a reasonable expectation of forgiveness.

But what Iqbal was proposing leapt a new moral barrier for

me. He was proposing that we murder, in cold blood, a score of unsuspecting men who had done us no harm at all, and who must be put to death solely because we wished to take what was under their guardianship. Or as Robin might have put it: because they stood in our path. We would take all these men had, and all they ever would have – we would make their wives into widows, render their children fatherless – and why? Because we wished to enrich ourselves.

I do not expect the readers of this manuscript to understand my shock and horror that this thought: *Silly young fool*, you will say to yourself, *how else do you lay hands a vast fortune that rightly belongs to another?*

I will admit that I had not properly considered the implications before that evening in the Riad al-Mansur. I believe I had convinced myself that Robin had some trick that he would employ to remove this portable wealth bloodlessly from those who possessed it. And there was indeed a measure of trickery involved. But at the core of this mission was black, brutal murder.

I slept badly and the next morning after breaking my fast I sought out Hanno, determined to sweat the guilt from my body in a long, savage training session – and so I did, with sword and shield, with my Arab dagger – my *janbiya* – and misericorde, and finally, with a little target practice with the crossbows and bolts that Robin had acquired in the haven of Qatran.

We practised for several hours in a quiet garden, away from the main area of the Riad, a place of flowers, trees and grass and – before we filled it with the clang of steel weapons and the grunts of battling men – a wonderful tranquillity. About half way through our session, Ricky came to watch our antics – having finished his stint as watchman on the dhow in the harbour below – and he cheered us on in our strenuous efforts as if we were a pair of noble knights engaged in a deed of arms before a royal court.

We finished our session and towelled ourselves dry, and were sitting on an old wooden bench, sipping lemon water, when Hanno remarked that he would cheerfully kill a man right now to have a gallon of good Bavarian ale.

"The Saracens do not hold with strong drink," I pointed out to my shaven-headed friend. "It is against their religion. Besides, you drink far too much ale. It's slowing you down, I swear you're already as sluggish as..."

I did not finish my profound thought because Hanno, lashing out a lightning-fast fist to the left side of my head, had just knocked me clean off the garden bench, tumbling me laughing on to the soft grass.

"They do have wine," said Ricky, a moment later, freezing Hanno and I in the midst of a playful wrestling bout. "It may be against the teachings of the Prophet Mohammed, peace be upon him," he went on, "but not all men of Islam adhere to the rule strictly, not always; some good men of the faith enjoy wine. But the Lady Tanisha has decreed it should not be served out."

"Wait! There is wine here?" said Hanno, releasing my right arm, which he had been twisting painfully behind my back.

"Where is wine? Tell me and I spare the life of this insolent child."

"It's locked in the cellar, o' course," said Ricky.

"Hmmf," said Hanno, scowling at the little sailor and sitting down again on the bench. "So why tell me? Is funny joke? You mock me?"

"You see that little door over there?" Ricky pointed to a low, wooden door set in the interior marble wall of the Riad. "That door leads to the cellars. It is locked but, if I had but a few thin lengths of iron, I believe..."

The former wharf rat was a man of some rare skills, it seemed. With nothing more than a bent crossbow bolt and an old iron nail, levered free from the bench, he soon had the door open and, a short while afterwards, we were in the cool, cobwebby depths below the house, rapping our knuckles on a number of wooden casks and selecting one small barrel as our prize of war.

The wine was superb, a light red that slipped down like nectar. We sat in the shade in the furthest corner of the garden and sampled it with pleasure.

After a cup or two, I happened to mention my deep unhappiness with the murderous aspects of the plan to steal the gold.

"It already has a good deal of blood on it – that gold," said Ricky. "It is thoroughly gore-stained, you might say. The precious metal comes from the hot lands far to the south of the great African desert, I am told. The gold is wrested from the deep earth by thousands of wretched mine-slaves in the Kingdom of Sosso – whose ruler uses gruesome sorcery, animal-sacrifice, they say, to maintain power over his people. Slaves die like flies in the mines so the King may have his gold. I was chained to a man, in the gal..."

Ricky swallowed his wine in one and reached out a hand for a refill. He was suddenly very pale under his tan and seemed almost overcome with a bout of violent shaking at the memory. He muttered, "God preserve me from that evil..." and drank the wine in one straight draught. Then he seemed to recover. "In the galley, I heard that the only place worse to be a slave was the mines of Sosso... If that is true, I can hardly conceive of the suffering."

I caught Hanno's eye, and raised one questioning eyebrow. "Should we make him talk about this?" I asked him silently. Hanno shrugged. "Let the little man talk, if he wishes to," he seemed to be replying to me.

"The Almohad Caliph regularly sends thousands of slaves – Christian and Jew, mostly, but indeed any man who has the misfortune to be captured – in long, chained marching columns down to his partner, the King of Sosso.

"These wretches tramp for weeks across the vast, blistering desert, with little water or food and only the whips of the slave-masters to drive them on, and when they get to Sosso, the King feeds them into his ever-hungry mines. All perish there – eventually. In return, the Caliph receives gold – and rock salt. Jewels, too, rubies and diamonds, if the African tyrant finds them..."

Ricky seemed to be fully recovered now. "All I would say to you, Alan, is do not trouble your conscience over this matter.

All those involved in this filthy trade – they are guilty of the very worst crimes. They *deserve* death."

We watched from the high walls of the Riad al-Mansur as the cavalcade of dust-shrouded horsemen approached.

I had seen these men – or men very like them – before. On the plain of Arsuf, where the great battle had taken place in July, these men had fought with skill and bravery against us. They were Berber lancers: big men on fine horses, wrapped in mail under their once-white robes and armed with one stabbing spear, similar to a Christian knight's longer lance, and two light but deadly javelins. I could also see curved scimitars hanging by their sides.

I counted nineteen men, which was the approximate number we had been told to expect, and as they halted outside the gates, waiting for them to swing open, I examined them covertly from the walkway that surrounded the courtyard. They looked like what they were: tough, professional soldiers – Saladin's men, who had travelled from his Egyptian Sultanate along the harsh North African coast nearly two thousand miles to Tunis, to take charge of the consignment of the Caliph's gold, which had been brought up from the mines in the Kingdom of Sosso. They were not expecting to receive the gold today. The rendezvous was set for two day's time, the full of the moon, at a large oasis, a terminus of the camel trains, to the south of the city. They were here at the Pleasure Garden of the Conquerer, the house of their ally, to rest, to eat and sleep after their journey in perfect safety. Or so they thought.

We shot them down the moment they were all inside the courtyard; the moment the double wooden doors had closed upon the outside world.

Two dozen of Robin's men, as well as, a dozen of the black-clad house guards and even a few of Iqbal's crew of seamen, rose up from their positions of concealment in the walkways above and raised their crossbows and loosed. The quarrels whizzed and thumped into the tired Berber lancers, skewering flesh, hurling men from their saddles, six or seven men falling before the rest knew what was happening. Javelins too sped down like thunderbolts from Heaven. Robin stood tall with his long bow and quiver of scavenged Qatran arrows and slew the poor Berbers with a chilly precision.

I stood with Hanno and we loaded our crossbows and loosed, again and again, taking care not to damage the horses – we would need them. But I believe I killed at least three men. It was a massacre – no other word for it.

When every saddle was empty and the courtyard was filled with corpses and the writhing quarrel-stuck bodies of the wounded, Little John came out of the door in the wall, coming from the heavenly garden, and with Gareth and three of the other Sherwood men, they dispatched the wounded swiftly, slicing throats with a dry, casual indifference born of long practice.

We killed them all, and lost only one man on our side. One of the Berbers, a young man, was quicker to react to the assault than his comrades and, plucking a javelin from the holster on his horse's withers, he launched it up at the walls, and caught one of the Black Guards in the belly, knocking him flat. An instant later, Hanno shot the young Berber stone dead with a bolt through his throat. We killed them all, every man... all except one.

He wore a distinctive red turban, while the other Berbers wore only white cloths over their spiked steel helmets, and we had been told to look for him and ensure that he was unharmed. His face was grey with terror, and he lifted both his arms in the air in surrender the moment the crossbow quarrels began to fly. He watched all his comrades die, with his black beard, plaited into a stiff rope, twitching like a nervous cat's tail at every strike. When the last throat had been cut by Little John and his murderous crew, and the courtyard fell silent, Red Turban was the only member of his troop still sitting a horse, hands in the air, gazing at Iqbal standing up on the walkway.

"Welcome to the Riad al-Mansur, Captain Hassan, peace be

upon you," said the pirate chief in formal Arabic. "I trust the long journey here was not too fatiguing, my friend. Would you care, perhaps, for a little refreshment?"

We stripped the bodies – the bloody white robes would need to be washed in cold water, I heard the little egg-headed steward tell one of his subordinates, and the holes made by the crossbow bolts neatly mended. Quickly now!

The horses, some terrified and quivering, were soothed, brushed, fed and watered and put into the stables. We hauled the dead men through the Riad to the garden behind the main house, where we buried them in a single huge grave. I muttered a prayer over the mound of fresh earth, for although these men were our enemies and not of the true Christian faith, it seemed wrong to put them in the ground without some message sent up to Heaven.

The massacre made me melancholy – and I was not the only one. As we ate our evening meal, our labours done for the day, even the sweet white wine that Tanisha provided as a celebration could not lift my sour mood. Nor the mood of the long table where the Sherwood men ate their rice and mutton and sipped their wine and nibbled their fruit; every man knew what we had done that day was mere execution. There was no glory in it. None.

Of our company, only Robin seemed largely unaffected by the bloody work we had accomplished. When all the other men had slunk away to their beds – despite the ample quantities of wine provided by our hostess, there was no call for revelry – I saw him still chatting in lively manner with Iqbal, Ricky and Tanisha and the Berber captain, Hassan, who seemed to be quite reconciled to the loss of all his men. I drifted a little closer to their group at the end of the table, and pretended to examine a candelabra and peel away an excess of dried dribbles of wax from the brass fittings. But it was a poor pretence: Robin noticed immediately that I was hoping to listen to his talk.

"Join us, Alan, if you will. Here, take another cup of this

wine – it is a rare vintage from the lady's homeland, from Valencia, I believe she said."

I hesitated just a moment. But since I did not believe I would be able to sleep at all that night, I sat down and accepted a brimming cup.

It seemed that Captain Hassan was telling my lord about the handover of the gold. I could not look him in the face, finding his treachery repellent, but I listened to what he had to say, and sipped the excellent yellow wine.

"It is no more complicated than presenting a parchment scroll, which was issued to me in Cairo by the Sultan's Treasurer, and which I have safely in my baggage," said the Berber captain to Robin, with Ricky translating.

"The scroll is marked with the seal of Salah ad-Din himself, and is a receipt for the gold and the ten she-camels that carry it."

"Is that all?" said Robin. "You hand over this receipt and accept the gold and it is all done? That seems..."

"They will recognise my face," said Hassan. "I know the camel captain, Musa, very well – we are old comrades of the desert. We have done this transaction three times before; every year this month at the full moon. And the route and cargo of this train are, of course, a jealously guarded secret."

"It still seems a little too easy..."

"There is a little formula of words to be spoken too – I say 'Old camels give the sweetest milk'; Musa replies, 'Yet old donkeys have the sweetest temper'. But that is all. My lord this *is* a simple exchange. Musa takes my parchment back to the Almohads; I take charge of the camels and the gold."

Robin frowned. He took a sip of wine. "What do you think, Alan?"

I had nothing to say except, "The gold is a vast fortune, worth more than any man could hope to gain in one lifetime. And, with such a glittering prize in the balance, we must be constantly on our guard against treachery."

A sad platitude, I know. But Robin said, "I agree. And I wish to say this now, this night, to all here at this table. Ricky you will translate this for me."

Ricky inclined his head.

My lord said, "I swear on my honour that if any man – or woman – plays me false in this affair, my vengeance will be truly terrible. Men will speak of it in generations to come. But I will proceed in good faith, and I will keep my bargain with you, Iqbal, until I am given cause to doubt it."

Later, as the gathering at the table broke up and we all retired to our respective sleeping quarters, Robin took my sleeve and drew me aside.

"There is something about this I do not entirely like," he said.

I nodded. I was beginning to feel uneasy, too.

Robin said: "Keep your eye on Captain Iqbal, when we go to the oasis, tomorrow night. If he means to play us false, it will be then, I believe. If he means us harm, if he means to cheat us, he will act when the camels are being handed over. Or shortly afterwards, in the desert, in the darkness..."

I said I would watch him.

"And Ricky too," Robin said. "He seems like a good fellow but..."

"We will go to the meeting at the oasis with our eyes wide open, lord, our weapons at the ready," I said. "Put your trust in me. I shall not fail you."

Robin smiled at me. "You're about the only person I do trust, Alan."

And with that kindly word, he bade me good night.

Chapter Fourteen

We dressed ourselves in the white robes of the Berber lancers – now miraculously cleaned of blood by the efficient household servants, with the rips and tears from the crossbow bolts neatly mended. In the early afternoon, mounted on the dead men's horses, which fortunately seemed to accept us docilely as their new masters, we rode out of the Riad in a column of twos.

Iqbal and Hassan were at the head of the column, side by side, both in their borrowed robes, with lances and javelins in the holster on the horses' withers. Next came Tariq and Ricky – who with his black beard and dark tan looked more like a desert warrior than anyone. And that was the point: the men at the head of the column must seem as Berber-like as possible, because behind them came Hanno and me – I had my blond hair covered with a steel helmet and shrouded in the white linen Berber head-dress, and, as I had taken a good deal of sun in the past six months, I believe I could have passed for a fair-skinned local, given that the meeting would be at night. I was, however, concerned by Hanno.

I would not say he was ugly, but his square face, scarred, battered and lined, with its pugnacious jaw, could never be mistaken for anything other than a warrior of the far north: a German, in short. Still, it would be night, and he would not be required, God willing, to do anything more than stand around looking tough – and he could certainly do that without effort. There was no mistaking Little John's Englishness, either, his merry blue eyes in his scalded face. Indeed, the more I thought about it, the more I fretted that the camel-train guards – a score of desert-hardened Almohad troopers, from one of the Caliph's elite regiments – must instantly recognise us all as imposters.

But then, why would they think that? Their captain Musa knew Hassan, and we had the formula of words, and the parchment receipt sealed by the Sultan's Treasurer himself. All will be well, I told myself. All will be well.

Robin rode at the back of the column, in the last pair of our twenty men with Gareth, as his lieutenant. He had told me that he wished to watch the road behind us, personally, as we made our way southwest towards the oasis of Najid, on the southern outskirts of the city of Tunis. I had not realised, until that afternoon, just how large the city was. Ricky had told me that it contained a hundred thousand souls – which was three times the size of London – and I had not truly believed him. But, as our column walked the horses on the long dusty road around the southern walls of this seemingly endless metropolis, I realised he had not exaggerated at all.

Ricky had also informed me that the gold came north from the city of Timbuktu, beyond the southern fringe of the great desert. It came north across the desolate rocks and sands by slow camel train to the city of Fez, which was about a hundred miles south of the narrow stretch of turbulent water where the Mediterranean meets the Atlantic, the strait called in Arabic *Jabal Tariq*, Tariq's Mountain, after a vast, high rock on the European side.

From Fez, the camel trains carried their loads east along the traditional coastal routes to Tunis, where the camels were usually changed or allowed to rest, feed and water themselves at the Oasis of Najid – our destination that afternoon. When the trains continued eastwards, they stopped once again at Tripoli, before braving the final exhausting leg to Cairo, the capital of the Sultan of Egypt. It was a stupendously long journey, covering thousands of miles of dry and dangerous wilderness, one that might take a walking camel some weeks or even months to accomplish. Yet, for generations of camel herders, it was no more than a stroll along the Pilgrim's Way to Canterbury.

We rode with the lowering sun in our eyes, and the high, white walls of the huge city, which reflected the sun's raw power, never seemed to end. For mile after mile we journeyed, all of us sweating like pigs in our iron mail and padded gambesons, under the borrowed loose white robes – and this was near the end of October. It would be quite unbearable, I reflected, to ride out clad like this in the scorching heat of high summer.

Eventually, we parted company with the white walls of Tunis and rode due south, and in only a mile or two we reached a dusty little town, no more than a large village, in truth, of low mud-built houses around a large greenish pond, shaded by ancient palm trees. I heard the noise of hungry camels roaring from one of several small enclosures, a fenced circle, made more impenetrable by a lattice of thorns woven into the wooden slats that made up the barricade. It was the only occupied enclosure and, as I stood in my saddle and craned my neck, I counted ten hump-backed beasts inside.

It was full dark by the time we climbed stiffly down from our horses, and tied them to rope lines – well away from the camels. Once we had watered our mounts and attached their feedbags, Robin gathered all of his Sherwood folk together. He said, very quietly, "Be ready, all of you, and if it comes to a fight, and you get separated, ride to the Riad. Rendezvous there."

I was ready; in fact, I was in a state of extreme alertness, prepared for the slightest hint of treachery. Iqbal, Hassan, Ricky and Tariq had made their own council group, and at a nod from Robin they set off on foot towards a low building in the centre of the town, a little back from the oasis. Robin and I, Hanno and Little John, followed on their heels and before I knew it we were passing under a striped blanket that served as a door and into low but wide and deep building lit by torches that reflected from whitewashed walls.

There were a dozen men inside, some heavily armed with spears and curved swords and standing by the white walls. Two men stood by a table in the centre of the room, and they too were armed, with scimitar and *janbiya* daggers, similar to but not as fine as the one in my own belt. Behind the table on the floor was a long mound covered in blue woollen blankets.

We four Locksley men stood back, allowing Hassan and Iqbal to approach the two men at the table, which I saw held a brass jug of some kind of drink and four cups. There was a brass plate of sticky brown dates, too.

No man spoke and the tension in the air was almost visible. I could see the knuckles on the wall guards tighten on their spear shafts and sword hilts. I had my hand on the hilt of my *janbiya*, ready to pull the blade and fight.

Hassan and Iqbal threw back the capacious hoods of their white robes to reveal their faces, and slowly, slowly, the stern expressions on the faces of the two men at the table changed into genuine smiles of friendly welcome.

"Peace be upon you, Captain Hassan," said the man on the right, who I assumed was their leader, since he spoke first.

"And upon you be peace, as well, Captain Musa," said Hassan. Then all seemed to be well.

The guards relaxed a fraction, although they did not move from their positions. Musa and Hassan exchanged news and good wishes – they behaved as if they were indeed old comrades. We were all invited to try the dates and take a drink of cool fruit juice from the big brass jug. Robin declined on behalf of all the Sherwood men with a smile and shake of his head. We stood back, while Ricky, Tariq, Iqbal and Hassan made friendly talk with the captain of the camel train and his lieutenant, nibbled and drank.

Hassan, with some joke I did not catch, produced the parchment roll – a plain brown cylinder, bound up with a scarlet cord. He untied the elaborate knot, unrolled the parchment and showed it to the other captain. I caught only a glimpse of it, a sheet of dense Arabic writing, with a large cipher at the bottom, a swirling jumble of coloured lines, more like a drawing than writing, but beautiful even seen at a distance. Once Musa had inspected the scroll, he stretched out his hand to receive it, but Hassan took back his hand, withdrawing the scroll just out of Musa's reach. He made a joke again, something about gold, and retied the red cord around the brown cylinder.

Musa nodded indulgently. The two men went over to the blue-covered mound and, with a casual flick, Musa pulled back the nearest blanket.

Suddenly the whole room seemed to be filled with a magical glowing light. Every eye in that place was drawn to the hoard.

Under the blankets, which Musa quickly pulled away with the flourish of a mountebank doing a conjuring trick, piled in groups of five hundred shiny ingots, were ten little stepped mountains of golden light. I could hardly tear my eyes from them: more gold than I'd ever seen in my life: five thousand pounds of in weight of pure African precious metal. The little bars, each one about three inches long and one inch high, seemed to be filled with an interior brightness – they shone, they actually twinkled in the torchlight; they seemed to fill the whole low space with a generous warmth and light.

Suddenly, shockingly, there was a loud crash from the table. The spell was broken. All eyes now whipped to Ricky who was standing shamefaced beside the toppled big brass jug, with a spreading stain of fruit juice on the floor. I had my blade half out of its sheath – and I saw that Hanno too had a weapon in his hand. But then all was well again. Someone over by the wall laughed, then all was laughter, and loud jokes about Ricky's clumsiness.

But in the general release of tension, I noticed one small thing. Hassan had been holding the scroll in his right hand. Now the scroll was in his left.

So what? I asked myself. He changed the hand in which he held the scroll. I watched him bend down and ostentatiously count the golden ingots in the nearest pile, aloud in Arabic. Five hundred little bars in each pile, ten piles in all. Five thousand pounds of gold. It took some while but when he was finally finished there was more laughter. Hassan with great ceremony then handed over the scroll to Musa, who bowed and tucked it into his robe.

All was movement now. The guards came away from the walls. Musa and his lieutenant bowed and embraced Hassan and Iqbal. Then in a flowing rush they all left the room, nodding politely at Robin and I as they passed us.

Iqbal and Hassan went with them, loudly calling out good wishes and sincere hopes for a safe and swift journey back to Fez. And I found myself in a room full of gold – a king's ransom, no less – alone but for my three closest friends. I went over to the pile of glowing metal on the floor and picked up one of the bars. So small, yet so heavy. It felt warm in my hands. And, though you may find this a fanciful word to use about metal, profound.

"All right, Alan, plenty of time for drooling later," said my lord. "We are not quite out of the woods yet. We need to get this lot back to the Riad in safety. Go and get the rest of the men and start loading up the camels, if a wealthy fellow such as you will condescend to undertake so menial a task."

I went out to gather the Sherwood men and set them to work, with the help of the ten camel herders, who went where the camels did. On the way, I stumbled in the darkness and accidentally bumped into Hassan, hitting him hard and almost knocking him to the ground. I apologised profusely in English, begging his pardon, and he, rather grumpily, seemed to forgive me.

Within the hour, we were on the road again. The ten, heavily laden she-camels plodding along in the centre of our column, led by their usual handlers, and with our horsemen, all with weapons drawn and as alert as can be, forming a defensive cordon around the outside. I noticed that Captains Hassan and Iqbal seemed to be having some sort of an argument as we jogged along. However, I was too far away to hear what was being said.

After two hours, about half-way home, Robin called a halt so that we could all take a drink, stretch our legs and give our beasts some water, too.

I saw Robin talking quietly with Little John but kept my eye on Iqbal, who still seemed to be arguing with Hassan, with Tariq and Ricky standing by. And then, miraculously, they were at the centre of a ring of Locksley men, spears levelled, swords drawn, and Robin said: "I think, Captain Iqbal, that we ought to have an honest talk about what just happened, don't you?"

The first thing Iqbal said was: "I did not play you false, my lord. I have kept my word and my bargain with you."

"And so how do you explain this?" Robin said, holding up the brown scroll with its distinctive red cord. "Ricky, translate this, if you please."

"He stole it from me – that one," said Hassan in Arabic, pointing at me. "He took it from my robe when he fell against me, the black-souled thief."

Robin seemed to understand the meaning if not the exact words. He ignored Hassan and looked directly at Iqbal. "This is not about my light-fingered young friend, Alan, but about why you seem to have sent that unfortunate Berber captain on his merry way with another, different scroll."

"It is not what you think," said Iqbal.

"What do you think I think?"

"I did not betray you. I swear it."

Robin said nothing for a long, long while. "I do not trust your oath, Captain. Tell me now, right now, do not waste any more of my precious time or I will cut out your eyes and make you eat them. I warned you about this."

Iqbal said, "It was not meant to hurt you. It is not an action against you. I wanted to give us some time. That is all."

"What does that mean?" I could see that Robin was losing patience. I wondered if he really would make Iqbal eat his own eyeballs.

"I gave Musa a forged scroll, a false receipt," said Iqbal, who was babbling now, "because I wanted to throw the blame on him. He will show it to his superiors, the Almohad commanders in Fez, and they will know, immediately, it is not genuine. The Almohad will then suspect that Musa is complicit in stealing the gold, for if not, why did he not notice that the scroll was a false one. The duplicate is deliberately poor, for this exact reason."

"You betrayed your friend?"

"He is a goat-fucker. No friend of mine. But yes, I sacrificed him to give us more time to escape. They will torture him, trying to get him to reveal who is behind the robbery – they would have executed him anyway for his incompetence – and that will take several days. He is a hard man. But he knows nothing except that he made the exchange as usual. While he screams under the hot irons in Fez, we will be sailing swiftly north for Marseilles.

Inshallah, by the time the Almohads realise Musa is innocent, we shall be in the Christian County of Provence, free, clear and very, very rich. All of us. I did this only to make us safer. You must trust me, my lord."

"I do not." But Robin seemed to be thinking. "And there is no ambush ahead?" he said. "Musa is not lurking in the darkness to retake the gold?"

"He is not. He knows nothing. He and his men are on their way back to Fez now, oblivious. I swear this. I swear by the Name of Allah, I swear by the souls of my children. I have kept faith, I have not broken our bargain."

Robin looked at him for a long time. He was not usually an indecisive man but I could see he was struggling to make up his mind. I fully expected him to order Iqbal's death, there and then. Or the eyeballs. But he did not.

"I choose to believe you," he said. "But do not do anything like this again. Next time: tell me first. This is your last warning."

I could see relief in Iqbal's eyes – and the sweat beading his forehead.

As the sky was turning a milky grey in the east, we came in sight of the high mud walls of the Riad. There had been no ambush and, having ridden all night to Najid and back, alert to every click and rustle and squeak in the darkness, we were all deeply tired, exhausted even. But deeply joyful, too.

I had spent much of the long journey greedily calculating how much of the gold would be mine, and what that precious metal would be worth. There were five thousand ingots, each weighing a pound, and each pound in weight worth roughly fourteen pounds of English currency. Iqbal and his men were due to receive half the gold – although that now seemed unnecessarily generous – and Robin, as leader of the expedition, was taking twenty-five shares. About sixty people were getting one share only – those who had gone directly to Messina. Thirty of us who had come with Robin were receiving three shares each. And each share was worth fourteen and one third ingots. So my three shares amounted to forty-three bars of pure gold.

In terms of money, that meant more than six hundred pounds. *Six hundred pounds!* My annual income from Westbury was, in a good year, about ten pounds in silver. This was a veritable fortune. I could live in great comfort for sixty years – should I survive to that great age – and never lift a finger again. Or I could buy land, or clear forest to make new lands, and build myself a fine castle... I could afford to buy myself a new destrier, a valuable war horse. I could buy a dozen horses, retain a dozen knights...

I was deep in this most pleasant of reveries, half asleep, when the gates of the Riad swung open and our cavalcade, horses, camels, gold and a score of fatigued men, clattered into the courtyard, and it was not until the gates swung shut again, and I was about to climb off my tired horse, that I became aware of the large welcoming party on the walkway above, surrounding us.

The Riad al-Mansur possessed half a dozen guards, whom we had left behind to guard our base and ward the Lady Tanisha, along with a similar number of servants and one or two Sherwood men who had been deemed surplus to requirements for the expedition to the oasis. Fifteen folk, perhaps.

But the walls above us were now were thronging with men: black-clad, with blackened steel cuirassiers gripping raised javelins, about a hundred of them; and a score or so of more lightly armoured men with recurved bows, and short Moorish arrows nocked and ready. I swear my mouth fell open.

One man stood a little apart from the rest on the crowded walkway. He was a tall, imposing, middle-aged man, handsome in a cruel, sharp-boned way, hawk-nosed with a short black beard, curled and oiled. He wore a black steel cuirass and matching greaves and a spike-topped steel helmet, wrapped in a black turban. A heavy black cloak hung from his shoulders to his ankles.

Tanisha stood beside him, looking calm, serene even, and

particularly beautiful, and I saw that the family resemblance was strong. I knew, of course, immediately who he was. It was Prince Khalil, master of this house.

He spoke French, which came as a shock. But my world righted when I remembered that he had married a lady from the lands of Burgundy, and his daughter spoke the language too. A very well-educated family, it seemed.

"Remain calm, all of you. There is no call for unnecessary bloodshed," he said in the Frankish tongue, lightly accented; then repeated it in Arabic.

I looked at Robin who was still on his horse, and staring up at the dark man on the walkway with a quite unreadable expression on his drawn face.

"Stand fast, everyone," said Robin in English. "Nobody move a hair."

"You must be Robert Odo, Earl of Locksley," said Khalil with a smile. "Peace be upon you. I cordially welcome you all to my humble house."

"You are too kind, sir," said Robin, returning the smile, though a little stiffly. "Upon you also be peace. You are, I believe, Abu Ibrahim Khalil bin Yusuf, Emir of Valencia. I thank you for granting us the use of your home."

Ricky was helping Captain Iqbal down from his horse; the little Londoner was shaking like a leaf in a gale, but I could hear him stuttering out a hurried Arabic translation in Iqbal's ear.

"You are most welcome, my lord," said Khalil. "Now, if you would be so kind, you will order your men to dismount and divest themselves of all their arms and armour. If you would then be good enough to pile all your weapons over there, on that sheet of canvas, I would greatly appreciate it."

"And if we do not choose to do so?" said Robin.

Khalil frowned. "That would be most unfortunate. The consequences would be ... well, I dislike the use of threats – so vulgar, don't you think?"

"I believe they have their place."

"He rarely ceases from making them," Iqbal said in Arabic.

"He is a violent man. But never mind that! Well met, brother – I had not expected to see you here. I understood the plan was that we should meet in Valencia."

"The plan has changed," said Khalil in Arabic. Then, in French: "Lord Locksley, you must immediately order your men to dismount and disarm."

"And if I do not?"

"If you obey me, no harm will come to you. Let me put it like that. I have a proposition I wish to put to you, a matter of business. There is a task that I wish you to perform; that only you and your men *can* perform. But I must ask you, first, if you please, to lay down weapons. If you do *not* do so, now, right now, I regret to say I will deal with you as decisively as I must now deal with my treacherous younger brother."

I was puzzled by the emir's words – but not for very long.

The tall, black-clad lord on the walkway said only one word:

"Tariq."

I saw the Assassin glide forward a step, there was a flash of steel in the air, a plunge of metal, and Iqbal was grasping his own collarbone, a little fresh blood gently seeping between his white fingers from the tiny wound.

The Locksley men were twisting and shifting, someone shouted, "Bastard!" I saw the dark archers on the walkway pull back their bowstrings. I caught a glimpse of Tanisha's lovely face and saw that she had not changed her expression at all at the casual murder of her erstwhile protector.

Iqbal sank to his knees, staring up in disbelief at Tariq, who was now casually cleaning the long dagger he always carried with a cloth. Iqbal slowly toppled forward and landed face first with a thump on the ground.

"Steady, boys, steady. Off your horses, now," Robin was shouting. "Come on, dismount. And let's get those weapons piled over there. Move!"

Robin's men, after a moment of confused staring, obeyed him. I slid down off the back of my mount, and with the greatest reluctance I unbuckled my sword and tossed it on the growing pile in the corner of the courtyard.

"You, Englishman," Khalil was pointing at me. "Knives too, if you'd be so kind," he said. I added my *janbiya* and misericorde to the mound.

"Tariq," said Khalil, and I confess I flinched. The emir pointed at Hassan. "That man is a traitor, too, to his comrades – which is far worse."

Quicker than blinking, Tariq had his dagger out again. One swift pace and the steel was buried hilt-deep in Hassan's guts. The Berber captain gave a soft moan, and blurted: "Lord, I was acting on your brother's orders..."

"You have a point but . . . but I hate a traitor worse than the plague. Make it quick, Tariq!" And the Assassin wielded his blade once more, silencing Hassan with one neat slice that opened his throat like a wallet.

The servants came out and cleared away the two bodies – and took with them the canvas sheet, clanking with our weapons. Grooms came and took away our horses, and the baffled herders silently led the she-camels, with their precious loads, through the opened doors and out of the courtyard.

I heard myself give a tiny whimper of disappointment as my fortune stalked out of the gates on the swaying humps of those ten beasts of burden.

I half-heard Khalil give an order in Arabic to one of his black-clad lieutenants: "Get it loaded in the dhow as soon as you can. We sail at dawn tomorrow." But I paid little heed. I was grieving for the sudden loss of my gilded life of ease and leisure – my stone castle, my fine destrier...

When the courtyard was empty but for Robin's twenty-odd Locksley men, all now disarmed, disillusioned, disconsolate, most a little fearful and all mightily resentful of the whole business, Khalil addressed us once again.

"Set your hearts at ease, my English friends," he said in his Arabic-accented French. "I mean you no harm. I have taken possession of my Caliph's gold, naturally – you have no right to it – but if you agree to my proposal, you shall not go unrewarded. You may yet go home wealthy men."

Chapter Fifteen

They locked the Sherwood men in the underground storeroom – along with Elise and two terrified sailors who had been part of Iqbal's crew. And they were provided with water, orange juice, bread and cheese and eggs boiled in their shells, so that they might break their fast after the long night's ride.

However, Robin, Little John, Ricky and I were taken to the dining room and asked to sit down at the long table. Warm water scented with roses was brought by the servants and, while we waited for Prince Khalil to join us, we washed the dust of travel from our hands and faces and dried them on clean linen towels: we were not to be treated as prisoners, it seemed, at least, not quite as prisoners. Now disarmed and surrounded by Khalil's bow and lance men, his Black Guards, we knew we were very far from free men.

Tariq loomed quietly in the corner of the room, watching us intently with eyes like chips of jet. That made my skin crawl. Our weapons, I had noticed earlier, had been hauled into the long central room with the tinkling pool and left in a tangled mass under an orange tree. The weapons were not guarded, I noted. I wondered if perhaps I might have an opportunity at some point to discreetly regain possession of my *janbiya* or my misericorde.

Khalil and Tanisha joined us just as the food was being served – eggs, cooked in butter and mild spices and fresh bread, a huge platter of mutton stew and rice. Six plump roasted capons. A pair of grilled ducks stuffed with dates. An array of soft cheeses, fruit and olives. No wine, sadly, but more of the delicious mix of sweet juice that seemed to flow like water in this house.

I was aware Khalil was trying to make himself pleasant to us.

But I could not understand why.

The Almohad prince graciously invited us to eat, and we did so, setting to with a will. I found I was actually ravenous after the long night of tension and hard riding. It occurred to me, only after I had finished my second plate of mutton stew and was mopping up the gravy with a piece of flat bread, that the food might be poisoned. I soon dismissed this notion – Khalil and Tanisha were both eating with almost as hearty an appetite as me. And Little John, it must be said, was making an absolute hog of himself, as usual.

When we were done, and the servants had come around once again with the hot water and towels, Khalil said, "I understand that you must be rather angry with me. I have taken the golden hoard away from you, by force of arms, and I'm sure you consider this an affront. But I have need of it. And, I assure you, if I can persuade you to fall in with my plans, you will be compensated – not to the degree of wealth that the gold would have given you – but in a not inconsiderable way. All I ask is that you trust me."

"That's what your brother constantly asked us to do," said Robin, sitting back in his chair. "Trust him. Did you ask *him* to trust you, too?"

"My little brother Iqbal – I believe I owe you an explanation for that."

"I believe I understand much of it already," said Robin, picking a shred of mutton from his teeth. "The idea for the gold robbery was cooked up between you two brothers. You, who are well connected at the Caliph's court, and involved in the business of Almohad rulers, supplied Iqbal with the times and dates of the arrival of the train and rituals of the gold transfer."

"You are as perceptive as I was assured you would be. I understand we have acquaintances in common, people involved in the frankincense trade."

"Seems likely," said Robin coolly. "Why do you need gold so badly?"

"All in good time," said Khalil, with a false little laugh. "First, I shall tell you, if you'll indulge me, why I was obliged to dispose of my brother."

Tanisha poured Robin a little more orange juice, and favoured him with a demure little smile; and I noticed my lord responded with one of his own.

"The simplest way to explain it to you is to say that he was a greedy and treacherous fool. As you correctly surmised, I arranged this little operation to take possession of the Caliph's gold, and my agreement with Iqbal was that we would split the proceeds equally between us. For reasons that need not concern you, I was obliged to ask my brother for a favour..."

To my surprise, Tanisha interrupted him, also speaking French. "They know, Father, that Iqbal rescued me. They know that part of the tale."

"Is that so?" he said. And for the first time I saw him express some emotion beyond the bland politeness that he seemed to exude like oil from his pores. He looked hard at Robin and said, "My daughter is a silly girl, headstrong and given to romantic notions. She was fooled by a man, once, a sea captain she trusted and... I was obliged to ask Iqbal to track her down and retrieve her from his grasp. I only wish *I* had caught the fellow alive."

There was a flash of black and terrible anger in his eyes, and for the first time I had a glimpse of why Ricky seemed to be so terrified of him.

Then Khalil mastered himself. "The price Iqbal demanded to rescue my daughter was the robbery you gentlemen have just so efficiently and successfully accomplished. I must offer you my sincere congratulations."

"But you still plan on denying us the proceeds," said Robin dryly.

Khalil smiled. "I do. But you may not go home empty-handed. First, let me finish telling you why I felt the need to wipe my younger brother from the world. We made a deal, and

Iqbal made all the usual promises that he would honour it. But I have known him all my life, and I know his nature." Khalil took a sip of his fruit juice, smiling genially at the whole table. Ricky, I noticed, kept his eyes down and his head humbly lowered the whole time,

"As must be obvious now, Tariq is my man, and has always been loyal to me," Khalil said. "Mistrusting my brother, I placed Tariq with Iqbal, and ordered him to work his way into Iqbal's confidence. This he did most cunningly." Here Khalil raised his cup high to the tall lean man standing at the wall of the dining room watching us with his dark killer's eyes.

"Tariq kept me informed, whenever he could, of Iqbal's plots and schemes. And he discovered that my brother was planning to ransom my daughter back to me. Not content with his half of the gold, he was planning to demand the whole shipment, in exchange for Tanisha, his own niece."

Khalil suddenly looked at Ricky. "You knew this, did you not, Rachid al-Basan?" he said in Arabic. "You knew my brother meant to betray me."

Ricky's face turned light green. In his terror, I genuinely thought he would vomit up his supper. His mouth moved silently but Khalil did not bother to wait for a reply. "I should have you flayed alive for that crime."

"Ricky is with us, now. He is one of our company," said Robin.

"Is he?" Khalil looked at my lord. "You would protect him from me?"

Tariq moved off the wall, coming forward on to the balls of his feet.

Little John let out a soft belch and shifted on the bench, which creaked under his bulk. His new position allowed him to keep Tariq under his eye.

"Finish your story, sir," said my lord. "And tell us what you want from us – and why you need this vast quantity of gold so very badly."

Khalil attempted a careless laugh. "There is not much more

to tell. My brother plotted to cheat me, to threaten my daughter's life in exchange for all of the gold. I could not allow that. I would have been made to look foolish and, far worse, look weak. Reputation, as I'm sure you know, is an armour."

"I understand your actions," said Robin. He had, after all, ordered the death of his own brother when that wretch had betrayed him to the sheriff.

"So, we have no quarrel over Iqbal?"

"None at all. I believe he would have tried to cheat me too."

"I swear I shall not do the same. My sacred word on it."

Robin did not reply. He took a slow sip from his cup.

"You do not know me, Christian – not yet. Why should you take my solemn word as truth? But you will find, I think, that I am man of honour."

"You were going to tell me why you needed the gold," said Robin.

"Was I? I don't think I was. Perhaps when we trust each other a little more. I believe I was going to make you a proposition. Will you hear it?"

Robin looked attentively at him.

"As you know, I am the Emir of Valencia. Do you know my lands?"

"I've glanced at a map," said Robin.

"You know, then, that my emirate lies on the east coast of the Iberian Peninsula abutting the Christian Kingdom of Aragon to the north..."

And he proceeded to give Robin a detailed description of the political situation of his part of Spain. I confess I did not give his dull lecture my complete attention. I was tired after another night without sleep, and now that the danger of swift death seemed to have passed, the mutton stew was weighing heavily on my belly. I gathered from drifting in and out of Khalil's droning exposition, that the emirs of the southern half of Spain, who were ruled from Seville by the great Almohad Caliph, Abu Yusuf Yakub, behaved much the same as the feudal lords of England or France. That is to say, that they were constantly jostling with each other for power, seeking favour and honours from the Caliph – who might be thought of as a great and powerful king. The Caliph had recently won a series of victories against the Christian knights in the west, on the Atlantic coast, in the southern region known as the Algarve, but he had since returned to Morocco with more than three thousand Christian slaves captured in the war: poor wretches destined for the mines of Sosso. In his absence, Khalil wished to win his lord's approval by expanding his own territory north into the realm of Alfonso, the King of Aragon and Count of Barcelona. In the spring, he said, he planned to launch a great campaign, and he wanted Robin and his men to help him to victory.

I sat up straight at that point.

"What?" I said stupidly. "You wish us to fight against Christians?"

"Alan, let the emir complete his proposition," said Robin.

"I will offer the equivalent of fifty English pounds in coin to each of your men who will fight under my black banner; and five hundred pounds in silver to you personally, Lord Locksley, as their noble captain..."

"No," I said, my temper rushing to the surface. "Absolutely not. We would never take service under a heathen lord and kill our fellow Christians. It would be a sin, a monstrous sin." I was on my feet, red-faced and raging.

"Alan, be calm," said my lord. "We will hear the gentleman out."

"No. Never. Robin, surely, you cannot contemplate this? Even for you, this is a crime beyond wickedness. I personally would rather die than..."

I saw Khalil looked over at Tariq; the Assassin straightened his spine.

Little John was instantly his feet. He aimed a huge sausage-like finger at Tariq, pointing it like a battering ram. "Don't even think about it, laddie," he said. "You take one step nearer, just one little step, and I'll put my right fist so far down your throat, you'll be sniffing the sweat on my armpit hair."

Tariq froze. He did not understand John's words – but the meaning was crystal clear. The promise of imminent violence vibrated in the still air.

Lady Tanisha said soothingly, "I believe we have allowed our passions to overcome us. Perhaps we should all retire to consider the matter further."

"Yes," said Robin. "We should like to consider your proposal, emir, to chew it over properly. May we have some time to debate among ourselves?"

"Certainly – you may have a day and a night to consider the matter. Tomorrow I depart for Valencia. I hope you will agree to accompany me."

"Just out of interest, my lord, what would happen if we should choose *not* to take you up on your most generous offer?"

"Ah, that would be most unwise," said Khalil, with a pained grimace. "Very soon, if it had not already happened, the regional governor in Fez and the Sultan's Treasurer in Cairo will be wondering what has happened to their train of gold. They will suspect it has been stolen. Then it would be my duty, as a trusted servant of the Caliph, to inform him who was responsible – a band of Christian vagabonds. And to deliver them to the Caliph's justice."

They locked us in the underground store room with the rest of the Locksley men, and the moment the heavy bar had been dropped into the iron brackets on the outside of the door, I rounded on Robin: "Lord, you know I am your most faithful follower," I began, "but I simply cannot, I will not allow . . ."

"Oh, be quiet, Alan," said Robin crossly. "For once, curb your flapping, old woman's tongue. We are not going to serve that puffed-up butcher. Of course not! How could you think it? The Moorish bastard stole my gold. *Our* gold, I mean. And I will have it back. But I must be allowed to think. I cannot think while you are yapping your schoolboy outrage in my ears."

I shut my mouth.

"Let us all sleep on the matter. I see that our captor has

kindly provided us with plenty of soft cushions and warm blankets. I will sleep and then we will think on how we may extricate ourselves from this makeshift prison."

"If I might be permitted to flap my old woman's tongue on more time," I said angrily, "escape is the least of our worries."

"How so?" asked Robin.

I told him then about the door that Ricky had opened two days ago with his bent crossbow bolt and nail, which led out to the tranquil garden.

"Is it still open?" Robin addressed Ricky.

"It is, my lord," said the Dowgate man. "I checked just a moment ago."

"That *is* a stroke of fortune. We may yet recover the gold. But we cannot move till darkness. Now, John, be so kind as to set a guard on the garden door, two men, two-hour watches. Thank you. I will still sleep on this – I urge the rest of you to do the same – but tonight, when it is full dark..."

We waited till nearly midnight, listening at the barred main door till the soft noises of the house died down and finally ceased. Then, when we were sure that the Riad was asleep, we all slipped out of the garden door, as easy as pie. A moment later, we were snatching at the pile of unguarded weapons in the room with the pool, and were soon fully armed and ready for battle.

I was just slinging on the scimitar and tucking the *janbiya* into my belt, when a black-clad guard came wandering out through an arch, yawning, scratching himself. He saw us and gave a loud yell. An instant later, a small dagger, expertly hurled by Hanno, was sprouting from his throat. But the alarm had been raised, and Khalil's warriors were appearing from all sides.

"Kill them," bellowed Little John. "Get every one of the bastards."

Robin echoed the command. "We cannot allow a single man escape to raise the alarm," yelled my lord.

The Sherwood men fell to the task with a will. They had

been robbed and imprisoned, bilked of a vast fortune the like of which they might never see again, and they were in the mood to slaughter the whole cheating world.

The Black Guards were disorganised, poorly led, and came at us in ones and twos, like simpletons. They died for their foolishness. I fought with scimitar and *janbiya*, slicing, hacking and found both weapons to have the delightful keenness of new-stropped razors. Khalil's men did not stand a chance against our pent-up fury, and once we had killed all those who came directly at us, we hunted their dark-clad brothers through all the rooms of the palace and its gardens like rats, and slew all those we found without mercy – two score of men at least.

In no time at all, we were masters of the Riad al-Mansur.

I came across a mound of bloody corpses in the kitchen areas and, with a sense of shame, saw that the half dozen servants, people who had brought us food and drink and who had posed no threat at all to our company, had also been killed in the frenzy. The egg-headed steward lay on top of the pile gazing sightlessly at the ceiling. I muttered a guilty prayer for their souls.

However, and although we searched high and low, every room, every nook, we found no sign of Khalil nor Tanisha, nor of the tall Assassin Tariq.

Robin immediately dispatched Hanno down the hill to reconnoitre the small harbour and, in less than an hour, he came back with his report.

The dhow was still there and guarded by four black-clad warriors – that was all the guards Hanno could see; but he admitted that there might have been more, hidden or just sleeping on board. There was also another ship in the harbour, perhaps a hundred yards away from the dhow. A slave-galley.

I twitched at the mention of this kind of vessel. But Hanno grinned at me. "It is not same Griffon boat," he said. "This one much bigger, painted black as midnight. With two red eyes, like an animal, on the pointy end."

Ricky said: "It is the *Khamsin*. I know it – oh God, oh God

Almighty, God preserve me . . . I know that ship well." And his voice rose and cracked alarmingly and his whole body began to tremble. He gripped his bloody sword with both hands, and took an even firmer grip on himself. "This black galley is Khalil's own ship, Alan, the one I was, I was . . . It is not the Cretan vessel. Your friend Nikos Phokas will be long gone. Back in Ierapetra, I imagine. Those small galleys are not built for long voyages, far from home."

Hanno was giving Robin what detail he could of the free personnel on board the *Khamsin* – he had seen some hundreds of crew, officers and Black Guards. But there was also some sort of jolly celebration taking place in the Harbour Master's house, which was filled with light and music and revelry.

Robin and Little John were conferring, trying to come up with a plan.

"Of course, they're bloody celebrating," growled Little John. "They've got all our fucking gold. God's great bleeding arse-grapes, I'd like to get in among them with my axe. Can't we just charge in and kill them, Robin?"

"There may be as many as two hundred men. It would just be suicide."

"I heard Khalil give orders to load the gold into the dhow," I said.

"Did you now?" said Robin. "You kept that very quiet, Alan."

"Didn't want to be accused of flapping my old woman's tongue."

Robin said nothing but gave me a chilly, silvery stare.

"Right," my lord said, a moment later. "Gather round, here's the plan."

Chapter Sixteen

We came down the hill as quietly as we could – which was, to say the least, not particularly stealthily. While we bumped and stumbled on the loose rock and undergrowth in the darkness, making our clumsy way down the road behind the Harbour Master's house, Hanno ranged ahead of the rest of us, a shadow slipping invisibly through the night. He had told me to watch him and learn stealth from his actions but I lost sight of his form early on and I only managed to spot him again as he flitted out of a patch of deep shadow, streaked across the well-lit quay, and leapt on to the dhow's deck.

He surged up behind one of the guards, who was standing oblivious on the prow and, with a vicious hand-axe blow to the back of his turbaned head, Hanno dropped the man to the planks like a sack of wet sand. A second guard in the waist of the ship must have seen something of the attack, or had sensed the violent movement, for he cried out in Arabic, words that I did not catch – and it was the last thing he ever said. Hanno launched his short-handled axe in a spinning arc and it thunked into the centre of his forehead.

The guard's cry had, however, alerted the rest of Khalil's men on the dhow – and black-clad figures were popping up all along the length of the ship, calling out for news, asking what was amiss. But Robin and I were at the bottom of the slope now, with a handful of Sherwood men all around us, and Little John was ahead of us, already charging like a bull for the side of the ship, bounding forward with his great double-headed axe in one hand . . .

We swarmed over the side of the dhow and swiftly dispatched the half dozen guards on board. There had been some cries – some of our men had unfortunately screamed aloud in their battle excitement, and I was aware that some of the men on the black slave-galley, a few hundred yards away, were now sounding the alarm. The lights of the Harbour Master's house blazed brighter and the great central door was opening, and dark figures were emerging from within, with spears and swords. But we had the dhow unmoored, by this time and, using the long sweeps, we shoved the vessel away from the side of the stone quay.

Ricky was at the tiller, issuing orders to the two Arab crewmen, and to some of our own fellows too, to drop the sails and haul on this rope or that.

Once the killing was done, I stayed well out of the way. Standing with Robin and a few of the others on the aftcastle with loaded crossbows in our hands. My lord had his own bow and half-full quiver.

"If any man sees that bastard Khalil, he is to shoot him down without mercy," he said.

But the dhow was under sail now, moving, gaining way, and fully fifty yards from the land. The quay was filling up with shouting, jostling men, waving weapons and torches. I only once caught a glimpse of Khalil at the back of the throng, too far to make a sure shot with an unfamiliar crossbow.

Robin, however, saw him too. He immediately nocked an arrow, drew back the cord to his ear and loosed the shaft in a smooth instant – and a big ugly fellow in a white robe fell dead two full yards from the emir's side, spitted right through the neck. Farther along the quay, there was a noisy commotion around the black galley, scores of men milling about and a blaze of orange torches. Drums were beating; there was the distinctive pig-squeal of a Saracen trumpet. They were preparing to launch the big vessel. They were going to come after us. Of course, they were.

Yet we were now a hundred yards out in the dark Bay of Tunis, the breeze filling the sails, deck tilting and a hiss of water along our flank.

Robin muttered, "I believe, at this moment, that I would hand over ten pounds of our precious gold for a sheaf of *straight* English-made shafts."

Then he turned to me and said: "Right then, Alan, let's go below and see if your tongue-flapping was worth it. See if we're princes – or paupers."

The sun rose on a glorious warm autumn day. The dhow was scudding along under drum-taut sails with the wind coming straight in from the east, and we had cleared the Bay of Tunis and were sailing northeast out into the wide – and blessedly empty – Mediterranean Sea. During the night we had seen the lights of the galley and heard the menacing heart-beat drums of the slave masters driving it onward, but our superior speed meant that the torches of Khalil's vessel swiftly disappeared, swallowed by the night. We sailed on.

I sat in the waist on the larboard side of the dhow with the rising sun pleasantly warm on my face, sharing a bite of elderly bread, a piece of hard cheese and a mouldy onion with Hanno. Yet I have rarely felt a greater sense of wellbeing than on that magnificent morning. Under me, packed along the spine of the dhow's hold in ten new wooden chests, were our five thousand gold ingots – eighty-six of which, delightfully, now belonged to me: it truly was, as Ricky had called it, wealth beyond the dreams of the moneylenders.

I was rich. We had slipped the grasp of Khalil, and his Black Guards and his fearsome Assassin, mostly unharmed, and were speeding towards Marseilles and a rendezvous with our friends. Then it was home to England.

I was amusing myself idly with thoughts about what I would do with my money, which, since Iqbal's death, and the demise of his half share of the haul, was now double the original sum – one thousand, two hundred pounds! Perhaps I would build myself a grand townhouse in London, as well as my fine new stone castle in Nottinghamshire. Perhaps I would take a wife – a lady of gentle breeding and elegant looks, with a large dowry to boot; although she might prove too high and mighty for a gutter-born thief such as me. Maybe, instead, I'd find a good, honest Nottinghamshire lass...

Hanno, who had an equal-sized share coming to him, said, "I like to have my own free company. Good men, good fighters all. I will hire in Bavaria – but I think Italy is the place for us to make our work. Plenty of different sides who pay us well but ... ach, who knows, maybe I just find a nice alehouse and a fat ale wife and drink and fuck till I am bored to death. Maybe I *buy* an ale house..." He tailed off and sank into a smiling reverie.

There was an air of celebration all over the dhow. After the noonday meal, some of the men began to sing and dance on the aftcastle watched and applauded by the others. Robin and I were persuaded to sing a duet together, an old country song called *The Thrush and the Honey-Bee* and, although I had lost my vielle, a stringed instrument which I usually played to accompany my singing, when the *Tarrada* was destroyed at Matala, my lord and I gave a decent rendition, and the cheering afterwards was enthusiastic.

By mid-afternoon, the coast of Sicily was visible on the horizon, with the peaks of its daunting mountains spiking the hazy blue sky. We planned to call in at the port of Palermo, on the north side of the island, and seek news of the *Santiago* and the Sherwood men under Owain's command.

If luck was with us, they might still be at Messina, a hundred miles east of Palermo, and we could join up with them, transfer the gold into the bigger ship, sell, sink or just abandon the little dhow, and then travel up the coast of Italy and round to Marseilles all together in one powerful vessel.

I was looking forward to seeing Owain, a kindly soul and a superb archer, and telling him about our adventures in Africa. It would be good to be back in the larger company of my countrymen again, too, and on a more roomy ship. And very much safer, should Khalil and his slave-galley catch up with us. With another sixty or so tough Locksley men under Robin's command, I was sure we could see off any threat from the emir with ease.

If I am totally honest, that bright afternoon at the end of October, I truly believed my adventure was over, and that I'd be home in England, a wealthy man, by Christmas. I should have remembered the old saying, a favourite of Little John's: Man makes his plans – God just pisses himself with laughter.

We did not notice the galley until it was almost upon us. Our lookout, our only sentinel, who was posted at the top of the main mast, had been looking down at the antics on the aftcastle, instead of watching the sea for enemies.

Robin would have whipped the man raw for that crime, had he lived.

The galley came round a headland, rowing straight into the wind at a furious pace, and when shouts of alarm belatedly rang out on the deck, the vessel was only two hundred yards away and coming on like a racing horse.

It was Kavallerios Nikos Phokas. I could tell by the white standard with the golden bull fluttering above. It was evident he had been lying in wait for us in Sicily, in some cove, with watchers on the cliffs. I cursed our stupidity.

The Cretan knight knew our destination – Marseilles – we had even discussed it with his father the Archon. And the route there from Tunis was as obvious and as well trodden as a king's highway. All he had to do was await us, like a footpad on the road, and we would eventually come to him.

Ricky had assured me that the Griffon galley would not be able to sustain a long search, and it had not. While it waited for the dhow to come north, it had obviously revictualled, restocked its water and rested in these waters. The Archon obviously had good friends in Sicily, fellow Byzantines.

"Christ's sweaty crotch-cloth, that fellow is *persistent!*" said John, who was standing beside me in the waist, rolling his shoulders to make ready.

The galley was a hundred yards away and closing.

I had just finished struggling into my old mail hauberk, and was tying my sword belt very tight to take some of the weight of the heavy iron links.

"It's a matter of honour," I said, tucking the *janbiya* into my belt.

"You don't think he knows we have the gold?"

"I don't think he cares much about money. He thinks we dishonoured him. By tricking his father and breaking our arrangement, he feels that we have offered him a grave personal insult. He guaranteed our integrity to his father. He vouched for us to the Archon because we had participated in the Great Pilgrimage. He thought we were decent Christian men-at-arms."

"More fool him," said John, hefting his axe and a round wooden shield.

The galley was seventy yards away, still heading straight into the northwesterly breeze. If we were to try to use our speed to escape, the only direction we could run in this wind would be northeast, or due east, all these directions would take us closer to the oncoming enemy.

There was nothing for it. We were going to have to fight him.

Robin was on the aftcastle, with Ricky at the tiller; my lord with his bow and half a dozen Sherwood men with crossbows or lances. At the prow, the other extreme of the ship, stood Hanno in mail with a similar force of Sherwood men, similarly equipped. Little John and I and a dozen men-at-arms had the waist of the ship: where the enemy were most likely to try to board us. Our duty was to hold them off with sword and shield, while Robin and Hanno bombarded them from either end with lethal missiles.

It was a weak plan. But the best that could be managed. I saw Robin conferring with Ricky at the tiller, agreeing something between them.

Ricky had told us that Nikos had about a hundred marines on board the galley; we had a mere two dozen fighting men. I said as much to Little John.

"What are you complaining about?" he said. "We only have to kill four Griffons each. I'll have some of yours if you're going to be wet about this."

I felt a great hot wave of affection for Little John just then. Nothing daunted him. Not ever. Not overwhelming numbers of enemies, not Death itself. Just the sight of his huge, happy, beaming face made me feel a hundred times braver. Just four men. I could do that. I could manage four.

The galley was forty yards away now. I could see the faces of the marines in the front rank, I might even have been able to identify them, had we met before. There was no sign of Nikos. Perhaps he knew that the front rank faced the most danger. No.

He was no coward. Of that I was sure.

There was a blast of whistles. With no more warning than that, the ship went about, the heavy booms of the two sails swinging dangerously over our heads. I ducked only just in time. The ship changed its direction in the alarmingly sudden way of vessels at sea. The prow swung round and we were suddenly heading towards the galley, fast, like a thrown spear; the dhow leapt forward with the wind full behind and, with the galley coming on at a cracking pace, the blue water between us was shrinking fast.

Robin was shouting: "Brace yourselves. Brace, men, brace!"

And I knew what was in his mind.

We were going to ram the galley, slice into her like a battering ram, and hope to sink Nikos's ship before her Cretan marines could get over our side.

Closer, closer; a flight of javelins soared up from the enemy vessel, scores of light spears arcing up into the pale sky, and raining down on the ship. Our men had their shields up, over their heads, and the steel javelin heads clattered against our wooden protectors. But I heard one man scream, "Jesus God!" and out of the corner of my eye I saw a Sherwood man with a yard-and-a-half long shaft sticking out of his leg above the knee.

We endured only one more shower of javelins and then, with a tremendous crash, the pointed nose of our dhow punched into the side of the galley. Our momentum crushed the double bank of rowers, snapping the pine oars like kindling, tossing them this way and that – I could hear the poor slaves screaming inside the body of the ship – and the dhow carried on, forcing its way into the side of the galley like an axe strike. With a shriek and groan of rending timbers, the galley seemed to open under the assault.

But before the dhow had come to a halt, their marines were leaping at us, crossing on to the beak of the dhow where only Hanno and a handful of his men-at-arms were there to oppose them.

But these were Locksley men.

The Cretan marines – in leather cuirasses and kilts, with red-plumed steel helmets and bronze greaves on their shins – boiled out of their vessel and leaped across to ours and they were met with a barrage of crossbow bolts and our own javelins, hurled at a distance of only two or three yards. The Cretans were spiked and skewered, some slain in mid-air as they jumped from one ship to another, the quarrels smashing through their leather chest armour and penetrating deep beneath. Three or four men never made it to the dhow, swept aside and into the sea. One man, a giant, a fellow who perhaps thought himself a hero, landed on the prow, raised his sword with a cry of rage – and Hanno put a crossbow bolt neatly through his open mouth.

But more marines were coming behind. More heroes. With a shower of enemy javelins that knocked two of our men to the deck. The two sides clashed then, mashing together into a knot of struggling bodies in the confusion and timber wreckage where the two ships were enmeshed. It was hard to tell friend from foe. But our side had only a few men still standing, Hanno was slaying left and right, axe and shield. Gore spraying everywhere; men falling like bowling pins in an ale-house alley to his lethal skill.

I shouted, "Westbury!" and flung myself towards the prow, fear giving my feet speed and sureness. I was aware that Little John's great bulk was beside and slightly behind me. His bellow of "A Locksley!" was deafening.

I sensed rather than saw an arrow whistle past my waist. It took a marine officer in the groin, just below his cuirass. The man tugged at the embedded shaft, tripped and fell into the sea. Hanno was still fighting, his blood-covered face in a snarling mask, hacking wildly into the mass of foes like a woodsman tackling undergrowth, when I hurled myself into the melée beside him. I fended off a sword strike from a screaming man, and jammed the crossbar of my sword hilt into his face. Another fellow sprang up before me, and I sliced him down with a looping backstroke. A marine jabbed at me with a spear, I fended off the strike with my shield, the point skidding across the painted leather – and before I could riposte an arrow thumped into his cuirass-covered chest with the noise of a drum and plucked him away. I could hear Robin yelling: "Push 'em back, men. Push them all back."

His bowshot had carved me a little space. I swung the sword full strength at the next man, slicing through helmet and lopping the left ear clean off his head. He screamed, helmet falling apart, blood pissing from his ruined head and turned away. Disappeared into the crush. Another man reared up before me and I felled him with a straight lunge to the throat.

We were holding them, I realised. They could only come at us across a narrow bridge of broken timbers over the tossing sea, and we had stopped their attack dead. But it was not enough. It could not be enough. We were losing men – and we had none to spare. The space between us was filled with writhing bodies, wounded and dead, marine and outlaw. They had coalesced, formed a line of sorts. No more reckless diving on to our blades.

"Push forward, lads," shouted my lord. "Take the fight to their ship."

I realised he was right on my shoulder, the bow abandoned, and striking doubled handed over my head with a long spear he'd gained somewhere. Jamming the point into enemy faces. Dropping their men, one after another.

But it was Little John who broke them. He simply jumped across the wrecked timbers and crashed straight into the midst of their line. It was a bizarre, almost suicidal move, to hurl himself bodily into the crush of scores of his armed enemies. No man could reasonably expect to do that and live to tell of it. Yet fearless John Nailor did so and he broke their cohesion. His huge mail-clad bulk crashed through their front line – half a dozen marines, shoulder to shoulder – then he shoved a man away and started swinging that huge hellish axe. He took wounds, for sure. I saw a dagger plunge through the iron mail and deep into his broad back, and a spear piece his massive thigh. Yet he simply ignored the pain and hurt and carried on swinging that devastating axe, slaying his foes, splashing their blood in great red sheets in all directions. And, of course, we Locksley men came charging after him.

Now we were on their deck – and killing them.

My wooden shield took blow after blow, and I felt each ringing strike reverberating up my left arm. But with my right, my strong sword arm, I was slaying, chopping, killing, putting down man after man. And all about me were my comrades. Hanno on my left, Little John on my right – and behind us Robin and the rest of Sherwood crew, bloody-faced, raging, spitting, snarling, ever surging forward to kill and maim and slaughter our enemies.

We were greatly aided by two things: the design of the galley and the proximity of the Sicilian coast, which was no more than half a mile away.

The galley had no deck to speak of in the waist of the ship; just a central walkway over two cavities on either side where the slaves toiled at their benches. The walkway was only wide enough for two or three men to walk abreast, and Hanno, John and I filled it completely with our bulk.

And we advanced – slowly, surely, killing them all as we came.

The Cretan marines were no cowards, but they came at us in twos and threes, urged on by their screaming officers, and Nikos, who I could now see at the far end of the galley on the quarterdeck, shouted louder than them all.

They all died. Even those lightly wounded.

The galley slaves, still chained to their benches, played no part in the battle above them, except when a marine slipped from the walkway, by a misstep or from being wounded by one of us, and fell among the slaves – upon which he was immediately kicked and stamped and punched and torn until he was a tangle of bloody rags: a horrible way for a soldier to perish.

Behind us, Robin and his men were loosing crossbow bolts and javelins, showering the mass of enemy on the rear deck, but we were taking missiles too. Hanno took a javelin to his helmet, which caused him to stagger, and Robin seized him and pulled him back into the crowd of our fellows. My lord himself took his place in the line of three, and on we went.

I chopped and hacked, sliced and slew, cutting out way forward. The noise was hellish – screams and cries and the clash of steel, and the smell of opened bowels, and piss and fear clogged our nostrils. But we were moving forward. I saw we were nearly at the end of the walkway at the galley's quarterdeck itself. Some of the marines, I noticed, and there were only a score or so left, were slipping off their leather cuirasses and greaves and diving into the warm blue sea, swimming hard for the safety of the Sicilian shore, but Nikos was still there roaring for his men to stand and fight. They outnumbered us, even then, yet we clearly had the upper hand – then Little John stumbled, fell to his knees, the loss of blood taking its toll even on his great strength. And Gareth immediately stepped over him, into his place.

We surged onward. More and more marines were quitting the quarterdeck, embracing the safety of the sea. And we were there, at the end of the ship, and Nikos standing with only two terrified marines beside him.

My arms and legs felt like lead. My shield was a crumpled mess. I shrugged it off my arm. And I pulled the *janbiya* from its sheath and advanced on Nikos, sword in one hand and Arab dagger in the other. The two remaining marines were surrounded and overwhelmed by our men in a few moments. I yelled, "He is mine, I claim him." And advanced on Nikos.

The Cretan knight was slack-jawed with amazement, but he had a drawn sword in his hand, unsullied and shining bright. He stood alone on the blood-drenched quarterdeck of his own galley. His marines were all dead, mortally wounded or had fled into the sea, and he was confronted by a dozen blood-soaked savages, who had just ripped his little command to shreds.

"Surrender, my friend," I said. "Or you will surely die."

Nikos gaped at me. I was covered in blood, with a dagger and sword in either hand, and I must have presented a terrifying sight.

Robin said, "Dispatch him, Alan. You spared him once, and how has that turned out? Badly. We cannot take prisoners. End this foolishness now."

I ignored my lord. I looked into Nikos's terrified eyes. "Throw down your blade," I said, "and I swear you will be well treated. Surrender – now."

And Nikos's sword clattered on to the bloody deck.

Robin sighed. "Why, Alan, why do you always have to make things so much more complicated?" Then he gave orders for the Cretan knight to be securely bound and taken back to the dhow.

I sat down on the side of the galley, utterly spent, and gazed at the bloody carnage we had wrought. The timbers of the galley were thickly painted with gore. There were dead and dying everywhere I cared to look. But there was no time for maudlin reflection – one of the Arab sailors on the dhow was yelling something, something urgent.

"Alarm! To arms!" Was that was he was saying? It seemed absurd – the battle was over. We had won. I could not understand what he was shouting, or why. There was a sudden current of activity all along the two vessels, still mashed together, inextricable entwined. Men were running here and there. Shouting. Even the wounded were sitting up and looking wildly out to sea.

To the west.

I got wearily to my feet, grunting with the effort, looked west and saw, with a plunge of my heart, the dark shape of a galley, larger than the one on which I now stood, heading directly towards us, and no more than a quarter of a mile away. With a pair of demonic eyes painted on its jet-black prow.

The Emir of Valencia, it seemed, had finally caught up with us.

PART 3

Chapter Seventeen

There are some periods in a man's life that are so painful to recall that his outraged mind wipes them almost completely from its folds, until only a few lodged fragments and images remain. Such was the time that I spent as a wretched galley slave aboard the Emir of Valencia's ship, the Khamsin.

We made no effort at all to resist the boarding by Khalil's black-clad guards; nor to protect the gold that still rested in the hold of the dhow, which the emir's men swiftly discovered with cries of delight. There would have been no point since we only had a handful of unwounded men, I think I counted fifteen survivors of the battle against the Cretans, and almost all of those men, including myself, were utterly spent. We faced at least two hundred fresh enemies and to resist would have meant our certain death.

Robin said only this to us before the first Black Guard jumped aboard: "Whatever happens next, try to be strong, endure what you must, and wait for Fortune's Wheel to turn. Remember who we are: men of Sherwood."

He was answered with bold shouts of "A Locksley! A Locksley!"

Only Little John, now pale, shrunken and bandaged, seemed to be dissatisfied with the decision to surrender without a fight. "Could we not kill a dozen or so of them – then surrender? Teach them to respect us a little."

"We could, but we will not. This is my order. They already tally the deaths of the dhow guards to our account; if we make a dozen more widows, we create hundreds more enemies. And we are at their mercy. We must endure, survive, keep our minds strong, and live to fight another day."

I never discovered if Robin was right – or whether Little John was correct. For the emir's men showed us no respect whatsoever. We were deprived of our weapons, stripped completely naked and our hands were bound. Those among us who could walk were herded at spear point on to the demon-eyed galley and shoved below decks. Those who could not – Cretan marine and Sherwood man alike – were simply tossed into the sea to drown.

The bodies of the dead were similarly disposed of, and soon the sea around the three ships was a churning cauldron of feeding sharks. Robin caught a glimpse of Prince Khalil up on the quarterdeck of the *Khamsin* as we were being taken below, and called out to him. The emir, tall and dark in black cloak and armour, affected not to hear – he was conversing with Tanisha – but Tariq the Assassin looked over at us with his murderer's eyes.

The spear points were pricking Robin's naked back so he bowed his head and went uncharacteristically meekly below. I was beside Ricky as we stumbled down the wooden steps, and I saw he was shaking uncontrollably again, muttering, "I knew it, you fool, Richard, you God-damned fool . . ."

I gripped his shoulder, and told him to have courage. "Robin will find a way out of this," I said, with a confidence I did not feel. "Robin will save us . . . he will make some arrangement, or dream up some brilliant new plan."

"He will not. We will all die down here," said Ricky, his teeth wildly chattering despite the warm day. "You have no idea what horror lies ahead."

The first impression that remains in my mind is of the stench below decks: an almost solid invisible wall of faecal matter, urine, old sweat and rotting meat. I could feel my eyes smarting from contact with the noxious fumes – they truly felt as if they were bleeding. It was dim down there, too, and much hotter than above, and I was astounded to see so many naked men all crowded together in such a small space. I later discovered that there were two hundred rowers, all slaves, from a motley of all nations and creeds, packed tightly in a space a stone's throw long and two spear-lengths wide.

The rowers were on two levels, two men to each oar, with fifty oars on each side of the ship. It was not fully dark down there for the deck above the rowers was not solid wood but a latticework of square holes, which allowed in a grey twilight. My bare feet splashed in foul, swampy bilge water, and the movement sent a dozen black scurrying shapes leaping out of my path.

We were herded by our captors to the centre of the ship and forced to sit down in the raised central area where the big kettledrums were situated. The wooden boards under our bare arses were gelatinous with years of filth. The drums were silent now but two men, squat, furry, well-muscled brutes, sat before them on stools glaring at us, emanating a pure, mindless loathing.

The galley slaves, in contrast, entirely ignored us. Most were slumped over their oars, resting their heads on their folded arms, apparently asleep. Some just gazed into space, blank-eyed, lean, pale faces clawed with misery.

The slave-masters were a different breed to the Black Guards we had faced above, and it was clear that they had dominion here in this lower Hell. They were stripped to the waist, torsos gleaming with sweat, and wore filthy, baggy trews of canvas or linen. Over their shoulders were curled loops of black, gleaming leather whips. The chief slave-master – a huge hairy fellow wearing a sleeveless leather jerkin – was giving orders in gutter Arabic, and I saw that the other slave-masters were searching through the rows of slaves, seeking out the dead, unfixing their fetters with heavy keys, and hauling the bodies into the central walkway, roughly piling them. One man, who was dragged limply from the benches, proved not to be completely dead. He stirred and gave a weak cry, and one of the guards, immediately smashed his head three times with the heavy butt of his whip until he was still. The bodies were then dragged along the slimy walkway and up the steps through the square hatch and away into the light. I thought I could hear the splashes as they were dumped over the side to fatten the circling sharks.

They began to slot us Locksley folk into our places, the places vacated by the dead. Nikos Phokas who, like us, had been roughly stripped and bound, stood up and cried out in bad Arabic: "No, sirs, not me. I am not with these men. They took me captive. I am a knight of Crete, a nobleman..."

The whip smashed across his shoulders, breaking the unmarked skin, and Nikos screamed like a pig at slaughter. I doubted he had ever felt the cut of the lash before. But he continued protesting. "I am the only son of the Archon of Messara, in Crete. My father can pay you..." He went down under the hiss and crack of leather, his flesh sliced into a bloody mess by the whips of the slave-masters – yet still he insisted on his rank and privilege.

"You're a knight of Crete?" said the chief slave-master, coming over.

Nikos rose up again, bleeding heavily and babbled that he was, saying: "Ransom me, sir, my father is a great lord who will pay handsomely..."

The slave-master laughed. "Not any more. You're no lord's brat here."

He slapped Nikos hard across the face, a full strength blow from his meaty hand, knocking the boy down to the boards. Then he put a foot on his neck and squashed his face into the slime. "You're a worm, that's what you are, a filthy worm; and, if you say one more word, I'll silence you for ever."

I was next. I knew better than to protest. I was seized by two burly slave-masters and bundled roughly on to a low, hard bench. My right foot was clasped in an iron ring and chained to a bolt sunk deep in the ribs of the ship. Nikos, who by now had discovered the wisdom of holding his silly tongue, was chained on the same bench right next to my left elbow.

He looked at me, his eyes huge and filled with horror. I tried to smile encouragingly but also put a single finger to my lips. He nodded dumbly.

It took a surprisingly short time to fix all of us in place. Less than an hour, anyway. And, all the while, above us we could hear Khalil's men taking possession of the dhow and the Cretan galley; wrenching the two ships apart, somehow, and then the bang of hammers and rasp of saws as repairs began.

Of course, we slaves could see nothing of all this in the stinking gloom below decks. Nikos and I were on the lower level of benches, with two naked ancient wretches on the level above; their feet at the height of our heads. The Cretan knight and I shared a single, thick, very long pinewood oar, dark and oily-smooth from the many horny hands that had wielded it before us. My friends were scattered all along the ship on both sides – Robin a few rows ahead of me, near Ricky who was already slumped in the rower's resting pose, head on his crossed arms over the oar. Little John and Hanno were somewhere behind me on the other side. I was gravely worried about those two. Both had taken wounds in the battle and, while they had been salved and bound up tight with linen bands while we waited for Khalil to board the ships, I did not know if they would be able to pull an oar. The alternative, if they could not row, was to be dumped over the side of the ship for the sharks – there was no mercy in this place. None. And very little rest. How would they ever heal their torn flesh and recover their full strength?

There was one glimmer of hope, a very faint one. When all the new slaves had been chained in their benches, there was a flurry of fresh activity. And a dozen or so Black Guards came down the rowing deck, and they were carrying large wooden boxes, very heavy. They passed by our benches and stacked them at the rear of the ship in raised alcove, out of the filthy bilge. I watched them work and, when I turned away, I caught Robin's eye. He gave me a grim little smile and a lightning fast wink. I knew exactly what my lord was thinking: "At least the gold is still with us."

That meant that my lord was already scheming. That meant he would get us out of this alive. Somehow. I was sure of it; almost sure, anyway.

How can I describe the life of a galley slave? Simply put: it was a Hell on Earth. Perhaps worse than the real Hell, I shall only know that when I meet my Maker and if I am consigned to the Fire for my sins. But whatever the Almighty has in mind for me, however much He chooses to torment me, it cannot be all that much worse than the life of a captive rower on a Moorish warship. As I have already said, I blocked most of that hideous time from my mind. But I will tell you only this: we rowed for four hours without a break, then rested four hours. We did this again, again, and again, for ever.

We were driven by the beat of the kettledrums, which throbbed out almost continuously, like the very heartbeat of the ship. I shall never forget that awful sound: boom, boom, ba-boom, boom; boom, boom, ba-boom, boom ... on and on, never ceasing, until it became the rhythm of my own heart, pulsing in my veins, the music of all the aches of my body, whether I was awake or trying to snatch a few instants of feverish half-sleep at the oar.

At the end of the first hour, my arms, my back and my legs were burning with agony; my palms were bloody and blistered, my naked arse rubbed raw. I had sweated several pints and my mouth was as dry as I imagined the great southern desert to be, and I was seriously wondering if Death was not a sweeter alternative than this endless hauling on that slippery smooth, God-damned oar, pushing the weight forward, dipping the oar, pulling back against the sea; pushing it forward, dipping, pulling back...

Any mistake was punished with the whip: if you were out of time with your fellows, even a fraction, the lash cracked down and split the skin on your shoulders or back; if you slowed even a fraction, they sliced your skin – sometimes on your tender belly or thighs; if you complained or spoke out of turn, or said almost anything, in truth – again you were corrected with the lash. Few of the galley slaves spoke at all, for fear of incurring the slave-masters' wrath. But I braved a short whispered conversation with the two men above me on the first day. They were both Italians, I discovered, fishermen who were captured off Otranto and sold as slaves. I asked how many years they had been rowing like this – they both looked to be old men, of at least sixty years – and discovered they had been chained here for only nine months; they were both twenty-six years old, and wished to die, as soon as possible, but could find no way of ending their misery.

When my first four-hour stint was over – and it seemed like I had endured a full day of the hardest toil I had even done, worse than fighting a pitched battle – we were given a few scraps of stale bread and a kind of watery bean stew, which I wolfed down in a few moments. And water, a great deal of water, a whole wooden bucketful for each thirsty rower.

Water, I was to discover, was the one great necessity on a galley, and each vessel had to carry oceans of it to keep the rowers fit enough to perform their labours. Without water, the oarsmen simply died. And that was inconvenient for the slave-masters: it meant hauling out the lolling dead and replacing them with fresh men – if they could find them. It was easier to give the living ones plenty of water – and plenty of the lash.

Only half the oarsmen rowed at one time – every other file rowed while the other men rested – unless there was a battle or some other sea emergency that required full speed. I discovered *that* on the third day of my captivity, when an autumn storm blew up out of nowhere. I can only surmise it was the third day for time had already lost its meaning by then in that nightmare existence. Day and night blurred into one stretch of lighter or darker agony.

I had just finished my four-hour stint, and had slumped gratefully over my oar, drowsing like all the others, when the ship began to sway and rock alarmingly. I could hear the loud slap of waves breaking on the wooden ship's side, not a yard from my ears, and the shouts of alarm came echoing from above through the lattice of the gratings, along with torrents of water.

The whips cracked out and our section's drums began to beat once again. One Locksley man shouted out in English, saying that this was unjust, that they had already done their part ... and was flayed into submission with a few licks of the cutting leather. And we were all forced to row again; our tormented arms and legs screaming with every pull of the heavy pine oar.

The chief slave-master walked down the central aisle, calling out in Arabic that we must all row for our lives – row or die. The storm would take all of us if we did not row harder, he said, and no man's chains would be loosed if the ship began to founder. So we rowed. Exhausted bodies writhing in ever-fresher agonies, our poor muscles screaming, even if our mouths were clamped and silent, teeth grinding against the constant burning pain.

It is astounding what a man will do – what he *can* do – when his very life is at stake. We ran before the storm, toiling hard for two hours or more, and I guess that we outran it, for we came eventually into a place of calm seas and quiet – a harbour, someone whispered; Sardinia, said another, and the buzz of words spread throughout the decks; for once not silenced by the slave-masters. And there we stopped. The drums ceased their hideous pulse. And I slumped over my oar and immediately fell into a deep death-like sleep

We rested for a blessed day and a blessed night, while the rain splashed and trickled down through the holes in the latticework above. It was the only wash I had during that hellish voyage. They pumped out the bilges, two slaves freed to this new labour, a constant stream of putrid brown water was sucked from below our feet and splashed over the side of the galley, even as the blessed rain fell, and fell. I had long since grown used to fouling myself where I sat, like every other galley slave, wallowing in my own shit and piss. They fed us later, too: double rations, fresh, soft bread straight from the port bakers, no doubt, with a few hunks of gristly goat bone mixed in the usual slop. The food was gone in an instant, as always, and I was ravenously hungry still. I didn't complain. Instead, I slumped and slept on my oar again.

I remember several short whispered conversations that I had with Nikos during that long nightmare journey across the Mediterranean Sea. I don't remember when the first conversation took place, after we had endured two full days on the bench, I believe, somewhere between Sicily and Sardinia.

He whispered, "It is your fault I am here. This is all of your making."

We hadn't spoken much before then, only practical muttering about the timing of our strokes, or general murmured oaths and desperate prayers for salvation, but the searing venom in his voice that time took me quite aback.

He said, "If I were not so tired, I would *kill* you with my bare hands."

I said, "If I were not so tired, I would defend myself. But, think on this, Griffon, if you killed me, you would have to pull this oar on your own."

That shut him up.

A day or two later, I convinced myself he had died. When our stint was over, he crashed down on the oar and did not move at all for some hours.

I whispered his name. He did not respond. I poked him with a finger, still nothing. I shoved him harder. He lifted his head with a jerk and said, "What? What is it?"

"I thought you were dead," I said.

"What of it?" he replied.

I couldn't think of a reply. He said, "I was dreaming, you English bastard, and you woke me. I was dreaming that I was lying under an olive tree in Crete with a girl I know, and we were drinking cold white wine . . . And you woke me. To this Hell. God, how I hate you. You woke me."

I begged his pardon, and meant it. I too knew the sweet respite of a faraway dream. But he refused to let it drop.

"It is all right for you – you were born to drudgery; you are no gentle, you have no honour, no noble family lineage, you were born for servitude. This is your rightful lot."

I felt my own rage rising then. I thought about smashing him in the face with my fist, maybe more than once, maybe until he truly was dead. But managed to control myself; the slave-masters would bring down the lash on us both. I had seen it before when a fight broke out on the benches. Instead I said, "You speak a great deal about your honour. Too much, I would say, for a Cretan. Why, after so many years of Saracen rule over your dusty little backwater, I wouldn't be surprised if you were at least half Moor, by blood."

He struck me then, a weak slap, and his other hand raked at my eyes. I ducked and punched him once, a short pop to the chin that rocked him back, but we both subsided when the slave-masters began to shout. We'd learnt by then not to provoke our captors. We stared at each other in furious silence.

"What would you know about honour, anyway?" he muttered.

"I know a galley slave has none," I said.

"You and your oath-breaking lord have taken even that from me."

I felt like hitting him again. But I could see one of the slave masters watching.

"No talking," he said, and lifted his whip to emphasise his point.

A little while later, when we were once more labouring at the oar, I whispered to him, "My lord did not take your honour; if you wish to blame someone, blame Prince Khalil, master of this vessel. He is your true enemy."

But Nikos did not choose to reply.

After something like a week – I cannot say for certain in the blur of pain and exhaustion that was our existence below decks – the Cretan began to weep into his water bucket. He was sobbing and slobbering, the snot running down his chin, moaning about mercy and Death, and cursing the world in general and me in particular. He did not stop. It went on and on. No one else in that fetid box paid him the slightest attention, sunk as they were in their own all-consuming misery. Tears were common. Some wept or wailed or muttered, or prayed aloud, to whatever God they believed in. I prayed to Saint Michael, the warrior archangel, more than once a day, begging him to save me. Some slaves screamed out in their agony – or begged guards to have pity and end their horrible lives. They got the whip – nothing more.

But when Nikos began sobbing, I was unnerved. I expected him to cry himself out and then sink into a deep sleep – it was during our four hours of rest. But he went on and on, and I genuinely thought he would never stop.

After a while, I hissed at him to be quiet. If he did not wish to sleep, there was no reason why his moaning and snuffling should keep me awake.

He said, "Kill me, choke the breath from my body. I will not resist – I swear it. I beg you, Alan, in the name of Our Lord Jesus Christ, finish me."

I was struck with a pang of sorrow for him – for me, for all of us.

"Hush now," I said, "do not despair. Robin will come up with a plan. Look yonder, he is speaking with Ricky, who knows the benches better than any man – doubtless between them they will think of some way out of this."

"Even if he did think of a plan – and I cannot see how he could – why would he save me? We are enemies. You're my enemy. Your perfidious lord will take you away, up to the light and air and leave me in this pit to suffer."

"He is not your enemy. He will not leave you here. I swear it. I will not leave you here. When we get out, I promise, Nikos, we shall all go together."

His snuffling slowed, he gave a few more wets gulps and stopped.

"Do you mean that, Alan? You will take me out of here?"

"I swear it, Nikos. We are Christians, men of the True Faith. We have quarrelled, it is true, and we have fought and shed blood in the name of our quarrel. But on this foul bench we must be comrades. I shall not abandon you to this earthly torment. Hold fast, man. Keep your courage. Robin will save us – you wait and see. The Earl of Locksley will take us from here."

I even convinced myself that this was true, that Robin would save us.

But my lord did not. He could not.

Robin could do nothing to end our agony.

Chapter Eighteen

Our salvation, when it eventually arrived, came at the hands of our enemy.

"Land! Land off the starboard bow," the whispered report came down from above and sped along the benches like a wave. Those who were asleep were nudged awake, those rowing instinctively sat straighter, and pulled their oars more willingly. Even the slave-masters were cheered by the news.

"Where are we?" I asked the Italians on the bench above, as quietly as I could. "Spain," came down the reply. "The city of Valencia, I believe."

Valencia – the emir's domain, the base of Prince Khalil's power.

We came into calmer water and the usual rocking of the galley, the rhythm of the sea, died away. We still pulled the oars but there was a distinct sensation of more speed and less resistance to the hull of the ship. Another rumour came rippling along the benches: we were entering the huge harbour of Valencia, on the eastern coast of the Iberian Peninsula, one of the great trading ports of the Almohad Empire. And before too long the slave-masters were calling for us to cease rowing, and the water buckets began to pass all along the benches and we drank and drank.

The mood among the rowers was, if not exactly jubilant, then a good deal less miserable than before. Valencia was the demon-eyed galley's home port and we would surely rest here for a day or two, perhaps more, even if the emir meant to continue his voyaging. There would be messages at the palace that the great man had to deal with, affairs of state to attend to. The rumours flashed and whizzed along the benches, each one better than the last: we were staying a week! A month. The ship would be emptied of its slaves for the whole winter, the storm season now in full swing. The slaves would all be rested until the spring – three or four months of blissful idleness! The guards allowed this chatter to continue and, as if to confirm this last and most wonderful rumour, I saw that the slave-masters were using their keys to unlock some of the rowers; even now Robin was being released from his ankle chain. My lord stood up from his bench and nearly fell again at the unfamiliar standing position. He conferred briefly with the chief slave-master, the fiend in the leather jerkin – who was being, if not actually courteous to Robin, then a good deal less domineering. Robin pointed to Ricky, and the two slave-masters with the keys went to work on his chains.

My lord came hobbling down the central aisle, walking with difficulty, and I saw how terribly thin he now was. His face was almost skeletal, his collarbones and ribs horribly prominent, poking through the flesh, and his knee joints looked twice the normal size. He pointed out two Sherwood men to the slave-masters, who dutifully set them free. He came to my part of the ship and pointed at me, smiled and said, "That young one, as well, I certainly will have need of *him*," and made to move on. Behind me, Nikos gave a despairing cry, a choked incoherent sound. Robin was already past me by now and pointing out three more of his Locksley men to our guards.

The slave-master was already crouched at my feet, wielding

the big iron key, unlocking the padlock on my ankle fetter.

I said to Nikos, "Are we enemies? Answer me quickly."

He said, "No, no, never. Do not abandon me here, Alan, I beg you."

"Will you serve my lord of Locksley?"

"I will serve him faithfully. I swear it. Do not leave – "

I called out to Robin, who turned and looked back at me. "My lord," I said, "you've forgotten our comrade Nikos. Have them set him free as well."

Robin frowned. "Our *comrade*?"

I raised my eyebrows and whispered, "For me, lord, as a boon."

He paused for just a heartbeat and then said to the nearest slave-master: "Forgive me, but I neglected to indicate my other faithful servant there."

And he pointed at Nikos.

We were brought out on the deck and, even though the skies were heavy with cloud, the brightness of the open air was painful to my eyes after so long in the dim hold. We were all naked and filthy, crusted with ordure, sweat and grime and I do not think we could have fought off a gang of urchins armed with sticks at that point: but we were off the benches and it was wonderful. The port air tasted cold and clean. I took it in great lungfuls.

There were only a dozen of us still alive, and I saw that Little John and Hanno were both in a bad way, very thin, barely conscious and caked in dried blood and puss from their mistreated leaking wounds. Robin had ordered two of the stronger Locksley men to stand either side of them and support them. He would not allow them to sit – a precaution, and a wise one, knowing well how the emir's men treated those who were too sick to row.

We were marched off the ship and onto a wooden quay, now shivering with cold and for the first time I looked up and around to take in the place we had landed. The port was huge and crammed with ships of all sizes and shapes: galleys and dhows and cogs and fishing craft, snake boats, busses, rowing hulls and swift little single-sailed smacks – a thicket of masts and rigging, a floating town of hulls and decks. There must have been two hundred vessels all crowded into a wide semi-circular bay at the mouth of a wide brown river that day, and five thousand people to man them.

I saw a gang of slaves, far healthier looking than us, being stripped of their clothes at spear-point, and realised with a sinking heart that they were destined to take our places on the benches – there would be no miraculous three-month respite over the storm season for the wretches left in the galley.

The slave-masters had disappeared and a squad of the black-clad troops of Khalil's personal guard now surrounded us. I wondered where they were taking us, as we shambled and hobbled along the quay, beside a row of imposing stone built dwellings, shops and warehouses. The people were mostly dark-haired with tanned faces, in all kinds of Arabic dress, long robes or loose tunics and baggy breeches; their heads were covered with caps and white turbans and capacious black hoods with dangling tassels at the back. But here and there I saw half-familiar faces that might have been English or German, pale eyes and hair the colour of straw. We were given no opportunity to speak to them; the Black Guards were formed up around us, and hurried us on with the butts of their spears. There were few women visible in the harbour, and those we did see were all veiled enticingly, their midnight hair draped in dark cloth. Others wore a cloth mask over the lower parts of their pale faces and their dark eyes were painted and jewel bright.

No one we passed seemed to pay the slightest heed to a gang of a dozen naked men shambling along the cobbles, their fish-belly white bodies filthy, bruised, bloody and scabbed and marked all over with whip-cuts and sea sores. We were infidel slaves – beneath the notice of free men and women.

We left the harbour and travelled up a sanded road along the southern side of a wide, slow river; there were shacks here and there, with small boats outside upturned for repairs, and homely little plots of land where people were growing vegetables. Here and there were olive trees, their trunks ancient, twisted and gnarled like the grey-green bodies of petrified ogres.

We soon turned off the sandy road and passed down another track that led to a long white wall, smooth as marble and punctuated with square towers every fifty yards or so. Inside the walls I could see red-tiled roofs, the tops of waving green fronds of palm trees, and a slim minaret with a golden dome at the top that reflected the weak sunlight.

There was a grand gatehouse set in the white wall about halfway along its length, two square, crenulated towers with Black Guards on the roofs, and a wide wooden door between them, and there we paused while the chief guard of our contingent went inside a little portal set into one of the bigger doors.

"What is this place?" I muttered Ricky, who astoundingly seemed to have come through the ordeal on the galley better than most of our men.

"This is the Russafa Palace, residence of the Emir of Valencia."

"But why have we been brought here?"

"I have no doubt we will discover that very soon," said Robin.

An hour later, as the sun was sinking, we faced the emir himself. We were standing awkwardly in a large garden in the middle of a space surrounded by several cool-looking stone buildings. I could smell oranges and roses and the odour of spicy food cooking, which made my mouth run with saliva. We were all still as naked as babies, and about as weak as newborns too, although we had been issued with a few rough blankets to preserve our modesty and ward off the mid-November evening chill.

The Black Guards had retreated to the corners of the large garden, where they stood like sentries around the perimeter, and the Emir of Valencia faced us alone, with only tall Tariq standing mutely at his shoulder.

"Once again, I've given you cause to be angry with me," Khalil said.

Robin made a little choking sound: "I think we have sailed way past anger by now," he said in French, the same language the emir had used.

"We surrendered ourselves to your mercy. Yet we were not treated with any courtesy. And three of my men died inside your damned galley – two or three more may not live through this night. Not to mention the repeated insults and injuries we have all suffered at the hands of your slave-masters."

"True. Yet you stole what was mine – do you know what I usually do to people who steal from me? I do not believe you would care to find out."

"It was not yours. You stole it from us; we stole it from the Caliph."

Prince Khalil chuckled. "The gold is certainly mine *now*. It is snug in my treasury not a hundred paces from where we now stand."

He seemed to find the situation vastly amusing. "Let us move on, Lord Locksley. Let us forget the past. I hope you can find it in your Christian hearts to forgive me. Does not your prophet Jesus Christ preach forgiveness of the sins of others? Turning the other cheek. Let us speak of the future."

"Just say your damned piece," said Robin. "You fished us out of that hellish pit for a reason – why don't you tell us what you actually want."

"But I have already told you…" said Khalil, pretending to be amazed at our ignorance.

Robin is right, I thought, *we are past mere anger now.* I wondered if I had the strength to leap on Khalil and choke the life from him. I knew I had not. The Assassin would surely get me before I got within three feet. One day, I vowed, I'll gut him like a freshly caught trout and watch him flap.

"Tell me again," said Robin. He sounded utterly exhausted.

"I wish you to fight my enemies to the north. I wish you to

help me to expand my realm. Surely you cannot have forgotten my little proposal?"

Robin glanced quickly at me. He said, "We have not forgotten."

"Well, I will make it simple for you. I wish you to serve me as mercenaries – paid fighters – and you will be handsomely rewarded. Indeed, in view of your previous reluctance, I will generously increase my offer. If you will fight for me, and faithfully do my bidding in the war against the Christians, if you will serve me for, say, one year and a day, from this night, I shall pay you one tenth of the gold that you, ah, liberated, from the Caliph's camel train outside Tunis. One tenth of five thousand ingots of gold – is five hundred ingots, which is still a magnificent, even a princely sum."

It was. By my calculation, five hundred ingots of pure gold would be worth seven thousand English pounds! Ten thousand, five hundred marks!

Robin seemed unmoved by the new offer. "And what guarantees do we have that you will honour your side of the agreement?"

Khalil frowned. "You must take my word. As I will take yours."

"Nothing more?" said Robin.

"You do not seem to fully comprehend the situation, my friend," said Khalil. He seemed a little irritated with Robin. "Let me put it plainly. The choice before you is straightforward: on the one hand, you agree to serve me in my struggle against the Christians of Aragon, willingly and to the best of your abilities, and I will pay you a small fortune in precious metal for that military service. Or, on the other hand, I send you back to the galley, right now, tonight, forget I ever laid eyes on you, and attempt to locate another company of fair-skinned Christian men-at-arms for my particular purposes."

"One fourth share of all the gold," said Robin. "In advance."

"No. One tenth after your service had been satisfactorily completed. And I shall not give you a day and a night to ponder the question either and make another attempt to flee. I must have your answer today, right now."

Robin looked around at the naked, shivering, filthy wretches – our bodies wasted and broken, scabbed, lousy, white as maggots. He looked every man in the face and no one said a word. Even Nikos just shrugged.

"We shall not go back to the galley. Yet we are not strong enough to fight for you. We will need food and water, clothes and weapons – and time. Time to recover our strength and heal our wounds. Time to train our bodies."

Khalil smiled at my lord. "You will have plenty of opportunity to eat and rest, to heal yourselves and train. Now, will you all give me your oaths?"

We did: all twelve of us swearing solemnly one after the other to serve this murderous Moorish warlord and betray our Christian brothers.

Chapter Nineteen

Food and rest, new clothes, fresh air and warm water to wash in – and time.

"Christ's clenched sphincter, Alan," said Little John. "These Moors may be poor, benighted heathens but they certainly know how to live. I can't remember when I ate so well and so regularly. Maybe never in my life."

I could not disagree; we'd been lavished with food and wine, assigned comfortable – if well guarded – quarters and issued fresh clothes. We were allowed the freedom of a large walled-in section of the Russafa Palace, which contained sleeping rooms, courtyards with splashing fountains, a huge garden lush with fruit trees, flowers and greenery, a bathhouse, with steam rooms and cold plunge pools and silent servants who washed us, sluiced us down, and rubbed sweet oils into our poor, wasted bodies. Lavish meals were provided three times a day, and nothing was demanded of us save that we rest and heal. After the Hell of the galley, it was a kind of Heaven.

I was particularly cheered by Little John's swift recovery. Three weeks had passed since we had accepted Prince Khalil's shameful proposal and John had put on a great deal of flesh in that time and the two cruel wounds he had taken in the sea battle – in his upper back and his right thigh – had closed up and were now healing nicely. I could hardly believe that he had managed to pull an oar in the galley on our journey from Sicily – a journey I subsequently learnt had lasted eleven days. The suffering of exercising his torn muscles hour after hour must have been indescribable. But John was very tough. He had survived and now, miraculously, he was on the mend.

One member of our company, whom I'd believed to be dead, had given Little John a great deal of unceasing care, day and night. Elise, the wise woman, had been taken under the protection of Tanisha when the demon-eyed galley had captured our dhow. The two women had apparently formed a bond of sorts while travelling to Tunis – and Tanisha had reached out her hand in friendship when the Locksley men had been cast into the hellish-depths of the *Khamsin*. Elise was now the maid-servant of the Lady Tanisha, as we were now obliged to call the emir's daughter, the mistress of the Russafa Palace, and their friendship was the source of our comfortable state.

Christmas arrived and the emir, or perhaps his daughter, favoured us by providing a feast of roasted goose. Even more unexpectedly, a priest came to our quarters, a wizened fellow called Revemund and, although he spoke no French or English, he conducted a Mass for us in Latin to celebrate the birth of Our Saviour, which most of our company duly attended and for which they were deeply grateful. Robin, characteristically, did not bother to come.

I was surprised to see a Christian holy man in Moorish Spain, and took the little old fellow aside after the service to satisfy my curiosity.

"Oh, there are still a few of the Faithful left in these lands," he said in his odd Spanish-inflected Latin. "In centuries past, we lived beside the followers of the Prophet, peace be upon him, in relative amity – the Jews, also. They called us *dhimmis*, or 'protected people'. We were not considered the equals of the followers of the Prophet but we were granted a little respect as People of the Book. The Moors revere parts of the Holy Bible, my son. Did you know that? They venerate Abraham and Moses, as we do. But when these new warlike people came up from Morocco in my father's time, these Almohads, all that changed in Al-Andalus. This fierce new regime is far more fanatical. Now the Caliph is forcing all our people to convert to their faith or face death. Yet there are a handful of us who have not succumbed."

After the celebrations of Christmas had passed, we began to train in earnest. Robin told us we would be fighting in the spring; and we'd better be ready.

The emir was away on his foul galley down the coast somewhere about the business of his master the Caliph, but his Arab steward issued us with our own weapons and mail. Our war gear had apparently been salvaged from the dhow, and kept in store until this moment. Our blades had even been oiled against any damage caused by the salt. I noticed that a rent in my old mail coat had been expertly mended, and the rust patches had been carefully scrubbed from the iron links. It struck me then that Prince Khalil had been planning to recruit us for some months and had made elaborate preparations.

I said as much to Robin as we were lying on twin slabs of wet marble sweating in the steam room of the bathhouse after exercise in the gardens.

"I think he has been looking for us – or for a small company of Frankish men-at-arms like us – for at least a year or more," said my lord.

"How can you know that? Did he tell you?"

"Not exactly. But it was not too difficult to piece together."

"I don't understand, lord." The fog in the small hot room

made it difficult to see Robin's face.

"How much do you know of what Khalil will ask us to do for him in the spring?" he said.

"Nothing – but that we must fight our fellow Christians. In the north."

"I will tell you but you must keep this to yourself for now. Agreed?"

I nodded.

"Our target this spring will be the fortress of Ulldecona, which lies a dozen miles to the south of the Ebro River, which has long been the border between the Christian Kingdom of Aragon and the Emirate of Valencia."

I nodded again, only vaguely aware of the region of which he spoke.

"Ulldecona is a stone castle on a hill – a powerful fortress – and it dominates the main road north into the Christian lands. It is on this side of the river – in Moorish territory – but that was not a significant problem until a little more that a year ago. The Montcada family of Barcelona owned the castle but it had been abandoned, neglected for many years. They had not the strength to defend it against the Moors. Then the Montcadas granted it to the Order of Knights of the Hospital of Saint John of Jerusalem about ten years ago. A gift to ensure the entry of one member of their family into Heaven."

"The Hospitallers?" I said.

"The same. But they too did nothing, at first, with Ulldecona – until just over a year ago. The summer before last."

"What happened then?"

"The Hospitallers sent a new and energetic commander to the castle. A man named Sir Charles de Bearn, a devout man, a ruthless man, I am told. He took with him a strong force of knights – men dedicated to pushing the True Faith into the lands of the Moors, bringing them the light of Christ."

I thought of a Hospitaller friend I had known in the Holy Land, a good and kindly fellow, a godly man and a superb warrior, called Sir Nicholas de Scras. I wondered if this Sir Charles de

Bearn was perhaps another of his ilk.

"The knights worked hard, they brought in peasants to farm the region, they collected their tithes; they fortified the castle, made it almost impregnable. Before the Emir of Valencia fully grasped the danger, he had a Christian enclave – a fortress filled with fanatical knights – in his domain."

"The emir allowed this to happen?"

"Khalil's father was emir then, and he took his liege men north and attacked the castle of Ulldecona. He failed. He tried again a few months later, but he was a sick old man by then and he died before he could succeed. Now his son Khalil wishes to try once more to excise this Christian cancer from the body of his emirate. And he wants us to help him achieve this end."

"How do you know all this?"

"Some of it Khalil has told me. Some I knew already. Some I worked out by myself."

I thought about what he had said. And sat up on my slab. The heat and steam was making me feel light-headed.

"And we must fight these Hospitallers in the spring, in only a month or two's time?" I said, getting unsteadily to my feet. "And somehow capture their impregnable hill-top castle which has defeated the Moorish armies?"

"Yes. But do not tell the others yet, Alan."

"We have our weapons back, lord, even our mail. Why do we not just break out of here and make a run for it?"

Robin got up too. He glanced at one of the slabs a dozen yards away where one of the palace servants was soaping his own back and shoulders.

"Let's take a cold plunge in the pool," he said.

We splashed luxuriously in the cool waters and I reflected that this, along with the fine food, the elegant gardens, the flowers, the abundant fruit and tranquillity, was yet another example of the vast gulf between the quality of life in Valencia and that at home in my own manor of Westbury. I bathed infrequently at home, perhaps once a week – and it was a dull chore. Water needed to be boiled up in great cauldrons, which took some time, and I sat glumly in a barrel before the fire in the hall and scrubbed myself raw.

Here it was one of my greatest joys. I bathed every day after exercise, and looked forward eagerly to the servants massaging my muscles with oils after a good supper and before bed. It was almost sinfully pleasurable.

Yet enjoyable as it was, I feared this luxury was making me soft.

I swam over to Robin. We were the only folk in the pool at that hour, which gave me some comfort. No one could possibly overhear us here.

"So, my lord," I said. "Shall we make a break for our freedom?"

"We are twelve men – and Elise," he said. "And not all of us are back to our full strength. I do not see how we can escape and live to tell of it."

"I am sure we could scale the walls," I said. "We could make decent ropes from our bedding, fabricate some sort of hook, or a grapnel..."

"I don't mean escape from Russafa, Alan. That would be child's play: yes, ropes, hooks... we could probably simply fight our way out the front door. But afterwards? None of us is an accomplished sailor, save for Ricky, and I do not think we could steal ourselves a ship and sail it out of Valencia harbour without being stopped very soon. Even if we did, I'd not like to wager on out-sailing the vessels at the emir's command. And if caught..."

"Back to the oars," I said with a little shudder.

"The other alternative is to run north, and try to reach the Kingdom of Aragon before we were recaptured. Thirteen folk on foot, some still weak from their injuries, trying to cover a hundred miles of unfamiliar territory with the emir's men on our heels. No, I don't think so, Alan. We can't do it."

I was disappointed. I was used to Robin providing solutions to all of life's problems but he seemed to be stuck.

"So we must do the emir's bidding? Fight these good Hospitallers?"

"Let me think on it, Alan. We have a little time in hand. And this new incarceration is not too unbearably irksome, is it?"

It had been our practice since Christmas for Hanno and I to exercise together in the garden, when it was not raining – which it did surprisingly seldom for winter, the weather here being far more mild and dry that it would have been in England in January. Hanno was now almost fully recovered from his wounds and he decided to begin instructing me in the arts of stealth.

It was fun, to be honest. And I rarely describe combat training in those terms. Hanno and I made a great game of it in the extensive Russafa gardens, usually with Hanno guarding an object, a peach, for example, or a dagger, and setting it on a table or branch of a tree. My task was to approach the object without being seen by Hanno and claim it. Hanno armed himself with a crossbow, with quarrels blunted with pieces of cork, and if he saw me he shot at me with the weapon, and if he hit me he was declared the winner. If, instead, I managed to snatch the object before he could touch me, I won.

He gave me a demonstration. Starting from the far end of the garden, a hundred paces away, he told me to close my eyes and count to twenty. When I opened them he was gone. I hefted the crossbow and kept close to the object, an apple, which had been balanced on the top of a low circular wall surrounding a blue-tiled fountain. For the man guarding the prize, it was difficult to maintain concentration, for nothing happened for great stretches of time. A hour might pass and nothing appeared to have stirred in the garden, then, from an unexpected direction, sometimes even from behind me, a blurred figure would rush out of leafy concealment and seize the prize.

It was like magic – but a kind of magic that could be taught. So Hanno taught me all that he knew about stealthy movement. He had me creeping inch by inch, on elbows and toes, through the parts of the garden in the deepest, darkest shade. He showed me how to wrap my body sinuously around a tree branch or trunk so that I was invisible. He taught me how to move over ground littered with dry twigs and leaves without making the slightest noise. And after a couple of weeks of painful failure – Hanno's crossbow bolts did not penetrate my skin but they each left a large bruise – when I finally succeeded in rushing out from under a ornamental bush and snatching an egg balanced atop a helmet on a patch of lawn, I've rarely felt more pleased with myself.

The one event that stuck in my memory of those months in Spain, occurred when I was moving stealthily along a line of thick yew hedge in the southern part of the garden one afternoon in late January, and I heard voices: two voices, a man and a woman, conversing in French. I peeped out from behind the hedge and saw Robin and Tanisha sitting on a bench behind a small stone table. There was wine on the table, dried figs and dates.

My lord and the mistress of Russafa Palace were deeply engaged in conversation, and while a veiled Arab maid and Ricky, who had been taken on by Robin as a personal servant, were standing only a few yards away. I heard the lady tell my lord at great length about her carefree youth, her schooling and upbringing in Valencia, and the wonders of the ancient city.

"I should love to see some more of it," said my lord, "but we have, understandably, not been allowed to leave the compound since we arrived."

Tanisha said that she would see what she could do about arranging a visit to the city, with a suitable escort of the Black Guards, and then they moved on to other matters. Robin began to describe the green beauty of his homeland and tell a few comical tales of his life in Sherwood as an outlaw.

He told her an old one about disguising himself as a potter and selling his wares in Nottingham. He sold his pots so cheaply that the wife of the Sheriff of Nottinghamshire herself was intrigued and invited him to dinner with the Sheriff. He ended up winning an archery contest, tricking the King's man and making the law look ridiculous. It was a fine tale, and my lord told it well – but I happened to know that it had no basis in truth at all.

It was based on a *canso* that I had composed myself, as a comic tribute to my lord.

In other circumstances, I might have enjoyed the spectacle of my lord appropriating one of my fanciful yarns as a true event in his life, but for one thing – the expression on Tanisha's face as she listened to Robin tell the tale.

It was clear to me that the young lady was besotted with Robin. I was green myself then, with little experience of the world, but I could clearly see that Tanisha was hanging on his every word. She gazed at him, her head tilted slightly upwards, her dark eyes huge, from time to time touching her full red lips. I was amused at first, then irritated. Finally I became angry.

What was Robin doing? He was clearly setting himself to charm this impressionable young lady – yet he had a good wife and a baby son back in England. Marie-Anne, his countess, was a wonderful woman, lovely and kind, and I adored her – in a strictly sisterly way. And while I knew men who were separated from their wives on campaign for long periods often found comfort elsewhere – the Sherwood crew were notorious for their lusty exploits – I had not expected this sort of goatish behaviour from my lord.

I stepped out from behind the hedge, ready to give Robin a piece of my mind about his infidelity. I believe I was about to remind him of his sacred marriage vows to Marie-Anne. But when I opened my mouth to speak those very words, something flickered in the corner of my eye and I was struck hard in the belly, and immediately doubled up winded, gasping for breath.

"Apologies, lord, for to disturb you," said Hanno, emerging from beside a tree like a slab of bark come to life, a crossbow dangling casually from his hand. "This clumsy youngling and I make our training today."

I only had one proper conversation with the Lady Tanisha during my time at the Palace of Ruffasa. And it was she who initiated it. She summoned me to her apartments, which were in a different part of the sprawling palace, and a squad of Black

Guards escorted me there one evening in early February.

"Lord Locksley tells me that you are a famous musician," she said.

I admitted this was true but told her that my favoured instrument, a five-stringed vielle, had been lost in a shipwreck off Crete.

"But you can sing, can you not? I believe I heard you singing with your lord on the dhow. Quite tunefully, if I recall; I wish you to sing for me now."

I did not much care to be summoned and ordered to sing like some performing monkey by this chit of a girl. But I was hardly in a position to refuse her. I was, in a way, her prisoner. Displeasing her seemed unwise, and also somehow discourteous. But it was an unusual request.

I looked beyond Tanisha – who was lounging in a loose gown on a pile of cushions, her face unveiled, her black hair unbound, completely at her ease – at the stiff upright figure of Elise who gave me a distinct nod. The young crone was urging me silently to do my duty.

So I sang for the princess. To be honest, I was proud of my singing and I have found it no great hardship to have a beautiful girl lost in admiration, hanging on your every drawn-out note. I sang a few slow, formal *cansos* in French, rather well, I thought; and then two or three more jolly English folk tunes, the words of which she did not understand, nor did she seem to care for the tunes much. I do not recall exactly what compositions I sang for her but I was aware that she seemed oddly impatient for me to complete my performance, and was quite unmoved by my fine singing, which seemed rather odd given that she had summoned me solely for this private musical entertainment. She yawned discreetly; she drummed her fingers lightly on the cushions; then she began to examine her long painted nails in detail.

"Do you wish me to sing another tune, highness," I asked in French. "Or have I perhaps already delighted you enough?"

"That's quite enough," she said. Then, smiled prettily, "And I thank you for sharing your music with me, sir. It has been very . . . ah, pleasant."

She was certainly a beautiful girl. That could not be denied but I found I did not care for her at all. "Shall I take my leave then, my lady," I said.

"No, no, sit down here." She indicated a cushion by her feet with an elegant wave of her hand. "Now you must tell me *all* about yourself."

I was perplexed. I knew I was a young, well-made fellow and had even once or twice been described as reasonably handsome. But I could not understand what she truly wanted. Not romance, surely. I frowned at Elise.

"Sit down, Alan," the wise woman said. "Tell my lady about yourself."

I told her a few details of my early life in Nottinghamshire but it soon became obvious that she did not find me even the tiniest bit fascinating: the person she wanted me to talk about was Robin. She asked me how I'd met my lord; she asked me about his years as an outlaw, and I duly recounted some adventures – but most of all she wanted to know about Marie-Anne.

I obliged Tanisha as well as I could: describing Marie-Anne as a great beauty, with a sharp wit; an intelligent woman and a model of wifely virtue.

This did not seem to please her at all.

"My Lord of Locksley has a son, is this so?"

I said it was, and named him as Hugh, a vigorous and noisy child.

"And is he Robin's true son?" she asked. "Born of his seed?"

I froze. Hugh was, in fact, the fruit of a forced coupling between Robin's lady and the Sheriff of Nottinghamshire, a Norman shit-weasel called Sir Ralph Murdac, who had captured Marie-Anne and raped her. Hugh was a bastard – although Robin claimed him as his own. One of our Locksley men had been gossiping and word had evidently reached Tanisha's ear. If Robin found out about it, the gossipmonger was a dead man. I'd also beat quantities of blood and shit out of the man, if I discovered his name.

"He is Robin's true son, of course, he is," I lied. And, may God forgive me, a treacherous blush began to creep from my neck up to my cheeks. "A fine boy, very healthy, he'll no doubt grow to be a fine warrior, just like his father, like father like son . . ." I realised I was babbling, and shut my mouth.

Tanisha smiled at me, happy as a cat before a bowl of fresh cream.

"I thank you, Alan," she said. "You have been very helpful. Well, I grow weary now. You may take your leave."

I stood up. I wanted to say something to repair my mistake. But my mind was utterly blank. What good would repeating the obvious lie do?

"My lord loves Marie-Anne more than life itself," I said. "He will always love her, and only her, whatever has . . . happened in the past."

Tanisha stopped smiling and for a moment I caught a glimpse of the young woman who had stabbed the importunate ship's captain in the eye.

"You may take your leave, musician," she said in a voice of iron.

I was half way down the corridor, inside a phalanx of Black Guards, when Elise came running after me. "Wait, Alan, wait a moment," she said.

"What?" I was in no mood for any more womanly conversations.

"Don't snap at me, Alan Dale," she said. "I come to bring you tidings, a warning from the spirits, from the otherworld."

"I don't believe any of that nonsense."

"Nevertheless, I am bound to pass on the warning."

"What is it, then?" I was still fuming from the thought of that silly girl thinking that she could have my lord and displace my lovely Marie-Anne.

"I dreamed of you. I dreamed of you and John Nailor and some of the other Locksley men. You were marching bravely into battle – all together."

"So?"

"Behind you was a terrible beast, stalking you, and you were unaware of it, quite unaware. It was a twisted creature out of Hell – the body of a lion, the head and claws of an eagle. This fearsome beast was hiding in the darkness behind you. And then it struck, clawing at your unsuspecting backs with its terrible talons. Cutting you down from behind."

Despite myself, I felt a shiver of superstitious awe at her words.

"Beware, Alan Dale. Beware the beast that lurks unseen behind you."

The captain of the Black Guards, a fairly decent fellow called Zeyat, said something in Arabic. I didn't catch it but the meaning was perfectly clear. "Come along, man, back to your quarters. We haven't got all night."

"Tell you what," I said, "if I see a hellish monster that is half-seagull, half-pussycat, I'll be sure to give it a really wide berth, how's that, Elise?"

"You may mock," she said. "But now you have been duly warned."

I nodded at her, and glanced over at Captain Zeyat.

"Shall we go back now?" I said in English.

"One more thing," said Elise.

"What? Should I now worry about a half-dog, half-maggot?"

"Those things my lady said about Marie-Anne. Don't tell Robin. Keep it to yourself. You will be poking a sleeping bear. Say nothing, for *his* sake."

I thought about that for a moment. Then I nodded. She was right.

"I'll hold my tongue," I said.

As promised, Lady Tanisha arranged for Robin to visit the city of Valencia, which was apart from the Ruffasa Palace, a mile north, on the banks of the River Turia. I was beset with a heavy cold, my nose streaming, my throat raw, and was minded to stay in our quarters: Ricky persuaded me to go.

"There is an apothecary you should visit in Valencia, near the street of the silversmiths, and he will make your illness disappear like mist in bright sunshine," he said cheerily. And I was glad, in the end, that I went: the city was a wonder to me, an exotic jumble of narrow winding streets, towering mosques, each one extravagantly decorated in a different style, and with many thousands of people thronging the thoroughfares and the wide squares.

A large number of the people we passed were soldiers, men-at-arms of all kinds: swaggering oak-skinned men with broad scimitars swinging freely at their waists; tall, pale Berbers in violet robes using their long spears as walking staves; Turkish cavalrymen with recurved bows on their backs and quivers of arrows at their sides, forcing their tough little ponies through the crush with high cries and indiscriminate blows from their riding switches.

The dust, noise, stench and heat, even in the cool month of February, were oppressive and even a little intimidating. I found the gabble of a dozen different tongues unnerving – but also strangely exciting. It was like being in a dream world, filled with inhuman unknowable folk; a world in which we were not quite welcome. Our party consisted only of Robin, Ricky, me and Hanno and any notions I had of escaping were dashed immediately since we were unarmed and surrounded by a dozen of Khalil's alert Black Guards.

"I see the emir has been spending our gold," Robin muttered, as we passed a group of Nubian swordsmen, big bare-chested warriors from the southern lands below Egypt, faces dark as rock oil, except when they smiled their brilliant white smiles, as they often did. I did not really understand what my lord meant by "spending our gold", and asked him to explain it.

"Mercenaries," he said, smiling sardonically, "men like us. Hired with the Caliph's gold. Have you not noticed that the city is full of fighting men?"

I had indeed noticed but I had not thought any more about it.

I visited the apothecary, and was given a bitter, foul-smelling potion to drink then and a bag of dried orange peel, which I was supposed to steep in boiling water to make a medicinal night-time drink. Then Robin did something strange: he asked if we might be permitted, as infidels, to climb the very tall and spindly minaret, which was adjacent to the Great Mosque.

I was taken aback. Robin had never shown the slightest interest in the Moorish religion or its architecture. The Black Guards were also surprised and unsure what to do: it was clear that they had been told to indulge our wishes by the Lady Tanisha – but would this visit be a kind of defilement?

They discussed the matter among themselves, and then after conferring with an elderly imam, who seemed to be the caretaker of the minaret, we were ushered in, told to remove our boots – for some odd reason – and allowed to climb up the winding staircase of the tallest tower in the city.

The aged imam gave a rambling speech to Ricky as we climbed, who did his best to translate the history of the minaret to us. It was very old and very holy – that was all I gathered. My cold-blocked nose and ears made breathing difficult on the long climb to the top. But when I emerged snotty and sweaty into the noon sunshine, I was amazed by the magnificent view.

The city of Valencia was laid out beneath us and I could clearly see the thick encircling walls punctuated with massive stone gates and the broad roads leading out to the rest of Spain. The maze of little streets made mad whirling, intricate patterns and up here, away from the stink and din, the design seemed oddly beautiful. We could see the round bodies of trees in the many plazas, and dim courtyards inside the walled houses, cool oases of shade and quiet. The River Turia was a thick green snake to the north, winding around the city and heading out to the harbour where we had been landed as slaves, nearly three months ago. The road along the southern side of the river was thick with traffic at this hour: bands of horsemen in bright cloaks, armour gleaming, and big lumbering wagons pulled by oxen teams.

To the southeast, I could see the walls of the Russafa Palace – I could even make out the lush garden in which Hanno and I had spent so many hours practicing our craft. Robin came to stand beside me, and looked in the same direction. "You see the palace," he said. "You see our quarters?"

I said I did.

"Now look beyond them, over the wall at the end of our garden."

I saw a part of the palace beyond the high garden wall that was quite different to our compound. It was protected in the same way, high, white stone ramparts on all sides, with dozens of sentries walking along the top but the interior of the space held one very large square building, strong-looking and with a score of violet-robed spearmen at the door, and three smaller ones, barracks for the Black Guards, by their looks, and the rest of the space was an open sandy area rutted by the wheels of vehicles over many years.

The gates of the enclosure, set between two stone towers, were wide open but heavily guarded – by fifty men at least – and an overloaded wagon pulled by eight oxen was trundling into the wide space before the building.

"What is that place?" I asked.

"That is the treasury. Inside that strong-house, watched day and night by many hundreds of his Black Guards, is a little room where the emir keeps all his wealth. Barrels of coin, boxes of jewels, works of art, fine silks..."

"And our gold," I said.

Chapter Twenty

Whatever the apothecary put in his foul potion, it was powerful stuff, for my cold cleared up nicely in a matter of a day or two. Indeed, I never got around to making the hot drink with the dried orange peel. And my return to good health was doubly fortunate because three days after our visit to the city, at the tail end of February, the emir returned to Valencia from his sea travels and summoned us to a council of war, at dusk, in the larger of the two dining rooms that had been placed at our disposal during our incarceration.

We filed into the room, a very different crew to the one that had been addressed by the prince three months before. We were no longer naked, maggot-white, wretched, cowed by the galley, fainting with hunger and exhaustion: we were healed and whole, rested and well fed. Most of the Locksley men-at-arms had been training just as hard as Hanno and me.

I remember the candle-lit faces in that semi-circle before Khalil and his tall Assassin Tariq, with a wall of Black Guards behind them, watching over us. Robin's face was alive with adventure, his odd eyes sparkling like polished silver in firelight. Little John had put on great quantities of weight and was once more his beefy, jovial, red-faced self. Hanno had shaven his round head that very evening and was toying with a long stabbing dagger, cleaning his fingernails with the point. Nikos had washed and combed out his long black hair and grown a small pointed chin-beard that made him look like a saturnine goat. Gareth had managed to acquire a black eye from somewhere: a training accident, or a quarrel with one of his comrades.

We were twelve men, dressed in European-style tunics, hose and calf-length soft leather boots, with long green Sherwood riding cloaks falling from around our shoulders, our winter-pale faces were scrubbed and shaved and unnaturally clean-looking for former outlaws – I was not the only man who had discovered the delights of the bath house. Even Elise, who was standing next to Tanisha had wetted and combed down her dandelion frizz of hair until it formed a shiny grey helmet on her narrow head.

Khalil spoke: "I do not think you are as angry as you were when we last met," he said in French, a language most of Robin's men could understand.

No one said anything for a little too long, until Robin coughed and murmured: "You've been generous, sir. We thank you for your hospitality."

"I do not seek thanks, but your service. You remember your oaths?"

"We remember," said Robin. "What service do you require from us?"

"I shall tell you. In the meantime, let us take our ease and have some wine." He clapped once and a Black Guard slipped away to obey his order.

Wine was brought and little delicate honey cakes, and we all helped ourselves, then the servants carried in a sandbox – a flat, square container about a yard by a yard, filled with fine pale grains – which was laid on the table and on which Khalil began to sketch out a map of the eastern coast of Spain with the point of his jewelled dagger, with the principal cities marked by little black pebbles, which he dropped into place from a small pouch.

"Here is Valencia," Khalil said, pointing to the southernmost pebble. Robin, Little John, Hanno, Nikos and I crowded around the box. There was no room for the rest, who wandered off happily to enjoy their wine and cake.

"Here is the fortress of Ulldecona, held by the Knights of the Hospital of Saint John. I wish you to capture the castle for me by subterfuge."

He drew a line between Valencia and Ulldecona with a dagger. "From here to there is about one hundred of your English miles..."

"Subterfuge?" I said. "What kind of subterfuge?"

"Peace, Alan," said my lord. "Hold your tongue and allow the emir to outline his plans to us. I'm sure he will answer all your questions at the end."

I clamped my mouth shut.

Khalil was drawing again in the sand with his dagger. "This is the main road north to the Kingdom of Aragon. Here is Tarragona, where they are building a grand Christian cathedral – less than fifty miles from the River Ebro, here, which has always been the line between our people and the Christians. The cathedral is important as a symbol – they thumb their noses at us building it so close to our border. But I shall not trouble you with that."

We all stared at the box of sand with its lines and pebbles.

"As you can see, the castle of Ulldecona dominates the road to the Kingdom of Aragon. All trade – and any large armed force, for that matter – would have to pass under its shadow if it wished to reach the Christian lands.

"I cannot allow Ulldecona to remain in Christian hands. Quite apart from the fact that it is on my territory, and so constitutes an insult to me personally, I have been given permission by the Caliph to invade the north and expand my territory into the kingdom of Alfonso, King of Aragon and Count of Barcelona. Yet I must take Ulldecona before I move on Aragon.

"The Caliph, may he live a thousand years, triumphed in the east of this peninsula last year, capturing the region known as the Algarve and is pushing up into the belly of the Kingdom of Portugal. He desires me to push north on this eastern flank. The central plains of Iberia, held by the Christians, will be menaced on both sides and cannot hold out long. And if all goes according to plan, we will push up from Cordoba next year and take Toledo and Madrid by the winter. In a few years, the wise and powerful Caliph means to have the whole Iberian Peninsula, from the straits of Jabal Tariq all the way up to the mountain passes of the Pyrenees in his hands."

There were some murmurs of surprise from around the table.

"He is certainly ambitious, your thousand-year Caliph," said Robin.

"I am not saying this to boast of the greatness of the Almohad – though I believe our dynasty is mightier than you can imagine. Neither is it a secret – the Caliph has sworn an oath to this effect in public. He means to have the whole of Spain under his enlightened rule, or perish in the attempt."

It was clear the Locksley men there were feeling uncomfortable by Khalil's talk of conquest. There was murmuring from around the side of the chamber and I saw the Black Guards stiffen their backs and lift their chins.

"I tell you this because our ultimate triumph in this land is assured," Khalil continued. "It is the will of Allah. The Caliph had nearly a hundred thousand troops under arms. And how many can the Christian kingdoms of Spain muster? A bare ten thousand men-at-arms, if that. I tell you this because you may be reluctant to serve me wholeheartedly, to aid me with all your strength to capture the castle. You may feel that you are betraying your fellow Christians. I tell you now the outcome will be the same whether you aid me or not. Ulldecona will fall. The Caliph will rule there sooner or later."

Prince Khalil paused; he looked hard at all the men gathered around the sandbox. "You have given your oaths, and I trust you will honour them. I do not have to remind you what will befall you if you try to play me false."

"You have made your point, emir," said Robin. "And we have given you our oaths. Now tell us *how* we shall capture the fortress at Ulldecona."

"You cannot guess? I was told you were a clever man, Lord Locksley. Why do you think I went to the trouble of dressing you in Christian clothes? Why did I preserve your equipment, mail and arms from the sinking dhow?"

Robin smiled. "You wish us to enter the castle of Ulldecona dressed as Christian men-at-arms – perhaps claiming to be shipwrecked on the Spanish coast on the way home from the Great Pilgrimage. You wish us then to open the gates and let your men inside to slaughter the unsuspecting Hospitallers."

"You do not disappoint me, Lord Locksley. Yes, that is it, in essence."

"And our payment? You promised us one tenth of the gold."

"Once the castle is captured, you will be given five hundred ingots of gold, and sufficient beasts to carry them, and set free inside the Kingdom of Aragon to return home as you see fit. Now, you and I, my lord, shall retire to discuss the finer points. But before I leave you, I wish to know that you all agree with my plan, and will try to achieve it to the best of your abilities."

Robin said, "Does any man choose to go back to the galley?"
He looked round the room at each of his followers.
No one said a word.

Robin was gone for some hours, while I fretted and frowned and wrestled with my conscience. We had no choice, really. To return to the galleys was a certain death sentence for Robin and all of us. Yet to betray our fellow Christians, holy warriors of Christ, no less, and offer them up to death was a terrible crime and a mortal sin as well. True, I did not know these men. I had never met them. They were not my comrades, nor my fellow countrymen. They were not friends. But, still, it was a foul thing to do to any good man.

Robin returned at a little before midnight, looking exhausted. I was sitting up in the dining room waiting for him with a jug of wine, a stack of flat breads, sliced onions in vinegar and a boiled capon with a spiced sauce.

My lord plonked himself down and poured himself a beaker of wine.

"I know what you're going to say, Alan," he said. "You are going to tell me that this is a dishonourable course, a cowardly trick to play on the good Hospitallers and you will never countenance it – something like that anyway. You're going to demand that we refuse to do the emir's bidding."

I opened my mouth. Then closed it again. He had stolen my words.

"It might shock you to learn that, for once, I entirely agree with you."

I stared at him.

"However, we are *not* going to be sent back to the galley to be worked to death, I can tell you that as well," he continued. "I've not forgotten the experience – neither have I forgiven that arrogant bastard for subjecting us to it. I am minded to make Khalil pay for that insult. And I have a plan to accomplish it, but there's one element that I cannot fit into my schemes."

"Is it the gold?" I said.

"Well done, Alan," he smiled at me. "It is the gold. He took me to see it in the treasury tonight, to confirm that he has not spent it all. There are still three boxes of gold inside that stronghouse. He actually let me look inside them. But the gold will remain there, locked up tight, while we go north to fight. But I cannot for the life of me work out how we can remove all the gold from the strong-house, guarded by hundreds of men, and still escape with our lives. It's too heavily guarded. What I really need is for them to *give* me the gold, freely, just hand it over to me... But why would they ever willingly do that? Don't worry, Alan, I'll think of something..."

"Forget the gold, lord," I said. "Just get us out of here with whole skins and back to England – that is enough. None of our men would complain."

Robin fixed me with his stare; his silver eyes glinted like a blade in the dark of an alley. "That is *my* gold," he said. "I have bled for it. It is *mine*."

I could not hold his terrible gaze and looked down at the table.

After an awkward pause, Robin laughed and said, "No matter, Alan; that is a problem for me to solve. Give me some of that capon and I'll tell you what the emir has in store for us... and what we will really be doing."

We spoke until the small hours, discussing the problem, this way and that, going over a host of different possibilities until I was yawning, barely able to keep my eyes open. Robin, on the other hand, was full of life and fire and at one point went off rummaging in cupboards to find quill, ink and parchment.

It was not until nearly noon that I awoke, with Hanno kicking the frame of my bed. "The Earl wants to see everybody. Now. In the garden."

Rubbing my eyes, I stumbled out, unwashed, into the bright garden sunlight. Our whole company was gathered there, looking bemused. It was clear Robin had not slept, yet there was no diminishment to his inner blaze.

Without any preamble, he said, "We march tomorrow. Every man is to rest well tonight and we muster at dawn right here. Pack the belongings you wish to carry on the march – and be prepared to abandon the rest. We shall not return to Russafa. Rations for three days will be provided by the emir, along with canteens of water for every man, but you are responsible for your weapons. Make sure they are clean, oiled and sharp. We are going to war!"

We did as our lord bade us. I ate as much as I could and slept in the afternoon and for much of the night. Between times I sharpened my *janbiya* and my sword, and made sure that the point on my misericorde was as keen as a needle. I oiled the straps on my kite-shaped shield, repainted its surface with Robin's wolf-mask device, black on white, and put on the mail coat for the first time in three months. In an instant, I felt like a proper soldier again.

The Emir of Valencia came to salute us before we departed with the rest of his army. We lined up in all our war finery and the emir came down the line looking at every man. I noticed that there was a company of Black Guards hovering nearby and Tariq the Assassin prowled beside him, alert for any attempt on his master's life. We stood like stone statues and received his inspection impassively. However, I'm sure I wasn't the only man in the garden who considered snuffing out the life of the one who'd humiliated us.

Prince Khalil addressed us then. "Once you were galley slaves," he said. "Now you are proud warriors again. Remember your oaths to me and you will be richly rewarded when the battle is won. Know this, you Locksley men, I have utter confidence in you to fulfil the task I have given you. But I am not a fool. So I have decided that I need a little more security, an extra safeguard to ensure you keep your side of the bargain. And therefore, I tell you now, that there had been a small change to our previous plans."

The Sherwood men were turning and looking at each other

mystified.

"Your liege lord, Robert Odo, Earl of Locksley, shall remain here under close guard at the Palace of Russafa, until your mission is accomplished."

I gaped at the emir.

"As I say, I have full confidence that you Christians will do your duty at Ulldecona. But all men are frail, apt to waver from the righteous path, and if, for example, it should come into your foolish heads to betray me, perhaps to inform the Hospitaller garrison of my stratagem, then think on this..."

Khalil seemed to be looking directly at me; looking into my heart.

"If you deviate from the orders that have been given you, your lord will die. If you break faith with me, Robin of Locksley will be immediately put to the sword. If you violate your oaths to me, I shall make it my business to hunt each of you down – then, life at a galley oar will seem like a mercy."

Chapter Twenty-one

It took me several miles of marching before I could fully comprehend what had just happened to us. Robin and I had thought we'd been cunning – our late-night scheme had indeed been to betray Khalil to the Hospitallers. We planned to enter the castle, pretending to be pilgrims returning from the Holy Land, as agreed, but then to inform the Castellan of Ulldecona, Charles de Bearn, immediately that Khlail meant to introduce his men into the castle by stealth, and that we had been coerced into helping him. Once we had confessed, we'd join the defenders and defy the Moors from the ramparts.

At the end of the first day's march, more than thirty miles of rough coastal road which, despite our training, left us all foot-sore and dog-tired, we gathered round our small campfire to discuss what was to be done.

It felt strange to be in the midst of an army of our enemies, and we naturally stuck close to each other on the march and in camp. The military might of the Khalil, was evident all around us. The Almohad troops were mostly cavalry, white-robed Berber lancers on huge chargers, and Turkish-style light horsemen armed with bows; but about one fifth of the force was infantry, a regiment of tall Nubian swordsmen, and companies of swift-footed Moroccan spearmen. The advancing Caliphate army was at least a thousand men strong, by Little John's calculation, and he did not, like other men, exaggerate numbers to reflect his secret fears of the coming action.

"I haven't seen such a gathering of leather-arsed fighting men since we left the Holy Land," he said, stirring the pot of soup that bubbled over the fire. He was the band's cook, since Elise had remained in the Russafa Palace with her mistress. Ricky, too, had stayed behind with Robin, as his servant. The former wharf rat was a fine sea-going sailor and brave as a lion but our training exercises had revealed that he was a sadly indifferent man-at-arms.

"This seems too great a force to seize one small castle," said Nikos. He had been decked out on the march in his dazzling scale-mail coat and plumed steel helmet, and once more looked like a brave Cretan knight, son of a powerful lord. He had removed the armour now that we were safely in camp, of course, but his pride in himself as a man had been returned to him.

"The bulk of the force is not to take the castle but to cross into Aragon and capture the city of Tarragona," I said. "I'll tell you what Robin told me he had discovered about the emir's plans for the cathedral being built there."

I saw that I had every man's attention in that circle of firelight. "You must keep this to yourselves. If the emir realised that we knew this, all our lives would not be worth that pan of broth, which I see is now boiling over."

Little John rescued his soup – a fine-smelling concoction of leeks, barley and mutton – while I looked around to check that no hostile ears were listening. The nearest neighbours were a dozen yards away, a group of red-robed Moroccans laughing uproariously at some crude joke – and I doubted any of those men spoke English. I admit, I was enjoying the attention: I was the youngest there yet the veterans were all agog to hear what I had to say.

"Spit it out, youngster," growled Little John. He was in undisputed command of our little group of ten men-at-arms, as Robin's deputy, although he was often kind enough to listen to what I had to say on matters of import.

"The King of Aragon and Count of Barcelona – Alfonso is his name – will be in Tarragona on Shrove Tuesday at the new cathedral hearing Mass."

"Did Robin tell you that?" asked Edwin, the smallest man in our band. "How does he know what will happen in a far-away city in days to come?"

"Robin was granted a little more freedom in Valencia than the rest of us," I replied. "I think we all noticed that. He told me that the Lady Tanisha allowed him to visit the harbour and the docks – with a full escort of Black Guards, of course – and he spoke to several of the Christian sailors whose ships were moored there. They told him this news; indeed, it is the talk of the whole of the western Mediterranean. The cathedral at Tarragona is said to be the wonder of the age – a beautiful new basilica is under construction. But I believe Robin worked out the rest of the emir's plan by himself."

"Get to the point, Alan," said John. "Tell them why Alfonso's presence is important." I knew that the big man was also privy to our lord's secrets.

"The King of Aragon has paid out huge sums to construct this fine new cathedral in Tarragona," I said. "He is attending a great feast there on Shrove Tuesday with all the local Spanish nobles, and a Mass of thanksgiving for him and his high-born friends, before travelling back to his capital Barcelona for the beginning of Lent. Today is Thursday, if you've lost count of the days, and I may tell you that this Sunday is the Kalends of March, so..."

"In five days' time," said Little John evidently losing patience, "on Shrove Tuesday, the King of Aragon will be in Tarragona, a hundred and thirty miles from where we now sit, only lightly guarded and unprepared for an attack. The emir means to make a swift lunge north across the border with his cavalry, take the city of Tarragona by surprise, seize the new cathedral, seize the King himself and any stray nobles he can conveniently scoop up."

"That is why the Emir of Valencia has been hiring troops all winter from all over the Moorish lands... with our gold," I said. "He means to conquer this whole part of Spain in one fell swoop – capture King Alfonso at Tarragona and force him to cede large swaths of the Kingdom of Aragon to him. Maybe the whole kingdom. And Ulldecona is the key to the scheme. He cannot advance safely on the city of Tarragona if a near-impregnable fortress filled with fanatical Christian knights is left unsubdued in his rear. Once they have snatched the King and are moving south again, they will be pursued, and if the Hospitallers and their troops were to sally out and attack his retreating men, Khalil could be caught between two fires. So he *must* take the fortress of Ulldecona before he makes his lunge for Tarragona."

John took over again. "He will leave a few hundred troops, well hidden, below Ulldecona to take possession of the castle when we open a gate for his men, and he will continue north with the rest of his army. He has little time to get to Tarragona. If he is late, and the King has departed for Barcelona, all will have been in vain. He cannot tarry at Ulldecona. He must push north."

"But what will *we* do at Ulldecona?" asked Gareth. "If we betray the emir, and inform the Hospitallers of the plot, Robin is surely a dead man."

"If we don't betray Khalil," I said, "the Hospitallers will die, Alfonso will be captured, and the Kingdom of Aragon will be lost to Christendom."

"What then shall we do?" said Nikos looking at me.

"I honestly do not know," I said. We all then looked at Little John.

"God's great bleeding bum-grapes – how should I know?"

I marched beside Little John the next day along the coastal road, skirting little fishing villages, and more substantial settlements on hilltops; past skeletal vineyards, dormant after winter, and ancient silver-grey groves of olives. The spring barley was just showing green in the fields and, on our right, the sea was a deep vivid blue. But for the occasional brief rain shower, the weather remained kind to us.

At noon we stopped for a bite of bread and cheese, and a flask of red wine, well watered. "Have you thought on this matter some more?" I said.

"I've thought of almost nothing else," said John with a sigh. "Robin said something to me, the night before we left, and I think it is important: he said, 'Stick to the plan, John. Whatever might happen on the march, adhere to our plan.' I think he suspected that Khalil might yet have a trick to play."

"He said something similar to me," I said.

"What do you think we should do, Alan – stick to the plan and let Robin die? Or obey Khalil and consign the Kingdom of Aragon to its fate?"

"I do not think I could allow Robin to be slaughtered for the sake of a foreign country that I do not know, and do not love," I said.

"But Robin insisted we should follow his plan," Little John replied.

"He couldn't know that Khalil would hold him as a hostage. He couldn't know that keeping to the plan would mean his death. I say our first loyalty must be to our liege lord. Therefore we must obey Khalil. There is the matter of our oaths, too. The oaths must also be weighed in the balance."

"So we betray the Hospitallers to their deaths?"

I felt sick to my stomach but I knew the decision must be faced: "Yes, John. We must betray them. If we keep faith with Khalil, if we do *not* break our solemn oaths to him, Robin will live, and we will at least have our gold."

"So be it," he said. He chuckled and slapped my shoulder. "The gold. Yes, mustn't forget the gold. I'll make a mercenary of you yet, Alan Dale."

The cavalry left us that evening, galloping off to the north and the west in small companies of horsemen. I gathered that they meant to travel in small groups and get into hidden positions well before the Shrove Tuesday feast so that, when the time was ripe, they could attack the city from several sides.

The Emir of Valencia remained with us, with a large company of his companions, Berber lancers, perhaps thirty men strong, the kind of unit that a Christian knight would call a *conroi*. He came to visit our campfire that night, bringing a full skin of wine as a gift. We were civil to him in return, although I noted that the Assassin was never far from Khalil's shoulder, and there were more of his Black Guards looming in the darkness beyond the circle of firelight. He need not have bothered with these precautions, we had no stomach to attack him – Little John had made our decision known to the whole band, and we were all reconciled to following the emir's orders.

"Tomorrow we will approach the castle of Ulldecona," he said in French. "If the Hospitallers are watching the roads, and we must expect that they will be, your band must appear to be genuinely fleeing in fear from us."

He accepted the cup of wine that Nikos passed him with a gracious nod of thanks, although I noticed that he did not drink from it.

"We will travel a little more slowly than you," Khalil said, "stopping to search every village, house and barn, asking the local peasants if they have seen a group of infidels who exactly match your description. They will know we are coming and their own spies can corroborate your story. When you are inside the castle, tell them as little as you can. The fewer lies you tell the better. Speak of your own true experiences in the Holy Land, of the battle of Arsuf, perhaps. These kinds of stories will be the most convincing. Mention by name any of their brethren you might happen to know from that time."

He knelt down and pulling out his dagger he scratched a plan of the castle in the dirt. We gathered around, looking down at the rough drawing.

The Hospitaller fortress was situated atop a steep conical hill with commanding views of the countryside for miles on each side, Khalil explained. The entire summit of the hill, an area of about two acres in size, was surrounded with a twelve-foot high curtain wall, with a walkway running all the way around the inside.

"Inside this enclosure, this bailey, as you Christians might call it, are several store houses, a stables, a barracks, the kitchen, all the usual buildings to support a castle with nearly a hundred inhabitants, as well as a kitchen garden, several goats, pigs and chickens running wild, a number of mature olive trees and one venerable lemon tree."

Khalil's people had reconnoitred the place thoroughly, I realised – and I wondered how he had got a man inside to spy it out so well.

My question was answered almost immediately. "Tariq will now tell you more about the bastion inside the curtain wall," the emir said. "He spent several weeks working there as a labourer earlier this year, digging a well."

The Assassin came forward, and took the dagger from Khalil's hand. "The bastion is on the southern side of the outer bailey," he said in Arabic, and Khalil translated it into French. "It is a fortified compound with a square tower on the eastern side, very high, very strong – this is the keep, the refuge of last resort. They call it the Tower of Saint John. There is a smaller round tower built by our people a hundred years before the Christians came – here," Tariq marked the square tower and the round one and drew curving lines linking the two. "There a long church here," he said, "next to the tower, and also very well fortified."

The whole castle looked to be a formidable defensive structure. No wonder Robin had described it as almost impregnable. While Tariq drew in some more buildings and indicated the main gate in the curtain wall, and the only gate in the inner bailey, I calculated how difficult it would be for an attacker to capture this fortress without the subterfuge we were planning.

The attacker would have to approach in full sight of the defenders, coming up the steep hill to the curtain wall. This would be the first obstacle. The defenders could mass their strength to stop them here. And in most cases they would succeed. If, however, the enemy did manage to get over the curtain wall and into the outer bailey, the defenders could retreat to the even more powerful inner bailey, and defy them from there. If that fell, the defenders could fall back on the square tower – or they could put garrisons in the smaller round tower – or even the well-fortified church. In short, it would be extremely difficult for any attacker to prevail without having overwhelming numbers and ample time – weeks or even months, in fact – to capture the different parts of the castle one after the other. The reality was that news of the Moorish attack on the fortress would bring reinforcements down in a few days from Aragon. Ulldecona Castle, I reckoned, was a tough nut that would be almost impossible to crack by ordinary assault, provided the defenders had enough numbers and the determination to hold it.

"Here, on the northeastern side of the curtain wall, is the sally port," Tariq was saying, while poking at the outer circle on ground with the dagger. "You men should be welcomed inside the castle tomorrow afternoon, *inshallah*. At midnight, the following night – it is the dark of the moon, by the blessing of Allah – you must open this small door here, this sally port. It is locked with two bolts, top and bottom, and I shall be waiting outside."

"How many men will you have with you?" I asked in French.

"Initially only two dozen," said Khalil, answering for him. "But they will be my best and strongest – men of the Black Guard, with whom you are more than familiar. Two men will hold the sally port open and wait for the rest of our force – more than two hundred men – to arrive at the summit of the hill. Tariq and the Black Guard will join you in the outer bailey and together you must immediately attack and secure the gatehouse here." He pointed to the gate in the west wall of inner bailey, beside the round tower.

"Do not delay. Speed is vital. You must take and hold against attack the gatehouse of the inner bailey until my troops arrive – perhaps half an hour. Is that clearly understood?"

"It not first time we do this work," said Little John in his bad French.

"Once my men are inside the inner bailey, your work here is finished. Your lord will be returned to you – unharmed, *inshallah* – you shall have your gold and leave to depart Ulldecona with my thanks and my blessing."

Khalil was smiling genially at us, as if the deed were already done.

"What about the square tower?" I said. "Those Hospitallers will no doubt barricade themselves inside and you will not winkle them out easily."

"If they refuse to surrender, I shall burn the tower with them inside it."

I felt a sick, sour feeling in my belly. Even though these men were not my comrades. It seemed a terrible fate for any good Christian man to suffer.

"Is every man clear about what is required of him?" said Khalil.

We nodded.

"Midnight, two nights from now," said Tariq. "This place. Yes?" He pointed at the scuff in the dirt that indicated the sally port in the curtain wall.

"Must I remind you of the perils of breaking your oaths?" said the emir.

We shook our heads. I had a mad vision of drawing my *janbiya* and plunging it into his belly. That would have been sweet. But I did nothing.

"Then may Allah guide your footsteps," said Khalil, and took his leave.

Chapter Twenty-two

The gate was huge and built of heavy oak reinforced with iron bands and broad-headed iron nails. A dozen faces looked down at us from the high walls on either side, and a voice said in French, "Tell me again, sir – you claim to be an Englishman, from... England?" He sounded incredulous.

"I do serve the Locksley Count," said Little John in his own mangled version of that language.

"Sir Knight," I said, "we flee from the soldiers of the Emir of Valencia. They are on our heels, sir; and we would fain take refuge in your castle."

Some of the heads disappeared and I could hear an angry conversation beyond the solid oak. A head in a conical steel helm popped up again.

"Wait here, until we summon our lord," the helmeted man said.

We Locksley men all looked at each other.

"What if they do not let us inside?" I whispered to Little John. "Do we go back to Prince Khalil with our tails between our legs?"

John merely shrugged.

The emir had once again confounded us. We had assumed he would go north with the rest of his cavalry to seize Tarragona and the King. But he remained with his force of some two hundred Moroccan infantry and Black Guards in a wood, hidden from view, about three miles south of the castle.

"If we fail to get inside this big pile of rock, that evil heathen bastard will have no more use for us," said Little John. "Do you think he will greet us when we return with a big kiss and a cup of honeyed ale? No – if we go back to him, he will throw us once more into the pit of that fucking galley."

Hanno said quietly to me, "It will be dark soon. The sea is only five miles away, over the high mountains yonder. I say we make for the sea, find a fishing boat then..."

I would not go back to the galley – I decided die. But running for the sea in the vague hope to carry us seemed absurd. Then there was no back in Valencia under sentence of death. I closed my eyes, offered up a prayer to Saint Michael, my guardian: *Let them open the gates, holy one. Persuade them. And forgive the base treachery I will thereafter commit. Or, if that cannot be, allow me to die with a bloody sword in my hand, not a God-damned oar.*

There are some folk who claim that prayer has little effect – that the saints are deaf to the pleas of Man. I know this untrue, for Saint Michael heard me. And with a loud creaking noise, like the tearing of a tree in sunder, the massive gate of the fortress of Ulldecona slowly began to open.

We walked through the gate and found ourselves surrounded by a gang of hard-faced men in black surcoats with large white crosses on their chests.

They were brother sergeants of the Order of the Knights of the Hospital of Saint John of Jerusalem – and a number of them, perhaps a dozen, were ominously holding loaded crossbows pointed at the ground. The sergeants formed a sort of corridor on either side of the open gates. As the portal creaked closed behind us, I saw two knights, in helms, mail, black cloaks with white crosses, standing at the end of the corridor, waiting to greet us.

I looked at Little John.

"Tell them who we are, Alan," he said. "And why we're here."

I stepped forward but before I could speak, Nikos pushed past me.

"Sir, these Englishmen mean to betray you," he said a little breathlessly in his Greek-accented French. "I beseech you: do not trust a word they say."

I stared at him, completely astounded.

"Why you treacherous little shit," said Little John. "I ought to rip you a new..."

There was a ripple of movement all around. Some of the

...ants had raised their crossbows; they were moments away ...n skewering us. I saw that Hanno had a hand on his hilt, as if ...e meant to slaughter a dozen crossbow-armed Hospitallers all on his own. I belatedly reached for my own.

"Halt," shouted a commanding voice in good French, and one of the Hospitaller knights stepped forward. "Let no one move. Be still, all of you."

"Stand fast, men," roared Little John.

The knight who had spoken was a slim, short, clean-shaven man, his face marked by hardship and advancing middle age. But there was an unmistakable athletic bounce in his step as he came forward towards us.

"You, sir, you in the fish-scale mail – step away from the rest of them, if you please." Nikos took a few steps closer to the Hospitallers.

"Keep a close watch, Sir Arnold, on our English visitors." The middle-aged knight waved a finger at our little group. "And if a single one of them draws his weapon, you have my permission to kill them all."

I took my hand off my hilt. Little John beside me was muttering dire threats under his breath and glaring at Nikos.

"Now, sir, speak up. Say your piece. You claim these men are traitors. Not to be trusted. Explain yourself."

The Cretan puffed out his chest. "I am Kavallarious Nikos Phokas, eldest son of Lord Ioannis Phokas, Archon of Messara, in the Province of Crete. I was captured by these men in a sea battle off the coast of Sicily three months ago. I was made a slave in a galley owned by the Emir of Valencia, and we were subsequently sent north, by the infidel emir, to trick our way into your castle and betray the fortress to the benighted armies of Islam."

There was a stir of muttering and half-conversation in the Hospitallers ranks but the pointed crossbows did not waver for an instant. I felt my heart sinking into my boots. How could Nikos do this to us? We were comrades; I saved him from death in the galley; he'd sworn to serve Robin faithfully . . .

"The Emir of Valencia lies yonder," Nikos said. "Hidden in the wood by the main road with all his men. And these fellows – these traitors to their Faith, and to God Himself – have agreed with him to trick their way inside this Christian fortress and open a gate to let your enemies in. They seek your deaths, Sir Knight..."

"Indeed? Yet you are with them. You travel with traitors. Why is that?"

The Hospitaller's words stopped Nikos. He stammered: "I... I ... You see, I..." and seemed quite shaken up by the old knight's question.

"My lord," I said, "if I might be allowed to explain..."

"Quiet!" said the knight. "I wish to hear from this man. You, sir, how come you travel in their company, if you believe them so untrustworthy."

"We were imprisoned together by the heathens," said Nikos. "And the emir said that we would all be allowed to go free if..."

"If you all agreed to take part in this plot. Yes? All of you."

"Uh, I never intended, sir, to . . . In fact, I always secretly meant..." Faced with the knight's hostility, Nikos appeared unsure of himself.

"I believe I've grasped the essence. Sir Arnold, you will disarm these men and lock them in the dungeon below Saint John's Tower. I will interrogate their leader later. This Greek knight here must also surrender his sword. Conduct him to my chamber, I will draw the truth from him there."

"Sir Knight," I said, making a last attempt. "Allow me to tell you how things truly stand. We meant to tell you all about the emir and our..."

"I will allow you to speak, young man, in due course. If you are innocent, you will have nothing to fear from me. But if you meant to do us harm..." he turned to his fellow knight. "Sir Arnold, call out the rest of the brothers, and double the guards on the walls and atop all the towers. If what this young man says is true, the Moor is nigh and we must ready for him."

We were locked in the dungeon below the great square tower, which was on the eastern side of the inner bailey, just as Khalil and Tariq had described it. Indeed, the whole castle was exactly as they had drawn its plan on the sandy floor of the camp. Scrubby olive trees and dun coloured rock, strong outer walls and fortified buildings. The sergeants treated us decently, though, and while they removed all our weapons, they did not molest us in any way.

Nor did we have to wait long.

I had time for one swift conversation with Little John before I was summoned by the Castellan – for I soon discovered the knight who had ordered our imprisonment was the lord of the castle, Sir Charles de Bearn.

"Has it occurred to you, young Dale," Little John growled, with a ferocious depth to his voice, "that if we had just dispatched that Griffon in the Red House last autumn, we would not have had any of this grief?"

I stared at him. Griffon. I had not thought of Nikos by that disrespectful epithet for a long time. A griffon was a mythical beast, wasn't it? I searched my memory. Yes: a griffon was a hybrid, a beast made of two others. But what were they? Suddenly Elise's odd prophecy sprang into my mind: the terrifying beast lurking in the shadows, waiting to claw us from behind, half eagle, half lion. A griffon. A Griffon who had now betrayed us.

"If we'd just knocked off Nikos in Crete, we would have sailed straight to Marseilles with a shipload of stolen gold, got drunk as bishops for a couple of days, then we'd be heading off home to England rich as kings."

"I can't see into the future, can I?" I said angrily. "I'm not bloody Elise." But Little John's shaft had gone home. It *was* my fault.

"No galley; no Ruffasa; and Robin would not now be facing the chop."

I looked at my boots, close to tears. I had no reply for my friend.

"All right, Alan; I'm just teasing you," said Little John, in a much more friendly tone. "Just a little jest. It's the fortunes of war. Ups and downs. We'll all have to make the best of it."

"I make that Nikos pay, Alan, worry not," said Hanno, at my shoulder.

It was little consolation. But should I really have allowed them to kill Nikos in cold blood? Had my squeamishness sentenced my lord to death?

I must have looked distressed for John said, "Don't fret, lad, Robin is a wily bird, and tough, you know that. I've seen him extricate himself from tighter corners. Go, mend this, talk to the headman. You know what to say."

Two brisk sergeants showed me into the Castellan's chamber, which was on the second floor of Saint John's Tower. And these two men remained inside the door, guarding it, watching me. It was a comfortable, rectangular room with a fire burning in the hearth and a long table covered in a mess of parchments and scrolls. A flagon of wine sat there with several dirty pewter cups. The Castellan was standing with his back to me holding his hands to the fire – the nights were still chilly in March – but he had removed his long black cloak to reveal the equally dark surcoat worn underneath.

"You have been chosen to speak for the others, hmm? My advice to you is this: trust in God and do not lie to me. Now, tell me your name and where you hail from. Recount how you came to be at my gate this evening."

He turned to face me as I began to speak, and I felt a powerful urge to tell him the whole truth. But it had to be resisted. I recalled Robin's words when he told me about the "holy relic" he had sold to the Archon: mix in as much truth as you can. So I told the Hospitaller as honestly as I could how we came to his castle in Spain. I told him about the march from England to Outremer, about the battles we fought there, and about our sea travels...

"So you admit that you planned to steal this camel-train of gold from the Almohad Caliph?" he said. "A bare-faced theft of his treasure."

"We saw it as a way of depriving the Sultan of Egypt, our enemy Saladin, of the resources he needs to wage war against our holy armies." I struggled to keep a straight face as I repeated Robin's reasoning for the theft.

Sir Charles actually laughed. "Oh, that *is* good. You told yourself that, did you?" I saw that when he smiled he was actually a kindly looking man.

I said nothing at his remark. He cordially invited me to continue so I recounted how we had been ambushed by Nikos and his Cretan galley, how we had captured him and, in turn, been taken and imprisoned on the slave-galley belonging to the emir. I told him of our comfortable confinement during the winter in the Russafa Palace and how Prince Khalil had forced us to swear to help him conquer this Christian fortress of Ulldecona.

"You admit the charge is true, then," said Sir Charles, frowning at me.

"Yes, sir, however, my lord the Earl of Locksley and I concocted a plan that we should tell you immediately about the emir's plan. Indeed, I have a letter, written by Robin of Locksley, addressed to you personally, outlining the plot, and explaining that we were forced to give the appearance of going along with it in order to deceive the emir. I have this letter in my pouch."

Sir Charles did not look very impressed but I dug in the leather pouch attached to my belt and handed over a much-folded piece of parchment.

He read the inscription, which was indeed made out to him by name and title, and then he read the document slowly. I blessed Robin's foresight in writing the letter. The all-night discussion of our strategy at the Russafa Palace had, it seemed, this time, borne fruit. At least, I truly hoped it had.

"Hmm," Sir Charles said. "And yet your lord is not with you. Did he then willingly choose to remain with the emir?"

I said: "Ah... ah, well..."

"Or did the Emir of Valencia, whom I know from my own informants to be a man of deep guile, choose at the last minute to retain possession of your lord so that you'd indeed be forced to carry through the plan to open the sally port and let our enemies into this castle. Had you, in fact, decided among yourselves to follow the emir's plan and betray us all to our deaths?"

I thought about lying to the Castellan then. I considered telling him that our love for Christ, and our fellow Christians, had dictated that we abandon our lord to his fate. But I could not. Sir Charles stared at me in chilly silence.

"Whatever our intentions might have been, whatever thoughts may or may not have been in our heads," I said eventually, "we have done nothing against this castle – we have not acted against you or any of your people."

"True," he said. "A man may have evil thoughts yet not act on them."

I was encouraged by his words. "Furthermore," I said, "your castle is likely to come under attack within days, or even hours. Might I suggest that it would profit you to have a few extra men-at-arms to bolster your defence."

"But how could we ever trust you?" he said.

I raised my head and looked full into his face, locking my eyes with his. "You can trust us, sir. On my honour. I will swear an oath of loyalty to you, if you wish it, and so will the other Locksley men – although I cannot speak for Kavallarious Nikos Phokas. You have the full truth before you now, sir. But I would say this, before you make your decision: we have been forced to make a difficult, even impossible choice, in recent days, and I am sure you can comprehend that. If we chose wrongly, should we not be given a chance to make amends, a chance to redeem ourselves and earn your forgiveness?"

He inclined his head, as if to say, "maybe".

He considered for a while, just looking at me quietly and calmly.

Then he said, "In your travels, in the Holy Land and in your struggles against the foe, did you ever encounter a man named Sir Nicholas de Scras?"

I was thrown by his question. "Ah, yes, I met Sir Nicholas. He was one of your brethren – a Hospitaller. I esteemed him greatly.

Indeed, I will also say I considered him a friend, as well as a fine comrade on the battlefield."

"You may or may not know it, but we Hospitallers quite regularly and comprehensively communicate with the other brethren of our far-flung Order. Every house of the Order in Christendom must submit reports of local activity, intelligence and political news, even gossip, to their superiors, who pass along a digest to the other houses. We like to know what is happening, as much as is possible, in all four corners of the world, and at all times."

I wondered why he was telling me this. The Order of the Poor Fellow-Soldiers of Christ and of the Temple of Solomon – the Templars – a similar elite organisation of fighting monks, were famous for their wide intelligence networks. I had always assumed that the Hospitallers, their greatest rivals, would possess similar structures. *What point was he trying to make?*

"Your master's name is known to us – Robert Odo, Earl of Locksley – as is his reputation. Not a high reputation, as it happens. He is a known thief – and some people suspect him of the brutal murder of a Templar knight."

I said nothing. *Was Robin's murder of Sir Richard at Lee coming back to haunt us? Would it condemn us all to death at this holy warrior's hand?*

"And your name is known to us as well."

He paused for an awkward length of time.

"Your reputation, in stark contrast to your lord's, is very good – one might even say it is excellent. I do not believe you have lied overmuch to me tonight – although a lesser man might well have been tempted to do so to save his skin. You're a fellow of undistinguished birth yet you behave with as much rectitude as a nobleman of the purest blood. You are a good Christian, I am told, which cannot be said for Lord Locksley, and you are also swordsman of some renown. I think I also recall from my reports that you were invited to join King Richard's *familia*, his inner circle of chosen knights, which would have meant money and fame and rank – yet you politely refused, preferring to honour your original oath and remain with your own liege lord. This tells me you are a man of the highest principle, and despite your low birth, a man with a deep sense of honour."

I was feeling slightly embarrassed at all this praise. And I muttered something about Robin giving me all that I had, and how I felt grateful...

"So I have decided that you and, by extension, your nine comrades, *can* be trusted to fight alongside us when the heathen descend on Ulldecona. But first, there is one thing you must do to prove your loyalty beyond doubt..."

"What might that be?" I said warily.

And he told me.

Chapter Twenty-three

The sally port was an arch-shaped, man-sized door in the northeast side of the long circular curtain wall. It resembled a gate you might find in a walled garden, and was overshadowed by a cypress tree of the kind often found in consecrated burial grounds in these southern lands.

I shuddered when I made out the elongated oval shape of the tree in the dark night – was this a bad omen? An omen of death? I stood to the right of the sally port and stared up at its looming presence. *Would I die tonight?*

It was a little before midnight and, as Tariq had foretold, the night was moonless and pitch black. On the walkway of the curtain wall above the port, was a squat black shape darker than the night. Hanno was keeping watch over the wall for the approach of Tariq and the Black Guards.

A dozen yards away, Little John and Gareth were crouched behind the thick trunk of a venerable olive tree, little Edwin was up in its branches, audibly uncomfortable and trying not to move, and around and about, in a semi-circle around the sally port, concealed under shrubs, and in corners of the wall, and folds in the ground were the rest of the Locksley men. They were rested, having slept most of the day, fed and once again well-armed.

All save Nikos.

We had not seen him since his denunciation at the main gate the night before, and I suspected that Sir Charles was deliberately keeping the Cretan away from us for fear of our violent reprisals. Rightly so. I felt nothing for him now but a sour hatred. He had betrayed his friends – it might have been out of love for Christendom or hatred of us, I did not know. But he had broken the most basic rule of a man-at-arms: be loyal to your company; protect your comrades. If I had the chance, I'd rectify my mistake at the Red House and murder him in a heartbeat. I knew Hanno and John felt the same.

"They come now," a Bavarian voice whispered from above me.

I went to the door and began to feel for the bolts, top and bottom. They were rusty and ancient, and it took me several moments to wrestle them both open. Then I swung open the door. I stepped through it and found myself on the steep slope of the hillside. I had a dark-lantern in my hand and fumbling slightly, I opened the little door in the side to reveal a gleam of candle-light.

I heard a rustling sound, a click of a stone under a boot and then Tariq rose up before me – I swear that man could move more quietly than a ghost.

He said nothing but clapped a hard hand on my shoulder and went through the door. And suddenly there were Black Guards all about me, big men in dark turbans and cloaks, filing past and through the door. When the last had passed me, I followed on in and pulled the door shut behind me, shooting the bolts.

"No!" hissed a voice in Arabic. "Leave it open, infidel."

There were Black Guards all around, visible by the faint gleam of my dark-lantern. I hesitated, feigning not to understand the language.

"Open the door, infidel," said Tariq. "Open it now." One of

the Black Guards shoved me roughly towards the door.

I pretended to fumble with the top bolt. Then turned, quick as a weasel, and lashed out with the heavy iron lantern at the head of the man who had shoved me. The metal box exploded, its iron sides coming apart on contact with the fellow's hard skull to reveal for an instant the full light of the candle inside, which was almost immediately extinguished as it hit the ground.

But it was enough to give me a glimpse of two dozen Black Guards all staring at me, and tall Tariq glaring hardest of all.

A Black Guard rushed at me, cursing in Arabic, scimitar in his hand, but I had my *janbiya* unsheathed by now and, as he came swinging at me, I ducked under the scimitar blow and plunged my razor-sharp curved blade into the fellow's belly, ripping it across, through his tangled guts and feeling his hot gore spurt over my hand. He screamed and staggered away.

Just then, from all around that part of the outer bailey, a dozen red-orange pine torches sprang into life. There were men in mail everywhere.

It was instant mayhem. I saw Little John charge out from behind his olive tree, huge axe already swinging, and Gareth coming on just behind him, sword in hand. Above and behind me, I heard the *spang* of Hanno's crossbow. The guard who I'd knocked down with the lantern had got back to his feet and was in the act of swinging at me with a sword when Hanno's timely quarrel took him in the centre of his chest and put him down again.

As I hauled out my arming sword, I saw the other Sherwood men were barrelling forward on all sides, their faces shadowed and grotesque in the red flickering torch-light. Two Black Guards rushed me at almost the same time. I sidestepped the first man, his scimitar swishing an inch past my shoulder, and hacked my sword into the back of his neck, as his momentum took him past me. The second man cut at my head and I ducked down beneath the blow, then bobbed up and feinted a long-armed overhead diagonal slice with my sword, which he dodged by skipping sideway . . . moving exactly into the space

I wanted him to occupy, where he received the curved point of my *janbiya* deep in the base of his throat, slicing in and through his windpipe.

There were Hospitaller sergeants joining the mêlée now, competent men, in black surcoats with the familiar white cross on their breasts, armed with sword and shield, and some with crossbows, mailed in iron links or padded gambesons and crowned with steel broad-brimmed helmets, known as sallets. They surged into the area by the sally port, erupting from the surrounding darkness, more than a dozen of them, racing forward to join the battle. These sergeants fell upon the Black Guards like wolves loose in the sheep fold, cutting down enemies with a swift, grim professionalism.

Out of the corner of my eye I saw lanky Tariq drop his sword and sprint for the curtain wall. A Sherwood man called Hal, an older fellow, a father of three daughters, steady and decent, boldly challenged Tariq, sword in hand.

I saw the Assassin reach up to the back of his neck and pull out a long, slim black knife from a sheath in the upper part of his robe. As he was running, without breaking stride, Tariq hurled the blade straight at Hal and the spinning steel smacked exactly into the poor man's right eye, dropping him like a stone. Tariq was past him a moment later and leaping with arms outstretched for the walkway. I looked up and called, "Hanno, stop him!"

The Bavarian heard me. But his crossbow was unloaded and, as he shoved his foot in the iron stirrup and hauled back the cord, the Assassin was already up on the walkway and had one leg over the top of the wall. Hanno, a dozen yards away, slotted the quarrel into its groove, raised his bow – but it was too late, Tariq was gone, vanishing into the darkness on the other side.

He was the only man to escape our ambush. The mêlée was over now. The remaining Black Guards were swiftly dispatched, the wounded men too, and in the red glow of the pine torches, I saw the carnage we had wrought.

There were black-clad bodies everywhere and puddles of

blood glinting wetly. I saw another Locksley man – Dickon – bleeding from a terrible wound below his navel, and a Hospitaller sergeant was crouched over him, examining the damage. I did not expect him to live – lower belly wounds were almost always a death sentence. But if he could be saved, the good Hospitallers, famed for their medical skills, were the men to treat him.

Sir Charles de Bearn came striding across towards me, looking grim. I had not seen him fight but his sword blade was spattered with fresh blood.

"I hope we have proved our loyalty to you," I said. My whole body was trembling uncontrollably, as it often did after a bout of action. I felt close to tears, too. But I wouldn't allow myself to weep in front of this warrior monk.

"Beyond doubt," he said. "You have done well, Alan. I think we got them all – which means that when the rest of the Moors come up the hill to join their comrades we shall be able to give them a nice little surprise."

"Not all of them – a man called Tariq, one of Khalil's lieutenants, escaped. We could not stop him. You should be wary of him, sir, he is a very dangerous man, a genuine Assassin from the high mountains of Syria."

"Truly? I have heard tell of these men. Well, I shall be wary then."

He scratched at an itch under his helmet. "It is a pity this Assassin escaped. Khalil will know that you have played him false this very night. I had hoped we might have longer to prepare ourselves. But, it is no matter."

"It may be a grave matter for my master, sir," I said. I felt the prick of tears behind my eyelids, and found I could not look at the Castellan directly.

"Yes, yes," said Sir Charles. "I am sorry for it. And I shall pray for Lord Locksley. It may be that he will find some way out of his predicament. Do not lose hope – hope is a weapon, too, and powerful one. Hope brings victory; hope can even sometimes change the shape of the world around us."

We cleaned our weapons; we cleaned and bound our wounds; we ate, drank and slept a little. Just before dawn, Dickon died, and as the pale sun was rising we buried him and poor old Hal, the father of three, in the castle's graveyard – which was, in fact, not far from the sally port where we had fought so successfully the night before.

The bodies of Tariq's men had been removed from the field of combat and buried in a mass grave outside the cemetery – the heathen should not lie in consecrated ground, the Hospitaller priest had said – all that was left to show that twenty-six men had died in that corner of the outer bailey were some rusty patches of blood, already soaked into the earth, and the scrapes and scuff marks made by men struggling with each other for their lives.

We all joined the Hospitallers, the knights, sergeants, their chaplains and male servants – there were no women at all permitted in the castle – for the service of Prime in the large, thick-walled stone church inside the inner bailey. I was surprised how sparsely attended the service was, about thirty worshippers, not including our seven surviving Locksley folk, and assumed that all the castle's other fighting men were on the walls or in the towers, watching for the enemy. I gave it no more thought then, but offered up heartfelt thanks to God and Saint Michael for my deliverance. I offered up a prayer for Robin, too, begging God to keep him safe from Khalil's wrath.

Sir Charles invited Little John and me to break our fasts with him in the refectory, a long wooden-beamed building in the inner bailey, where he also proposed that we make an impromptu council of war with all his knights.

"Kavallarious Nikos Phokas will be joining us for the repast," Sir Charles said casually as we were coming out of the church. "I trust you'll behave in a civilised manner. No recriminations. Let bygones be bygones."

I stopped dead, and stared at the Castellan.

"Truth is, Alan, we need his sword," he said. "I trust you will be civil."

I called to Little John who was talking to Sir Arnold, a Hospitaller knight who, unusually for the Order, hailed from England, from Winchester.

"Nikos will be at breakfast with us and we must be civil to him, Sir Charles says. Apparently, we urgently need his sword to defend the castle."

Little John sucked in a deep breath. He didn't say anything for a dozen heartbeats and then he let out the air in one loud whoosh. "Very well, yes, I can play nicely for a while. At least till we fight off Khalil's crew. Then, I swear by Saint Peter's pink, well-pimpled prick, I'm going to chop off the fucker's treacherous head and take a long, luxurious shit into his lungs."

"Sounds like a fine plan," I said. "I may join you in the endeavour."

Sir Charles had the grace to seat Nikos at the far end of the table from Little John and me. He scowled sulkily at us down the length of the table, occasionally curling his lip to show his contempt. We ignored him as best we could. But it was not the presence of the traitorous Cretan at the meal that disturbed me so much as the number of Hospitaller knights attending.

"Where are the rest of your knights, Sir Charles," I said as I sat down. There were seven men in black tunics, including the Castellan, at the board.

"These are all of our brethren, Alan," he said, looking puzzled. "Sir Tomas died last year, and Sir Luis left the Order after a special dispensation from our Master. This is the full complement of the brethren at Ulldecona."

He introduced me to the other six men but, in my dismay then, and due to the passage of many years since, their names have slipped from my mind – all save that of Sir Arnold, the English knight. Now I could clearly see why the Castellan was so quick to overlook the charge of treachery against the Locksley men. And why he said we desperately needed Nikos's sword.

We ate bread, cheese and eggs and drank good red wine, and

the knights made conversation, but I remained silent, pondering our situation.

"How many sergeants are there in the garrison?" I asked Sir Charles.

"Twenty-four sergeants; divided into three watches of eight men."

"Can any of the castle servants fight?"

Sir Charles shook his head. "Neither can any of our chaplains be persuaded to wield a sword and spill heathen blood – even in God's name. We have only the few men-at-arms we have to repel the Moors. No more."

"You are aware, sir," I said, sinking a cup of the rough red to give me strength, "that the Emir of Valencia has two hundred picked men outside your walls, right now, and many hundreds more that he can call on to aid him. We have fewer than forty men-at-arms here to oppose him. If we tried to guard the walls of the outer bailey with our full strength we'd have . . ." I did a calculation " . . . one man every ten paces. We'd never keep them out."

"We have managed to do so perfectly well before now," said Sir Charles, with a maddening air of calm. "We do not place our brethren all along the outer wall, evenly spaced. That would be unwise. We watch from the towers, and when we see the attack shaping up we concentrate our force to repel it. You have much to learn about defending a castle, young man."

I admitted I did. But the disparity in size between the garrison and our Moorish foes still greatly alarmed me.

I ate a little more and listened to the conversation, holding my peace: Sir Charles, it seemed, truly did know his business. He discussed the creation of three watches of his men-at-arms, each watch commanded by two knights; two watches would always be on duty on the walls while one rested. He briefly enquired about the provisioning of the castle with the cellarer knight, and apparently there was plenty of food and wine; the arbalester reported a goodly store of crossbow quarrels in the armoury. Sir Charles then informed the table that, the morning after we had arrived, he had dispatched a pair of swift riders to deliver the news of the emir's advance, and his plan to capture the King of Aragon at Tarragona cathedral.

It was Monday morning and the King would be celebrating Mass in Tarragona cathedral tomorrow at noon. I wondered if the messenger had reached there in time to warn of the danger. It seemed likely: Tarragona was sixty miles away, a distance that could be covered in one hard day's ride, providing he had a change of mounts and managed to avoid the emir's men.

"Will Alphonso come with troops to help fight the Moors?" I asked.

"Certainly the King will come. This castle of Ulldecona lies within his God-given kingdom. He is honour-bound to come and fight for it..."

My spirits lifted at this news – a moment later they were dashed.

"...though it may take Alphonso a little while to muster his knights. I expect we shall see his banners in the next five or six days. A week at most."

A week! I goggled at the Castellan. Khalil had a thousand or so Moorish fighting men at his command between here and Tarragona. We had just forty. There was no way we could hold out here for a week. A day, maybe; perhaps two. Then we'd be overrun. I could not contemplate our fate if we fell into Khalil's hands again. He'd said the galley would seem like a mercy.

"Don't be downhearted, young man," said Sir Charles. "Remember, we do always have one unanswerable advantage over our heathen foes."

I perked up. "Yes?" I said eagerly. "What is it? Pray tell me, sir."

"The Lord of Hosts will be with us. God Almighty will be on our side."

Chapter Twenty-four

The Emir of Valencia came to Ulldecona in the late afternoon. He came with a dozen riders, all fully mailed and armed, and under a large flapping white flag. A sentinel atop the round tower gave the alarm with a blast of his horn, and Sir Charles, Little John and I scrambled over to the gatehouse set in the southwest side of the curtain wall and watched Khalil and his men walk their horses up the steep curving road that led to the castle's main gates.

Beyond the small group of Moorish horsemen, looking south, was a patchwork of fields, woods and olive groves with a few distant scattered houses and barns. There were troops on the move down there. I could see small contingents of infantry, twenty or thirty men in dark clothing, marching on the farm tracks between the little fields. Some were heading east towards the sea, others coming northwest, each company of marching men throwing up a small cloud of dust. It was clear what was taking place. Khalil was sending out his men to encircle the Hospitaller castle on the hill.

The emir stopped his horse a dozen yards from the closed main gate and stared up at us on the battlements of the gatehouse.

He was wearing a steel helmet with a spike wrapped in a black turban, a black cloak, iron mail and a decorated chestplate of blackened steel. The flag of truce in his right hand was in fact a long spear with a white sheet tied to it. At his right hand side was a rider I recognised, the captain of his Black Guards, a fellow named Zeyat. He kept his horse close to the emir's and his shield ready in case we should attempt to loose a crossbow bolt at his lord. I wondered where Tariq was. Had he been wounded in the sally port fight?

"What brings you to my gate, Moor, armed and accoutred for war?" said Sir Charles in French. "Speak your piece, then return to your land."

His voice was booming, commanding, unlike the soft conversational tone he used in the castle. I could feel my courage swell with his authority.

"Ask your new friends," said Khalil in the same language, his darkly handsome face twisted in anger, "ask those two piss-haired vipers standing beside you why I am here. But do not believe what they tell you. Do not trust them. They are both liars, born only to deceive honest men of God."

"I know these two – and I know that they agreed, under duress, to open this castle to your men. But Christ Our Saviour is merciful, and we must try to be so as well. Your plan has failed, emir. Your stealthy warriors who crept up here in the night are dead. The King of Aragon is alerted to your plot, and he will be gathering his knights to come to this place and punish you for your arrogance. So I say this to you: let no more blood be shed. Go now, and leave us here in peace, and these lands shall be untroubled once more."

Khalil laughed. It was not a pleasant sound. He stroked his oiled black beard for a moment, then turned to the captain of his guards and said quietly to him in Arabic, "Mark well this closed gate, Captain Zeyat. Once we have smashed through here, we will mount all the Christian heads on the top."

Then, in French, he continued, in a louder voice, "The Englishmen broke faith with me, and they attempted to betray you. Give them to me, all the Earl of Locksley's men who yet live, and I shall trouble the knights no further. Give me the English and no more blood need be shed here today."

I shifted nervously and glanced at Sir Charles to see his reaction to the emir's offer. He was smiling, shaking his head at this foolish suggestion.

"Hand these good Christian souls over to you, sir? So that you may torture them, make them your bloody playthings? No, sir. That I shall not do. Go now, lord of the Moors, go back to your lands – or prepare to do battle. Let God decide who shall have victory – and who shall bleed in the dust."

"So be it," said Khalil. "But do not expect speedy deliverance from the King of Aragon. He will not save you. He knows nothing of your situation."

He looked at Zeyat, and said in Arabic, "Throw them down here."

The captain of his Black Guards, bent to his saddlebow and untied a large-ish bundle, which had been hanging there. He unwrapped it, partially, and then flipped the two heavy objects it contained towards the castle gate.

They were a pair of severed heads.

On the battlements, we all stared in horror at the heads, their blank eyes, the lolling tongues, already blackening; the scabbed stumps where they had been separated from the necks. "I do not think King Alphonso received your message," said Khalil in French. And he laughed humourlessly again.

Then he leaned over to Zeyat, and said quietly in Arabic, "The next time I am at this Christian portal. I wish to ride straight through it without hindrance. You *will* take the gate for me – understand? Whatever the cost."

Then he half-turned his horse and, looking back over his shoulder, he looked directly up at me and said in French, "Hear this, you English oath-breakers, I have sent word of your treachery to Valencia, and given my orders for the death of your lord. *My* messengers will not be intercepted. It will not be a swift death for Robin of Locksley. Neither shall your deaths be quick. When I possess this petty fort, and it will be very soon, I swear it, you shall, all of you, come to comprehend the true meaning of the word pain."

We made ready for war. The armoury in the castle was, happily, as well stocked as the cellars. I put on a gambeson, a quilted tunic, underneath my own mail hauberk, and tied chausses around my thighs, covering both my legs in mail from toe to groin. A felted-wool coif, with a mail coif over the top, protected my head, and a light chain ventail covered my throat and chin; even my hands were covered with leather-palmed mail mittens.

I selected a kite-shaped shield, painted black with the Hospitaller cross on the front, and a fluted steel cap with a full-face visor. When I had tied my old sword belt around my waist, and tucked the *janbiya* into the belt and my misericorde in the top of my left boot, I was armoured from big toe to top-knot in almost impenetrable round, iron links, and in some places it was two layers thick. Yet when I looked at my companions – the remaining Locksley men and the Hospitaller knights and sergeants, who were similarly accoutred – I was struck by just how few we were compared with Khalil's hordes.

These Hospitallers might be formidable – I recalled the outstanding skills of my friend Sir Nicholas de Scras – but what chance would we have against so many foes? And the King of Aragon was quite unaware of our situation. No help would reach us before the Moors overwhelmed our walls with their numbers. All we could do was to fight, and die, as best we could.

We manned the walls, but lightly, and put lookouts up on the roof of the round tower and the square, and on the main gatehouse, too. And we waited.

The sun sank in the west, the light faded and died, and we could see blocks of men marshalling in the south, and the glow of many campfires.

We waited a little more, but it soon became clear that Khalil did not plan come at us that night. Night attacks are very difficult; it is hard to tell friend from foe; men are fearful in the darkness and often do not fight well.

I presumed that Khalil was waiting for some of his cavalry to return from the north. And that was fine by me. The longer he delayed, the longer we would breathe air. I was in no hurry to die here in this remote place so far from home.

Although we did not think he would come that night, we kept our guard up, and a good watch on the walls and towers, but in shifts; some men went into the refectory to eat a little and drink wine and some of us retired to the wooden barracks in the inner bailey to sleep for a few hours.

I was lying, still in my full armour, in a narrow cot in the half-full barracks, trying to snatch a little rest, when something occurred to me. Khalil had indicated to his captain that they meant to attack the gatehouse with all their strength, and I thought it might be worth sharing with Sir Charles my understanding of their Arabic conversation. If we put all our men on the gatehouse, if we massed our strength there, we'd have a better chance of fending off their attack. It felt important to tell Sir Charles, and since I could not rest, with the idea buzzing in my head, I went to seek him.

He was neither in the refectory, nor in his quarters in the Saint John's Tower. Eventually, about midnight, I asked Sir Arnold, whom I found on watch on the southern part of the curtain wall. He told me that the Castellan had probably gone to the old church to pray, as was his habit before a battle.

I pushed open the double door and walked into the gloomy interior. The long nave of the church was lit only by two candles burning on the altar at the far end. The soft yellow light made the large golden cross in the centre of the altar gleam alluringly, and I thought briefly of the Caliph's gold that we had once had in our possession – now, of course, long gone. I wondered too whether Robin was still alive, and felt a shudder of guilt. Could we have saved him? I did not think so. I muttered a prayer for his poor soul, anyway.

My eye was drawn by a figure kneeling in front of the altar, his arms propped on the rail, in the attitude of prayer. I could tell it was a Hospitaller knight by the cross on his dark surcoat and I guessed it was the man I had been seeking. I advanced on soft feet, reluctant to intrude on his devotions.

But when I got closer, I noticed something odd about his stillness. And his posture: he seemed to be slumped against the rail as if fast asleep.

I wasted several moments vainly waiting for him to move; then I went a little closer. He was dead, of course. And a name leapt into my mind: Tariq!

I saw that the mail between his right shoulder and neck and had been rent, sliced open a few inches only by a hard downward blow from a sharp dagger, and saw that there was a tiny amount of blood on the iron links.

I immediately recalled the method the Assassin had used to dispatch Nasir, the pirate chieftain in Qatran, and the way he killed Iqbal in Tunis.

For a moment, I marvelled that he had been able to get so close to the experienced Castellan to make the lethal strike. But the man had been at his prayers – who would be on their guard in a church? Then, suddenly spooked, I whirled around and whipped out my sword. There was no one there, just the shadows dancing in the corners of the space outside the pool of light.

I sounded the alarm, running from the church, calling the castle to arms. Armed men came pouring out of all the buildings in the inner bailey.

While the chaplains and their servants tended to poor Sir Charles's body, stripping it and washing it and laying it under a white sheet on a bier in the nave of the church, the rest of the garrison searched the castle thoroughly, from the tops of the two towers to the dank dungeon we had been kept in when we first arrived. There was no sign anywhere of Tariq.

He had manifested himself out of thin air, and struck out and killed our noble leader, and then disappeared again like smoke on the breeze.

I was partly awed by his extraordinary skills – but mostly they terrified me. If he could do that, then none of us was safe. How could we defend the walls when at any moment we might be murdered by an invisible wraith?

"He is the best, yes?" said Hanno, who seemed to be a little too pleased by the Assassin's work. "He kill, he disappear, he kill again. It is perfect."

I scowled at him and it was on the tip of my tongue to ask if he understood which side he was fighting for. But I held my peace. Having searched the whole inner bailey twice, he and I were now making a tour of the outer, where there were far fewer places to hide. We came round to the sally port in the curtain wall and I went over to check it was bolted shut. It was – and I knew it could only be locked from the inside.

"If you had been quicker with your crossbow," I said, "and shot the murdering bastard when I asked you to, we would not be in this mess."

Hanno just looked at me. I had enough sense to hold my tongue.

"Open little door," he said. "I want to see wall outside."

We went out on to the bare hillside, our weapons drawn. I could see the campfires of the Moorish army below, a wide scatter of fiery pinpricks. Yet they were flaring into greater life, one by one, as the soldiers dumped wood on them for the morning meal. Dawn could not be far off, an hour at most.

The enemy was waking up. Today, I was sure of it, we would fight.

"Hey, Alan!" said a voice from above me. I turned and in the faint grey light I could see that Hanno had half-scaled the wall. His head was now level with the top. It had taken him no more than a few moments and he had used nothing more than the natural cracks and fissures in the ancient stone.

Hanno jumped down, landing like a cat. "I do not think this a big mystery," he said, "how this Tariq comes in and out, unheard and unseen."

I had to agree with him. We did not have enough men to watch every section of the curtain wall and a man with Tariq's – or Hanno's – skills could easily slip over the top in the dark and wreak mayhem inside at will.

That revelation made me feel even worse.

They swarmed up the hill at us an hour before noon, hundreds of black-clad infantrymen coming up in the spring sunshine. They paused for a few moments at a safe distance of a hundred paces, then, at the pig-squeal of trumpets and the rattle of their drums, they charged the gatehouse *en masse*.

I stood on the walkway on a part of the curtain wall, a few yards to the east of the main gate, with a loaded crossbow in my hands, and another bow, also primed and ready propped up against the curtain wall by my knee.

Nikos stood beside me. He had disdained the crossbow as a grubby peasant's weapon, which irritated me, but he was fully armoured in is fish-scale hauberk and a plumed steel helmet, with a sword at his waist and a vicious spiked mace in his gloved hands. I had barely spoken to him since the day of our arrival at Ulldecona, for obvious reasons, but at this hour, with battle at hand, it seemed churlish to continue my silent animosity.

"God be with you today, Nikos," I said, gruffly.

He nodded at me, unsmiling. "And also with you."

I had persuaded Sir Arnold, the English Hospitaller who had taken command of the garrison after Sir Charles's death, to concentrate almost all our men at the main gate. I had told him of Prince Khalil's words in Arabic to Captain Zeyat at the gate the day before and he agreed with me that this is where the hammer blow would most likely fall. Half a dozen fellows were scattered around the rest of the defences but we had more than thirty men-at-arms here to face the Moors' main charge.

Nikos and I were stationed here with two Locksley men – Gareth and Edwin – as well as two Hospitaller knights in full armour and four grim-looking brother-sergeants armed with crossbows. On the far side of the gatehouse, the western side, Hanno and Little John, and the two remaining Sherwood men stood with two knights and another four sergeants.

The rest of our force, a mere dozen fighting men, was gathered atop the gatehouse with Sir Arnold in the centre.

The black tide of Moors hurled themselves, screaming, at the gatehouse and the walls on either side. They came with ladders and grappling ropes, and in the centre I could see a score of well-armoured men carrying a huge tree trunk with a hammered steel cap covering the front end: a battering ram.

I waited till the enemy were at the base of the curtain wall and beginning to climb their ladders before leaning out and loosing the first crossbow. I took a snarling man in the chest. At such short range, the bolt easily penetrated his mail and he was punched off the ladder by the force of the blow. Another man immediately took his place and, by the time I had dumped the first bow and reached for the second, three men were on the ladder and climbing for the top of the wall. I skewered the top man, an evil-looking fellow with one glaring eye, putting the bolt right through his throat. He stumbled back and carried the men behind him when he fell.

I dropped the bow, seized the top of the ladder and by twisting it, I managed to shove it away from the wall, the very bottom fellow stepping off the falling rungs as if he were stepping down from a horse's back.

All along our part of the wall, the same thing was happening over and over: the sergeants were shooting down at the climbing Moors, felling them one after the other. The two knights were pushing the ladders off the stonework, tumbling men with every massive shove. But there were too many of them. Scores of them, perhaps as many sixty black-clad men were boiling with rage below our little part of the wall, and ladders were popping up faster than we could dislodge them.

The noise was deafening – the cries of "Allahu Akbar" and the screams of the wounded, those with smashed legs from their falls, or deep puncture wounds from the scything crossbow bolts. I could hear the booming of the battering ram against the wooden gate and the bellows of Sir Arnold, urging his men to "Kill them for Christ, send them all to Hell where they belong".

I shoved another ladder away and out of the corner of my eye I saw a turbaned head surge up to my left. Nikos stepped forward and with a one mighty chop of his mace, crushed the man's skull, leaving him draped over the wall, lifeless, blood pooling in his dented helmet. Nikos shoved him off the battlements with his foot, but there were Moors everywhere now along our line, rolling over the wall and coming up with their scimitars in hand.

I pulled out my sword and engaged the nearest man, a giant with a fat-bladed weapon, who carved the blade down towards my head screaming a heathen challenge. I parried the massive blow, forcing the scimitar to my right to clang harmlessly on the stonework, and powered forward, smashing my steel-armoured forehead into his face. He reeled back and I shoved my sword point deep into his throat, the steel bursting out the back of his neck.

I got my shield round from its position on my back and slid my arm into the straps – and just in time. A Moor with a crossbow, one of a dozen enemies now on the walkway, loosed and I only just got the wood up in time to take the quarrel dead centre. He now had a useless weapon in his hands and I could see that he knew it by the fear in his eyes as I advanced on him. He hurled the whole crossbow at me. It bounced off my shield and he tried to draw a long dagger, but I cut him down swiftly, before he could even get the blade clear of the sheath, two fast hacking blows, left and right, that laid his left shoulder and face wide open.

I felt a massive blow across my mailed back, whirled round, shield up and ready, and took another sword cut across the width of the leather-faced protector. This fellow was a wizened warrior of forty summers or more. Very skilled. He parried my sword blow, and blocked the next attack easily too. It was only when he stumbled on a dead body at his feet that I was able to get a cut into the back of his thigh; a slashing swipe that severed the tendon, crippling him immediately. I dispatched him with a thrust to the ribs.

I looked for a fresh opponent.

The Hospitaller knights were magnificent. As I paused for a moment, panting, I watched in awe as they killed and killed. Their elegant sword work was the stuff of dreams – or nightmares, if you happened to be their enemy. Swift, slicing cuts, lightning lunges, and ripostes, nimble-footed speed and enduring strength – every enemy that came under their blades died in a few pounding heartbeats. The sergeants, crossbows now discarded, were almost as surefooted as the knights, and killed with a similar ferocity.

But Nikos was the most magnificent – he fought like a man

possessed. Mace in one hand and sword in the other, he took on opponents left and right and slew them all, his arms whirling. I had not seen him fight like this before and was amazed. A fellow blundered past Nikos, his lower jaw smashed and bloody from the Cretan's swinging mace, and he came stumbling towards me. I split him from shoulder to waist with one mighty blow of my sword.

Then they were gone. There were no more living enemies upright on the walkway, and a writhing carpet of wounded and dead at our feet. I peered over the wall and saw that the ladders were now abandoned, and the Moors were steaming away. The battering ram lay untended before the main gate. It was wondrous, a God-given miracle, we had actually seen them off.

We had beaten them.

I heard cheering breaking out all the way along the curtain walls. Wild shouts of joy, and somewhere else a trumpet sounding, pealing incessantly.

The trumpet was sounding the alarm.

I turned around and saw, with a huge bursting shock deep inside my chest, that there were Moors inside the inner bailey; scores of them advancing slowly across the open space from the direction of the sally port. Not our black-clad foes from the walls before us – they were still running – but Berbers in pale violet robes, and Moroccan spearmen in green and short, bow-legged Asiatic men with stubby recurved bows in their hands.

The realisation was like a slap to the face. While we had been valiantly defending the main gate – concentrating our forces here on my advice to Sir Arnold – the real attack had taken place on our unguarded rear and, while we were distracted by the feint, the emir's much larger force had simply scaled the undefended curtain wall behind us and were now inside the castle itself.

Chapter Twenty-five

Sir Arnold was shouting, "Back, men, get back! Retreat to the inner bailey!" and the trumpet on the round tower was still blasting out notes of alarm.

I looked at Nikos and saw shock and fear in his eyes, too. We scrambled down the stairs to the sandy ground of the outer bailey and with all the rest of our comrades ran for the wide-open gate of the inner bailey.

There were Moors everywhere. A tall, purple-veiled spearman stood in my way and jabbed at me with his long weapon. I flicked the point aside with my sword and charged into him with my shoulder, knocking him sprawling to the ground. I had no time to stop and finish him. The open gates of the inner bailey were only thirty paces away, and I ran with all my heart, long strides, blood pounding, the Hospitallers and my friends all around me.

A pair of Hospitaller knights and three brother-sergeants had formed a sort of flimsy shield wall to the south of the gate of the inner bailey, standing heroically between our running men and the advancing wave of cheering Moors. They beat on their shields with their swords, trying to draw the enemy towards them, to halt them, and give the rest of us time to get inside.

But Prince Khalil's men merely skirted around the shield wall of five Christian swordsmen, coming round the side of this feeble line of knights and sergeants to crash directly into the loose mob of our men who were streaming away from the main gatehouse. One Moor came too close to Little John, who flipped him away, with a sideways flap of his axe, like someone shooing a fly away with his hand, leaving the warrior staggering a few steps, bleeding, stumbling before finally dropping to his knees into the dust.

The Moors by then had surrounded the five swordsmen. One fellow with a recurved bow, nocked a shaft, aimed and loosed at a distance of only seven yards. The arrow sank fletchings-deep into the side of one of the knight's chests, punching through mail and ribs, knocking the man down. Nikos, who was still beside me, yelled, "No, no!" and veered off the route to the gate to go to the aid of the five embattled Hospitallers.

I hesitated; I stopped dead. *Should I go to help them? Was it my duty?*

"Don't be a bloody fool," roared Little John, picking me up, physically lifting me by a handful of my ventail at the scruff of my neck, and thrusting me towards the gate of the inner bailey, which was now beginning to close.

A scrum of men was at each of the two big wooden doors, shoving them together; and half a dozen crossbowmen were standing in the centre of the closing gap, loosing at any Moor who came into their line of sight. One of them, I saw, was Hanno.

I hurtled past him, with Little John a half-pace behind me, and came skidding to a halt inside the inner bailey. A Hospitaller sergeant standing beside a tangled pile of military equipment handed me a crossbow and a bag of quarrels and said, "Up on the walls, man. We'll stop them from up there."

I hurried up the steps, and at the top on the battlements I hastily loaded my crossbow, shoving my foot in the stirrup, hauling back the cord, slotting a bolt into the groove; then I looked down at the scene in the outer bailey.

There were dead and wounded men scattered everywhere, mostly theirs, by the grace of God, but here and there one or two of our comrades. Nikos and the remaining Hospitaller knights and sergeants had formed a loose circle, back to back, twenty paces from the gate and were completely surrounded by a crowd of Moors, who were raining blows on them from all sides. Whenever he could get a clear shot, a Turkish bowman would loose a lethal shaft into their midst. There were only four Christians still standing out there but they fought on; they fought like caged, yet still dangerous lions.

Nikos was laying about with his sword and mace, his blows becoming wilder and less effective. He had a quarrel sticking out from his mailed side. And he was slathered in blood, the mittens of his armour clotted with gore.

A brother-sergeant went down when a scimitar blow

clanged down on his helmet; three Moors fell on him, daggers flashing, coming back bloody.

I aimed carefully and loosed my bolt at a man who was duelling with Nikos. Hit the Moor squarely in the spine with the quarrel. But no sooner had he fallen, arching in pain, than a spearman ran in from the side and plunged his long weapon deep into the Cretan's thigh. Nikos staggered under the impact, recovered and lashed his attacker across the face with his spiked mace, crushing cheekbone and ripping away the man's nose. Nikos straightened, somehow, and blocked another man's swinging sword blow, and shoved his screaming opponent away with some force, but the Cretan's leg was now a mass of wet blood, and would not bear his weight.

A Hospitaller knight went down next to a flurry of sword blows. He did not rise. Nikos and a brother-sergeant were the last two men standing. They pressed their backs together, stood as straight as they were able, and raised their bloody weapons. For a moment, for a long, breathless moment, they defied their enemies. Then it was over. The bowman aimed deliberately and shot the sergeant full in the face, and he was down. The scimitar men fell on Nikos all at the same time, like a gang of peasants threshing the chaff from the wheat at harvest time, felling him under a dozen swift downward cuts.

As I loaded my crossbow again, I could not but feel a twist of anguish for the death of Nikos. Not a friend, but nearly a friend. He had done us wrong – yet he proved beyond doubt he was a worthy companion at the last. He sought honour and glory all his life. Perhaps, at its end, he found them.

With the death of Nikos and the Hospitaller brethren, the mood in the outer bailey became less frenzied. The gates were firmly shut and barred. We had almost all our surviving men up on the walls of the inner bailey by now, most armed with crossbows, and we took lethal pot shots at any Moorish man-at-arms foolish enough to come within fifty paces.

This was the effective range of those weapons, the distance

at which one might expect to accurately hit a man-sized target. Beyond the fifty-yard mark we let the Moors be, and they milled around on the west and north sides of the outer bailey beyond an invisible arc that stretched all the way from the captured main gates to the now-open sally port in the curtain wall.

I watched them most of the afternoon, expecting at any moment for them to organise and come at us on the walls in a howling mass, just as they had come at the main gate. But they did not. I made a rough count of the visible enemy and decided that they did not have enough manpower to carry off a successful assault on the inner bailey – they had about a hundred men unwounded, perhaps a hundred and twenty, in the whole of the outer bailey.

They must be waiting for reinforcements, I thought.

More importantly, they seemed to lack proper leadership. I wondered if all their captains had been killed in the fighting. There was no sign of Khalil, although I saw that the main gates of the castle had been thrown wide open as a symbol of their success in capturing the outer defences of Ulldecona.

I thought about Khalil's simple trick – and it clearly had been a trick, which I had fallen for like a simpleton – to speak in clear Arabic to Captain Zeyat about capturing the gate in my hearing. I'd done the rest myself: it was I who had influenced the commander of the castle in the disastrous placing of his meagre forces. How long, I wondered, had Prince Khalil known that I understood their heathen tongue?

When the sun began to sink, they had still not come against us in the inner bailey, and I realised that I was weak both with fatigue and hunger.

Little John came round from his part of the wall to speak to me as the last gleams died in the west. He brought pine torches and a pot of pitch to keep them refuelled. He also brought bread and ham, a skin of good red wine – and a small, shivering, tonsured chaplain.

As I munched bread and ham gratefully, John said, "Father Miguel here is going to keep an eye on the enemy for us, Alan –

got your horn, Father?"

The chaplain nodded mutely. He looked absolutely terrified. "Keep these torches burning all night," John continued, "no snoozing, mind, Father, and you just tootle on that horn if you think they're up to mischief, yes?"

The little man nodded glumly again.

"We've been summoned to the church for a full council of war," he said to me. "Sir Arnold wants to discuss our options." He gave a snort of derision. "Anyway, we're all meeting in the church in one hour's time."

It was a much-depleted gathering in the church. And as gloomy a meeting as any I have attended. The cold body of Sir Charles de Bearn lay on its bier by the altar, completely shrouded in a white linen sheet and illuminated by two candles in tall golden stands, one at each end.

After his death and that of the two knights who sacrificed themselves with Nikos outside the gates, there were only three Hospitaller knights left standing to defend the inner bailey – another had been killed in the assault on the main gate – and sixteen brother-sergeants. We had also lost two more Locksley men in that brutal mêlée and now only Hanno, Little John, Edwin and Gareth and I survived from the original English contingent.

We numbered twenty-five fighting men in all, about half of whom were in the church that chilly evening. A dozen brother-sergeants had been posted to the walls of the inner bailey, all round its hundred-yard length, to stiffen the watch of the chaplains, priests and a few servants, those curious folk who could not bring themselves to shed Moorish blood, even to ward their own.

The rest of us gathered round Sir Arnold to hear his words.

"This cannot be a council of despair," Sir Arnold began in a strong, confident voice. "We must do everything we can to keep our hopes alive."

Then he paused for a long moment, too long, in fact; I

looked questioningly over at Hanno and Little John. The big man just shrugged. *What hope could there possibly be?* I thought. There can be no hope of salvation in this earthly realm. Robin is most likely dead or, worse, dying slowly in agony; the two Hospitaller messengers sent to the King of Aragon have both been intercepted and decapitated; and today is Shrove Tuesday: Khalil's men will have surprised the city of Tarragona this very morning; they might already have captured the King and his nobles and be bringing them all back to Valencia in chains. What hope can there possibly be?

Sir Arnold said, "We cannot know what is happening in the rest of the world. But God is with us – he may have warned the King of the danger from the Moors. We do not know. All we can do is to hold fast, to resist the foe with all our strength and courage and put our faith and trust in the Lord."

There was some muttering from the exhausted men standing around. *Is that all you have to say?* I thought. *Put your trust in God; keep hope alive?*

Little John cleared his throat and said, "If that fine, pious thought doesn't get your dicks hard, think on this: we have ample food and wine; we have plenty of crossbow bolts, more than we can use, and masses of other kit and weaponry. And that keep yonder is as strong as any I've seen. We could, if we chose to, retreat to the Tower of Saint John and defy Khalil for weeks."

That was more like it. The holy knights frowned at Little John's crude language. But he was right. The keep was strong. We could hold out there.

"We shall make the Tower of Blessed Saint John our last redoubt, for sure," said Sir Arnold. "But I also say we should hold these bailey walls as long as we are able. Time is on our side. This battle cannot go unnoticed for long. The Aragonese will hear of it, and our brother Christians will come to our aid. It is just a matter of time. I say we hold the walls and retreat to the tower only when forced from them. In the meantime, I plan to make a night-long vigil in this church – to earnestly pray for our deliverance from a power stronger than any on this Earth. I invite any Christian man here to join me."

I call myself a Christian but there was no way I was going to spend the night on my knees praying in that chilly church. After the council had concluded, I went quickly up to the walls to check on Father Miguel, and finding the outer bailey quiet, and the little chaplain alert, if rather jumpy, I went to my cot on the barracks and swiftly fell, fully dressed, into a heavy sleep.

Hanno woke me a little after midnight by kicking the soles of my boots.

"He come again," he said. It took me a moment to comprehend.

"Tariq?" I mumbled, rubbing the sleep-sand from my eyes. I felt, if anything, even more tired after just a few hours sleep than before I lay down.

"Come see!"

I followed Hanno out of the barracks and across the inner bailey to the long stone church. The body of Sir Arnold lay in a pool of blood before the altar, not far from where I had found the corpse of his master Sir Charles de Bearn. Three chaplains knelt beside Sir Arnold's remains, eyes closed, deep in prayer for his departed soul. Two sergeants and another Hospitaller knight were staring down at the body, seemingly unsure what to do with it now.

"He is very, very good," said Hanno. "He come over the wall, make his kill, and disappear again like ghost. He is a perfect killer."

One of the sergeants gave him an angry look.

I took Hanno by the arm and led him to the door of the church.

"I think Tariq remained inside the castle between the two kills," I said. "He can't have come over the wall, no matter how good he is; there were far too many watchful eyes. He was already here. He's still here. Somewhere."

Hanno nodded. We found Little John, and the other Locksley men, asleep in the straw of the stables, waking them as roughly as was necessary.

"Hunt in pairs," Little John said when we'd explained our conclusion. "We know how good he is; don't take any chances. You see him, kill him – two against one; no mercy, no hesitation. Just cut him down, yes?"

So it began. Hanno and I, and the rest of the Sherwood men, with help from six of the sergeants, went through every room in the castle, searching slowly and carefully: every cupboard, every chest, the shaft of every privy.

We found nothing.

We looked into dark corners and under beds, in the round tower and in the square tower, in the stables, the barracks and cook-houses, we searched the church and its tiny vestry, pulling away the altar and looking behind it. We looked in the laundry, looking under piles of dirty chemises, braies and hose; surcoats and robes; peering in the empty boiling vats. Again nothing.

Gareth and Edwin, on Little John's orders, reluctantly prodded at the pile of dead men stacked like logs beside the church, feeling the temperature of their flesh to make sure none was faking. They were all genuine corpses.

We went all around the walls with torches and spears, thrusting the blades into the dark spaces that were too small to hide a cat. We looked at the roofs of the outbuildings, and under the eaves; we searched haylofts.

And then we did it all over again.

If Tariq the Assassin had been inside the castle during the early part of the night, he was no longer there now. I was sure of it. I would have bet my life on it.

Hanno disagreed. He seemed possessed by the idea of finding Tariq.

"He is here, Alan. I can smell him."

At dawn, we ceased our searching. There was nowhere else to look. The kitchens made bean soup and fresh bread for us to break our fast and Hanno and Little John and I sat on the battlements above the gate looking down over the outer bailey, eating in silence. The Moors, those who had slept inside the curtain wall, were waking. We watched our mortal enemies wash hands and faces, lay out mats and, facing east, get on their knees and bow down to their god.

"They'll come at us this morning," Little John said, getting to his feet with a small grunt of tiredness. "And they'll break through the gate, I'm certain. I'll make sure all is ready for our retreat to the Tower of Saint John."

Hanno and I said nothing, merely shrugging in agreement.

"When the word comes," said Little John. "When they have nearly broken through the gate, don't hesitate at all, run like hares for the big square tower. Don't stop for anything. Run. You hear me? No heroics."

We both nodded. I was trying to think of something encouraging to say, as Little John left us, something to lift our spirits – but nothing came to me. A moment later, a Moorish trumpet sounded. Hanno and I leapt to our feet.

We looked out over the parapet and there was Prince Khalil, riding a fine grey stallion at the head of scores of his Black Guards. Not scores, hundreds: a thick river of dark-clad warriors on foot flowing through the open main gate and into the outer bailey. And they brought their stores and provisions with them, loaded in wagons. There were carts full of barrels and boxes, too, masses of fodder and firewood. And among them I could see a squad of infantry man-handling a long dark shape, a heavy trimmed tree-trunk capped with steel – the battering ram.

No parlay this time. No fancy words or threats. I saw Khalil conferring with Captain Zeyat, and the man saluting, and they just came straight at us.

They brought the battering ram up to the gate, twelve men wielding it, two score of Black Guards covering them at their labours with shields, two shields to a guard, one held high over the ram to make a kind of carapace of leather and wood and the other shield covering the flanks. It looked like an armoured centipede as it scuttled up to the gates and began immediately pounding at our doors, striking up a hideous rhythm.

Bam…bam…bam…

We were not just gawping like bumpkins while this was occurring. The alarm had been sounded and sounded again, trumpets rang out from all sides the inner bailey summoning the fighting men to battle. Folk ran here and there. We grouped soldiers above the gate and on either side of the battering ram and immediately began hurling down stones, spears, javelins, pots of boiling water and slamming crossbow quarrel after quarrel into the attackers. We pelted the armoured caterpillar with lethal missiles, smashing skulls and bones, skewering Black Guards, when we could get past the shield defences, every now and then punching a quarrel through the leg or shoulder of a ram-man, but mostly clattering our missiles uselessly against the large black-painted shields. When we did drop an enemy, we all cheered, but it seemed to make no difference for another man would sprint forward from the Khalil's massed ranks behind to take his place. We loosed into them until our back muscles ached from hauling the cords and our fingers were raw.

But only twelve of our men were defending the gate.

Bam … bam … bam … The ram continued its deafening assault.

We had taken the decision – that is, Little John and the senior knight had – that we could not concentrate all our fighters at the gate, as we had done so disastrously before; the rest of the wall of the inner bailey had to be manned as well, in case the gate attack was a feint. So half our men were at the gate and half scattered around the rest of the defences, with chaplains and servants to watch for a second attack. At the gate, we loaded and loosed, loaded and loosed, but it seemed to have little effect. We killed a dozen of them, wounded a score or more – but they had hundreds of men to take the place of the casualties. And the pounding never ceased. I could even feel the vibration of the very wall itself, hear the constant ominous creaking, groaning and cracking of the wood of the fragile gate beneath my feet.

Bam…bam…bam…

At one point I saw Hanno take a long crossbow shot at Khalil himself who was sitting on his horse only seventy yards away by the curtain wall. He missed by a good two yards, the bolt digging itself harmlessly into the dirt.

I yelled at him to kill the men on the battering, not waste his shots on distant targets.

He shouted back, "Look Alan, look! Tariq is not with the emir. He is always beside him. Always. But in this battle – where is the Assassin?"

"He could be anywhere," I shouted. "That doesn't prove anything." Hanno opened his mouth to reply but just then there was a tremendous screeching of torn wood. The Black Guards below us gave a great shout of victory. I could see Khalil lift a hand and order a general advance of his men. And our own trumpets were suddenly calling the retreat.

"We must go," I said. "The gate has given. Everyone – to the tower."

We began scrambling down the stone steps beside the gate – which, as I neared the bottom, I could now see was shattered and hanging half open.

Bam . . . bam . . . bam . . . The assault did not relent in the slightest.

They would be through that shattered portal in just a few moments.

Hanno had stopped dead. He was staring at the pile of corpses beside the church. He grabbed my sleeve. "Look," he said, "look at that face!"

He was pointing at a corpse lying at the edge of the pile; a man with a bloody tonsured head and grey-white skin; a cadaver; no more, no less.

"I know where he is," Hanno shouted. "I have it now." He began to run.

We were the last two of our men by the juddering gate in the inner bailey, the rest steaming towards the redoubt, most already safe inside.

Hanno was running the wrong way; not east towards the square tower and safety, but south towards the church. I looked behind me at the gate. I could now see daylight through one half-battered-open section. I could see the mob of Black Guards hammering outside; make out the individual faces.

Bam . . . bam . . . bam . . . A large chunk of wood flew off the gate and landed at my feet. They would be inside in less than ten swift heartbeats.

I was paralysed with indecision. Hanno was at the church door by then. He turned. "Come Alan, please. We find him. I know where Tariq hides."

"Christ's cum-crusted cock," came the bellowing familiar yell from the still open door of the Tower of Saint John, "get a bloody shift on, Alan."

I forced myself to move. I ran.

I ran towards the church and the urgently beckoning figure of Hanno.

Chapter Twenty-six

I burst through the doors of the church, two steps behind Hanno, and I could hear the shouts behind me of the Moors as they exploded through the gate.

It was dim in there. The candles had been extinguished with the dawn. But Hanno had an axe in his right hand and was hurrying heedlessly towards the altar. I stopped to let my eyes adjust to the gloom, put down my heavy unloaded crossbow, and reached for the door's heavy wooden locking bar and slid it into the two iron brackets either side of the portal to God's House.

It would not take them very long to chop through that bar, if they were determined to get in here, but it might just give us a little extra time to live.

Hanno's boots were clattering noisily on the polished stone flags of the church and my eye was immediately drawn to the white shape of the corpse of Sir Charles de Bearn to the side of the altar.

It seemed to be moving.

I rubbed my eyes, some trick of the dim light. No. The white sheet was rising up in the air. The corpse was coming back to life.

Not a corpse, in fact, but the tall form of Tariq the Assassin, wearing a white linen burial shift, belted at the waist. I was stunned speechless. I did, at least, have enough sense to draw my arming-sword.

Hanno, naturally, was a great deal more self-possessed. He had solved the puzzle of Tariq's hiding place. The Bavarian cocked his right arm and hurled the axe in a flat spinning arc directly at Tariq. I'd seen Hanno throw these small weapons before. I'd seen him cleave a skull with one of them from twenty paces. He hurled the axe at Tariq's head as hard as he could.

The Assassin caught the spinning axe in mid air.

He grinned at Hanno. "Now we shall see," he said in Arabic.

Tariq pulled the long dagger from its sheath on his belt and advanced on Hanno. The Bavarian drew his sword. I closed in on the pair of them.

At the back of my mind, I could hear the roaring of Moorish voices in the courtyard outside the church; someone was banging on the church door.

Tariq's dark eyes flicked between Hanno and me, both of us armed with swords, both advancing on him with death written on our faces.

"You and me, alone," Tariq said to Hanno in Arabic. "Only us two. I will not fight this young one." He inclined his head towards me. "Tell him, boy, I know you speak our tongue, tell him I shall fight him, and only him, now, man to man, a duel between skilled warriors, with all mutual respect."

I had no need to translate. Hanno fully grasped the Assassin's meaning.

"Push that up your hole, Moor," he said. "This no child's game."

And we both fell on him at the same moment.

A man without mail or armour of any kind, no matter how

skilled or quick he is, and equipped with only a dagger and a small hand-axe, is usually no match for two experienced swordsmen clad in good mail from head to toe.

We laid into Tariq from two opposite sides and any other man would have been meat in a few heartbeats. But Tariq managed to block Hanno's first sword strike with a deft flick of his captured axe and, a fraction of an instant later, as I swung at him from the other side, he parried my lunge at his eyes with a twitch of the dagger, which sent my blade hissing harmlessly over his head. Hanno came at him again from his left, a chop at his neck; I attacked his right leg, and he had to leap madly out of the path of our blades.

We said not a word to each other, but Hanno and I advanced on the Assassin as a team, instinctively: we were slowly backing him towards the wall, like a pair of mastiffs cornering a bull. When his back was a yard from the stone of the church wall, Tariq looked wildly between the two of us, head jerking left and right – and leapt at me, ignoring Hanno completely.

He got past my sword point – with a little jink and a twist – and his dagger was suddenly licking out towards my belly, like a striking snake, a foot away from my flesh before I even knew what was happening. In the very last moment, I swivelled my hips, turning sideways, and the slim dagger blade scraped over the links of my hauberk just below the ribs.

Tariq already had the axe, in his left hand, ready to chop down at my head. He was impossibly fast. I was still recovering my wits from the last lightning blow, the dagger strike, trying to bring my long sword around for a desperate cut at his waist. But I was slow, far too slow. The little axe went up and back, began its downswing, and I thought, *My God, this is my death!*

Then his left hand, the hand holding the short axe, jumped from his hairy wrist in a wide spray of red and I saw Hanno's grim Germanic face behind the handless arm, and the silver sweep of his sword through the air.

Tariq screamed: a long and terrible howl at the loss of his hand. And I whipped my blade right into the midst of that bellow of pain, slicing the sharp sword deeply into the muscle of his right thigh, just above the knee.

And the Assassin was done.

Hanno gave him two vicious thwacks with his axe at the very top of his spine, making a noise like a wood-chopper as the blade hit bone. I levered my sword out of the meat of his leg and plunged it into his belly, punching through, liver, lights and organs till the steel burst out the other side. He fell then, bleeding hard; his body losing shape and carriage as he slumped and curled on the floor. We stood for a few moments, breathing like broken men, watching the blood pool and spread about the killer we had killed.

Then Hanno knelt down beside him, looked into his dark, dying eyes, and said, "Not bad, Moor, but . . . not perfect!" and Hanno sawed open his throat with his sword to speed him onwards.

There was a banging noise, a hammering. Sword pommels on wood. It had been there some time. Coming from the church door.

Hanno, still on his knees beside the corpse, looked up at me and I stared back. There was nothing to say. We were in perfect agreement. I have fought several duels with men, with knights and lords, even, and there has, on occasion, been honour in those combats. But I do not regret that we combined our strengths to slaughter the Assassin: he was our enemy. He had lurked in the shadows to strike down decent men without warning. Tariq was a murderer, plain and simple. It had been, you might say, an execution. More importantly, I believe that neither Hanno nor I could have beaten him alone.

The hammering at the door had grown in volume, and now there was the sound of axes splintering against the wood.

Hanno said, "This way!" and I followed him into the small vestry, which abutted the wall. We climbed out of a small window and, with a little effort, a leap and a clamber, we found ourselves on the southern part of the wall that ran all the way around the inner bailey. The courtyard below us was now filled with Khalil's black-clad troops; the gates were open, hanging drunkenly on their huge brass hinges, and I could see that the iron-studded door of the Tower of Saint John was firmly closed. But there were men at the narrow windows, our men, plenty of them, and armed with crossbows.

I saw Edwin lean out and loose his crossbow down at a Black Guard who was battering at the tower's door with the flat of his scimitar. The quarrel slashed down and took him in the top of his head, punching through his steel helm, and he fell down dead immediately. I called out to my little Locksley comrade and he saw Hanno and I running along the top of the wall, pointing us out to his companion at the window, a Hospitaller sergeant.

A few moments later we were opposite a similar window in the southern side of the tower, still on the wall and ten paces away, and friendly faces were throwing us a strong rope, and we were jumping, crashing into the stones of the keep, and climbing – and helping hands were reaching down to haul us up and inside the bulk and safety of the square tower.

A quarter of an hour later, I was gulping down a cup of wine in the former quarters of Sir Charles de Bearn, at the same table where the Castellan had interviewed me just four days ago. It seemed like a distant age.

When my nerves were a little steadier, I told Little John about Hanno and Tariq – how the Assassin must have moved the corpse of Sir Charles into the common pile of bodies, disguising the Castellan's face with a little blood, and then how he had taken his place on the bier, covered in the sheet.

"That must have taken some rare self-discipline," said Little John. "To lie completely still while your enemies discuss their strategy all around you. But it was a clever move. No one willingly disturbs a knight's corpse."

"Well, he's not looking so clever now," I said.

"If you want me to say 'Well done, Alan', you can think again. You disobeyed my orders. The only reason I'm not beating you bloody is that I will need you to fight. And I suppose you did remove a dangerous piece from the board. But don't get cocky. Your punishment is sentry duty. Drink up that wine, grab a bite of bread and cheese, and get on the roof. You're doing a four-hour stint. Any sign of attack and you sing out. Understood? No fucking about, Alan, I'm serious. Keep a good watch or I'll make you pay."

It was oddly peaceful on the top of the Tower of Saint John. It was a dry, cold day and I could see for miles in all directions. The Black Guards had pulled back from the door of the tower below me and were busy looting the buildings they had just captured. There were hundreds of them out there but the fighting had all but ceased for the moment. We were conserving our crossbow quarrels; they were staying out of range. I could see Khalil just beyond the gate in the outer bailey conferring with a crowd of his officers.

Twenty yards behind him, coming through the gates were more and more wagons, some stacked with provisions, but others carrying nothing more than firewood for the troops' campfires. They were clearly settling in for a long siege. That increased my sense of despair. I did not know how long we could hold out in the tower. Surely a matter of days only, with the great forces arrayed against us. We simply did not have enough men. That had been the problem from the start. With a hundred knights and the same number of sergeants, we could have held Ulldecona till the stars fell from the sky. But with only a handful of knights we were doomed. We'd always been doomed. Soon we would all perish. Perhaps worse would befall us.

My heart was in my boots so I lifted my gaze to the beauty of the surrounding countryside. Perhaps King Alphonso would ride over the horizon soon with an army of knights and put Khalil to flight. I did not expect it. The King was, for all I knew, a wretched prisoner. As we were.

Khalil had triumphed, Ulldecona was lost; we were as good as dead.

I looked at the northern horizon anyway, and saw that it

was empty. No long column of Spanish knights with bright armour, glittering arms, snorting horses and gaudy fluttering banners. Nothing. And to the south I could see another contingent of Moorish reinforcements coming in from the east: a company of a hundred or so dark-clad men on foot, and a dozen horsemen, probably Moroccan mercenaries, coming to swell the emir's numbers for the final assault on the keep. More enemies pledged to accomplish our deaths.

I began to sing to myself softly: a lament called the *Song of Roland* about a Frankish hero who fought the Moors in the high mountains to the north of where I now stood. Roland dies tragically in the end, blowing his horn to summon help. I wept as I sang to myself: I wept for Nikos, who had sought glory, and found death; for Robin who might well be wishing for death even now; for all my comrades who had died on this journey, on this quest for gold. And for myself; for my own imminent demise far from home.

As I neared the end of the lament, I noticed something that wiped all self-pity from my mind. I could now see clearly how we would be defeated. For in the outer bailey, I could see Khalil surveying a caravan of wagons.

Eight wagons. Each wagon piled high with brushwood and straw, and his men were pouring a green liquid over the tightly packed loads. My mind flashed back to Hanno's departing trick at the beach in Matala – the way he had kept the Archon's men at bay with a wall of olive oil-fuelled fire. And I remembered Khalil's grim words in our camp on the march from Valencia: "If they refuse to surrender, I shall burn the tower with them inside it."

I leapt down the stairs, tumbling, tripping, bashing into the sandstone walls in my hurry. I found Little John on the ground floor organising the barricading of the only door to the tower. I told him what I'd seen and we went up to the second floor to look out of one of the windows.

There were Black Guards trotting into the inner bailey, lining up with their crossbows behind enormous oblong wooden shields – as high as a man and twice as wide – which were sometimes used as portable walls to give cover to bowmen. Edwin, who stood beside us, loosed his crossbow and it slammed into one of the giant shields. The response was immediate – a dozen bolts arced through the air and clattered against the window frame, one snagging the sleeve of Edwin's mail hauberk.

We all stepped back from the open window.

Edwin started to reload his bow. Then, to a loud trundling of wooden wheels and the squeal of ungreased axles, the first of the oil-soaked wagons, emerged through the shattered gate, pushed by a dozen armoured men. The quarrels flew thick and fast now. The Black Guards loosing at us in a lethal torrent, trying to prevent us from shooting at the oncoming wagon; or the one behind that; or the one following that one. Edwin bobbed out into the window frame, loosed his weapon, and hit one of the men pushing the leading wagon. He turned to me with a grin of triumph at the exact moment an enemy bolt thumped into his cheekbone, transfixing his smiling face.

Little John and I dragged him away from the window; he was unconscious and bleeding heavily. I picked up his crossbow and untied the bag of quarrels from his waist. Then I stepped over to the window, bent to load it and a bolt pinged off my helmet. It skittered across the wooden floor.

"Don't bother," said Little John. "We've no chance of stopping them."

I heard a thump from below as the fire-wagon crashed into the door.

"What sha... shall we do then, John?" I asked, trying unsuccessfully to keep the shake out of my voice.

I could well imagine those piles of oil-drenched wood and kindling set alight and the fire consuming the whole of the tower. It would be like being locked in a bread oven. No air to breathe, just choking smoke, red hot stone; anything not made of stone would burn, the beams, the furniture, our clothes. The skin would roast to crackling on our living bodies. The end, when all went dark, and the screaming stopped, would be a blessed relief.

"We have only one chance, as I see it," said Little John. "Just one. Get everyone together now – all the men who can still run and hold a sword or a crossbow – gather them all downstairs in the hall. Go now, Alan. Quickly."

I could feel the heat already, and hear the roaring crackle of the burning wagons on the other side of the stone walls. Inside my gambeson, worn beneath my full suit of mail, the sweat was running down my chest and back like rivers. We were a dozen men, all more or less unwounded, all armed just as we chose. I had my drawn sword in one hand and a fresh, black-and-white Hospitaller shield in the other. Despite the excessive heat, my teeth were chattering so hard I had to clamp my mouth shut. A Hospitaller sergeant came jingling down the stairs in full gear, mailed from head to toe.

"He's still there," he said. "To the right of the gate, by the grain store."

"Of course, he is," said Little John, who was pulling on a pair of thick leather blacksmith's gloves. "The bastard is longing to watch us burn."

John slapped his heavy gauntlets together. "Everybody know what to do?" he said, looking over the group of a dozen strained, frightened faces. We nodded mutely. "Ready to repay that smug prick what we owe him?"

"Let us do this damn thing," said Hanno.

Little John pulled back the iron bolts and tugged open the heavy oak door – to an inferno. The wall of red-orange flame outside was a living, rippling monster. The heat punched at us, an invisible blow, I even took a step backwards, bumping into one of the last surviving Hospitaller knights behind me. I could just make out the blackened, burning skeleton of the fire-wagon, pushed up hard against the door, blocking our path out of the tower.

Little John surged forward. He seized the side of the wagon in both his gauntleted hands and shoved with all his massive strength. And by God's grace the wheels on the wagon turned. The burning vehicle began to roll slowly away from the door. John gave a huge shout of pain and fury, bunched his muscles and pushed again. The wagon shot out into the space behind it. Suddenly I could see into the inner bailey, see the astonished faces of the Black Guards standing beside their huge crossbow shields.

Little John was burning, his green cloak was a mass of smouldering wool, but he was actually gaining speed – God knows how he stood the pain – he drove the rumbling, fireball of a wagon a good fifteen yards and straight into a knot of black-clad soldiers, who scattered at the approach of the flaming vehicle. We surged out of the tower right behind Little John and his burning wain, a tight wedge of fully armoured men wielding swords, Hanno and I to the fore, shrieking our war cries, and aiming the wedge straight for the figure in a dark cloak on a fine horse beside the grain store, a little to the right of the shattered gate.

As we hurtled past John – his face red and blistered, his eyebrows burnt away, I saw one of the Hospitaller sergeants toss him a linen towel heavy with water, and place his axe into his blackened, leather-covered hands.

Then I was past him.

Our plan was simple. Prince Khalil was right there in the inner bailey – hoping to watch us burn – and we would cut our way to him and make him our prisoner. With a dagger at his throat, the Emir of Valencia would be forced to allow us to leave the castle. And if he refused? Well, slicing through his windpipe would be a consolation when we came before the face of Almighty God. It was a simple plan, not a good plan. It was our only plan.

A Black Guard appeared in front of me, and I smashed him down with one slashing sweep of my sword; another man came in from my left, swinging a flanged mace, and I took the crunching blow square on my shield. I threw his mace-arm aside and plunged my blade into his groin.

I was in a knot of enemies now, hacking, shoving, using the sword's pommel and cross-guard as often as the blade, crashing my mailed right fist into bearded, screaming faces. I was aware, but only vaguely, that Hanno was behind me, at my left shoulder, killing and cursing in German, slicing and punching, spitting his defiance; then a splatter of gore across my face made me aware that Little John too had joined the fray, and was wielding his axe to my left and dropping men like barley under a harvester's scythe.

Prince Khalil was only ten yards away from me now, and he was staring in amazement as we shoved and cut and hacked our way through the thick crowd of his soldiers towards him. A Black Guard with a crossbow about three yards to my right, aimed at my chest and, while I was beating off a challenge from a lunging Moroccan spearman with my shield, he loosed. I felt the strike of the quarrel in the meat of my right shoulder like a kick from a horse. I staggered back a step or two and, glancing down I could see the black bolt jutting from the iron mail just above my bicep.

I felt no pain. All around me people were shoving, cursing, spitting and dying in a vast deadly scrum of mingled friends and foes. I lifted my sword.

I slashed and hacked. I shoved and swore. One fellow tried to seize my sword with his hands, and I simply pulled the blade back and he screamed and fell away, scattering fingers. A short fellow in a red turban slammed up against my chest, inside the protection of my shield arm. I had no idea where he came from. He began to pound my chest and belly with a curved dagger, striking once, twice, three times, before I shoved him blundering away and hacked my blade down into his shoulder. I thanked God my mail was well-made, for though he gave me horrific bruises, he did not pierce the links.

Red Turban fell to his knees, staring at me in disbelief, his neck slashed deep, wet blood sheeting his chest-armour. I kicked him down, and stepped into another battle, clanging swords with a Black Guard, who looked familiar: Captain Zeyat.

He sliced hard at my head, clipped the top rim from my shield, and his steel clanged on my helmet. But I had my blade in his guts by then, and, as I twisted it, he squirmed and died before my eyes.

But no matter how many we killed, there always seemed to be more. A Hospitaller sergeant on my right fell to a sword blow to the back of the head that stove in his steel helmet. I nearly tripped over one of our knights who had fallen at my feet, gored in the belly by a spear. My friends now each seemed to be surrounded by enemies, our wedge formation broken apart. I swung the sword and lashed out with my shield; I kicked and butted. I felt blows battering my mail with every step. I struggled through the crush.

Yet Khalil was moving farther away. He had seen that we were coming for him, and was moving his horse towards the gate, preparing to flee. I parried a vicious swinging blow, and took another crashing sword strike from a second man on to my crumpled shield. Something struck me in the back – hard. I could feel my strength fading. A blow from a mace crashed down on my battered helmet, which set my ears ringing. My knees felt weak and I had to force myself upright – and Prince Khalil was now almost at the gate. Out of reach. I roused myself, calling his name, calling him to come and fight, batting a spearman out of my path, smashing a bearded face away with my shield. My sight was dimming, shimmering, coming in waves.

I had no idea where Little John and Hanno were. Or even if they lived.

Then a horn rang out. A pure high note; a glorious, golden note, as I recall it now. I heard the sound of cavalry, the thunder of many hooves on stony ground. Prince Khalil turned his horse aside from the gate, instead of leaving, riding across its open space towards the church. There was a flicker of movement, high up above the gate. A crossbowman on the wall gave a shout of panic and loosed his bow. But he was aiming outside the walls, he was aiming at something in the outer bailey, something I could not see. Then I did see something that made me gape in surprise – and nearly get skewered by a charging spearman. The crossbowman on the walls was hit by a missile and knocked backwards, thumping to the ground three yards from my feet.

I just managed to dodge the spearman's lunge, and flailed wildly with my sword as he pounded past me, hacking weakly into his mailed right arm.

I stared, swaying, at the body at my feet. The man was dead. An arrow was sticking from the middle of his chest: an honest-to-goodness English arrow, a yard long and unmistakeably adorned with grey-goose fletching.

Chapter Twenty-seven

Robin's small cavalry force pounded through the shattered gate of the inner bailey. His men – and he only had a dozen horsemen with him on this tightly formed charge – swept into the remaining Black Guards and utterly destroyed them. Their razor-tipped lances came down and they punched through the fragile bodies of the emir's men – armoured or not – hurling them about like a child's discarded dolls, this way and that, without the slightest mercy. When their long spears had been wetted with blood, the English cavalry abandoned them, as often as not still in the bodies of their victims, and drew their long swords and the terrible slaughter continued.

There were bowmen now, too, entering the inner bailey on foot. Men in forest green cloaks. I saw Owain and two score of familiar, well-loved faces. The Sherwood archers nocked and loosed, nocked and loosed, picking their targets, killing their men, and Black Guards fell and fell and fell around me.

And, in truth, I could barely keep my own feet. My vision was coming in and out of focus. My head was singing a weird sad melody, the pain was roaring in my right arm, and there was a raging fire, so it seemed, in the small of my back. I could not understand where Robin and his men had come from. Brought by angels, or sent directly from Heaven. But they were here. Praise God. And our desperate fight could now be won. Indeed, it *was* already won. I lifted my leaden sword with the greatest difficulty, my right arm seemed not to function any more. All my strength had fled from my body – but, mercifully, there were suddenly no more enemies about me to struggle with. I stood alone, swaying like a drunkard, dazed and done.

I could see Little John sitting alone on the ground a dozen yards away, covered in blood, the steel twin-blades of his axe drenched in gore. The bodies of a dozen dead and wounded Black Guards surrounded him, a small mound, in fact. He saw me looking at him and smiled tiredly, lifted a hand. He looked very strange, an odd sort of surprised expression on his blistered and blood-streaked face. It was only later I realised this must be due to his lack of eyebrows. Hanno too was alive, thank God. He was standing by the grain store beside the gate, leaning against the wall, with a skin of something – wine, I expect – already held up in the air while he gulped thirstily.

Robin, dismounted, was standing with a drawn sword in front of Prince Khalil, who had also climbed down from his horse. Khalil, terrified, held his hands high in the air. I thought: *Good, now kill him, Robin. Open his belly.*

But my world was slowly dissolving around me. I felt sick and faint, my vision blurred. My mouth was dry. Owain came to me, grasped my arm and said: "Alan, you live! Saints be praised. But you don't look very..."

Then I remembered no more.

I awoke in a cot in a dark place in a small wooden room that seemed to be moving gently. Robin was beside me, sitting on a box, peering into my face.

"Water," I said. "Give me water, for the love of God."

My lord handed me a bowl of blissful water mixed with a little wine and helped me to drink. I looked at my body. My right arm was bandaged at the bicep, and a thick white swathe of cloth was wrapped around my middle.

"You took a crossbow quarrel in the arm, and a spear, I think, in the lower back. Not deeply. Neither wound is serious," said my lord.

The pain was bearable. But I thought for a moment about taking issue with his assertion that my wounds were not serious. I felt as weak as a crippled baby mouse. It seemed too much effort to argue with him.

"You took a couple of nasty knocks on the head," said Robin, "which had us all worried for a time, but you seem to be much better now."

I nodded – a stupid thing to do – and something red and white flashed behind my eyes and the pain stabbed through my skull in a sickening wave.

When I could speak again, I said: "Where are we?"

"Come on deck and see. Elise says you should not sleep too much."

"Elise?"

"Come on, get up, Alan. I'll help you."

Stopping only once to be sick in the filthy bilges, I came out into bright sunshine on the slightly canted deck of the *Santiago*.

The first thing I saw was the form of Prince Khalil, slumped against the ship's side. The Emir of Valencia was trussed with many ropes and had been stripped to his braies. His smooth, lean, white body was also marked with a large number of rather fine, purple bruises. It looked as if someone, possibly more than one person, had been kicking and punching him repeatedly.

Robin saw where I was looking. "Ah yes, the emir wisely surrendered to us at Ulldecona. If you look yonder, you will see the town of Valencia. We shall be there within the hour. We're returning the emir to his own city."

I looked at Robin. "Why?"

"We are ransoming him back to his family."

I looked again at Prince Khalil, eyes tightly closed, bound, naked, bruised and battered, sunk in his own deep misery.

"You should have made him row us here," I said.

I took some wine and a little soup at the table on the aftdeck, and Robin told me what had happened since we had departed from Valencia without him. The Palace of Russafa had been unusually quiet without the Sherwood men, and Robin had spent much of his time with Lady Tanisha. When the news reached the palace that a ship of infidels – a hundred green-clad men-at-arms, many of them archers – had arrived at the port of Valencia seeking their lord, Robin slipped over the walls of the palace one night, with Ricky and Elise, and they had all simply walked to the harbour to find their friends.

"I could probably have talked my way out of the main gate," Robin said. "Khalil took most of his Black Guards with him when he went north. And Tanisha had given me the run of the whole palace in their absence."

"Wait up, Robin. Why had Owain and our men come to Valencia? How did they know? I thought they were supposed to wait for us at Marseilles."

"I sent them a message. Tanisha was kind enough to allow me certain freedoms, even before you left for Ulldecona – one of which was visiting the docks at Valencia. I paid a Provençal sailor I met there to take a message to the *Santiago* at Marseilles, summoning our men to Valencia with all speed."

I looked at him with renewed admiration.

"If Owain had arrived earlier," said Robin, looking a little shamefaced, "we could have avoided all that business at the Hospitallers' fortress and just escaped. Although, I suppose we would still have had to fight Khalil at sea."

"How did you find us at Ulldecona?"

He told me that they had sailed up the coast and, hearing of the battle from some fishermen, had dropped anchor at a little village called Alcanar, and marched the five miles to the castle. I had even seen them approaching from the top of the Tower of Saint John with my own eyes while I was singing my lament, mistaking them for reinforcements for the emir.

Robin had been rather surprised to find the main gate of Ulldecona wide open, and they had attacked immediately. The massed volleys of the skilled Sherwood bowmen had decimated Khalil's troops in the outer bailey, and by the time they charged into the inner one, the battle had been decided.

There was good news from the north, too. Robin had dispatched another message from Valencia, even before we left, to the Christian city of Tarragona. It was a warning, alerting King Alphonso to the attack that Prince Khalil was planning at the cathedral on Shrove Tuesday. The King prepared an ambush in the streets of Tarragona and slew hundreds of Moorish troops in a bloody battle. And the Aragonese knights were now occupying Ulldecona, with the few surviving Hospitallers.

The Emir of Valencia, of course, was now tied up like a bundle of washing in the waist of the ship.

"Why not just kill him?" I said. "After what he did to us."

Robin avoided my eyes. "I promised Lady Tanisha that I would not kill her father," he said. "She was very generous to me and so . . ."

I expected to feel rage at Robin's merciful actions. Oddly I did not. I found, when I looked deep into my heart, that I did not care all that much whether Prince Khalil lived or died. I would have prefered the emir to be punished for his treatment of us in his ship and his behaviour at Ulldecona but, if Robin said he must be ransomed, so be it. Much blood had been shed in the past few days. It was time the killing ceased.

The most important thing, I told myself, as I felt the cool salty breeze and sunshine on my face, was that I was alive, and safe among my friends.

I did not see the ransom exchange with my own eyes. I felt suddenly weak after my conversation with Robin and returned to my cot in the hold of the ship. But Hanno told me much later that my lord had met the Lady Tanisha with all courtesy in a small pavilion a little set back from the main harbour.

Robin was accompanied by a strong retinue of mailed men-at-arms – Owain had recruited a dozen master-less Norman mercenaries from the brothels and taverns of Marseilles – and a squad of twenty bowman, too, in case there should be any trickery on the lady's part. Yet the handover went well. Prince Khalil was sullen and angry, not penitent in the slightest, when he was reunited with his daughter, and after all the polite formalities had been observed, the two sides parted without violent incident and our men returned to the ship with Lady Tanisha's permission to sail on the tide.

Just before we departed, I was awoken from my feverish slumbers by the clumping of big, booted men not far from my cot. A dozen burly bowmen were heaving a good deal of cargo, boxes, bundles and barrels, down into the hold, and stacking them and very close to where I was trying to sleep. I sat up and began to complain angrily at being disturbed, and saw Robin's lean face grinning at me over the nearest barrel.

"Don't be so grumpy, Alan," he said. "It doesn't suit you at all."

I glared at him. "I am gravely wounded, lord," I said. "Perhaps near death. I should at least be allowed a little peace during my final few hours."

"I think 'gravely' is pushing it," said Robin. "You've taken a knock, that's all. But we won't argue. This, I think, might sweeten your mood."

He opened the lid of the barrel, reached inside, and pulled out a handful of silver coins. He watched my expression as the coins trickled through his fingers and fell chinking back into the cask. "I received five barrels of silver just like this," he said, "from the Lady Tanisha for the person of her father."

I goggled at him. Five barrels full of silver – it was a vast fortune.

"However, I also insisted that I should also be given those as well."

He gestured with his head at the central aisle of the hold. And I saw three large dark wooden strong-boxes lined up in a neat row.

My heart stopped for an instant.

"Is that what I think it is?" I said. I swung my legs out of the cot and stumbled over to the nearest box.

"Open it and look," said Robin, handing me a crowbar. "I couldn't find a way to steal it, you see; the treasury was too heavily guarded. There was just no way to do it. I did, however, find a way to make her *give* it to me."

It may have been purely my imagination, but when I managed to lever open the lid of that first heavy box with my shaking hands, it seemed as if the whole of that dark hold was filled with a pure and shining golden light.

The End

The adventures of Robin Hood and his loyal lieutenant Alan Dale will continue in "Robin Hood and the Castle of Bones"

Printed in Great Britain
by Amazon